SHE STOLE
MY BUDDY'S
STARSHIP

MY BUDDY'S STARSHIP
BOOK 2

SHE STOLE MY BUDDY'S STARSHIP

MYLES CHRISTENSEN

MOON
ZOOM
PRESS

For the Dreamers
If we can imagine it, we can make it reality.

Chapter One

With the grayish-brown of intra-space swirling outside the flight deck of our starship, I glanced at my co-pilot, Vrynn, and she gave me that familiar look. I certainly saw it often enough. It was her exasperated look. Or maybe it was her frustrated look. Either way, I could tell she wasn't happy with me.

"How much longer until we get to Taphus Epsilon?" she asked. Her normally fair complexion had a deeper tint of blue when she got frustrated, or excited, or nervous. Pretty much anything that would make someone from Earth blush would bring out the blue highlights in Vrynn's skin.

Vrynn had been my co-pilot ever since she had unsuccessfully attempted to commandeer my starship and then refused to get off. Of course, a lot had happened since then. And, technically, it wasn't my starship. My best friend, Gabe, had found it.

"Ten minutes until the jump ends," Tera, the ship's holographic AI, replied, saving me from saying something stupid.

Vrynn let out a prolonged sigh. "I wish we could get there faster."

I let a few seconds pass, the grayish space still swirling around us outside the glass. "I have been working on it, you know," I muttered quietly.

"I know, Mitch," she said with a patronizing pat on my arm. "I'm just anxious."

We sat for a minute in silence with Vrynn checking the time readout every few seconds. Finally, she turned to me. "Won't it be amazing when we can travel instantaneously? Just think of how many people we could help."

"Yeah," I said, "I'm sure the Quake Drive will be amazing once it's installed."

Like most other starships in the Bonara cluster, our ship, the *Starfire*, could arrive at distant locations faster than light by traveling through alternate dimensional planes using the intra-space drive. It was tedious and boring, but much faster than travel through normal space.

The Quake Drive, on the other hand, was something entirely different. Tera said it allowed for instantaneous travel between two points through a portal in space-time. I'd never used it personally, but it sounded amazing. That's why Vrynn was so anxious to have it functional again.

A minute or two later, she turned back to me. "Do you have any idea when you might get it working?"

"Well, I guess I could go down to the engine room right now and work on it." I thumbed over my shoulder toward the flight deck door behind us.

Vrynn narrowed her eyes at my sarcasm.

Tera jumped in, her occasionally indifferent teenage attitude coming through. "You don't want to work on the ship's drive system while we're in the middle of a jump. With the plasma banks actively powering the drive, that would be like sticking a fork into a toaster."

She must not have caught my sarcasm. "I was kidding, Tera."

Between my tone with Vrynn and my retort to Tera, the flight deck suddenly felt as chilly as the space outside. Fortunately for me, our intra-space jump ended only a minute later.

Vrynn and I both sat forward in our pilot's seats.

"Sensors are reading thirty ships engaged in a battle on the surface of the moon," Tera said.

"Zoom in," I said as I checked the defensive systems.

A view of the surface appeared on the holographic display above my console. Dozens of ships swarmed around a small outpost, its defensive guns firing relentlessly back at them.

"That's more than we've taken on before," I observed.

"Can you read anything on the ships yet?" Vrynn asked Tera.

"They're Brooxika strikers," she replied. "No transponder signals."

That meant we were in the right place. Military vessels operating without their transponders broadcasting meant only one thing—Nexus-affiliated ships.

Still, thirty. That was a lot.

Vrynn must have sensed my concern. "Striker-class starships aren't heavily armored. We can easily take thirty."

"Automated distress call from the outpost," Tera announced. "It says, 'Our facility is under attack. Please render aid, if possible.'"

"They need us," Vrynn said. "Let's get down there."

I gripped the controls and pushed us into a dive. The ship over-rotated only a small amount before I corrected our pitch.

I was getting better.

We were still two minutes out when one corner of the outpost lit up in a giant explosion, and the defensive guns for the entire outpost fell silent.

"They must have hit the primary power generator," Vrynn said. Her face was a picture of intensity, her light skin showing even more blue tint than normal as she gazed at the battle below us.

Several strikers pulled away from the attack and rose to intercept us.

"Plasma cannons," I said.

Vrynn was way ahead of me, and the gun emplacements under our winglets erupted with streams of plasma rounds. The approaching strikers scattered in the face of our superior firepower. I banked the *Starfire* hard to chase the closest pair.

Vrynn fired a broad spread on the nearest craft. Several rounds tore into its engines, and the ship started to lose control, but Vrynn was already focusing on the next ship. Five seconds of concentrated rounds, and the second one exploded in a bright fireball.

Three more ships abandoned their attack on the outpost to engage us. That was good. Maybe if we could draw enough of them away, we could save the people on the ground.

Another pair of strikers swooped toward us, but they weren't coming directly in to attack. I banked right to close the distance. They turned away to escape, but I pushed the throttle hard. The *Starfire* was faster, so it was only a matter of time before we caught them.

"Mitch, let them go," Vrynn said.

"Why? We can take them." A solitary ship angled toward us but immediately peeled off when I shifted course. "See, they're scared of us."

"Maybe, but they're also leading us away from the attack." Vrynn replied as she focused her plasma cannons on another pair of strikers lurking behind us. "Get back to the outpost. That's what we're here to save."

"Good point." I forced myself to ignore the ships not directly between us and the beleaguered facility. As we flew down toward the small outpost, I could see a dozen strikers had landed next to a long squat building, the rest weaved back and forth, providing air cover. Pilots in full battle armor exchanged fire with ground forces defending the facility.

As I strafed the Nexus ground troops, three strikers flew over our position, dropping plasma charges as they passed. I dodged the explosions, but lost my line on the soldiers. "We can't attack the ground forces until we take out their air cover," I said as I turned my attention back to the airborne enemy vessels. I accelerated the *Starfire* upward to engage them.

"Can we hit them with atmospheric missiles?" I asked as several ships streaked by.

Vrynn pulled up the missile targeting controls. "I've got so many enemy ships in range, the system keeps switching the active target."

"Then let's shoot all of them," I suggested.

She gave me that familiar look. "Forget about the missiles; just get me close enough to use the plasma cannons," Vrynn said, focusing on the strikers in front of the outpost.

As we moved in low over the ground invasion force, the cover ships intensified their fire. Vrynn's melee took out one of the strikers and damaged a few others.

"Lateral deflectors are down to sixty percent," Tera announced.

I nodded and pulled the *Starfire* out of the fight. We flew past the facility, drawing several of the strikers away from their position. As I zigged and zagged, Vrynn continued firing. Amid the hailstorm of plasma rounds, she scored three direct hits on the nearest ship. Half of its fuselage fell off, and the craft spun out of control toward the ground.

"That's four," I said.

Vrynn nodded absently, her face the picture of concentration. "Get back to the outpost."

We needed to keep moving while also staying close to the facility to stop the invaders. Maybe it was time to see if the *Starfire* really could fly circles around every other ship in the Bonara Cluster. I banked back toward the embattled outpost, flying a wide arc around their position.

With a quick glance at my weapons console, I targeted the laser battery on one of the sitting ships. All the while, Vrynn filled the air with highly charged plasma rounds, keeping the swarming strikers at bay.

An impact warning blared on my display.

"Watch out, Mitch!" Tera yelled.

"I see them," I replied through gritted teeth. I swerved to avoid the incoming shells, and Vrynn immediately shifted her focus to the pair of strikers screaming toward us.

I kept the *Starfire* close enough to the outpost for the lasers to stay locked on the ship on the ground. But every time the enemy strikers would fire at us, the defensive battery would shift to destroying incoming rounds—that's what the system was designed to do, after all.

After several loops around the complex—and several downed enemy ships, thanks to Vrynn's work on the cannons—the engine of the striker on the ground erupted in flames. Just as I prepared to select my next victim, the attacking ground troops fell back to their ships and started taking off.

"Maybe we scared them away." That was Vrynn's optimistic nature shining through again.

"I doubt it," I said, bringing the *Starfire* into a hover over the site of the ground battle. I was about to land when Tera spoke up.

"The outpost is requesting that we stop the Brooxika vessels and re-cover the ferridium," she said.

With a quick shift on the throttle, I pushed us back into the air. "What's ferridium?"

"Ferridium is a volatile, high-energy compound used for cryogenic power transmission and magnification," Tera said. "It can also be used for—"

"The chemistry lesson can wait," Vrynn interrupted. "Go after them!"

I steered toward the clump of retreating ships, and Vrynn strafed them with plasma rounds. They scattered, but continued gaining altitude. I followed Vrynn's lead and pursued the ship she was shooting at, but she changed targets so frequently, it was difficult to know which to chase.

"That's another one down," she said as the ship in front of us exploded.

"If the outpost wants their ferridium back, don't you think we should stop blowing up the ships carrying it?" I asked.

Unfazed by my concern, Vrynn shifted her fire to the next striker. There were still over twenty enemy ships zigzagging back and forth as they rose through the atmosphere. A few seconds later, another ship exploded.

"Vrynn! The ferridium," I chided.

"Sorry," she replied with a sheepish look.

We were nearly out of the atmosphere now, and I zeroed in on another ship, even though it was obvious we could never stop all of them. A second later, Vrynn's plasma rounds found their mark, and its engine nacelle burst into flames. At least she wasn't blowing them up anymore.

We must have cleared enough of the atmosphere for intra-space drive operation because the lead strikers began jumping away. The ship I had targeted with the laser batteries jumped away, too, but I could have sworn it looked like it was on its last leg.

"Tera, are you tracking jump trajectories?" I asked.

"Of course." She sounded annoyed that I would even doubt it.

"Which ones are going directly to other planets?" I asked.

She gave me a puzzled look. "They're all going to other planets," she said.

"You can't jump to nothing," Vrynn added.

"What?" I said as I picked my next target from the dwindling fleet of tiny ships.

"There has to be a gravity anchor at the other end," Vrynn replied, still firing at the stragglers.

I frowned. "You've never mentioned that before."

"You never asked to jump to nothing," Tera said with a shrug.

Vrynn scored one more hit on the last ship before it jumped to intra-space. "Can we talk about this later?"

I studied the trajectory information. "Which one should we go after?"

"It doesn't matter. Just pick one and follow it," Vrynn said with obvious exasperation.

"Did any of them jump to Nexus-affiliated systems?" I asked Tera.

"The third ship to jump was aimed at Prentoro," Tera replied. "None of the others were headed for known Nexus systems."

"Perfect, make a jump to Prentoro," I said, trying to sound assertive and commanding.

A few moments later, we were on our way through intra-space and bored again.

"Do you think we'll beat them to Prentoro?"

Tera's eyes scanned the air in front of her. "We jumped on an above-average intra-space dimension," she replied.

"So, an above-average chance we'll get there first?" I asked.

"Except for the two-minute head start," Vrynn added with an annoyed huff.

We hadn't been doing this vigilante-of-the-star-cluster thing long, so we didn't work together like a well-oiled machine quite yet.

When we arrived in high orbit of Prentoro, there was no sign of the striker.

After about five minutes, I asked, "Any chance the Brooxika ship will still arrive?"

"There is a two and a half percent chance their intra-space dimension was so slow that they haven't gotten here yet," Tera replied.

"And what are the chances that they finished their jump and already jumped somewhere else before we got here?" Vrynn asked.

"Ninety-seven percent."

I did some quick math in my head. "Did you forget a half a percent?"

Tera shook her head. "There's a half percent chance that their drive overloaded and exploded during the jump."

I turned to Vrynn. "See, there's something to hope for."

She cocked her head and gave me a deadpan look. "Even I'm not that optimistic."

After another few seconds, I said, "I guess we better head back home."

Vrynn nodded. Then a moment later, she said, "We might have been able to catch them if we—"

I held up my hand. "I know. I know. The Quake Drive is going to solve all our problems."

Vrynn tilted her head, an enigmatic smile playing on her lips. "I have confidence in you. I know you'll figure out how to get it working."

If only I could be that optimistic.

Chapter Two

I flipped the futuristic spanner tool through the air, taking great pleasure in the sound it made as it clattered to the deck. I'd considered throwing it as hard as I could against the bulkhead, but the last time I'd done that, it had left a dent in the door of the engineering department.

The engineering department. That's what Tera wanted us to call the tiny room that housed all the drive systems and other engineering equipment that made the *Starfire* fly. But the small compartment that was wedged between the fabrication room and the medical bay just across the hall from the cargo bay on the lower deck of the ship was barely wide enough to walk around the various pieces of equipment and power systems. So calling it the engineering department didn't really make sense to me. The room was way too small to be considered a department.

Unfortunately, Engineering Walk-In-Closet didn't quite roll off the tongue, so I'd need to try out some other options.

"Careful with the equipment, Mitch," Tera said in her deadpan voice. "Some of these tools are one of a kind."

I blew out a breath. "Yeah. I know." I scrutinized the Quake Drive module. "Are you sure you don't have some sort of installation instructions somewhere in the computer's databanks?"

Tera cocked her holographic head to the side. "If there were installation instructions, don't you think I'd have mentioned it already?"

"Well, there have been times. . ." I trailed off when I saw the murderous look on my friend's face.

A second later, her expression relaxed, and she continued as if I'd never questioned her timing for conveying important information. "Besides, there are still parts of the databanks that are too damaged to read from. It's possible the instructions are there, and I just can't access them."

I leaned back against the bulkhead, shoulders slumped, and stared at the incredibly powerful, yet aggravating, drive system. I'd spent at least a week on it and still had nothing to show for my efforts.

Vrynn and I had worked so hard to get it back from Gralik, the leader of the militant faction that had stolen it from my buddy's farm back on Earth. In fact, this stupid piece of advanced technology is what had gotten my friend Gabe killed in the first place.

"Hey, Mitch. How is it going?" Gabe said as he walked into the engineering cubby.

I didn't even do a double-take when I saw him. Over the last several weeks, I'd adjusted to the idea that my dead best friend was alive and well again. Actually, alive wasn't the best word for it. The person standing in front of me with the curious expression on his teenage face wasn't really my best friend, Gabe. Sure, he looked like Gabe, sounded like Gabe, and sometimes even acted like Gabe. But in reality, he was a collection of circuits and servos stuffed inside a custom android shell programmed with some of my friend's memories.

The holographic Tera had been the one to customize his exterior, and given that she was a recreation of the teenage version of Tera, it was no surprise that she had picked a sixteen or seventeen-year-old appearance for the android version of Gabe. This android body was slightly more muscular than I remembered him in high school, but the six-foot frame and light brown hair were spot on. We had always stood eye-to-eye growing up, and that remained true. I wasn't as lean as my friend, but that had been the case with the real Gabe, too.

At first, my feelings toward this robotic Gabe had been conflicted, but now I just thought of him as my best friend, or at least a very naive, slightly artificial-looking version of my best friend. Sometimes I even forgot that this wasn't the Gabe I'd grown up with.

Gabe looked over at Tera and grinned stupidly. "Hi Tera."

"Hi Gabe," she said, brushing a strand of long, red, holographic hair behind her ear.

Gabe's artificial youthfulness wasn't the only thing that made me forget we weren't back in high school on Earth. AI-Tera and Robo-Gabe's awkward, budding romance had so many similarities to what had happened on Earth a decade or so ago, that I was almost willing to believe that some people were simply destined to be together. The real Tera and the real Gabe had crushed on each other on and off through junior high, fallen in love in high school, and married a few years after we graduated. They had been this sappy around each other as teenagers, so it was no surprise to see their high-tech stand-ins acting the same way.

I shook my head as I considered the bizarre life I now led. Just a few short weeks ago, I'd been fired from my crappy, dead-end job on Earth. It might have been longer. With all the excitement, I'd pretty much lost count of the days. Not to mention time wasn't measured quite the same in the Bonara Cluster.

I turned my attention back to the task at hand. "How much do we really care about having a functional Quake Drive?"

"I do not have any emotional subroutines," Gabe replied. "So my level of caring is a value that either approaches zero or could be considered equal to zero. But I can simulate emotions if you need me to."

I held up a hand. "That's okay, buddy. Tera's emotional subroutines are enough for everyone."

As if on cue, Tera let out a frustrated huff. "The *Starfire* was built around the Quake Drive as its primary means of inter-system travel. Without a portal drive, the ship is just lame."

"I don't know," I said with a shrug. "We've done pretty well so far."

Tera opened her mouth to argue.

I held up my hands in surrender. "Okay, I get it." I glanced at the drive module again. "We'll just have to figure out how to get it working."

"What seems to be the problem?" Gabe asked, moving closer to the module to inspect it.

I ran a hand through my hair. "Well, I've got the drive in place, and I've connected all the conduits and wiring—at least, I think I've connected them all. But it still doesn't work." I turned to consider Robo-Gabe. "You have the majority of the real Gabe's memories, right?"

He gave me a very mechanical lift of his shoulder. "I do not know the total quantity of the original Gabe's memories, so I cannot be certain that the amount in my neural processor is more than fifty percent, but I do have some of them."

"Didn't you—or the real Gabe—see what the Quake Drive looked like when it was installed? I mean, it didn't get stolen until after you were . . . you know . . . killed."

If my mention of Gabe's death bothered my android friend, he didn't show it. "The neural link that recorded Gabe's memories did not have that level of detail," he replied in a matter-of-fact tone as he continued to examine the cabling connected to the drive module. "Besides, the original Gabe did not have a photographic memory, so that information could not have been transferred in the link anyway."

I sighed again. "Well, it sure would have come in handy right now. Until we get this thing fully operational, it's pretty much just a massive—albeit extremely sought-after—paperweight."

Tera scowled. "Why would paper need a weight?"

Apparently, in all those video blogs Gabe had used to program the ship's AI, Tera had never mentioned a paperweight. I was about to tell her that it was just an expression when HelperBot rolled up to the doorway. In his chipper, 1960s announcer voice, he said, "This unit would like to assist in the installation of the equipment."

I glanced down at the wheeled smart cart and let out a short laugh. "Great. Do you have any electrical wiring diagrams for the equipment?"

"This unit is designed to be of service," HelperBot announced, clearly oblivious to my question. "Please give this unit instructions on how it can be helpful."

I held my hands out wide. "I don't know what to tell you, HelperBot. I can't give you any instructions because I don't even know how to fix it myself."

"This unit will remain nearby to assist in the installation of the equipment," the cart said.

"Perfect. That's just what I need," I muttered, forcing myself to take a calming breath. I glanced over at Gabe, who looked back at me with a placid expression. "Actually, HelperBot, could you assist Gabe in . . . uh . . . organizing the environmental suits in the mining bay?"

Gabe cocked his head. "I was not planning to organize the environmental suits."

I leaned closer to him and whispered, "I know. I just need to give HelperBot something to get him out of here."

Realization dawned on Gabe's face. "Ah. Good idea." He glanced down at the motorized cart. "Follow me, HelperBot, we have a new assignment." Gabe smiled broadly at Tera over his shoulder as he left.

The rover followed my android friend across the corridor to the cargo bay. "This unit can assist in a variety of tasks. Please give the appropriate instructions." Its voice faded as it rolled away.

I grabbed the discarded spanner and leaned in close to the drive module's upper interface panel. If I could only figure out a way to get the module to receive power, maybe we could diagnose the problem. The translator chip that Tera and Vrynn had implanted behind my ear was amazing at helping me understand alien languages—anything anyone said would just sort of appear in my brain in English a split second after they said it.

But it was absolutely no help at all with written words.

"Can you tell me again what this panel says?" I asked my AI friend.

Tera heaved a dramatic sigh. "It says 'Guard Against Plasma Flow Overload' or something close to that."

I stared down at the panel, spreading my arms out in frustration. "I'd love to avoid an overload. You're just not telling me how to do it!"

After a moment, Tera said, "Are you talking to me or the Quake Drive?"

"The Quake Drive," I muttered.

"You do know the Quake Drive can't . . . talk back."

"Yeah, I know." I chuckled to myself. "Maybe I'm getting a little too used to the machinery around me being able to think and reply."

At that moment, a clunky, humanoid robot lumbered from the cargo bay across the corridor into the engineering closet. Its face was expressionless—probably by design—and one of its arms was a different color than the rest of the body—bright yellow instead of gray.

"Speaking of which . . ." I muttered to Tera, trailing off when the mining robot stopped in front of me. "Hey, Slate. What's the situation?" I forced myself to ask clear, direct questions any time I interacted with the leader of the mining bots. Mostly because any time I acted casual and asked questions like "what's up?" or "how's it going?" Slate would go semi-comatose as his circuits processed all possible replies to the question.

Not only that, but I was anxious to avoid any repeats of the misunderstanding that had made the mining robots rebel and kidnap Vrynn.

The robot spoke in his very mechanical voice. "Mining operations are proceeding within acceptable tolerance. Palladium output has reached six parts per thousand. Platinum output is fluctuating in the range of—"

"It's okay, Slate. I don't actually need a full report." I considered what I could say that would help improve our interactions in the future. "You can summarize the mining report to just the part I need."

"Which part is needed?" he asked in his mechanical voice.

I stared at him for several seconds until I realized that he was serious. Finally, I shrugged. "Just go ahead with the full report."

Slate resumed his report, droning on about the quantities and yields of the various metals and minerals the mining bots were extracting from the moon's subterranean rock. I zoned out, thinking about how much easier it was to relate with him now that he had a real name.

I had named him Slate because his actual designation was translated SL8, and that looked like the word Slate to me. Besides, he dealt with mining and refining rocks all day long; it seemed like the perfect name.

"... transports are non-functional. You need a working vessel for the cargo."

That caught my attention. "What cargo are you talking about?"

"The mining output is as follows—" Slate began.

"No, no." I held up my hands. "Can you just tell me the size of the entire load?"

"Four thousand, two hundred fifty-seven steckl—" my translator chip hiccupped when it heard the units. Then a few seconds later, I heard, "eight hundred twenty-five kilograms."

For reasons I didn't quite understand, my translator was stuck in the metric system. It was probably set that way accidentally when Vrynn and Tera had installed it. And now that it was inside my head, I had no easy way to fix it.

Less than a thousand kilograms of refined ore. That could easily fit in the cargo bay, couldn't it? If a kilogram was two pounds or so, that would still be less than a ton. The real Gabe had a crew-cab pickup truck on Earth that could carry that much, and I was sure the ship could carry his truck and its payload several times over.

"The *Starfire* can handle that," I told Slate.

Slate glanced from me to the Quake Drive and back.

"This ship is not currently functional," Slate said in his monotone voice. "The drive system must be installed."

"Thanks, Slate," I said drily. "That's actually what I'm working on right now."

"Put the cables in the correct junctions." Slate pointed clumsily with his yellow arm.

For a split second, I had a glimmer of hope. "Do you know which connections they're supposed to go to?"

"Negative. But those are the plasma connections, and they must be installed there." He pointed again at the drive module.

"Yeah, I got that." I stared at him, hoping he would get the hint. He never had before, though, so I added, "Thank you for the mining report. You can return to your duties."

A moment later—without acknowledging that I'd said anything—Slate turned on his heel and marched awkwardly out.

I let out a long sigh and leaned against the bulkhead.

"You handled that fairly well," Tera said.

I rubbed the back of my neck. "Yeah, well, I've had some difficult co-workers over the years. At least I don't have to worry about hurting Slate's feelings."

Tera gave a little "hmph," probably annoyed about my attitude toward the bot's emotions—or lack thereof. She looked like she was about to say something when we got another visitor in the engineering room.

This tiny space was suddenly Grand Central Station.

A small, wheeled bot—about the size of a large RC car—rolled up to me. It was one of the robots that had come with the facility, meant to convey messages or play follow-the-leader or something. I'd never quite figured it out.

Using its single mechanical arm, it tapped me on the leg.

"What do you want?" I asked in an annoyed voice.

Tera made a tutting sound.

I glanced over at my holographic friend and saw her look of disapproval. I exhaled loudly. "Fine." I glared down at the wheeled bot. "What can I do for you?"

The bot tapped my leg again then gestured with its claw toward the drive module.

"You want me to fix the Quake Drive?" I asked.

Its claw arm twitched a little, tapped me again, and pointed toward the drive.

This constant stream of arm-chair mechanics was about to drive me crazy. "Can I have everyone's attention, please?" I yelled out the door. "I'm working on installing the Quake Drive!" I said very loudly and slowly. I turned my attention back to the wheeled bot at my feet. "Go tell everyone that I'm working on it."

The little bot faced me for a few seconds then sped backward out of engineering, just as Rascal lumbered in. The large beast—who was the size of a small bear with fangs like a sabertooth tiger and the heart of a puppy dog—sidled up next to me. He seemed to have a sixth sense—or however many senses he had—about my safety and state of mind. I'd saved him from the streets of Vasielle right after he'd sunk his fangs into a guy who wanted to kill me.

It was fair to say that one of us was the other's rescue.

He nudged against my hand, clearly wanting some attention.

"Hey boy," I said, patting him on the back. "Don't tell me you're coming to offer advice, too."

After a few scratches at the base of his neck, Rascal must have had enough, so he wandered back out of engineering toward his nest in the aft of the cargo bay.

I watched him go then returned to the task at hand. "If everyone could leave me alone for a few minutes, I might make some progress," I muttered.

A moment later, Vrynn walked in. "Hey, Mitch—"

"Before you say anything, yes, I'm working on the Quake Drive. No, I don't have it done yet. Yes, I'm trying to get it done as quickly as I can."

Vrynn chuckled. "Hard day at work?" she asked.

I folded my arms and leaned against the wall, ignoring her comment. "Besides, why am I the one in charge of fixing this thing? I don't really know what I'm doing."

"We could go back to the factory on Mela Suphoria," Vrynn offered.

"The one we destroyed on our last visit?" I asked.

Vrynn shrugged. "There might be something left to salvage."

"Seems like it'd be a waste of time."

"More than what you're already doing?" Vrynn replied with a smirk.

"Did you come down here to help, or are you just going to make fun of me?"

Vrynn's expression softened. "Sorry." She reached out and touched my arm. "You're doing great."

I couldn't help but notice the tingle of her warm fingers against my skin.

"Actually, I just talked to Slate," Vrynn continued, her hand dropping from my arm. "He said we'll have some ore to sell pretty soon."

"Where are we going to sell it?" Tera asked.

"Rulioa IV?" she suggested, glancing at me.

"Sounds good," I said with a quick nod. "We are trying to stay off Gralik's radar, after all."

"Exactly, and Rulioa IV is so small and out of the way, I doubt it even gets visitors from the central systems," Vrynn said.

I lifted a brow playfully. "How would you remember anything about the dock at Rulioa IV? As I recall, you were too busy punching me as I tried to dump you at the end of the cargo ramp."

Vrynn scrunched her nose at me. I wasn't entirely sure, but it felt like the equivalent of sticking a tongue out.

Tera brought us back to the discussion at hand. "There were two ships from different central systems at the Rulioa IV public docking port on our last visit."

Vrynn and I both turned and stared at her.

"How do you know that?" I asked.

"I remember our visit there," she stated, as if it should be obvious.

"Well, I remember it, too," I said. "I just don't remember all the other ships."

"She doesn't have to rely on a faulty memory," Vrynn said, throwing me a playful look. "She probably has a complete sensor record of everything that happens on the ship."

"Uh, not exactly," Tera replied. "The ship's sensors are constantly running, but my matrix only stores those things that I interact with—things I've experienced."

"Hang on," I said. "Did Gabe ever come into this room? After he reactivated you, I mean."

Tera's gaze became unfocused, and her holographic eyes scanned back and forth. "Yes, he came in here when he was first inspecting the ship for physical damage."

"Can you show us your memory of being with Gabe here in the engineering room?" Vrynn asked.

Tera pointed to the display on a nearby bulkhead. It lit with a video of Gabe—the real Gabe—opening the door to engineering and stepping inside. I watched for the moment that I needed.

"Right there. Stop," I said. The video paused just as Gabe walked past the installed Quake Drive. I leaned in, scrutinizing the plasma conduits and all the wires running from underneath. "Can you zoom in on this spot?" I pointed to the area I was interested in.

The view enlarged to show just the cabling and the interface. The resolution wasn't perfect, but at least I could see where most of the wires were supposed to go.

"Tera, this is perfect!" I exclaimed. "I wish I could hug you. I think you just saved the day."

Tera's holographic cheeks pinked, and she gave me a shy smile.

"Are you really going to be able to fix it?" Vrynn asked excitedly.

I shook my head and shrugged at the same time. "I don't know, maybe." I stared at the plasma conduits lying next to the drive module for several seconds, then looked up at Vrynn again. "At least we have a chance now," I said with a smile.

I always knew that Vrynn really wanted the Quake Drive running. She'd put her life on the line to steal it back, after all, even though she probably had different reasons than I did. She wanted to save the entire star cluster from a despotic uprising. I only wanted to avenge Gabe and cause as much trouble for his murderers as I could. But it wasn't until we had an actual plan to fix it that I really saw Vrynn's level of motivation. She spent hours in the engineering closet with me, tugging on conduits, scrutinizing the video recordings, and checking every system to make sure it was running at optimal efficiency.

We double and triple checked the location of each cable and conduit. Well, Vrynn did the first check; I did the double and triple. Even after all the checking, I was still nervous about turning on a device that could open a portal in the space-time continuum. I barely trusted myself to fix a toaster oven.

As Vrynn and I stood back, surveying our handiwork, Tera shimmered into view again.

"Did you finally finish?" she asked, sounding like a teenager who was doing her best not to act excited.

"Yes. It's time to try it out," Vrynn replied enthusiastically.

"Hang on," I said, holding a hand out. "Are we sure this is a good idea? Maybe we should check the wiring on the plasma input conduit flow valve again."

Vrynn let her arms flop dramatically to her sides. "Mitch, we've checked that five times already. It's time to dive under with our breath in." A moment later, my translator said. "Take the plunge."

Ignoring her, I said to Tera, "Are there any indications that we might not have everything wired right? I mean, can you sense anything?"

Tera squeezed her eyes shut, and I knew immediately she was just patronizing me. "Nope. Without connecting it to the power, I can't magically detect the drive module."

I sighed. Maybe it was time to dive in the water holding my breath—or whatever it was that Vrynn had said.

"If it's any consolation," Tera began, "the computer has calculated a ninety-seven percent chance that nothing will blow up when you activate the drive."

I shrugged. Ninety-seven percent wasn't bad considering I was currently hiding on a volcanic moon with a motley crew of robots, androids, and holograms, not to mention an alien woman with an optimistic streak and the general appearance of a water nymph.

A very attractive water nymph, to be exact.

"What's the other three percent?" Apparently, I couldn't help my masochistic tendencies.

"There's a two and a half percent chance that the drive will overload and catch the engineering room on fire," Tera said. "And a half percent chance that it will explode and rip a hole in space-time."

I shook my head. My mistake for asking.

"Maybe there's a way to switch on the control systems without actually allowing power into the drive core itself," Vrynn said.

"That sounds like a much better idea," I replied.

"Great. Should we disconnect this part?" She pointed to the plasma flow regulator.

My eyes nearly bulged out of my skull. "Uncontrolled plasma flow into an untested wormhole machine? That's your safe plan?"

Vrynn threw up her hands. "I don't know. What do you suggest?"

I let out a short huff and scrutinized the complicated jumble of conduits and wiring. "Well, the plasma comes from the main engine core, through the control valve and regulator,"—I traced the path as I muttered—"to the power conversion module which feeds into the Quake Drive." My brow furrowed. "I can manually decrease the plasma flow. That should limit the input power."

"Perfect," Vrynn replied. "Let's do that."

I shook my head as I adjusted the manual override settings on the plasma valve.

"Okay, Tera. Let's switch on the power connection," Vrynn said.

I held up a hand. "Hang on just a second." I turned and walked toward the cargo bay.

"Where are you going?" Vrynn asked as she trailed behind me.

I continued along between the racks of supplies to the loading ramp. Rascal must have sensed me coming because he rose from his nest and lumbered down the cargo ramp at my side. He gave me a guttural purr as I patted him on the head. A few seconds later, Skeeter, the *Starfire's* cat-like companion bot, who usually followed Rascal around anytime he went outside the ship, pranced down the ramp to join us.

"I'm going to wait out here while you turn the drive on," I called to Vrynn over my shoulder, "just to be safe." I took a dozen or so steps away from the *Starfire* and turned around. "Okay, you can fire things up now."

Vrynn stopped at the top of the ramp and stared down at me. "You know, if the Quake Drive does create a hole in space-time, you're not really far enough away to avoid getting sucked in," she said, her lips curled upward in a teasing smile.

"You think you're being funny," I called back, more loudly than necessary, "but you're really not."

"Come on back inside, Mitch," Vrynn said. "I promise we won't blow up the ship."

I let out a long breath, waited a few more seconds, then trudged back toward the ship and up the ramp, Rascal at my side the whole way. When I reached Vrynn I said grimly, "The only reason you can get away with making a promise like that is that if you do blow up the ship, we'll both be dead too fast to even know you broke your promise."

"You catch on quick," she shot back. Then, in a very exaggerated way, she closed both eyes and nodded her head.

Was she trying to wink at me? I couldn't help but smile at her attempt. It was adorable.

Rascal peeled off toward his nest while Vrynn and I continued on to the engineering cubby. I waved a hand in Tera's direction. "Go ahead and connect to the drive," I said. "I've lived my life with much worse odds than ninety-seven percent."

Tera nodded. A second later, I heard a relay click and the console in front of us lit up.

Vrynn bounced up and down with excitement.

I simply stared, dumbfounded, at the new readouts on the display.

"Whoa," Tera said.

"What?" I asked.

"A whole new array of propulsion selections just came online," she replied, staring off in the distance.

"That sounds promising," I said.

"What's it like?" Vrynn asked.

"There's actually an option to open a portal, but it's requesting spatial coordinates," Tera said. "I think the controls will even show up on your navigation panels on the flight deck."

"Let's go check." Vrynn was a blur, blue-blond hair fluttering behind her, as she zipped past me.

"Hang on, Vrynn. We need to be careful about this." I followed behind with much less enthusiasm. By the time I reached the flight deck, Vrynn was already passing me on her way out.

"We forgot to turn the plasma flow valve-thingy back on," she said in a rush as she ran back toward the ladder.

As she went blasting by me, I grabbed her hand and pulled her to a stop. "Vrynn, wait!"

She looked wild with excitement, and I had to admit, it was a little contagious.

"Vrynn." I repeated her name and then waited until she focused on my face. "We have to slow down here."

Vrynn frowned up at me. "Why? We've finally got the drive installed. We can finally start saving people."

I couldn't quite figure out why she felt so driven to get the drive working. I felt like we'd already made a huge difference in the Bonara Cluster, even without the Quake Drive.

I took a deep breath. "We don't even know if it will work. It's been installed and uninstalled three times, in two different Mark 7 ships. Not to mention the sub-orbital trip in the middle of a space battle around Zerlon Prime. It could be completely fried."

"Or it could be the key to saving entire planets," she shot back.

"But it won't do anyone any good if we kill ourselves in the process."

We stared at each other for several seconds, neither quite willing to back down. Then Vrynn's expression changed from defiance to desperation. "Please, Mitch," she said softly, gazing up at me with those deep eyes.

Her vulnerable, pleading gaze made me finally relent.

"Okay. Okay. Once we have the drive online and running safely, we can take the *Starfire* out for a test run."

Vrynn's face broke into a wide grin, and she launched herself at me. I assumed it was meant to be a hug of gratitude, but it felt more like a passionate tackle.

She pulled away from our embrace before I was quite ready and ran for the ladder. "Let's go!" she called back at me.

Snapping out of my daze, I followed Vrynn back down to engineering. She already had the plasma flow valve cranked back to full by the time I reached her. Three seconds later, she was back out the door.

"Don't do anything yet," I called after her as I frantically quadruple checked all the components.

Everything looked right. Hopefully.

After one last glance at the plasma flow rate and several deep breaths, I rejoined Vrynn on the flight deck. "I know I said we could do a test run, but are we sure we want to do it right now? We could wait and check that all the systems are running right. Maybe sleep on it."

"Mitch, we're going right now," Vrynn declared. "I already closed the cargo bay and sent the signal to open the hangar airlock."

"Wait, isn't Gabe coming with us?" Tera asked with a note of concern in her voice.

Vrynn turned to Tera with a sympathetic look. "Oh, I think he's in the middle of coordinating with Slate." She lowered her voice, as if sharing a secret with Tera. "Besides, after all the effort you went through to get his android body, we'd hate to put him at risk."

That sounded like a dumb reason to me. Gabe's body was way more durable than mine. "What about putting my life at risk?" I asked.

Vrynn waved her hand toward the seat next to her. "You have to put your life at risk; you're the pilot."

I slid down into my chair. "I don't technically have to be the pilot," I said, trying to ignore my growing sense of foreboding.

Vrynn shrugged. "You told Tera not to let me take control of the ship," she said nonchalantly. "I'm pretty sure that still stands."

We both glanced over at Tera.

"Uh, yeah, anything you tell me to do stays in effect until you tell me something else," Tera replied.

I scrubbed a hand across my face. "Okay, I know I said not to let Vrynn take over the ship, but things have changed since then." I considered Vrynn for a moment, thinking of everything we'd been through in the last few weeks, and how my feelings for her had changed. She simply stared back at me, one eyebrow raised, a placid expression on her perfect face.

"So Vrynn's allowed to fly the ship now?" Tera asked. "Without you?"

"Yeah, I can think of plenty of jams we might get in where I'll need Vrynn to take the ship." I turned to her. "You're not going to steal the *Starfire* from me, are you?"

A playful smile spread across her face. "Only if you force my hand," she replied.

I chuckled at her sarcasm. We both wanted the same thing, and there was no one in the Bonara Cluster I trusted more than Vrynn. In fact, my feelings for her went beyond mere trust. How far, I wasn't quite sure yet, but I certainly didn't worry about her killing me in my sleep anymore.

I turned back to Tera. "Yeah, Vrynn can fly the *Starfire* without me."

Tera nodded, and Vrynn sat forward on the edge of her seat. "Great. Let's get going."

I started to stand from my chair. "So. . . since you're allowed to fly now, maybe I should just wait here until—"

Vrynn pushed me back down. "You have to come with us. This is the moment we've been waiting for."

"If you mean the moment we'll explode trying to use alien technology that I've installed with my limited, Earth-man knowledge, then yeah, I guess this is the moment we've been waiting for."

A delicate laugh escaped Vrynn's lips, and I couldn't help but feel a little lighter. Or it might have been the hover emitters as I guided the ship out through the hangar airlock.

Vrynn acted relaxed, despite what we were about to do. Of course, she optimistically thought the drive would work flawlessly. I, on the other hand, understood my own limitations—not to mention all the mistakes I'd made in my former job back on Earth.

But I had to admit that Vrynn's hopeful attitude was infectious; it always had been. In fact, that was one of the things I liked most about her. I ended up being a more optimistic person just by being around her.

A few minutes later, we cleared the moon's atmosphere and flew away into the orbit of its gas giant.

"Where should we go?" Vrynn asked.

"We should start small," I said. "Like a jump to one of the other moons." I pointed in the direction of the next largest moon, its icy surface barely visible in the distance.

"We should think bigger than that," Vrynn countered. "Let's go to another system." She turned to Tera. "How far can the Quake Drive take us?"

"The interface will allow any destination to be input," Tera said.

Vrynn turned back to me, her face animated. "We could go anywhere. We could even—" She suddenly fell silent.

"What?" I asked.

"We could take you back to Dirt," she said somberly.

"Earth," I corrected her out of habit. Then it hit me, and the light-headed feeling had nothing to do with the hover emitters.

We'd actually had enough fuel for the round trip to Earth using the standard intra-space drive for several weeks—ever since we refueled at the Resistance base on Dreporox. The journey would have taken a week, but it had been an option.

A working Quake Drive meant instantaneous travel. I could be back in my Oklahoma hometown in just a few minutes. I gazed out the flight deck windows at the emptiness of space in front of us.

That was hard to fathom.

Vrynn must have seen the change in my expression. "Do you want to?" Vrynn asked, her voice laced with a fair bit of trepidation.

I turned to her with a wry grin. "Are you trying to get rid of me?"

A broad smile spread across her face, but it quickly turned somber. "I know what it's like to be away from your planet. To not have contact with your people for years."

Her words should have brought a feeling of homesickness or a sense of longing. Instead, I felt curiously empty at the idea of going back to my regular Earth life.

Vrynn needed me here. No one on Earth—with the exception of Gabe and Tera, who were obviously gone now—had ever needed me this much. And even though they weren't the real Gabe and Tera, if Vrynn took me back to Earth, I might never see this Gabe and Tera again.

I straightened in my seat. "Let's worry about Earth later. Right now, we need to figure out if the drive will even work."

Vrynn's smile widened, and she gave a curt nod.

I pushed the throttle forward, and we rocketed farther and farther out into the void. The star-speckled blackness was mesmerizing. Even if there weren't any constellations that I recognized.

Carefully—and quite expertly compared to earlier attempts—I rotated the ship back toward Thetis Max. From this distance, the gas giant Thetis looked like a large moon, and our volcanic home was like a tiny speck.

"Input the coordinates of low orbit over Thetis Max," I said to Tera as I applied the thrusters to line us up with Thetis Max, more or less.

"Coordinates confirmed." Despite the normally bored or flippant attitude of the personality overlay of my teenage high school friend, even Tera seemed interested in the results of our test.

I took a deep breath. We were about to bend the fabric of space—opening a portal between us and the moon below. "Okay, go ahead and turn it on," I said. It wasn't the most memorable command I'd ever given. Maybe I should have said something like "engage" or "activate."

Tera nodded, and Vrynn and I both leaned forward in our seats.

A tiny dot appeared a few hundred feet in front of the ship. Or at least, it looked like a dot when I first saw it. As I watched, the dot began to expand until it was about twice as large as the *Starfire*.

It felt like looking through a giant circular window floating in front of us. I could see the surface of Thetis Max, as if we were right above it.

It was incredible.

"The longer the portal is open, the more energy it drains," Tera said. "So, either take the ship through or tell me to close it."

This was the moment of truth.

Vrynn nodded encouragingly. "Let's do it, Mitch."

My grip on the control sticks tightened, and I nudged the ship toward the portal. As the *Starfire* slid slowly through the center of this bizarre window in space, I expected something momentous to happen—like a whoosh or a buzzing or something.

Absolutely nothing.

The ship coasted a few hundred feet forward and ended up a few hundred miles closer to Thetis Max.

"Wow." That was all I could think to say.

"This is amazing!" Vrynn exclaimed, bouncing out of her seat. "Do you realize what this means?" She grabbed my shoulders. "Mitch! This will change everything."

I smiled up at her. "Yeah, assuming it works over larger distances."

"I'm sure it will," Vrynn said confidently. "We could try it out right now."

I shook my head. "Let's go back to the hangar. I want to take a look at the drive to make sure everything is still okay."

"This is no time to be cautious, Mitch," Vrynn said. "Gralik and Nexus have subjugated entire worlds. We could end all that." I could hear the passion in her voice.

I scratched the back of my neck. "I know you want to go right now, but there's so much that we still don't know. Do we have a way to monitor the energy flow or the stability of the portal or its location?"

"I'm sure Tera can help us figure that all out as we go," Vrynn said.

As usual, I tried to ignore her optimism. "And what about the energy drain she mentioned? Do we have an unlimited number of portal jumps? How long can the portal stay open?"

"That's complicated," Tera said. "The Quake Drive draws plasma from our main engine core—which still has plenty of fuel—and feeds it to the power cells which get depleted any time the portal is open. Of course, they recharge automatically once the portal closes, but it takes a while. They were down to about ninety-two percent after that jump, but they're back up to ninety-six now."

"Let's go, then," Vrynn exclaimed.

"I'm sorry, Vrynn, but I'm not willing to jump right into combat with the Quake Drive yet." I tried to say it emphatically so Vrynn would know I'd made up my mind. "We'll do some more testing, and then we can figure out how to use it against Nexus."

Her expression flashed disappointment, which wasn't too surprising. "Okay, I guess I've waited this long; I can be patient one more day," she said, putting on a brave face.

I nodded and took the controls again, guiding us back to our base.

Despite my brain telling me I had made the right decision, I still had a gnawing guilt in the pit of my stomach.

Chapter Three

I had anticipated Vrynn would wake me up early saying that it was time to test the drive again, or that she would follow me around asking when we could go.

So I was surprised when I didn't see her all morning.

I spent some time in the engineering room, where Tera showed me the power cells on the Quake Drive and how to check their charge levels. They had all regenerated to full power, so that was a good sign.

After that, I went up to the flight deck and had Tera step me through the new display on my flight console. Entering the portal coordinates manually was way more difficult than just asking Tera to do it, but it was nice to know we had the option in an emergency.

Eventually, I left the *Starfire* to search the rest of the facility for Vrynn. I finally found her in the comm room of the abandoned mining complex. We had meant to repair the old communications equipment so that we wouldn't be reliant on the *Starfire's* systems only. Maybe that's what she'd been working on.

"Hey," I said as I walked into the small room. "How's it going?"

Vrynn's brow furrowed as she stared straight ahead, her gaze unfocused.

"Did you get the comm system working?" I asked.

She held up a hand to cut me off and pressed the headset harder against her ear. I waited patiently, growing more and more concerned based on her expression.

Vrynn glanced up at me a moment later. "I was checking some of the less-frequently used channels, and this came through." She switched the system to play over the speaker.

A garbled voice came out that my translation chip made even more choppy. I picked out the words assault, pirates, and something that I was pretty sure sounded like Ludros.

I looked at Vrynn, wondering if her translation chip did a better job than mine.

"Pirates are attacking a vessel at Ludros Beta Five. They're in danger of being overwhelmed and boarded," she said.

I frowned. "You got all that from a garbled transmission? I barely heard the word 'pirates'."

Vrynn stood abruptly from her seat. "We can save them from the attack!" She zipped past me into the corridor.

"Uh, yeah, that's a good idea," I said, but Vrynn was already long gone. I hustled out of the room and caught up with her about the time we reached the *Starfire*.

"What's going on?" Tera asked when we rushed onto the flight deck.

"We're headed to the Ludros Binary system," Vrynn explained as she activated her control panels. "There's a ship under attack by pirates."

Tera scrunched her holographic face. "Shouldn't the local law enforcement handle things like that?"

"The distress call said they need help," Vrynn declared as the *Starfire* hovered gracefully out onto the moon's bleak surface. "Maybe their planet's security forces aren't up to the job."

I shrugged. "In the line of duty, sometimes it's best not to ask questions."

"Is that from a TV show or something?" Tera asked.

"No, it's from me," I said, taking the controls.

Tera rolled her eyes in response.

Once we were in orbit, I angled the ship—slowly and carefully—in the general direction of the Ludros Binary system. "Okay Tera, set a jump to the Ludros—"

"Wait. What are you doing?" Vrynn asked.

"Jumping to the Ludros Binary system," I replied, not as confident as I had been a moment ago. "Didn't we want to save the day?"

"Yeah, but how long will a regular jump take?" she asked Tera.

"An intra-space jump to Ludros Beta Five would take twenty-three minutes," Tera said.

"That's too long," Vrynn said. "The pirates are taking over the ship right now."

I frowned. "Then we'd have to use the Quake Drive. Are we sure it can go that far?"

"How do you think this ship got to Dirt?" she shot back.

"Earth," I said with a scowl. But she did make a good point. "Okay, bring the Quake Drive online and target the portal for Ludros Beta Five."

"Portal target set," Tera said a moment later. "By the way, at this distance, the targeting error has a one-mile radius."

I nodded. "Good to know. Let's back the portal target away from the planet a few more miles, just in case."

"Done," Tera said.

"I can't believe we're doing this," I muttered, shaking my head. "Okay, open the portal."

A dot appeared in front of us and quickly grew to several times the size of the *Starfire*. A greenish-blue orb hung in front of us, so large that it was only partially visible through the portal. I remembered what Tera had said about the power drain from keeping the portal open, so I grabbed the sticks and pushed us through. The status on the Quake Drive panel indicated that the portal had closed and that the power banks were around eighty percent.

"Wow," I said. "I wonder if I'll ever get used to that."

"The Quake Drive is working perfectly," Vrynn said excitedly. "Now we can go anywhere we need to." She turned to Tera. "How fast can we do successive jumps before the power levels drop too low?"

"It depends on the total distance of the portal connection and how long it's open," Tera replied.

Vrynn nodded. "Let's assume super-short jumps, just enough for the ship to—"

"Hello." I waved my hand to get the attention of my co-pilot and AI assistant. "Shouldn't we be looking for pirates right about now?"

Vrynn stared at me for a second. "Oh, yeah, we need to do that." She glanced down at her console. "Let's scan the area for ships."

"I've already scanned the area," Tera said lazily. "There aren't any ships around us."

I frowned. "Are there even any ships in orbit?"

"There are nine different ships moving up into high orbit, likely preparing for intra-space jumps," Tera said. "At least half a dozen sentry ships are on this side of the planet, and a few ships have just entered the atmosphere on their way to various spaceports."

"Are any of them under attack?" I asked.

Tera shook her head. "Not that I can detect on my sensors."

I stared at the display in front of me. "How are we supposed to figure out—"

"We have an incoming call from Ludros Beta Five traffic control," Tera said.

I sighed. "Okay, go ahead."

A moment later, the holographic display above my console activated, showing the upper half of a frazzled-looking man. He wore a high-tech headset and a scowl. "Ludros Beta Five Control to Mark 7, please vector to Bantendra Spaceport at seven-one-five-zero."

My brows knit together. "We're actually here to stop a hijacking or pirate attack or something like that?" I knew it came out more like a question, but the whole weird situation had thrown me off my normal confidence.

The harried man stared at me as if I'd sprouted a horn from my forehead. At least that's what I imagined his expression might have been like. I hadn't actually seen any aliens with horns yet. "Acknowledge your re-vector to seven-one-five-zero." The controller cocked his head, waiting for my reply.

I turned to Tera. "Can you give me a waypoint indicator or something?"

Tera nodded, and a dot appeared on my navigation screen. I pointed the ship in that direction and gently applied the thrust. "Re-vector acknowledged," I said in what I hoped was an official-sounding voice.

The controller man dipped his head curtly, as if our conversation was over. But I didn't want to let the opportunity slip by.

"Is there a ship under attack?" I blurted out.

"What are you talking about?" He acted utterly perplexed at my continued conversation.

"You haven't had any reports of pirate attacks today?"

"No."

I glanced over at Vrynn, hoping she would give me some help on the details, but she sat silently staring at the projection of the spaceport controller-guy.

"Are you sure?" I asked. "Maybe you could double check. We received a signal that someone's ship was being attacked by—"

"I can assign your ship a berth at the spaceport, or I can vector you away from controlled space to search for some imaginary pirate attack," the guy huffed.

I scowled. "We definitely got a distress call about an attack from pirates, don't you think—"

Vrynn put her hand on my arm. "Maybe they said militants in the transmission, but it was translated as pirates."

I lifted my brows. "I guess that's possible."

The controller-guy muttered something like, "I don't have time for this."

I turned my attention back to the holo-display. "Sure, clear us for landing."

The controller-guy glanced down at a display in front of him as he tapped at the input panel. After a few seconds, he said, "Proceed to berth nine-seven-two."

"Thank you for—"

The connection terminated before I could say anything else.

I turned to Vrynn, puzzled. "Why would we receive a distress call from Ludros Beta Five that the planet controller doesn't know anything about?"

She tilted her head. "Maybe they sent the transmission during the attack, but they were still able to get away or land somehow."

I gave a small shrug. "Maybe."

Following the waypoint, I guided the *Starfire* down through the atmosphere. It was a stunning view. The surface of Ludros Beta Five was a patchwork of lush green plains crisscrossed with blue rivers and dotted with brown and gray mountain peaks. It felt like looking at a scene from Earth if someone had taken the Alps, the Caribbean, and the Amazon and squished them into one area.

The wild beauty beneath us abruptly ended with the beginning of densely packed streets and buildings. The city of Bantendra was hemmed in on all sides by what I assumed was the original nature of the planet. It reminded me of pictures I'd seen of Central Park, but in reverse.

I brought the *Starfire* low over the city, heading for the spaceport. Without the waypoint, I would have been completely lost. The flashing signs were utter gibberish to me.

Once settled in our assigned berth, I stood from my seat and moved to the door. When Vrynn didn't follow, I stopped. "Shouldn't we go out and investigate?" I said, motioning toward the spaceport concourse outside.

She looked up from her console. "Oh, maybe you and Gabe should take a look. I'll keep monitoring things from here."

I shrugged. "C'mon Gabe. Let's go check things out."

Gabe seemed happy enough to join me—assuming happy was the appropriate word for his algorithmic processes. We marched down the cargo ramp and around to the main concourse. It reminded me of the spaceport on New Talpreus, only newer and cleaner. And with fewer flea-market-style vendors.

"What are we looking for?" Gabe asked.

"The distress call said there was an attack," I replied as I scanned the ships we passed. "So, I guess we're looking for a ship that's been damaged or something."

We walked along the concourse, passing ship after ship that looked fine. Well, maybe not fine, per se. Most had maintenance crews working on some part of the ship. But I didn't see any with battle damage indicating a recent fight to repel pirates. Some of the docked ships were actually quite impressive, maybe not as large or well equipped as the *Starfire*, but still nice enough.

"No pirates so far," I said to Gabe. "But plenty of unhappy starship captains."

"I do not understand," Gabe replied.

"This area must be for ships needing repairs." I held my arms out wide. "Have you ever met a ship owner who's happy when the ship is broken down?"

"No," Gabe said. "But neither the original Gabe nor I have met very many starship owners."

I couldn't help but chuckle at that, particularly considering how much the real Gabe would have loved to have met even one starship owner.

I was about to say we should give up and head back to the ship when we rounded the corner of a dingy-looking freighter and came face-to-face with a gleaming-silver transport. It was about the same general size as the *Starfire*, maybe a little thinner and longer, though obviously not a warship. The exterior—that initially appeared silvery—actually had a multi-color sheen to it, almost like the underside of a video disk. I still preferred the menacing look of the *Starfire* and its bristling weapons, but this ship had an elegance that was hard to miss.

"Whoa, that's quite a ship," I said, not taking my eyes off the sleek vessel. "I wonder what she can do."

"I have always thought it was strange that ships are female," Gabe said.

My brow went up. "*You've* always thought that?"

"Well, I suppose the original Gabe always thought that. I only started thinking about it when I became operational a few weeks ago."

"You've given it a lot of thought, have you?" I asked with a grin.

"Less than one tenth of a percent of my secondary processing algorithms have been dedicated to the question, but yes, I have been thinking about it."

I was about to tell Gabe about the time his biological predecessor had made a similar observation, when the hatch of the luxury starship opened, and a pair of uniformed crew members—a man and a woman—stepped down the ramp and strode toward a nearby spaceport attendant. Based on their posture, I assumed they were military. Based on their scowls, I could tell they were upset.

I subtly tilted my head for Gabe to follow me, and we got close enough to linger within earshot of the conversation.

"... expected the mechanic to be here two hours ago. Why hasn't he arrived yet?" the man asked.

The flustered attendant glanced nervously down at her display. "I'm sorry, sir. Your request for a drive mechanic has not been finalized."

"Why not?" the female crew member asked in exasperation. "Do you not have mechanics on hand?"

"The mechanics who work within the spaceport are independently hired. You must request a specific mechanic for the hiring process to be completed," the attendant explained. "Do you have a particular mechanic that you would like me to ask for? I can process the order right now."

The man sighed. "We've never been to this spaceport. Who would you recommend?"

The attendant held her hands out. "I wouldn't presume to bias your decision with my opinion."

"We don't even know the names of the available mechanics. Can you at least tell us who most people choose?" the female crew member asked.

The attendant shook her head. "If you are unsatisfied with the service or if something goes wrong with your equipment after the repair, I could be held responsible. My job doesn't require me to take on that level of liability. Would you like me to transmit the full list of starship mechanics who are licensed to perform work in the Bantendra spaceport?"

"If that's our only way to get a mechanic, then go ahead," the woman said. She shared an exasperated look with her crewmate as they turned to leave.

As they walked past us on their way back to their ship, the man said, "Could she have been any less helpful?"

"I would have said she was an android, but that would be an insult to androids," the woman replied over her shoulder.

I did my best to stifle my laugh at her comment.

Two seconds later, Gabe said, "Oh, I get it."

His pitiful attempt at a solitary laugh was so mechanical and forced that it only made me laugh harder.

"But my logic subroutine cannot determine if that was an insult to androids or not," Gabe said

"Me neither, buddy," I said, as I got my laughter back under control. "But people can say strange things when they're under stress." I tilted my head in the direction of the retreating crew. "Maybe we should see if we can help."

Gabe raised an eyebrow but didn't protest. We tailed the two crew members to their ship. They both stopped at the bottom of the ramp and turned toward us, expressions immediately guarded.

"Can I help you?" the woman asked.

"Actually, we thought we might be able to help you."

I didn't miss the look of skepticism that passed between them. "Are you official Bantendra-registered starship mechanics?" the woman asked. I could tell from her tone that she already knew the answer.

"No. Just a fellow starship crew member," I replied. That was stretching the truth a little, but Gabe didn't correct me.

"Do you have any experience with plasma flow systems?" the man asked.

I shrugged nonchalantly. "Yesterday, I repaired the plasma flow regulator on a jump drive."

The man's expression shifted. He almost looked impressed. "Our drive's plasma injector module failed right as our jump ended. We have the replacement part, but the connectors are jammed."

"My friend has super strength," I said, indicating Gabe.

My friend smiled serenely back at them. "I am an android."

The woman's cheeks pinked slightly at this information, but otherwise, they gave no indication that they were uncomfortable with the idea.

"Come, we'll show you the system," the man said, waving us inside.

The luxury vessel wasn't that different from the *Starfire*, except that the rooms and corridors seemed to be made for comfort. Fortunately, their engineering room felt vaguely similar to the engineering cubby on the *Starfire*—and every sci-fi movie I'd ever watched.

Apparently, the engineering department was a universal constant.

Between Gabe's herculean strength and my helpful instructions, we had the new module installed and the plasma running smoothly in under an hour.

"Impressive work."

I turned around to see a woman standing in the doorway. She was probably in her late fifties or early sixties—in Earth terms—with a round, portly body and pudgy face. She had a swirl of iridescent hair piled on top of her head that didn't look even remotely natural, but maybe that was the vibe she was going for.

"But is it fixed?" the woman in the doorway asked. She had an easy, casual tone, as if she was used to people listening to what she said.

I scratched my neck and considered the newly replaced injector. "As well as I know how to fix it," I said with a chuckle.

"Maybe I should wait to pay you for your services, then, until after we test it." She arched a heavily made-up brow. I could tell the gesture was meant to be playful, but it was also slightly intimidating at the same time.

"Oh, you don't have to pay us." I gestured to Gabe and myself. "We were just looking to be helpful."

"I was looking for pirates," Gabe said in a matter-of-fact voice.

The older woman laughed lightly as she considered Gabe. She turned her attention back to me and took several steps forward. "My name is Shariamy Razome," the woman said. She was dressed in an opulent suit, glittering with beads and jewels. "I'm the fifth cousin of Chancellor Helvay and consul general to Invathea." Obviously, I was supposed to be impressed, though I wasn't sure who the chancellor person was or any of the rest of it.

"My name is Mitchell Foster," I replied. Feeling uncertain whether I should shake her hand or bow, I simply gestured to Gabe. "And this is my friend, Gabe."

She nodded at us in turn. Her smile seemed genuine, if a little guarded. "If you won't let me pay you, can I give you a ride somewhere? You did fix my ship."

"That's very kind, Consul General Razome—"

"Actually, you don't have to use my full title," she tittered. "You should just call me Shariamy."

"We have a ship," Gabe said shortly. "And it is faster than this ship."

Shariamy considered him. "Are you sure? Our recent technical difficulties notwithstanding, my ship has one of the best intra-space drives money can buy. It's the most recent release of the—"

"Ours has a portal drive," Gabe stated matter-of-factly.

I turned to him and gave a subtle shake of my head. We didn't really know this Shariamy Razome woman. Despite her insistence that she was related to some chancellor, it was probably best to not spill all of our secrets.

"Hmm. A portal drive?" Shariamy tapped her chin. "I had heard something about the Vanguard Dragoons trying to recover a ship with a portal drive." She eyed me thoughtfully. "Maybe the rumors are true."

I opened my mouth to redirect the conversation when Gabe piped up again.

"We also have a co-pilot." He cast me a sidelong glance. If I didn't know better, I would have thought my friend was feeling jealous on Vrynn's behalf. Did he think I was in danger of falling for the audacious flirtation of a woman who could easily be twice my age?

Shariamy frowned at Gabe's mention of a co-pilot. She tilted her head as if considering me. It seemed that Gabe's vague reference to Vrynn had distracted Shariamy's attention better than I could have.

"I was about to offer you a job as ship mechanic," she said. "It would certainly come with enviable benefits." Her expression slowly morphed into understanding. "But given that there's a co-pilot, then that would probably make you the pilot . . . unless it's your friend." She gestured to Gabe.

"I am not allowed to be the pilot," Gabe said. "I am an android."

"I wondered." She gave Gabe a patronizing, though not unfriendly, smile. "You seem far more intelligent—and realistic—than any android I've ever met. I don't suppose I could offer you a position on my ship?"

"Thank you. No," Gabe said.

Turning back to me, she said, "And if you work well with your co-pi-lot—"

"He does," Gabe interjected.

"—then you wouldn't want to lose that," Shariamy said. Her smile turned much more genuine and a little bit resigned. She reached into her pocket and produced a gleaming disk about the size of a silver dollar. "If you ever think of a way that I can repay your kindness, just let me know."

"Thank you." I took the disk, though I had no idea what to do with it. Gabe said nothing; he simply stared at Shariamy with an unruffled expression. "Well, we'd better get going." I pulled Gabe toward the door before he could get us into any more trouble. Shariamy waved us to the exit ramp, and we walked back down the concourse toward the *Starfire*.

"That was interesting," I said after a few moments.

"We were able to render assistance," Gabe replied. "But we did not find any pirates."

"Yeah, that's too bad, huh," I said.

"I also find it surprising that we must inform so many people that I am an android," Gabe said. "Can they not tell by looking at me?"

"Well, your tissue overlay was grown in the *Starfire* fabrication lab, which is pretty advanced compared to current tech in the Bonara cluster. It's probably more realistic than most people have ever seen."

"If the skin is meant to make me appear to be a biological, then perhaps telling people that I am an android is actually negating that goal. Maybe I should create an algorithm that would allow me to lie about my true nature."

I chuckled. "Let's not go quite to that extreme, either. You don't have to volunteer it to everyone, but if it comes up, be honest about it."

"Currently, I do not have any other options besides being honest," he said.

"Good," I replied. Remembering the disk in my hand, I held it out to Gabe. "Do you have any idea what this is?"

"That is a comm encryption token," he said. "It facilitates a direct transmission to the other person."

"We should probably hang onto it then."

"I have no desire to ever contact Miss Razome," Gabe said. "Do you?"

I shrugged and pocketed the token. "Probably not. But it never hurts to have a favor you can call in."

We had just turned the corner onto the row of berths where we'd parked the ship, when I felt something hard press into my back.

"Do not make any sudden motion that would draw attention," a man's voice whispered sharply from close behind me. "The same goes for your buddy." Though he didn't speak loudly, his tone was ice cold.

My first instinct was to raise my hands, but that's probably what he meant by not making any sudden moves.

Gabe turned to see what was happening. "It appears this man is threatening you. Should I incapacitate him?"

The guy pressed the metallic object deeper against my spine. I held a hand up to Gabe. "Thanks, buddy. Just hang on." I turned my attention back to the mugger. "What do you want? We don't have much money," I said.

The criminal let out a sinister chuckle. "You've got a ship that's way more valuable than money."

My stomach sank. Whoever this guy was, he knew who we were. My mind raced. How could some random criminal on Ludros Beta Five even know that we had the *Starfire,* much less that we were here in the spaceport? There had to be another explanation.

Before I even had a chance to figure out where this goon had come from, he decided to tell me more. Maybe villain monologuing was a universal constant, too.

"Wait till Ungar hears that Bantendra Station was the jackpot. When Gralik told us we had to watch Ludros, Ungar said it was the dumbest assignment ever. He said you'd never come to any of the planets in the Ludros systems. And now you can see how wrong he was."

"We have no idea what you're talking about," I gestured to myself then Gabe, hoping his android programming didn't have an anti-lying algorithm. He cocked his head to the side but didn't say anything.

"I might be stupid," the Nexus operative said dryly, "but I'm not that stupid. You're going to take me to the ship. And I'm going to be a hero. And Gralik is going to promote me to corporal or reward me or something."

If this guy got the *Starfire,* that would be bad, and not just because it would fall into Gralik's hands, but because he would almost certainly do something stupid like kill us.

"I should warn you that my friend"—I indicated Gabe—"is actually an android, and he hates it when people threaten me."

"That's even better," the Nexus thug grunted. "After I turn over the ship to Gralik, maybe I'll put your friend on display at the Caridyan tech show. I could even sell him to the highest bidder."

"He is going to be very upset if you keep talking like that," I said.

Gabe shook his head. "Mitch, you should know that I do not currently possess any subroutines for hate or anger or—"

The operative poked the weapon deeper into my back. "If he tries anything, you're a dead man."

"Oh, he'll be perfectly calm," I replied with more composure than I felt. "Unless you do something to hurt me. Then you're the dead man."

"Mitch I cannot—"

"Oh yeah? Who's got the blaster in the other one's back?" the operative replied, though the confidence in his voice had slipped a little.

"Seriously, though, you definitely shouldn't push me over," I continued, hoping to convey the plan to Gabe. "He might decide to use his super-strength to punch you across the concourse."

"Fine, I won't push you over," the guy snapped. "Just shut up and keep walking."

I glanced at Gabe out of the side of my eye and winked. That was all the signal I could risk giving him. Then I flailed my arms. "Hey," I said. "Stop pushing me!"

"I'm not doing anything!" the goon yelled back.

I intentionally scuffed my foot and tripped forward. When I hit the ground with my theatrical half-tumble, I got my first real look at my assailant. He had slightly yellowish-green skin, like a slimy bog or a baby's diaper. He wore a ratty, gray uniform that made him look like he'd just arrived for shore leave after months in space. His beady eyes stared down at me in surprise, then we both turned to Gabe. The thug probably wondered—like I did—if Gabe would do all those things I'd threatened.

Gabe considered me for a moment then turned to the Nexus operative, took one step toward him, and swung an open palm into the guy's chest. The goon sailed backward through the air—firing his blaster the whole way—and landed on a nearby exotic fruit stall. Fortunately for us, his aim was way off.

Another goon, who must have been trailing farther back, ducked behind a small transport shuttle and began firing at us, too.

I dove for cover on the other side of a stack of crates, pulling Gabe with me. I crouched low and peered around the corner of my makeshift barrier. Several blaster bolts hit the crate next to my head, and I immediately ducked. Aiming my blaster at the second goon, I fired off a few wild shots which kept him momentarily pinned down behind the shuttle.

"You don't happen to have a blaster with you," I said to Gabe.

"No," he replied. "But I am not permitted to fire one anyway."

I frowned, wondering how that had never come up before. It must have been our first time to fight anyone together outside the *Starfire*. It was probably our first time to fight anyone together at all, except for the private boot camp debacle back on Earth. But that was a different story.

I glanced around the other side of the stack and fired off a few shots at my original accoster as he struggled to free himself from a large pile of fruit. He dove back into the slushy mess to avoid being shot.

A moment later, the top crate in my defensive wall exploded. I covered my head to protect myself from a shower of wood slats and pieces of what had been some high-tech equipment a few seconds ago.

"I can't take on two by myself," I yelled.

"Retreat might be our best option then," Gabe replied. "Unless you would like to call Vrynn for reinforcements."

I shook my head. Though I knew Vrynn was good in a fight, I didn't want to put her in danger as well. "Let's get back to the ship," I said, crouching low, preparing to run. I took a deep breath, nodded at Gabe to start moving, then leaned out from behind the stack of crates and took multiple shots at both enemies. In the lull that followed, I pelted after Gabe.

At the sight of the approaching melee, the spaceport visitors in the concourse scattered like birds on a beach. Gabe and I had only gone about twenty steps before blaster bolts whizzed by, striking vehicles and ships ahead of us. "Cover!" I yelled at Gabe, and we both hid behind a nearby utility truck.

Turning back to our pursuers, I watched the second goon scamper toward my partially destroyed barrier. I fired off several rounds, catching him in the chest, and he crumpled to the ground. The first guy was now out of the fruit muck and in a much better position to cause trouble. I ducked just as several of his shots struck the edge of my hiding place.

"Perhaps these are the pirates," Gabe said, crouching next to me.

"What pirates?"

"We came to Ludros Beta Five to stop pirates. Maybe these are the ones."

I shook my head in disbelief as another pair of bolts struck the ground near us. "This is what your processors are thinking about right now?"

Gabe nodded. "That, and what steps I should take if a blaster bolt passes through the organic tissue of your body."

I barked out a short laugh as I took aim at our remaining attacker and fired off a few rounds. Leave it to my buddy to point out the worst that could happen. "I mean, maybe. These are Nexus operatives that Gralik sent to watch the spaceport, so I guess it's possible they got mistaken for pirates." I fired again.

"They certainly look the part," Gabe said, as if judging them for their fashion choices.

A moment later, I heard the deep rumble of ship thrusters approaching. I peeked over the top of the truck and saw a small gunship cruising low over the concourse, very intentionally approaching our firefight with the Nexus goon. I turned to Gabe. "Hopefully, that's spaceport security."

"Becoming involved with local law enforcement could be problematic," he said. "I am not fully versed in their procedures and requirements. We might be in trouble for using weapons in the concourse area."

"I'm sure we can explain what happened," I replied with a shrug. "Better than getting killed by one of Gralik's thugs. Or worse, having them steal our ship."

Gabe nodded his agreement just as dozens of plasma rounds struck the vehicle we were hiding behind. The top half exploded in a spray of shrapnel. The gunship shifted sideways to position itself for a better angle. Unless this planet had a "shoot all the suspects" policy, this ship was definitely not from spaceport security.

"Run!" I yelled, and we took off down the concourse again.

Behind us, the gunship settled roughly onto the pavement, and the original operative—still covered in chunks of fruit—jumped into the back of the open cockpit. A moment later, the ship roared into the air again.

Gabe and I were about fifty yards from the *Starfire's* berth when plasma rounds nipped at our heels again. I waved at the flight deck windows, hoping Tera or Vrynn would see us, before ducking behind a nearby cargo ship. Surely we'd caused enough ruckus in the concourse that our friends would know something was going on out here.

Suddenly, one of the *Starfire's* smaller dorsal plasma cannons sprang to life, swiveling toward us and firing a cluster of rounds at the gunship that had us pinned down. The enemy ship fired off a few more rounds at Gabe and me then swooped away, fleeing the *Starfire's* superior firepower.

I stood and ran toward our ship, Gabe close on my tail. As soon as my feet touched the bottom of the cargo ramp, I yelled, "Lift off! We have to catch that gunship!"

The ship shuddered under my feet as the hover emitters came online. Half a minute later, I burst onto the flight deck and jumped into the pilot's chair.

"What happened?" Vrynn asked, switching her controls to weapons as I took over flying.

"Nexus operatives," I panted. "Sent . . . by Gralik."

The light-blue highlights on Vrynn's skin nearly disappeared. "How does Gralik know we're here?" she asked.

"He doesn't," I answered as I pointed our nose upward and slammed the throttle to full. "But that'll change if the gunship gets away."

Vrynn brought up the controls for the atmospheric missiles and fired at the escaping gunship. Even with a missile outbound, I didn't let up in my pursuit. The ship was only one intra-space jump away from escaping. Hopefully, the pilot was too frazzled to consider composing a message to Gralik during a dogfight.

The missile streaked toward its target, and we followed in hot pursuit. For a moment, I thought maybe our job of keeping the gunship from getting away was going to be simple. The missile was locked on, and only a few seconds away from impact. But just as I was ready to celebrate an easy victory, the missile was met by a barrage of rounds from the gunship's plasma cannon, and it exploded just short of the mark.

"Ludros Beta Five flight control is asking us to stop firing our weapons within the lower atmosphere," Tera said. "They are threatening to revoke our docking privileges."

"Feel free to send our regrets," I said as I willed the *Starfire* to fly faster.

Vrynn unleashed a stream of plasma rounds from our cannons. The escaping gunship was still on the edge of the weapon's range, but I admired her for the effort. Besides, the deluge of fire forced the enemy ship to make evasive maneuvers, delaying it from reaching the upper atmosphere.

"I sent your regrets," Tera replied. "They're sending security ships."

"Great," I muttered. "Where were they when I was mugged in the spaceport?"

"Another missile?" Vrynn asked as her hand moved to the targeting controls again.

"Wait until we're closer," I said. "Can we target it with the laser battery?"

Vrynn shook her head. "Too much scattering in this atmosphere. We'd have to be much closer."

"Close enough for you to finish him off with the cannons?" I asked with a sidelong glance. I was pretty sure I knew the answer.

"Exactly," Vrynn replied, grinning.

I shifted our climb angle even steeper. We needed to reach a higher altitude first. That would give us a better shot, and would hopefully keep Ludros Beta Five's inept security off our backs.

Despite Vrynn laying down a veritable blanket of plasma fire, the Nexus gunship weaved and juked its way through, nearly clear of the steadily thinning atmosphere.

I tightened my grip on the controls. "We have to destroy that ship!"

A second later, Vrynn fired another atmospheric missile, but it was obviously too late. The gunship had pretty much left the atmosphere, and we weren't far behind. My steering became sluggish as the ship's control surfaces had less air to push against.

Despite my normally stubborn attitude about my less-than-stellar flying skills in zero-G, I decided this wasn't a time to let my pride get us in trouble. "Switch with me," I said to Vrynn.

She shook her head, attention fixed on the outbound missile's targeting screen. "Tera, calculate the enemy ship's most likely trajectory based on its current heading, and feed the intercept point into the missile's guidance system."

"It won't work," I said. "The missile needs air to be able to change course. They are called atmospheric, after all."

She spared me a small smirk, but kept her attention focused on the console. "That's why I'm making the last correction while we still have air." She tapped the screen. "There," she said and sat back to admire her handiwork.

The missile streaked forward straight as an arrow, its rocket motor still functioning despite the lack of air. Unfortunately, she'd sent the missile on a wild course, nowhere near the enemy ship.

Now above the atmosphere, I knew the gunship was only moments away from disappearing into intra-space. And all the while, the missile streaked forward, aiming for a point far ahead of the enemy ship. Could she actually be so lucky?

I wasn't sure why the pilot of the ship didn't notice the incoming missile. Maybe the gunship's tracking system was designed to ignore missiles as soon as they left the atmosphere. After all, what crazy person would try and use a missile that way?

I mentally counted down the seconds. The missile was almost there. Probably only three seconds away. It just had to hit the ship before it—

The ship shimmered out of view, starting its intra-space jump.

I sagged into my chair and grunted in disappointment.

We'd been so close.

A bright explosion lit the space in front of us. Much larger than the atmospheric missile would have created on its own.

"Yes!" Vrynn shouted, halfway leaping out of her seat.

I shook my head in disbelief. Had my gutsy co-pilot actually managed to hit the enemy ship just as it entered intra-space?

We floated out into orbit, approaching the coordinates of the explosion. "Did we get it?" I asked.

"The debris cloud is at least ten times greater than the mass of an atmospheric missile," Tera said. "Some of the ship might complete the intra-space jump, but most of it got left behind."

I turned to Vrynn. "That was an impossible shot! How did you manage to hit it?"

"Tera's matrix did the hard work," Vrynn replied with a smile. "But I must admit, it was a pretty good idea."

We spent the next few minutes talking about our narrow escape and sending an explanation message to Ludros Beta Five traffic control for the mishap before our discussion turned to our encounter with Consul General Razome.

"She offered Mitch a job as a mechanic," Gabe said.

I cringed. Gabe certainly got straight to the point.

"Did she?" Vrynn said, one eyebrow raised. She turned her piercing cobalt eyes on me.

"I'm sure she was just being polite," I offered.

"Very polite," Vrynn said with a small smirk.

"Also, the surface temperature of her skin fluctuated several times," Gabe said.

I shrugged. "That's probably just a unique characteristic of her species."

Gabe tilted his mechanical head to the side—a mannerism that he'd probably developed from watching us. "That is unlikely. It only happened during a few of your responses to her."

Vrynn's brow rose, her interest obviously piqued. "Really? What did Mitch say when her skin temperature changed?"

Before Gabe had a chance to reply—and completely embarrass me—I jumped in. "Vrynn, why don't we step through the Quake Drive targeting procedures? You mentioned wanting to learn more about that, didn't you?"

Vrynn's expression told me that she knew exactly what I was trying to do. I could also tell that she was torn between teasing me and actually learning more about operating the *Starfire*.

Fortunately, her desire to learn more about the Quake Drive won out.

With some generous commentary from Tera, we went through the commands for bringing the drive online, targeting a location, and opening the portal aperture. And because I wasn't sure she wouldn't just go straight back to teasing, I let Vrynn take command on our portal jump back to Thetis Max.

As the ship descended toward the derelict mining facility that had become our home in the Bonara Cluster, Vrynn turned and placed her hand over mine. "Thanks, Mitch," she said. "For everything."

The smile on her face made the whole experience worth it.

Chapter Four

Without the pressure to complete the installation of the Quake Drive, I suddenly found myself with plenty of time. The next morning, I wandered some of the corridors of the mining facility that I hadn't really explored yet. It was a relief to feel like I could use my time however I wanted.

I discovered a small room that, at one point, might have been a research lab. Most of the equipment was either too old or too broken to be of any use, but I had the strangest urge to transform it into a mad scientist's laboratory. Not that I imagined myself some intergalactic version of Dr. Frankenstein or felt any need to create my own re-animated monster. Besides, who would I resurrect? I already had Tera and Gabe back from the dead.

But I couldn't help wanting to have a place where I could tinker with things. My recent successes with the Quake Drive and the plasma injectors on Shariamy's ship made me want to build with my hands again.

Of course, cleaning out an abandoned lab was tiring work, so a few hours into the process, I decided to go rest on the couch in our partially remodeled living area next to the old mess hall.

I must have drifted off because the next thing I knew, I jolted awake to the sound of HelperBot's rubber wheels squealing. It's happy, announcer voice followed as it rolled away, out the door and down the corridor. "This unit has discovered the location of the human named Mitch. This unit has discovered the location of the human named Mitch."

I scowled. I hadn't been aware we were playing hide-and-seek.

I repositioned myself on the couch, hoping that if I could just lie still, my brain would drift back to sleep. A few minutes later, Slate came lumbering into the room.

I scrunched an eye open. "Do you require my assistance, Slate?"

The mining bot stopped in front of me. "The ore is ready to load."

I closed my eyes. "Oh, great. Thanks, Slate." Hopefully, if I acknowledged his report, he'd leave me alone.

Unfortunately, he didn't. "But there are no working freighters again," he said mechanically.

"Yeah, we only have the *Starfire*," I replied lazily. "But that should be good enough."

Without missing a beat, he continued. "There are no working ships in this facility."

"I know, Slate. I'll show you where to deliver the ore in a little bit." I wasn't quite awake enough to give detailed instructions on where to load the ore in the *Starfire's* cargo bay. I'd just have to take him there myself. "You can continue your work until then."

He spun on the spot and trundled out of the room.

After another ten minutes of trying—unsuccessfully—to fall back asleep, I decided I might be awake. When Rascal padded into my small room and basically sat on my legs, I knew I was definitely done with my nap.

My large—and quite over-protective—animal friend usually preferred his nest in the *Starfire's* cargo bay to anywhere else, but he did sometimes come out of the ship for important reasons. I patted his side and rubbed his lean shoulder. "Hey, boy, are you out for a stroll? Taking care of business?" I glanced around. "Where's Skeeter?" The feline robot didn't always follow Rascal around, just most of the time. Maybe Tera had her doing something else at the moment.

Now that I was sort of awake, I decided I might as well show Slate where to load the ore. I was still sitting on the edge of the couch when Gabe rushed past, heading toward the mining deck.

"Gabe," I called out.

He skidded to a halt and ran into the living area.

"Can you show Slate where to put the ore in the ship's cargo bay?" I asked, still feeling a bit groggy from suddenly being vertical.

"I cannot."

I sighed. "Is this one of those 'May I, Can I' arguments?" The matrix containing the real Gabe's neural imprint sometimes caught hold of funny things he used to say or jokes he would make. I didn't really have the mental bandwidth to deal with it at the moment, though.

"No. That would not really apply to this situation anyway because I said 'I cannot' rather than saying 'I can, but may I?' Even then, it would not necessarily be considered a good—"

I brought a hand up. "It's okay, Gabe. Just tell me why you think you can't do it."

"Because the ship is not there."

I snapped my attention to my android friend. "What? Did we leave it outside the hangar?" Even as I asked the question, I knew that wasn't right. We would have been forced to walk from the ship to the mining facility's external entrance through semi-toxic gases. And we definitely hadn't done that since my first visit to Thetis Max. Well, besides the time Vrynn and I snuck back into the mining level to disable the bots that had taken over that part of the facility. But we'd been wearing EVA suits for that, and I definitely hadn't put on an EVA suit since then.

"No. The ship isn't anywhere near the facility," Gabe replied.

My eyes narrowed. "This isn't some new, practical joke subroutine you're testing out. Is it?"

Gabe tilted his head. "That is an interesting idea that I will need to explore in the future. But, no. Currently, my statements are as truthful as I can make them."

I quickly got to my feet and hurried down the corridor toward the hangar. How could the ship have disappeared? When we reached the hangar, I skidded to a stop. There was definitely a huge empty space where the *Starfire* should have been—where it had been just a few hours ago.

I'm not sure how long I stood there staring at the patterns of giant prints on the dusty floor left by the ship's landing struts. Finally, I turned to Gabe. "Where's the ship?"

He clumsily shrugged his shoulders. "I do not know."

I ran back down the long corridor to the rest of the facility. When I reached the mess hall area, I called out, "Vrynn! Where's the ship?"

There was no response.

I looked in the room with the water reclamation unit.

Nothing.

I checked the hall by the power generator.

No Vrynn.

She had to be somewhere.

I descended the stairs to the mining deck, hoping to find Slate and ask if any of the bots had seen Vrynn. Halfway across the processing room, a thought occurred to me. Maybe Vrynn had taken the load of ore to sell it. I wasn't sure why she would do that without consulting me, but it was certainly possible.

I found Slate moving down the line of boreholes, monitoring the output at each station.

"Slate, have you seen Vrynn?"

"Yes. She is a biological of thirty-nine freezl—" My chip stuttered. "One point six meters in height. Her weight is estimated to be—"

"No, sorry. I should have asked when was the last time you saw her."

"I interacted with the biological called Vrynn sixty-five semlo—" Translation hiccup. "Two hundred seventy minutes ago."

At least the metric system didn't have a separate unit for time. Converting hundreds of minutes to hours was hard enough.

"Where and why did you speak to her?" I might as well ask specific questions.

"In the cargo bay when half of the batch of ore was loaded onto the starship."

I smiled. "Thanks, Slate. That's exactly what I needed to know." I turned back toward the stairs leading up to the main level.

I had been right. Vrynn had loaded the ore onto the *Starfire* so she could sell it. Maybe she had seen me taking a nap and decided not to wake me. The nearest inhabited planet was Rulioa IV, which was only fifteen minutes away by intra-space jump, give or take a few minutes.

How long did it take to offload and sell a few hundred kilos of ore?

Maybe she was doing some shopping while she was there.

I wandered back to the hangar to check.

Still empty.

I decided to pass the time in my little abandoned lab. I even contemplated cleaning things up, but my heart wasn't really in it.

After an hour or so, I headed toward the hangar again.

Nothing.

A few minutes later, Gabe found me. "Why did they not take us with them?"

"That's exactly what I've been thinking," I told him as I stared out the hangar portal at the desolate volcanic landscape. "And I'm worried they might be in trouble."

"We could send a message to them," Gabe said.

"Yeah, but we don't have a comm—" I stopped and glanced at my friend. "Hang on. We could use the facility's old comm system."

"Yes, that was my plan when I suggested it," Gabe said dryly.

When we reached the small comm room, I sat down at the desk where Vrynn had received the cryptic message about pirates. I found the main power switch without too much trouble. I was about to ask Gabe to translate the words on the primary controls when I noticed him paying particular attention to a nearby console.

"Look at this," Gabe said, pointing at a series of video feeds from the facility's security cameras. One of them was paused with Vrynn looking at the camera.

I slid over to the video controls and, after a little trial and error, activated that feed. The video of Vrynn came to life.

"Hi Mitch. I'm assuming if you're watching this, that you know what's happened."

"I definitely don't," I muttered.

The on-screen Vrynn continued, "Hopefully, you found this before you got too worried."

"We did not," Gabe said.

I smiled at my friend's reply even as I felt a growing pit in my stomach.

"If Gabe is with you, I'm sure he'll want to know why Tera would have left him."

"Yes, I do want to know that," Gabe answered.

I touched the control to pause the playback and glanced over my shoulder at Gabe. "You don't have to reply to everything she says."

"You did," Gabe said.

"Yes. And now I'm realizing that was probably a mistake." I tapped the panel to resume playback.

Based on the details in the background, she must have used one of the cameras in the hangar. I had to admit, it was a clever way to leave a message. I wondered where I had been during all this.

"Maybe I'm being a little too confident that things will work out, but that probably won't surprise you." Vrynn's expression shifted from playful to somber a moment later. She looked straight at the camera. "I just couldn't do nothing while my people suffered, not when I knew I had the way to save them." She gestured off-screen, presumably to the *Starfire*. "I know you'll be upset when you get this, but I couldn't risk telling you about my plan, just in case you said no. Besides, this is my fight. I don't want to put you or Gabe or anyone else in danger."

"She is putting Tera in danger," Gabe pointed out.

I nodded but didn't say anything.

"If we win, I'll be back soon," she said. "Then you can maroon me on Thetis Max again if you think I deserve it, which I probably do."

She glanced around as if searching for what to say next.

"Hopefully, you'll understand why I'm doing this, and hopefully you won't hate me for it." She leaned in toward the camera. "Goodbye Mitch. I'm sorry."

Vrynn stared at the camera for another moment, then disappeared from view.

I felt like my world was spinning. Or maybe this little, volcanic moon I was on had suddenly careened out of orbit. Either way, my brain simply refused to process what I just heard.

"She never explained why Tera would leave," Gabe said.

His comment momentarily distracted me from my turbulent feelings. I raised a brow. "No, I guess she didn't."

"She said she knew I would want to know," he said. "That implies that she was going to tell us the reason, correct?"

I let out a mirthless chuckle. "Yeah. She probably meant to but just forgot."

"She should not have said it then," Gabe observed.

"Well, we biologicals don't always get everything right, as you can tell."

"I will ask her to tell me the reason when we see them," he said in a matter-of-fact voice.

I wasn't nearly as confident as Gabe that we would see them again, but I didn't want to crush his hopes.

I leaned back in my seat and blew out a long breath, trying to wrap my brain around the situation. I still couldn't believe what she'd done.

Vrynn had actually stolen my starship.

"I can't believe she did this." I stood abruptly and stormed out of the control room. "How could she do this?" My voice rose. "What was she thinking?"

Gabe trailed behind me down the hall. "She said she wanted to help her people."

"Yeah, but did she ever stop to think that I would want to help her people, too?" I didn't stop walking. My anger was simmering, and I was doing my best not to take it out on Gabe.

"I would also like to help Vrynn and her people," Gabe said.

"I mean, why didn't she at least ask me? I would have listened. I might have been a little more cautious, but I would have tried to help." I wasn't really expecting Gabe to have any answers for me, but he was the only one within earshot at the moment.

Slowing to a stop at the main hallway, I watched Rascal wander past, not really going anywhere in particular. No wonder he had been walking around the facility. His nest was gone.

Vrynn had played a dirty trick on him, too.

Then I remembered something. "You know what?" I said to Gabe. "I bet that wild goose chase to Ludros Beta Five was all Vrynn's idea. She probably made up the whole thing just to get me to use the Quake Drive, and show her how it works."

"That is a definite possibility," Gabe replied. "Except the part about chasing geese."

"Why would she make up such an elaborate ruse? I would have taught her how to use it, if she'd asked. Did she think I would refuse? Does she not trust me?" I asked quietly.

Gabe stared back at me. "I do not know what Vrynn thinks or feels."

I barked a short laugh. "Me neither, apparently."

I considered Gabe for several seconds as the reality of our situation sank in. Glancing at the dingy mining facility walls, I let out a long sigh. "So now what?"

"Vrynn said she and Tera would come back after they are successful," Gabe said. "Are you asking what we should do while we wait?"

"What if they don't come back?" I asked softly.

A new fear swept over me. I had already considered how helpless we were, marooned on this moon without a ship. But what if something happened to Vrynn? What if she was injured or even killed in this fool-hardy crusade to save her people? Would I ever know it? Or had my goodnight to her the day before been the last time I'd see her?

"Vrynn seemed confident that they would be successful in helping her people," Gabe said.

I gave him a sidelong glance. "Yeah, but Vrynn's confident about everything."

Gabe stared back at me with an open, curious expression. He was waiting for me to decide.

My hands balled into fists at my sides. "We can't just sit here and wait for them to come back," I said. "We have to go find them."

"How will we *go* anywhere?" Gabe asked.

"The hangar," I said, striding down the corridor.

We hadn't made an inventory of the contents of the hangar, but I had seen the hulks of several derelict ships. Nothing that I had wanted to test out before. Who would want a jalopy when you had a sports car?

But I was desperate now.

Gabe and I hustled into the hangar and approached the first ship. It was a small craft about the size of a midsize car back on Earth. I wasn't sure it even had an intra-space drive. Not only that, but it had a gaping hole on the other side of the hull. A meteor, or perhaps a weapon, had punched straight through into the cockpit.

Gabe came around the small ship to look at the hole with me. "Could it be repaired?" he asked.

I shrugged. "When the *Starfire* crashed on Earth, Gabe—" I glanced at him. "I mean, the real Gabe, was able to patch up the hull. But that equipment is probably all with the *Starfire*."

"I do remember that part." Gabe tapped a finger to his temple.

I smiled at my friend before returning my attention to the rest of the hangar.

As we searched through the mess of decades of neglect, Gabe and I found a handful of other ships in similar condition as the first. But nothing I felt confident taking out into the vacuum of space.

"What is under this tarp?" Gabe asked from deeper in the hangar.

I negotiated my way around several piles of junk until I found him in the back corner. A giant . . . something—about the size of a shuttle bus—sat hidden under a dusty gray tarp. With a fair amount of effort—and grunting from me—Gabe and I peeled back the covering and stared at an ancient-looking transport ship. The gray metal of the hull was angular and dark. It didn't actually have rust—I doubt it was even made of a rustable material—but there were worn spots and repair patches scattered across the surface. It had definitely seen better days.

I approached the side hatch, pushed down the release lever, and pulled hard on the handle. The hinges squealed as the hatch swung slowly open. The puff of air that escaped smelled musty and slightly dead. On the bright side, at least that meant the ship's atmospheric seal was still intact. That was a good sign.

I pulled a flashlight from my pocket and stepped into the dank-smelling ship. It was tiny compared to the *Starfire* and reminded me of the little shuttlecraft on the Star Trek shows. The fact that I was living Star Trek in real life was a heady feeling.

Toward the front of the craft, I found a cramped flight deck, though it would have been closer to say it was a large cockpit—two chairs with no space between them. There were controls and sensor panels everywhere. Not that different from the cockpit on an airliner.

I turned back to Gabe, who stood just inside the main hatch. "Do you think we can get this hunk of junk flying?"

"It would certainly be possible to make it fly," Gabe said. "But I do not know if it would be advisable."

"Do you have a better idea for finding Vrynn and Tera?" I shot back.

Gabe glanced around the interior of the small craft, and his artificial brow furrowed. "If we have ruled out the possibility of waiting until they return, then this is the best option."

I gave him a wry smile. "Let's get going, then."

Chapter Five

It only took about a day to figure out how to get the power system on the tiny, old freighter working again. The control systems were a jumble of menus and indecipherable text. Initially, Gabe had to translate everything for me because the ship obviously didn't have an English setting. That was the first thing we fixed.

The jump drive was a completely different matter.

The plasma pump and manifold were shot. Even if I'd had the fabrication machines from the *Starfire*, it would have taken days to fix them, which was probably the reason the ship had been abandoned in the first place.

Unfortunately, I wasted an entire morning fighting with it before realizing that.

I slid out of the engineering crawlspace and unfolded myself. "I need a break," I said as I grabbed the lip of the main hatch and stretched out the stiffness in my back.

Rascal sat up from a nearby pile of scrap metal that he'd made into a temporary nest. He gazed up at me with large black eyes, as if to ask when I was going to fix his pitiful situation.

"Hang in there, boy," I muttered.

As I surveyed the rest of the cluttered hangar, I realized that even if we got the plasma feed to the jump drive fixed, we'd have to figure out how to extricate the ship from the back of the hangar. Why would they have put the freighter in such an inconvenient place?

I turned to Gabe. "I just thought of something."

"What is it?"

"I think this freighter was the first of all the ships to break down." I pointed at the rest of the junk in the hangar.

"That is certainly possible. Or perhaps the previous owners of this mining facility left a large space in the back corner and then hoisted the entire freighter over the rest of the broken ships and placed it here last."

I gave him a deadpan look.

"But based on my limited experience with biologicals' behavior, I would say that your explanation is more likely," Gabe added.

"That means there might be salvageable parts in these other ships that they didn't have when the freighter's plasma system went out." I glanced around the junk-strewn space. "Now we just have to find the parts we need."

It took the rest of that afternoon and part of the next morning to check the plasma flow systems on all the broken ships. In the end, we found two possible candidates. I decided to install the one that didn't look like it had been attacked with a hammer—not that I could blame the poor engineer who'd done it. These starship parts were frustrating to work on.

After a few days' work—and several dozen feet of makeshift plasma tubing—we had everything ready to go. At least, as far as my limited ability would get us.

With the help of a squad of mining bots, we cleared a path to haul the freighter to the front of the hangar.

"You have a functional ship again," Slate said. "Should the next batch of ore be loaded into it?"

"Yeah, that's a great idea, thanks. Also, while we're gone, continue at your standard mining rate so that we will have additional ore to sell when we return." I had nearly told him to "carry on," but he probably would have misinterpreted my meaning.

"Affirmative," the bot replied.

After the ore was loaded into the hold, we did one more double-check of the freighter's systems. As I walked around the back of the ship, I caught sight of Rascal in his nest. I walked over and sat down next to him. "Hey, boy. We have to leave," I said as I scratched him behind the head.

"Will Rascal come with us on our journey?" Gabe asked.

"As much as I hate to leave him behind, we can't risk bringing him." I turned my attention to rubbing Rascal's belly. "But we'll be back to get you as soon as we can," I said to my ferocious friend.

Gabe cocked his head to the side. "I do not believe that you are in a position to make such a promise."

I chuckled. "Probably not. But it hardly matters; Rascal can't understand English anyway."

That made me consider the feasibility of creating a translation chip for animals like Rascal. It probably wasn't a good idea, especially in situations like this. I gave him one last pat on his side. "Be good while we're gone, boy."

I walked back toward the freighter, my heart feeling like lead. I had already given Slate instructions to put food out for Rascal in our absence. There was enough to last about a month. He'd be in trouble after that, but then again, so would we.

Gabe and I boarded the freighter and sealed the hatch. We squeezed into the cockpit and settled into our seats, our shoulders still nearly touching. I cycled the hangar airlock, and a minute later we were out on the moon's surface.

Instead of a true hover system like the *Starfire*, the old freighter used reactive thrusters, which made it much harder to control the stability as we rose above the lava plain below. I engaged the main engines, and we slowly lumbered forward, gaining momentum. The cockpit shook as we reached orbital velocity.

"I hope she doesn't fall apart," I said to Gabe.

"You should. It would be difficult for your lungs to receive sufficient oxygen at this altitude," he replied. "You would probably die."

"Thanks for that," I said, shaking my head. "Of course, if the ship breaks up, you'd die on impact, even if you didn't hit an open lava field."

"I would certainly cease to function, but dying would depend on whether I am actually alive." Gabe turned to face me more fully. "You said we could continue our discussion about whether I am truly alive or not. This seems like a good time to talk about it, now that we are facing death."

I gripped the control yoke harder, wishing the ship would stop rattling so much. "I know it might seem like a good time, but right now I'm just doing my best not to completely freak out. Maybe later."

That seemed to satisfy Gabe, and he returned his attention to the status readouts. "At our current trajectory, we will be above ninety-nine percent of the atmosphere within thirty-six seconds."

Less than a minute later, the shaking subsided, and I was able to breathe a little easier, which was completely contradictory, considering the vacuum of space just outside the thin walls of the freighter's hull. But as long as there was air to breathe at all, I would make the most of it.

Without an AI—or really any autopilot function at all—I had to manually input the coordinates of the intra-space jump. We didn't know for sure where Vrynn had taken the *Starfire*, but her home planet of Mareesh was a solid bet.

When the computer displayed the estimated jump time, I did a double-take. Fifty-seven hours. I'd never seen an intra-space jump that long. At least, not since the one that brought me to the Bonara Cluster in the first place.

"This can't be right," I said, pointing to the display. "How could a jump within the Bonara Cluster possibly take over fifty hours?"

"You've only ever made jumps in the *Starfire*," Gabe replied. "This technology is much less advanced."

I shook my head. "We can't make a fifty-seven hour jump; I didn't bring any food with us."

Gabe considered the readout in front of us. "Not to mention that we do not have enough fuel to make it that far."

I pulled up the star map on the display. "The only planet in range is Rulioa IV."

"Maybe Rulioa IV is the best option," Gabe said.

I glanced sidelong at him. "Not hard when it's our only option."

"We could always return to Thetis Max," he said.

I considered that idea for a moment. Were we ready to commit ourselves to a one-way trip to the closest planet, hoping that we could figure out what to do from there? If I hadn't been so concerned about Vrynn's safety, I might have changed my mind.

I shook my head. "We have to help Vrynn and Tera." I took a breath and mashed the jump button.

As much as my first experience with intra-space had been underwhelming—just a slow fade-to-brownish-gray—this jump was weirdly disconcerting. The space outside the narrow cockpit window flashed several times, then it was almost as if space whooshed by and disappeared.

I glanced over at Gabe. "Did that seem weird to you?"

"The entire process of shifting our dimensional plane in order to travel large distances seems somewhat prone to failure," he replied.

That didn't help my state of mind, so I busied myself checking the flight readouts. "Everything seems to be operating normally. The system says the jump will take a little over nine hours."

We spent the next nine hours and three minutes alternately talking, sleeping, and going completely out of our minds. Well, I felt like I was going out of my mind. Gabe, on the other hand, seemed fine with the situation. Probably because—as he reminded me several times during those nine hours—he doesn't have an algorithm for feeling anxious or going crazy.

When we finally dropped out of intra-space, it felt like I could actually breathe again. Rulioa IV still looked like the dusty, arid, slow-paced, backwater planet it had been on our last visit, but I had never seen a more beautiful sight in my life.

We brought the ship down in the same spaceport where I'd tried to abandon Vrynn about five weeks ago. In fact, as we passed the short row of berths, I could have sworn the same guy was sitting on the wing of his ship as last time we were here. He was the one who thought Vrynn and I were having a lovers' spat. In reality, I was trying to ditch her so I wouldn't have to take a crazy woman who wanted to steal my ship with me.

Rather ironic, considering the circumstances.

I jumped out of my seat and opened the exit hatch. The hot, dry air was a welcome relief after so long in the small ship. "Let's figure out how to sell the ore and find a place to eat," I said to Gabe.

"I do not need to eat," he replied.

"After a nine-hour jump, I can eat for both of us." I slapped him on the back and started walking toward what looked like the small main street of the settlement.

The local metalworks proprietor gave us what I hoped was a fair price for the metal, and after browsing the shops on the main street, we found a place that looked like the fast-food version of an old-west saloon—the decor was rustic, the tables and chairs were worn and deteriorating, and the customers picked up their food at the front counter.

The fare was pretty basic. Some sort of vegetable and some sort of grilled meat mixed together with some bland seasoning. Apparently, stew hash was a universal constant. I ordered a bowl for both of us—less conspicuous that way—and we settled into a table.

Once I had food in my stomach again, I was ready to tackle our biggest problem.

"I'm not flying that freighter anywhere again," I told Gabe after switching my empty plate for his full one.

"I can agree with that," he replied. "Even without a subroutine for anxiety, I would rather not repeat a jump like that."

"We need a better ship," I said.

"Do we have enough money to buy another ship?" Gabe asked.

"I guess we're gonna find out."

When I asked the people at the next table, they told us that there was only one honest used starship dealer in the town. Following their instructions, we walked a few streets away and found a small field that looked like a junkyard but was actually the starship dealership.

As we approached the small building on the side of the yard, the door opened, and a young man came out—lean build, youthful face, and a mop of sandy hair. But it was his skin—not nearly as realistic as Gabe's—and the choppy, mechanical nature of his movements that hinted he was not biological.

"Please indicate if you plan to purchase a starship today or if you are here to do research for a future purchase or if you are only looking out of curiosity," he said in a slightly monotone voice.

"I'm glad you have a vocal inflection subroutine," I muttered to Gabe.

He nodded, gazing at the android car salesman with mild curiosity.

"We plan to purchase a ship, if we find one that we like," I said.

"What amount of money do you have available for the purchase? Ten to nineteen thousand Bonmarks, twenty to twenty-nine thousand Bonmarks, thirty to thirty-nine thousand Bonmarks, or greater than forty thousand Bonmarks?"

His questions made me feel like I was navigating an automated call system. I wondered what the equivalent of mashing the zero button would be. Could I talk to a biological person if I got the android salesman so snarled that he couldn't figure out what we wanted?

"We only have about three thousand Bonmarks." We had actually sold the load of ore for a little over four thousand, but I didn't want to spend it all. "What can you show us in that price range?"

"There are no ships available for that price," the android salesman immediately replied. "Please return when you have sufficient funds." He spun on the spot and walked back into the small building.

I couldn't believe he was about to walk away. We might not have a lot of money, but we definitely wanted to spend it on a ship. Maybe we could work out some sort of rental option.

I turned to Gabe. "Well, that didn't go how I expected."

"That salesman does not understand appropriate social interactions." Gabe scowled in the direction of the small building. "Also, he is not very good at selling ships."

"Right on both counts." I stared at the sandy mountains in the distance. "So, what do we do now?"

The moment the question was out of my mouth, the door to the sales office swung open and the same android salesman walked out. "Please indicate if you plan to purchase a starship today or if you are here to do research for a future purchase or if you are only looking out of curiosity."

I shared a look of disbelief with Gabe. Was this guy serious? Maybe he was programmed on a loop.

We gave the same answers as before, but this time I added, "We also have a ship to trade."

"Please describe the craft in question," the android said.

"It's a freighter with an old intra-space drive. We repaired some of the components so that we could get here," I said.

The salesman turned to Gabe. "You have superior mental acuity. Please give me more specific information about the craft in question."

I huffed under my breath. Apparently, now I wasn't observant or smart enough.

Gabe began spouting specifications—including some units of measurement that I hadn't even heard of.

"Based on those details, combining the trade-in value of the freighter with the three thousand Bonmarks, you have a single intra-space-capable option available." He turned and began walking down a nearby row of starships. I couldn't help but notice that it was the row with the oldest and smallest ships.

"At least being indecisive won't be a problem," I muttered to Gabe.

"You could still be indecisive about whether to purchase it or not. There are certainly other starship dealers on this planet, though they might not be in this town." Gabe still hadn't mastered the art of a low whisper, and I was sure our android salesman had heard him.

"There are two other dealers in this settlement. Neither of them will sell you a starship for a fair price," the salesman said.

He sounded quite sure of his statement. At least he knew we were considering other options.

After another minute of walking, he stopped and pointed to a small ship on our right. "This is the craft that you can afford to purchase."

We had passed some pretty rundown ships, but this one didn't even appear functional. About the size of a two-person fishing boat, with most of that size taken up by the engine in the back, it had to be the smallest ship on the lot. The cockpit didn't look much bigger than a lounge chair. In fact, I wasn't completely sure that the seat inside wasn't an old lounge chair.

"Does this ship still fly?" I muttered.

"I only sell ships that fly," he replied.

I scrutinized him. "Have you personally flown this ship?"

"No. But it has been certified by the owner of the lot, who is a test pilot."

That sounded impressive. "Does it have a good intra-space jump drive? I mean, will it actually make it to another planet?" I asked.

"This is a decommissioned scout-class Prulian fighter. It was damaged during a battle, but still has a fully functional jump drive that was released only five standard cycles ago."

I couldn't remember the conversion of cluster-standard cycles to years, and my chip always refused to translate it for me. But I knew that would have been within the last ten years.

The android salesman continued. "Because this dealership is not authorized to sell military-grade weapons, all armaments except the defensive auto-cannon have been stripped."

My brow went up. "How does that work?"

"The auto-cannon will attempt to neutralize any incoming offensive weapons."

Now I was curious. "Will it fire on the attacking ship?" I asked.

"It is not programmed to fire on other ships, but this dealership makes no guarantees about the accuracy of the auto-firing algorithms, and assumes no liability for accidental engagement of nearby craft," the salesman said.

"That's fine," I said, holding up my hands.

"Also, the radio communication system is not operational," the salesman added. "Perhaps you are skilled enough to repair it?"

I tried not to feel offended that he looked at Gabe again. But the comm was the least of our worries at the moment. "How long would a jump from here to Mareesh take using this ship?" I asked the salesman.

"Depending on the random intra-space plane traveled on, anywhere from seventy-nine to one hundred thirty brulon—" My translator chip tried again. "—eighteen to twenty-six minutes."

I let out a breath. "That's way better than fifty-seven hours," I muttered.

I considered the small cockpit again. Could Gabe and I stuff ourselves into that tiny space for half an hour?

Gabe must have understood my concern. He cocked his head. "Friends can sit close to each other, correct?"

"Yeah," I said. "I'd even be willing to squeeze in with a stranger if it meant saving Vrynn."

"So the familiarity does not determine your level of comfort?" Gabe asked.

"Oh, it does," I replied with a wry chuckle. "I'm just saying it would still be worth it."

Gabe nodded his understanding.

"Good thing we don't have Rascal with us," I added dryly.

It took about half an hour to walk back to the spaceport, pay our docking fees, and fly the old freighter to the dealership. We thanked our android salesman—despite his protests that he had simply offered a fair exchange—and loaded into the scout-class fighter.

It was an even tighter squeeze than I had guessed.

Fortunately, the real Gabe had always been on the lean side—and Tera had picked an android frame to match. With Gabe sitting on my left hip, I didn't have much room to maneuver and barely space to reach the flight sticks.

Somehow we made it into orbit without losing control of the ship, and I got us pointed toward the Barchee system.

"Can you see the rest of the control panel, Gabe? I can't see well enough to enter the coordinates."

"You should use the projected interface with vocal commands," he replied.

"Oh, I didn't know we had that."

"It is all explained in the user manual." He reached over and tapped a few buttons.

"What makes you think I'm suddenly going to start reading the vehicle owner's manual?" I asked.

A woman's voice began speaking. "Please indicate destination of intra-space jump."

"Mareesh," I said.

"Destination Barchee, set," the auto-pilot said.

"No. The planet Mareesh, in the Barchee system." I over-emphasized my enunciation, hoping the system would understand. Tera would be furious if I spoke that slowly and clearly to her. That thought made me suddenly miss my holographic friend, quirky personality and all.

"Destination Mareesh not available," the voice replied.

I frowned. "Why not?"

"Travel to planet Mareesh from your current position would pass through the Barchee star. Choose another jump location as a waypoint."

"I didn't know we couldn't travel through things in intra-space," I said to Gabe.

He shrugged. "Intra-space drives rely on large gravitational bodies like stars as the anchors of a jump. You can jump to them, but not through them."

"Huh," I said. "Well, I guess a jump to Barchee would be the next best thing."

"Ship's heading and velocity are within acceptable auto-pilot parameters. Please indicate when you are ready to jump."

"Proceed," I said.

The small ship made no sound at all as the stars outside faded away, replaced by the grayish-brown of intra-space. I let out a breath. Having made two jumps in unfamiliar ships, I couldn't wait to get back aboard the *Starfire* and travel through the stars the way I was used to. I chuckled at the idea that I was used to traveling through the stars at all.

"Is something humorous?" Gabe asked.

"Nothing. It's hard to believe I'm flying through a sub-dimension of space from one alien planet to another," I said. "Two months ago, if someone had told me I would be in this exact situation, I would have thought they were crazy."

"The original Gabe would have had a similar reaction to being told he would die and then have his consciousness loaded into an alien android."

I smiled. "He would have indeed."

A few moments passed, then Gabe spoke again. "Also, why do biologicals say 'nothing' and then proceed to actually say something? My memories of the original Gabe include many times when he would engage in this strange sequence. And you did it, too, just a moment ago."

"You know how sometimes I don't have great answers for the deep questions you ask?" I said.

"Yes."

"Well, this is one of those times."

It wasn't the fastest twenty minutes I'd ever endured, but compared to a nine-hour jump, it felt like waiting at a stoplight. Soon enough, we came out of intra-space near a beautiful blue-green orb.

I had seen several planets that reminded me of Earth, but this one looked like an over-idealized version of my home planet—oceans of deep blue, continents all green, and puffy white clouds dotting the atmosphere. Barchee didn't have a single desert or tundra on the entire planet. The only thing spoiling the beautiful view was my knowledge of what the Barchee people had done to Vrynn's people.

I steered our little craft into a wide orbit. "Let's set up the jump to Mareesh," I said to Gabe.

Gabe shifted so that he could see the readout. "With our current trajectory, we will be in position for—"

His abrupt stop caught my attention. "What is it?" I asked.

"Several ships are moving up from the surface to intercept us," he replied.

Were the Barchee so militaristic that they sent interceptors against every tiny ship that arrived in their system?

"How long till they reach us? And how many are there? Can you tell if they're armed?"

"Seven. Five. No."

I leaned over, trying to see Gabe's face. "What?"

"I thought it would be faster to answer all of your questions at once. They will reach us in seven minutes, there are five ships, and no, I cannot detect their armament."

I was about to tell him to remember that I wasn't a computer interface, but he spoke again.

"Wait. Maybe they aren't going to intercept us," Gabe said.

I held my breath, expecting him to elaborate. Now the seconds really did feel like they were creeping along. "Uh, Gabe?"

"Yes?"

"Did you want to tell me anything else about the ships?" I asked.

"Their course will bring them very near our current location, but they do not seem to be chasing us intentionally."

"I think Tera might be rubbing off on you. When were you going to tell me?"

"Soon," Gabe said. "The likelihood that they were still on an intercept course had not reached zero. I was waiting to be sure."

I supposed that made sense in an extremely logical sort of way.

"Also, I believe you gave me a compliment by saying that some of my personality algorithms are being affected by the time I spend with Tera. Thank you," Gabe said.

I didn't have the heart to tell him that, in this situation, it hadn't really been a compliment.

"Our scanners are picking up more information now," Gabe said. "It looks like three freighters and two fighters. They are definitely not on an intercept course."

"Sounds like a supply convoy," I said, craning my head around Gabe to get a glimpse. "How close will they pass by us?"

Gabe checked the readout on his side of the small cockpit. "Within a few kilometers."

"What is it with everyone and the metric system?" I said with a huff. "You know what, I'm not sure the real Gabe actually knew the metric system that well. Why would you tell me the distance in kilometers?"

Gabe twisted a little to look at me. "The metric system is a far superior method of measurement," he said in a haughty voice. "Length is actually based on the speed of light, so in reality—"

I held up a hand. "Actually, nevermind. Should we be worried about a collision?"

"No," Gabe replied. "But they will pass close enough to be targeted by our defensive auto-cannon."

That had me concerned. "Will it fire on them?"

Gabe lifted a shoulder. "Probably not. But as the salesman said, there is no warranty for the performance of the defensive systems."

"Can we turn it off?"

"The time we have before they are in range is an order of magnitude less than the time it will take me to figure out how to disable the targeting system."

"How much time until they're in range?" I asked.

"Nine seconds."

My eyes went wide, and I craned my head to figure out where the convoy was. I had visions of accidentally getting into a shooting match with a pair of heavily armed fighter escorts while flying this tiny scout ship.

With a quick tilt of the stick, I rolled us sideways so the belly of our ship faced toward them. This pointed the single auto-cannon—which was situated just behind our heads—away from the approaching convoy. It was the quickest way I could think of to make sure we didn't accidentally fire on them.

I peered over the edge of the canopy, trying to catch a glimpse of the other ships. Three freighters about twice as big as the *Starfire* loomed closer and closer. The two fighter escorts flanked them on either side.

I twisted the stick again to continue our inverted roll, holding my breath as the convoy cruised past. Fortunately, the maneuver worked, and the auto-cannon never tried to target them.

Once they were out of our immediate vicinity, Gabe said, "We can make our jump to Mareesh anytime."

"Let's wait and see where this convoy is headed," I said. I couldn't be sure, but it looked like they were heading straight for Mareesh.

We watched as, one by one, the convoy disappeared into intra-space.

"Even without Tera's tracking system, I could tell that was a jump for Mareesh," I said.

"You are correct," Gabe replied.

I activated the auto-pilot interface and gave the jump destination. A moment later, the ship smoothly entered intra-space. I had been watching the swirling grays and browns outside the canopy for only a minute or so when the auto-pilot announced, "Intra-space jump terminating."

A giant blue planet materialized in front of us. It might have been the moderately low orbit—or maybe it was because I was sitting in a tiny scout ship with a full canopy—but it seemed enormous. I could only see one horizon, as the rest of the planet was directly beneath the ship.

Mareesh was deep blue with strands and bunches of puffy white clouds scattered throughout the atmosphere. Despite what Vrynn had said earlier, I couldn't see any habitable islands. Maybe they were hiding under the clouds.

It was like staring at a giant scoop of homemade wild blueberry ice cream with marshmallow drizzled on top. Not that I had even seen that sort of flavor combination, but I would have been willing to give it a try if the opportunity ever presented itself.

I was pulled from my culinary pondering by a beeping alarm on my console. "What's going on?" I asked, shifting to get a better view of the part of the planet below us.

"The sensors are detecting weapons fire in the atmosphere."

I leaned farther forward, nearly pressing Gabe against the canopy glass. "Is it the *Starfire*?"

"The sensors of this ship must not have the Mark 7 in the databanks, but based on the volume of plasma fire, I would say it must be the *Starfire*."

My relief at discovering Vrynn and Tera alive was quickly tempered by the knowledge that they were in the middle of a battle with an armed convoy. "We need to get down there. Which way are they?"

Gabe rattled off the heading, and I clumsily pointed the ship in the general direction, which was no small feat considering my zero-G skills and the cramped quarters. I aimed for the general direction of the mid-air explosions, and once we hit the atmosphere, my piloting skills began to improve significantly. We raced across the tops of the clouds, closing in on the battle.

The *Starfire*—thankfully still in one piece—was engaged with the convoy, flying straight and steady in pursuit of the lumbering freighters as the escorts buzzed around it. But the escorts couldn't seem to score any direct hits because of the constant fire coming from the *Starfire's* plasma cannons.

"Do you think Tera is flying the ship?" Gabe asked, gazing at the firefight ahead of us.

"She must be. Either that or the auto-pilot," I said, smiling as I imagined what was happening on the *Starfire's* flight deck. "That's definitely Vrynn on the cannons."

I stayed a safe distance from the fight because I wasn't completely sure that Vrynn would know it was us. Maybe she'd think the escorts had a tiny, pitifully armed scout ship as backup for whenever a dogfight wasn't going well.

"Fighters approaching," Gabe announced.

I squinted at the battle. "What do you mean? They're still chasing Vrynn and Tera." The escort ships would never come after us while the *Starfire* was poised to attack the convoy.

"Not the convoy escorts," Gabe said. "Three additional fighters are coming out of orbit above the convoy."

"Can you identify them?"

Gabe tapped the situational display console. "Checking."

I held my breath and tightened my grip on the controls as I watched the *Starfire* strafe the freighters while simultaneously fighting off the escorts.

"Transponder signals identify them as Barchee Strikers." Gabe said. "Probably sentinel ships alerted to the battle."

I scanned the sky high above us until I caught sight of the bright fireballs of the Barchee ships braking as they entered the atmosphere. They would reach the *Starfire* in only a few minutes. Could Vrynn and Tera handle five enemy ships at once? There wasn't much that a small scout ship with only defensive weapons could do in a dogfight, but I wasn't willing to sit back and watch my friends be ambushed.

"We have to help them," I said.

"I agree," Gabe said firmly.

I jammed the throttle forward and sped toward the fight.

"We have a very low probability of surviving a direct confrontation with any of these fighters," Gabe said. "What is your plan?"

"I'm here as moral support," I replied, willing the little scout to fly faster.

Gabe cocked his head to the side. "Have you ever wondered why it is called moral support? You are not really supporting their morals, unless you consider Vrynn's choice to fight against her planet's oppressors a moral decision. It should really be called morale support."

I shook my head. "You know, buddy, I can't say I've ever thought of that."

As we drew closer, I heard the whir of the auto-cannon gimbal behind my head.

I glanced down at the control system. "It's targeting the escort ships," I said.

"Is that good?" Gabe asked.

"Definitely. Now, if we could just get it to fire on them."

As one of the escorts swooped toward the *Starfire*, it fired half a dozen slugs then veered away. Caught in the crossfire, our auto-cannon roared to life, targeting the passing slugs and then the enemy fighter. The escort dove to avoid our fire and the auto-cannon fell silent again.

"The auto-cannon fired," Gabe observed.

My heart pounded, being this close to the action. "Yeah, but do we dare try that stunt again?" It was one thing to sit in a comfortable pilot's seat on the flight deck, surrounded by several layers of armored hull plating. Flying this scout ship felt like hurtling through the air in a bobsled with a window—and definitely not the large, four-man kind of bobsled.

"Though the probability of failure is inordinately high," Gabe said. "It does seem to be the most effective action we can take at the moment to help Vrynn and Tera in their fight."

I shook my head, more at my own foolhardiness than anything. "Back into the fray."

Pulling up on the stick, I maneuvered us below the fight, into the space between the *Starfire* and the other enemy ship. But unlike our earlier effort, this time the auto-cannon took aim at the *Starfire* and fired several rounds.

"No, you dumb thing." I banged the console next to me. "Wrong ship."

"That was less than ideal execution," Gabe observed.

The *Starfire's* cannons swiveled toward us, lining up for a perfect shot. I winced, expecting to be annihilated in a hail of plasma rounds at any moment. The cannons stayed trained on us for what seemed like an eternity before finally turning away and taking aim at an approaching fighter escort.

I banked away hard, and the defensive targeting system lost its lock on the *Starfire*. I was able to maneuver close enough to the incoming escort that the auto-cannon fired on it. Several of our plasma rounds glanced off its cockpit, doing very little damage. I must have caused enough of a distraction, though, because it forgot about the *Starfire*. A moment later, Vrynn scored a pair of direct hits to its engine core, and the enemy ship exploded.

"The three strikers are less than one minute away," Gabe said.

Vrynn must have realized this, too, because the plasma cannons turned to target the incoming ships.

"There is still one escort fighter remaining close to the convoy," Gabe said, watching the tactical console. "However, it is directly below the *Starfire*."

"If we fly between them, the auto-cannon would try to shoot Vrynn and Tera," I said.

"That is a logical extrapolation, yes," Gabe replied.

"What if we maneuver below the escort?" I asked.

"That would allow the defensive system to correctly target the enemy ship," Gabe said. "But it might also overshoot and hit the *Starfire*."

"Not to mention, Vrynn might hit us if she starts shooting at the enemy escort," I said.

Then an idea occurred to me. It wasn't a terrific idea given that neither of us were wearing harnesses, but Gabe's artificial body was robust, and I was wedged in so tightly, I could barely move if I wanted to.

"Hold on to something," I told Gabe.

Twisting the controls, I tipped the scout ship over in a wide arc. We continued rolling sideways until we found ourselves underneath the *Starfire*, completely upside down.

The auto-cannon targeted the fighter below us and began firing. I did my best to keep us centered above the enemy ship to maximize the auto-cannon's efficiency. After scoring several minor hits in the escort's tail area, one of our plasma rounds found a weak spot and punched a hole through the rear stabilizer. The escort ship lost control and spun downward into the vast ocean below.

"It is fortunate that I do not feel discomfort," Gabe said, "because I believe this unusual position would have caused it already."

I glanced over at Gabe, who was pinned against the side of the canopy. "Sorry about that, buddy," I said as I brought the scout ship back to level flight.

Vrynn and Tera had already moved to engage the incoming Barchee ships. They fired an atmospheric missile right as the Barchee Strikers fired a salvo of rockets. My hand instinctively gripped the controls, wanting to mirror the *Starfire's* movements as they weaved and dodged.

The first striker went down with the impact of the missile, and Vrynn switched back to plasma cannons. The rounds raked across the second ship, and it exploded in a bright fireball.

Without realizing it, I must have let the little scout ship drift too close to the action. The final striker turned its attention on us instead of the larger *Starfire*. I pushed our little ship into a steep dive in an effort to avoid the incoming plasma rounds. The scout rocked with a glancing impact to the aft hull.

"I do not think we should engage the striker," Gabe said.

"I'm trying not to," I said through gritted teeth.

Warning sounds went off in the small cockpit as the striker fired another barrage. I zigged and zagged as best I could, but we took another hit.

Suddenly, the *Starfire* loomed over us, slicing in front of another salvo of rounds from the striker, blocking us from what would certainly have been the death blow. A moment later, they let loose a veritable storm of plasma at the enemy ship. The craft exploded in multiple places and drifted toward the ocean in pieces.

I glanced down and saw that the surface of the water was much closer than I anticipated. Pulling back hard on the controls, I set the scout ship on a level course again. I could just barely see the remaining two ships in the convoy as they approached a large caldera-type island that seemed to have materialized in front of us.

This must be one of the inhabited islands Vrynn had told me about. I couldn't see anything of the city inside, though, because the top of the caldera was covered with a grid or shield of some kind, sort of like the grill on a round barbecue.

The freighters flew through a narrow gap in the caldera wall, and I just caught a glimpse of a landing strip inside. The *Starfire* peeled off pursuit, and we followed their lead. Vrynn shifted the ship sideways and slowed, allowing us to fly up next to them.

"Any luck on the comm system?" I asked Gabe.

"I have not focused any of my efforts on troubleshooting the communications," he replied. "I decided it was more important to help you fly the ship and find the *Starfire*. Was that a mistake?"

I chuckled. "No. Helping me not die was definitely the better choice." I glanced over at the *Starfire*, though it was hard to see in through the reflective glass of the flight deck.

Gabe and I waved and yelled, not knowing whether they could see us—they definitely couldn't hear us.

The glass of the flight deck suddenly went transparent.

I turned to Gabe. "I didn't know it could do that."

"Perhaps Vrynn found the *Starfire's* instruction manual and decided to read it," he replied.

I opened my mouth to say that I was pretty sure we would have found an instruction manual, if there was one, when I realized my friend was making a joke. "Ha ha. Point taken."

With theatrical hand waving, Vrynn motioned toward the back of the ship and made an opening gesture with her hands.

Did she want me to land the scout ship inside the cargo bay? While we were in the air? To me, that didn't seem like the easiest way to reunite the gang.

She made the same hand signals again, more emphatic this time, so I shrugged and moved the little scout back into position behind the ship. The *Starfire's* speed began to drop, and I matched it. A moment later, the cargo bay door opened. Vrynn pushed a small stack of bins aside—with HelperBot's eager assistance—and waved us in.

I wished I could tell her that the laws of physics weren't affected by her optimism, but that would have to wait. Shaking my head, I guided the small ship into the bay, clumsily bumping it into a stack of crates as I scraped along the deck. As soon as we touched down, I killed the engine and hit the button to raise the canopy.

My feet had barely contacted the deck when an energetic blur of lithe limbs and blue-blond hair barreled into me. Vrynn wrapped her arms around my middle as we banged into the side of the small ship.

"I'm so glad you're safe," she said, looking up at me with those gorgeous eyes.

I winced as the sharp edge of the scout's winglet dug into my back. "I was, until that welcome."

She grinned and buried her head in my chest, hugging me even harder.

I knew there were other thoughts in my head, emotions I had been feeling earlier, but at the moment, all I cared about was that we'd found Tera and Vrynn, and we were together again.

Tera shimmered into view just as Gabe jumped deftly out of the scout ship. She shook her head as she gave him a look of relief mingled with mild annoyance.

"Hello Tera," Gabe said with a forced smile. "I am happy to see you."

Tera rushed forward and flung herself into Gabe's embrace. I did a double-take as I watched him tentatively wrap his arms around her, Tera's holographic red hair cascading naturally over his shoulder and down his arm.

"Uh." I pointed, unable to verbalize my question. "How is that . . ."

Vrynn's grin widened. "I'll explain later."

Adding to our welcome, Skeeter bounded in with catlike grace and began a systematic search of the cargo bay.

"What's she doing?" I asked.

"She's looking for Rascal." Tera said, shaking her head sadly. "She does this whenever something happens down here. Her algorithms associate movement in the cargo bay with accompanying Rascal outside."

"Where *is* Rascal?" Vrynn asked.

"Back at the facility, obviously," I replied.

"You didn't want to bring him with you?" she teased.

I gave her my best are-you-kidding-me look. "Did you see how cramped Gabe and I were?" I pointed to the scout ship's cockpit. "There's no way a giant pantoboar would have fit in that tiny compartment with us."

Vrynn stifled a smile, probably imagining what it might have looked like.

"And why did you leave Rascal behind anyway?" I asked. "It's not like he would have tried to stop you from stealing the ship."

Her expression turned mock-serious. "I would never steal a man's pet. That's going too far."

I let out a bitter laugh. "That's funny, considering what you did steal."

Now that the adrenaline from the dogfight had begun to wear off, and the relief at finding Vrynn in one piece slowly ebbed, the anger that had been simmering beneath the surface started to bubble over. All the unanswered questions, the days of hurt at her betrayal, came flooding back.

"How could you do this, Vrynn?" I paced a few steps away, running a hand through my hair. I whirled back to face her. "How could you abandon us without even a word of explanation?"

She turned defensive. "I did leave the message."

I narrowed my eyes at her. "You abandoned me."

"I didn't abandon you."

I laughed. "That's funny. It sure felt like being abandoned."

Vrynn cast her gaze around the cargo bay, not really meeting my eye. "We were going to come back."

I threw my hands in the air. "When? Once you played around being the pilot for a while? Once you had a chance to shoot down some ships above your home world and make everyone think you're the hero?" I knew I wasn't fighting fair, but the emotion of the moment had all of my thoughts gushing out at once.

Her gaze turned ice-cold, shooting daggers at me. "I knew you wouldn't understand," she said in a fierce whisper.

I glared right back at her. "You never gave me the chance."

We stood facing each other in silence for several seconds.

"Mitch, these aren't your people," Vrynn said softly, gesturing toward the surface below us. "You don't know them. You have no connection to them. How could I expect you to put your life on the line for them?"

Now that I had vented my feelings, the anger ebbed a bit. I still felt the sting of her betrayal, but I could sort of understand her perspective. What could I say to help her understand mine?

I chuckled and stepped back toward her. "Well, there is one Mareesh that I'm sorta close to. And she *is* pretty important to me."

From the look of pain I saw in Vrynn's deep blue eyes, I could tell she felt guilty for what she'd done. Hopefully, she could see that I wasn't going to leave.

She gave me a hesitant smile. "But this is my fight," she said softly.

"What if I want it to be my fight, too?" I asked.

Vrynn seemed ready to tackle me in one of her fierce hugs again—and I would have let her—but unfortunately, Tera ruined the moment. Apparently, her emotional subroutines weren't finely tuned enough to realize when two people were right in the middle of a very important reconciliation.

"You're not the only one who's upset here, Mitch," Tera said, looking from Gabe to me. "How could you bring Gabe with you?"

Vrynn and I still needed to fix things, but there would be time for that. I turned my attention to my holographic friend. "There's no way I could have found you if I hadn't brought Gabe along." Now that I wasn't feeling so upset, I couldn't help a bit of playful banter. I tilted my head toward Vrynn, still speaking to Tera. "You know, I'm not really surprised that Vrynn stole my ship; that's sorta what she's wanted from day one, but I never expected you to turn on me, Tera."

Vrynn let out a short gasp and opened her mouth to object, but I stopped her with a quick wink so she would know I was just teasing.

"The only reason I went along with this plan was so that Gabe wouldn't get hurt," Tera said softly. She turned to Vrynn. "You said this mission would be dangerous and that the only way to keep Gabe safe was to leave him behind." Then she rounded on me, her voice rising. "And now you ruined it."

Gabe reached out and touched Tera's arm, though I could tell now that he wasn't actually *touching* her projection. "I *am* still safe," he stated. "And I would choose to face danger if it meant I could be helpful to my friends." He paused as if considering his next words. "And if it meant I could be with you."

Holographic tears welled up in Tera's eyes and began to spill down her face.

I smiled and turned my attention back to Vrynn. "That's how I feel, too."

"Are you sure?" The hesitant look in Vrynn's eyes told me I hadn't completely convinced her yet.

I reached out and took her hand. Despite the light blue tint to her fair skin—which made it look like she was perpetually cold—her hand was warm in mine. "Vrynn, you're pretty much the reason that I didn't take the *Starfire* and fly back to Earth as soon as we had enough fuel." I couldn't help but smile at the reminder of that decision. "I'd rather fight by your side, freeing your people, than anything else in the universe."

She gazed up at me with those beautiful eyes. "Really?"

I nodded. "A hundred percent."

Vrynn's brow knit together. "The entire amount?"

Her translation chip must have had trouble with that expression.

"Yes. The entire amount. I'm all in. Wholeheartedly. Fully committed." I smiled, knowing her chip would definitely stumble on those idioms.

Vrynn shook her head, the confusion still evident in her expression. "You say some of the strangest things, dirt boy." The pleasant smile on her face slowly faded to a look of earnest longing. "Thank you, Mitch." Vrynn squeezed my hand and pulled me a little closer. "I really do care for you." She paused for a moment. "That's why I left you behind."

"I know." I pulled her into my arms and held her tight. "Just don't ever do it again." I swept a hand to Gabe and Vrynn. "We're a family now. We have to stick together."

"Stick together?" she repeated back to me. Apparently, her implant hadn't even attempted to translate that one.

"Exactly," I said, holding her even tighter.

Chapter Six

I hefted my end of the scout ship as Gabe and I carried it across the cargo bay. I had the distinct feeling, though, that Gabe could have carried the small ship on his own, and he was only sharing the load to humor me.

The *Starfire* was perched at the base of a cliff on the small remnants of an atoll several hundred miles from Mareesh's inhabited islands. It was really just a tiny rock jutting out of the sea, smaller than a football field. But it did offer some shelter from the wind.

"I still don't understand how you two are able to touch," I said to Tera, who stood nearby as Gabe and I rigged the harness around the scout.

"Vrynn and I have had a lot of time together. This was an idea we had in one of our late-night chats."

"Yeah, but how is it possible?" I asked.

"Gabe's android body regularly interfaces with the ship's systems—not to mention that the *Starfire's* internal sensors can detect an object's location to within millimeters," Tera explained. "So, it was easy enough to program my matrix to interact with Gabe's body."

"Huh," was all I could manage for the moment.

With the scout ship strapped firmly against the bulkhead, Gabe and I stepped back to admire our work. "That's not going anywhere," I said, almost out of habit. I glanced at Gabe and Tera to see if they'd understood the reference.

Tera—the real Tera—would frequently make fun of Gabe and me for saying that exact phrase. Soon after they were married, she had found a pair of old couches at a garage sale, and Gabe and I had come to load them into the back of his pickup. The couches had been too long for the truck's short bed, so we'd been forced to improvise with straps and an old extension cord. When we'd gotten everything tied down, Gabe and I had said, nearly in unison, "That's not going anywhere."

The sudden resurfacing of the memory sent a flash of painful nostalgia through my middle. I'd never have those days with the real Tera and Gabe back.

Oblivious to my internal turmoil, my android friend nodded at my comment. "I think that was a funny day. Would you agree?"

Tera rolled her eyes—holographically speaking. "It was silly, is what it was."

I looked from Gabe to Tera and back. "You both remember that day at the garage sale?"

"The original Gabe's memory of that experience was strong enough to be part of the neural transfer, though there are gaps in my record of some of the details," Gabe explained.

"I don't have actual memories, but the real Tera thought what you two said was so hilarious that she actually made a video of it. That's how I know about it." Tera moved to stand next to Gabe, probably without consciously processing it. After all, she was based on a collection of videos that—along with other teenage-girl things—had chronicled the real Tera's feelings as she fell in love with the real Gabe.

My chest flooded with warmth and fondness for these two friends—the original and the current versions of them—enough to wash away some of the pain of having lost them. In an effort to ward off the tide of emotion that I could feel coming on, I decided to change the subject.

I pointed to their arms as they gently—and adorably—nudged against each other. "So I can understand how Tera's matrix gets projected right next to your body, but how does her movement affect you? I mean, your body shifts when she bumps you."

Gabe looked down at their arms as if examining the results of a scientific experiment. "Tera's location is being transmitted to my autonomous motor algorithms, preventing any part of my body from moving through her holographic projection and creating an automatic, physics-based response when her projection approaches me. I am also receiving signals into my feedback loop telling me I am touching something." He tilted his head and said to Tera, "This is very interesting."

"Do you like it?" Tera asked, a shy smile lurking in her expression.

"I do not have any algorithms to process happiness," Gabe observed, "but I am fascinated by the experience."

Tera pulled him into another embrace, and Gabe heartily hugged back.

"I must say, I am a little bit jealous. The rest of us can't hug Tera." I said.

"Perhaps if anyone needs to hug Tera, they can tell me, and I will do all of the Tera-hugging," Gabe said.

"Great idea, buddy," I said with a smile.

Vrynn joined us a moment later. "No ships in the area. It looks like we avoided their tracking systems again."

"I'm curious. Why are we making camp under a precarious overhang instead of just going back to Thetis Max?" I asked her.

Vrynn gave me a sheepish smile. "Originally, I didn't dare go back to Thetis Max for fear you would take back the ship. And I couldn't really go anywhere else because I'd have no way to know when the convoys arrive."

I frowned. "Why are you attacking the convoys? Why not attack the Barchee on the ground? I assume they have a base or something."

Vrynn nodded. "They do. It's on Mardrys."

"What's Mardrys?" I asked.

"Mardrys is the large central island where the capital city is located," Vrynn said. "But we can't attack the base because there's a defensive grid over the top of the caldera."

"Oh, I think I saw that from the air," I said with a nod. "So you're trying to shoot them down before they reach the base?"

"Exactly. We'll cut them off and starve them out," Vrynn said.

"How many supply ships have you stopped?"

"Five," she said proudly.

"Out of how many?"

Her expression turned sheepish. "Oh, I don't remember exactly how many times—"

"We've attacked thirty-four convoys," Tera said.

My brow went up. "Is that enough? I mean, will that have an effect on the occupiers?"

Vrynn's back stiffened. "I'm sure it is. They wouldn't send the transports if the occupiers didn't need them. We just have to keep at it."

There was that undying optimism.

Later that evening, I sat down at the kitchen table to eat. At least, my body thought it was evening; I still hadn't bothered to ask the time or how long a day on Mareesh even lasted. Two bites into my Caridyan tart, Tera appeared next to me.

"Transport ships entering the atmosphere," she said.

I took faster bites, figuring I had enough time to finish my meal before we took off. Half a second later, Vrynn burst from her room and streaked past me toward the flight deck.

"Hurry!" she yelled.

Apparently, this was more like a fire department.

I stuffed my tart in a small bin under the counter, hoping it survived whatever kind of maneuvers we were about to do so that I could finish it later.

Just as I jumped over the back of the pilot's seat, Vrynn launched the *Starfire* from our perch on the tiny rock. By the time I could take over the flight controls, we were already skimming along the surface, just a few feet above the waves. Once we were a safe distance from our little island, I pulled back on the controls and angled the ship upward to meet the incoming convoy.

The holographic display above my control panel tagged the ships in the convoy with flashing squares. The largest was on the closest fighter escort, heading straight at us on an intercept course.

"This is about the time we portal jump right behind the convoy and shoot up the escorts," Vrynn said.

I nodded. "That could definitely work. But see these?" I pointed at another pair of flashing squares behind the transports, hanging back to protect the rear of the convoy. "We'd have to fight through those escorts before we'd get a shot at the transports."

"You have a better plan?" Vrynn asked, obviously defensive of her chosen tactics.

"What if we jump here, above the convoy, where they don't have escorts?" I asked.

"But if we're flying upward, and we portal jump to the other side, we'll be going the wrong direction. Away from the convoy."

I shrugged. "I can pull a tight turn."

Tera jumped in. "Actually, that's not entirely true."

"What. You don't think I can turn fast?" I asked.

Tera rolled her eyes. "I'm sure you're an amazing pilot," she said drily. "I meant that we wouldn't still be flying up if we don't want to. I can shift which way the portal on the other end is pointing."

My brow furrowed. "You mean we can go in the portal, heading one way, and come out in a different direction at the other end?"

"Yeah, pretty much," Tera said.

"Let's do that," Vrynn said excitedly.

I took a deep breath. "Target the area above the convoy, heading toward them, and open the portal."

"Portal open," Tera said as the familiar aperture expanded in front of us.

Except this time, it didn't feel familiar at all. Instead of seeing a view that was just closer to the one we already had, the view through the portal was of a patch of ocean floating up in the sky. I experienced a brief moment of vertigo as we approached. My eyes were telling me I was about to fall forward out of my seat, but my body was telling me that I was leaning back.

A split second later, we passed through the portal and my body discovered that my eyes had been right. The force of gravity instantly shifted forward, dragging me toward the front of the ship.

And the convoy was right below us.

I tapped my weapons console and fired off a pair of slugs from the rail gun. The transports weren't exactly expecting us to suddenly appear above them, not that the lead ship could have dodged from this close anyway. I glanced at Vrynn. "Why aren't you shooting already?"

Vrynn quickly snapped out of her amazement that my plan had worked and raked the second transport with the plasma cannons.

Both of my shots hit the first transport, slicing clean through the ship. Fire exploded from the holes, and the vessel broke into pieces as it fell toward the ocean. Vrynn's stream of plasma rounds from point blank range punched through the hull of the second ship, causing massive damage to the drive section. A few seconds later, the fire breached its power core, and the ship exploded.

The pair of trailing escorts recovered from their shock—but not soon enough to save the transports—and fired on us. I banked hard while Vrynn strafed them with the plasma cannons. I turned again, heading directly toward the two fighters, and split the gap between them.

Vrynn swiveled back and forth with the cannons, apparently trying to shoot both of them simultaneously. One of the fighters veered quickly away from the fountains of plasma, but the other got a little too much of Vrynn's attention. The round tore into its flank, and it quickly disintegrated.

"Escape portal," I called to Tera, and the Quake Drive aperture swallowed us moments later.

Before I even had a chance to process what had happened, we were gliding low over the water toward our tiny island.

"That was amazing!" Vrynn exclaimed. "Why had I never thought to use the Quake Drive like that?"

"It was just a fresh perspective," I said, grinning back at her.

Vrynn jumped across the aisle and threw her arms around me. "Mitch, this is perfect. Now we can finally free my people."

I could feel the warmth in my cheeks at her effusive praise. I attempted a nonchalant shrug. "It's okay. Just trying to help."

She pulled back from our embrace, but left a hand on my shoulder. I couldn't help but notice the way her touch always seemed to warm me. She glanced at her hand then turned her gaze on me with an intensity that made my stomach feel like we were still in the middle of a dogfight. After several long seconds, she leaned back into her own seat.

If that was the reaction I got from getting the jump on a few freighters, I could only imagine what she would do if we actually succeeded in driving the Barchee from her planet.

After finally getting a good night's sleep in my own bed—the one on the *Starfire*, anyway—I felt ready to take on Vrynn's enemies again.

I padded out to the kitchen and fixed myself a bowl of Varusian hash. It had a flavor like oatmeal, but with a texture more like tapioca pudding. Vrynn had already informed me that no one but the poorest street urchins ate it, and even then they never ate it before midday. That seemed like a pity, considering its similarity to one of my favorite breakfasts back on Earth. Besides, I was eating it in the privacy of my own starship. What did I care what anyone else thought?

Vrynn settled into a chair across the table from me. "I don't know how you can stomach that stuff," she said, wrinkling her adorable nose.

"Maybe you're right," I said as I savored another gloppy bite, "now that we're heroes, we can afford a more expensive menu."

She laughed. "Since when are we heroes?"

"Since we started The Battle of Mardrys," I said it with a dash of gusto to give weight to my declaration. I had actually just made that name up on the spot.

Vrynn's brows went up. "You just said the name of the original battle when the Barchee attacked my people." Her expression turned suddenly somber.

I didn't want the conversation to veer into depressing topics, so I continued with my false bravado. "Oh, well then, we'll call it The Second Battle of Mardrys."

"That's what you think the history books will call this?" She held out an arm, indicating our current situation.

I shrugged. "Sure."

"You're suddenly the confident one now," she said with a small smile.

I shrugged. "I feel pretty confident. We're back together, fighting to save your people."

"Actually, I am, too," Vrynn said, leaning toward me slightly. "I think it'll only be a few more days, and the Barchee will be forced to negotiate. They can't survive without supplies, right?" Her expression turned mischievous. "Unless, of course, they resort to eating urchin's hash." She glanced down at my bowl. "In that case, we might have to blockade the planet for months."

"You're gonna keep giving me a hard time about this, aren't you?" I pointed at my breakfast.

"Only as long as you keep eating it," she replied with a wide and captivating smile.

I decided to redirect the conversation to something more productive. "You know, I was thinking about all this flying the *Starfire* around, jumping back and forth through portals, saving planets."

"Yeah?" Vrynn prompted.

"What if Nexus finds out that we have the Quake Drive installed in the *Starfire*?" I asked.

"If they come after us, we can always jump away. With the Quake Drive functional, they'll never get the *Starfire* from us."

I gave her my skeptical look.

"Besides, as long as Dack got away with the other Mark 7, Nexus already thinks we have the Quake Drive."

"Unless they just destroyed the other Mark 7 without finding out that it was only Dack on board," I offered.

"Unlikely," Vrynn replied.

"Oh, I hope they didn't destroy Dack," Tera said as she materialized nearby.

Gabe climbed the last few steps of the ladder and joined us in the living area. "Who's Dack?" he asked.

"Dack was the default AI matrix in the only other surviving Mark 7," I explained. "He helped us steal the Quake Drive back from Gralik."

Gabe's expression turned serious—though that wasn't a big change—and he said to Tera, "If you have feelings for Dack, I will do my best to not impede any potential relationship you would desire to have."

Tera made a face like someone had soured her power supply. "Ew! Why would I have feelings for Dack? He's, like, ancient."

I couldn't help but chuckle. Dack's holographic projection had looked somewhere between forty and fifty by Earth standards. But to a teenage hologram, he might as well have been a fossil.

But Tera wasn't finished. She squared off with Gabe, a hand on her hip. "Do you think I'd go to all the trouble, bartering and trading to save up enough Bonmarks to buy an android body, then download your personality to it, and reprogram both of us so that we could touch just to then run off with some stuffy old AI whose holographic projection is too bulgy in the middle?"

"That is a complicated compound question that delves into your motivations and desires," Gabe replied. "I am not sure I have a sufficient answer."

"Uh, the answer seems pretty obvious," I piped in. Gabe merely cocked his head to the side as if asking me to elaborate. I stood and walked over to him. "C'mere, buddy." I put an arm around his shoulder and pulled him across the room to a private corner.

"I have access to all the ship's internal sensors," Tera said. "I'll still be able to hear you."

"Let them have their man moment," Vrynn told her.

I shot a quick wink of appreciation at Vrynn. Returning my attention to Gabe, I lowered my voice. Not that it made much difference. "Listen, she doesn't want anyone else. She's not ever going to want anyone else. Bringing you back was a fulfillment of a dream for Tera. That's how devoted she is to you."

He nodded stiffly. "My logical circuits had come to a similar conclusion, but I was confused by her reference to the other hologram."

I smiled. "It's okay to feel a little jealous from time to time, especially at the beginning." I nearly laughed at the absurdity of me giving Gabe relationship advice. He'd already married his high school sweetheart by the same time I'd had my first serious girlfriend.

"My algorithms are not currently capable of processing jealousy," he said. "But after she programmed our ability to simulate physical contact,

I decided to reciprocate by creating an algorithm that would allow me to develop romantic feelings for her," Gabe said.

My brows went up at that. "Really? Did it work?"

He tilted his head. "It has only produced what I would describe as a sympathetic attachment to her presence," he said in a voice that was nothing even close to a whisper.

"That's not a bad start," I replied. I nodded toward Tera. "I suggest you go show her what the new algorithm can do."

He nodded, and we returned to the group. Tera rolled her eyes at the whole thing, but quickly changed her attitude as Gabe stepped over to her and awkwardly took her hand. There wasn't a romance novel or romcom in the world—or universe, actually, assuming romcoms were a universal constant—where that would have been enough to satisfy a woman. But Tera was a holographic representation of a teenage girl, and she seemed thrilled just to be finally holding hands with her crush.

I smiled. My two friends were well on their way to recreating the interstellar version of the Earth-Tera and Gabe's wonderful relationship. Not for the first time—though maybe the first time with the artificial versions of my friends—I felt a little jealous of what they had. Without even thinking, I glanced over at Vrynn. For some reason, she seemed to be watching me instead of our teenagers. I raised a brow. "What?"

"Nothing," she replied, but she continued looking at me with an expression I couldn't quite figure out.

The thought occurred to me that I'd probably need to take some of my own advice and let Vrynn know how I felt about her.

As soon as I figured out how deep those feelings actually were.

"Convoy coming out of orbit," Tera said.

We had been sitting in the flight deck, all systems up and running, waiting for this exact thing. Six seconds later, we were in the air, skimming low across the water.

I checked the tactical readout. Staying so low to the surface helped hide us from enemy scanners, but it also limited our own ability to detect enemy ships. I could see two cargo vessels high in the atmosphere, but no escorts yet. The scanner resolution improved as we got closer, showing they had six fighters with them.

We hadn't seen six escorts with a convoy yet, but we'd faced more than that in other battles. Even so, a little pit of anxiety formed in my stomach.

We watched the tactical scanner as we flew closer to the approaching convoy. Once we were close enough to the ships, and far enough from our island base, we would pop up and attack. Or maybe we would just portal jump. The Quake Drive gave us such an advantage in battles that it almost seemed unfair.

A series of new targets suddenly appeared on my console. "What are those?" I asked.

"More Barchee fighters," Tera said. "Four of them."

"They're flying search patterns low over the water," Vrynn added.

They were learning from our tactics.

"Ten fighters," I muttered under my breath.

"They must really be getting desperate," she replied with a hopeful smile. "Our strategy is working."

"Do we take on the surface escorts first?" I asked.

Vrynn shook her head. "No, it's the transports we care about."

I nodded, but my mind was whirling. What was the best strategy? We could jump straight to the convoy, but then we'd have six escorts to deal with, not to mention these four on the surface quickly joining the fight.

"What if we match the speed of the transports and portal jump right between them?" I said. "The escorts would have a hard time attacking us without hitting their own ships. We could pretty easily take out both transports before they could get us."

It would be risky considering those transports were at least twice the size of the *Starfire*. But of course, Vrynn wouldn't think it was risky.

"Great idea," she said.

"Set up the targeting," I said to Tera. "Let me know once you've got it ready and how fast I need to be flying."

Tera's eyes scanned the space in front of her. "Targeting set. Increase speed by twenty percent."

I pushed the throttle forward and waited for Tera's approval.

"That's probably close enough," she said. "You can adjust when you come out of the portal."

"The timing is critical, so I'll just keep flying straight ahead, and you open the portal when it's right."

"Acknowledged," she replied.

A second later, the Quake Drive aperture expanded in front of us. It happened so quickly and so close to the ship that I barely had time to realize there was a portal in front of us before we were already through.

Vrynn fired twice with the rail gun at point blank range, and both rounds disappeared down the engine nozzles of the freighter in front of us.

"The aperture didn't close normally," Tera announced.

"What do you mean the aperture didn't—"

The lead transport exploded in a giant fireball. I dodged the largest pieces of the ship as they fell below us, but dozens of smaller chunks of debris pinged against the flight deck window.

"Target the second transport," I said to Vrynn as I tried to bring us through the last of the debris cloud.

Vrynn panned her controls toward the rear, but then just sat there staring. She didn't squeeze the trigger, and I didn't hear the plasma cannons.

"What's wrong?" I asked.

"The second freighter isn't there," she replied.

"How can it not be there?"

A warning blared on my console. Incoming rounds.

I pushed the sticks forward, sending the *Starfire* into a steep dive. The tactical console showed the six original escorts swarming around us, but no transport ship. In my peripheral vision, I could see Vrynn panning her targeting display left and right, up and down. She even stood up in her seat and literally looked out the window.

"It's gone," she finally declared.

I reversed the *Starfire* into a climb, dodging incoming fire as I doubled back to where the second transport should have been. "Unless the Barchee have developed a more maneuverable freighter design, or some kind of cloaking device . . ."

"That's what I was telling you earlier," Tera said in an annoyed tone. "When I tried to close the aperture, the Quake Drive wouldn't shut off."

"Why not?" I asked.

Tera shrugged. "It's probably a safety feature meant to keep the aperture open when something big is passing through," Tera said.

"What could have been passing through except us?" I asked.

"The second freighter," Vrynn said.

I let that sink in for a moment, still keeping my eye on the approaching fighter escorts. "Hang on, you're saying the other transport passed through the portal before it closed. Does that mean it jumped to the entrance aperture?"

"Correct," Tera replied.

"We need to find that transport." Vrynn leaned over her tactical console. "Where was our entrance portal?"

My warning alarm blared again. "We have bigger issues right now," I said.

"Stopping the cargo is the only issue," Vrynn said.

"And staying alive," I added, not surprised when Vrynn completely ignored my addendum.

"There it is." Vrynn pointed at her screen. "Just above the water. It's heading toward Mardrys."

I let out a sigh and pushed the *Starfire* into a steep dive. Going after the transport would mean fighting our way through the four escorts on their way up to intercept us, not to mention the other six currently pursuing us. Despite our success in destroying the first freighter, our plan had inadvertently put the second transport farther out of our reach.

I angled the *Starfire* toward the escaping freighter while Vrynn let loose a barrage of plasma rounds against anything that got close enough. The second transport was still several minutes from Mardrys, but I wasn't sure we'd be able to fight our way through the escorts in time.

I didn't want to pull Vrynn's attention from defending us, so I activated the weapons menu on my secondary console and selected the rail gun. This particular weapon didn't have much freedom in terms of aim—only within a few degrees of the direction we were pointed—but it could pack a punch. The targeting system tracked the transport, flying straight and low over the water, and gave me a positive lock. I fired a five-round star cluster plus one in the middle, something I'd learned in my first encounter with aliens.

We couldn't break off pursuit until we knew whether my shots had found their mark, so I weaved back and forth in an attempt to give Vrynn an advantage on the cannons. Toggling back to the weapons system, I selected an atmospheric missile. The tracking system selected a nearby fighter attempting to engage us. I didn't really know which one, but I wasn't picky. As soon as the lock flashed, I pulled the trigger on the control stick and watched a missile streak away and veer toward its target.

The sound of the incoming threat warning suddenly changed tone. Imminent impact.

I jammed the control sticks forward and gritted my teeth, just as an explosive slug streaked past the view port and detonated above us. As the ship dove, Vrynn and I both floated up against our harnesses. Tera had no mass to worry about, and Gabe could hold himself down against the bulkhead with the strength in his pinky finger. But there would probably be a mess in the cargo bay to clean up later.

"Two slugs hit that second transport," Tera announced.

Vrynn panned to the transport. "It's going down!" she said exuberantly.

I juked and weaved with the *Starfire* as the imminent impact warning continued to blare annoyingly. My dive had brought us too close to a pair of fighter escorts. They both fired, and slugs exploded just behind us, shaking the *Starfire's* frame.

"Rear ion deflectors took a hit," Tera announced. "But they're holding steady at ninety percent."

There was a lull in the impact alarm as I aimed the *Starfire* for the nearest bit of open sky. Vrynn stopped firing and stared at me. "What are you doing?" she asked.

"I'm getting us out of here."

She pointed back toward the ships still on our tail. "We could stay in the fight and take out more escort fighters."

I let out a short laugh, though her suggestion shouldn't have surprised me. I rolled the *Starfire* into a figure-eight loop, taking us right back at the enemy fighters I was trying to get away from. Vrynn had taken out several of them, but the remaining escorts had regrouped and were coming at us en masse.

I made a hard turn and zipped across the path of a pair of enemy ships. I knew it was a horrible naval tactic to present your broadside to an enemy ship, but with Vrynn working her magic on the plasma cannons, it wasn't much of a disadvantage.

The escorts scattered haphazardly, firing on us when they dared.

"Incoming enemy fighters," Tera announced.

"Yeah, we know," I shot back. "They're all around us."

"Not the escorts," she replied. "Five additional Barchee fighters are coming out of orbit above us."

"Can you identify them?" I asked.

"Barchee heavy attack fighters," Tera said. "Strong defensive shielding. Not highly maneuverable, but heavily armed."

I turned to Vrynn. "Have you ever taken on a Barchee Heavy?"

She immediately swiveled the cannons forward, lined up on the incoming ships. "Nope."

Apparently, she was up for the challenge.

I scrutinized their attack formation. They were coming in hard, head-on, hoping to catch us in the chaos. Regardless of whether it was a planned strategy to have the smaller escorts force us to fly straight up into the oncoming attack fighters, we would have done it anyway. The heavies were the real threat. Our cannons roared to life, and Vrynn sprayed the air in front of us with plasma rounds. Maybe we could use the chaos to our advantage, too.

I switched to the rail gun and fired a spread of explosive slugs dead ahead. The enemy heavies unleashed a barrage of their own, and I was forced to veer away, dodging incoming rounds as best I could. The heavies' initial volley exploded around us, and my console lit up with impacts and warnings.

"Lateral deflectors down to sixty percent," Tera called out. "Dorsal deflectors at fifty-two percent. And we've had a hull breach in the aft section of the top deck, just forward of the engine nozzles."

I spared Vrynn a quick glance. "Now are you ready to disengage?"

Vrynn nodded. "Yeah, let's get back to the island."

"Tera, activate the Quake Drive," I said. "Put the portal right in front of us and get us back to the island."

"Acknowledged," Tera replied.

A heavy fighter swept in close, flying across our path, just behind us. I pointed at the video displays. "Vrynn. Watch that one."

Vrynn fired on the approaching enemy just as the aperture appeared in front of us. The heavy swept near our tail, dodging the incoming fire. A second later, we were through the portal into peaceful airspace.

I slumped back in my chair and blew out a long breath. "That was a close call."

Vrynn nodded. She was smiling, though, so I wasn't sure she fully appreciated how precarious our situation had been.

The incoming fire warning shattered the relative calm of the flight deck. I stared down at my console, glad to see that it was mostly blank. Had a slug made it through the aperture with us?

It was more than just a slug, though. My tactical display showed one of the Barchee heavies still on our tail. I banked hard to avoid the incoming shots.

"What happened?" I yelled at nobody in particular.

"The heavy must have come through the portal with us," Vrynn said as she continued firing.

That was bad.

Not only did it mean we couldn't land on our little island base with this guy around, but we had to make sure he didn't get away and tell anyone else where we had jumped to.

And we had to do it fast.

I punched the throttle hard and pulled the *Starfire* into a steep climb. The heavy matched our maneuver, firing on us with its forward cannons. Vrynn fired back, but didn't do much damage against the heavily armored spacecraft.

I pushed the *Starfire* down, bringing us low over the water. "Remember that time you kicked up a dust cloud for us to hide in?"

Vrynn glanced at me. "Yeah?"

"Can you make a wall of water?"

"Definitely," Vrynn replied.

Despite never having done it mid-dogfight, I activated the hover emitters. Then, using my ever-improving zero-G skills, I spun the *Starfire* halfway around so that we were now flying backward.

Vrynn blasted the surface of the water between us and the heavy, and plumes of foam and mist erupted from the surface, blocking our view of each other.

Figuring that if we couldn't see him, he couldn't see our incoming slugs, I fired a spread of three rounds from the rail gun. The enemy heavy emerged from the curtain of water just as the first slug sailed past.

He wasn't as lucky with the second shot, though. It plowed straight through his main fuselage and detonated near the engine core. By the time the third slug exploded, it was only adding insult to injury. Pieces of the enemy ship splashed down, creating a wide debris patch that I hoped would quickly fade away.

I let out a long breath.

"Nice move!" Vrynn said with an affectionate tap on my shoulder.

"Thanks," I said with a wry grin. "You're still a crack-shot on the cannons."

She tilted her head at the initial translation, then smiled when the actual meaning made it through.

I turned the ship forward again and guided us the last few miles to our little island base. When the skids touched down, I finally let myself relax.

"Let's just focus on taking out the transports from now on," I said, rolling my neck to release the stress.

She gave me a mischievous grin. "I was just thinking how much more efficient we are when we can take out the entire convoy at once. They can't have an infinite supply of escorts."

I shook my head. "I'd hardly call that taking out the entire convoy. We didn't even destroy half of the escort fighters, and only one heavy. The rest got away."

Vrynn shrugged. "Some fish are slippery."

I waited for my chip to give me another translation, but nothing came. Apparently, the literal translation was clear enough.

I walked out of the flight deck into the living area, and Vrynn followed quickly behind me. "Since you got here, the missions have gone so much better. I don't think a single transport has made it through."

I offered Vrynn a wan smile. Obviously, I was happy that things were going well. But it felt like I had a sudden weight pressing down on my shoulders. We had no guarantee that our success would continue, and the Barchee escorts seemed to adapt each time we tried a new strategy. Could I keep coming up with new ideas and tactics? Would Vrynn be disappointed with me when we eventually let a transport slip through?

I glanced around, suddenly feeling very trapped inside the few rooms on the *Starfire*. "I need to get some fresh air," I said.

"We're near the south pole. It's only slightly above freezing out there." She sounded genuinely concerned for my sanity.

"I won't be out long," I said. "Besides, some crisp air might do me good."

I grabbed a jacket from my quarters and walked to the upper deck airlock. After the abbreviated cycle finished, I pushed open the heavy outer door and got my first real look at the surface of Mareesh, and my first breath of crisp Mareesh air. It smelled like a mix between a beach and a muddy forest.

I climbed halfway down the steps in the hull and hopped the rest of the way to the rocky surface of the tiny island. A flaky, bluish-green substance crunched under my feet, probably Mareesh's version of moss or algae.

Walking the fifty or so feet to the lip of our small landing plateau, I peered over the edge at the water below. Tall waves crashed against the rocky cliffs. I wasn't sure if Mareesh had anything like tropical islands, but this certainly wasn't one of them. It reminded me more of the islands near Ireland or Scotland.

The longer I watched the waves, though, the more alien they seemed. The foam on the caps wasn't white, it was tinged blue, and the waves were huge. They battered against the cliff side and sprayed bluish foam dozens of feet into the air. It was a mesmerizing sight.

A high-pitched whistling sound reached my ears, and I glanced around. Vrynn stood hanging out of the airlock hatch, waving and screaming at me. I couldn't hear her over the sound of the crashing waves, so that didn't explain the whistling sound.

Then the stony peak high above the *Starfire* exploded, raining down rocks all around the ship. I ran toward the ship, pebbles and debris from the exploding cliffside peppering the plateau around me.

"What happened?" I yelled up at Vrynn once I was in earshot again.

"The Barchee ships found us," she said as I began climbing the steps. "They're not quite in range, but they're firing anyway." She pulled me the rest of the way into the airlock and pointed over my shoulder.

I glanced back to see the fiery plumes of three atmospheric missiles. We swung the outer door closed and quickly cycled through the airlock.

"Emergency launch!" I called out to Tera as I rounded the corner into the flight deck.

The ship rumbled to life, and the deck shifted under my feet. I jumped into the pilot's seat and strapped myself in. Two seconds later, Vrynn landed beside me.

I grabbed the control sticks and jammed the throttle to full power.

The ship rocketed forward just as another missile slammed into the cliff. The rock shards pounded against the hull, sounding like hail on a tin roof.

"Any damage?" I asked Tera.

She shook her head. "Some minor dents, but nothing serious."

I turned to Vrynn. "Do we fight them off?"

The expression on her face betrayed the emotions warring within her. She didn't want to run away, but she knew it was the smartest choice. Finally, she glanced out the view port and said, "Let's get out of here."

Apparently, common sense had won out.

I pulled back on the sticks and flew the ship straight for the stratosphere.

"Open a portal to the Thetis system," I said to Tera.

"Affirmative," she replied.

"We're going all the way back to Thetis Max?" Vrynn asked incredulously.

"Where else would we go? I doubt there's anything left of the island." I thumbed over my shoulder.

Vrynn slumped into her chair, her arms crossed.

I was sorry to upset her, but we didn't have many other options at the moment.

The ship sailed through the portal into orbit above Thetis Max. The blackness of the Thetis system was a peaceful contrast to the combat we had just escaped. I let out a long breath of relief, knowing that we were several light years away from the Barchee ships that had just pulled the rug out from under us.

As we floated down to the surface of the volcanic moon and approached our mining facility, Vrynn turned to me. "Just know, we can't stay here. We have to get back to Mareesh as soon as possible."

"Can we at least stop long enough to pick up Rascal?" I asked with a heavy note of sarcasm.

"Obviously," she replied, as if I'd been the one to leave a family member behind, not the other way around.

As the inner door of the giant hangar airlock opened, I expected to see Rascal bounding around, excited for our return. That part was actually true; the large beast could barely contain himself. What I hadn't expected was the mess.

In our absence, my animal friend had torn holes through half a dozen derelict spacecraft and scattered the shards throughout the hangar. The *Starfire's* skids nudged aside one particularly large pile of newly created scrap metal. I rushed from the flight deck and down through the cargo bay, jumping from the loading ramp before it fully lowered.

Rascal bounded across the messy hangar and tackled me to the ground.

"Yeah, yeah, I'm happy to see you, too, boy," I said as he repeatedly nuzzled his large head against my neck.

"Looks like your pet may not be house trained yet," Vrynn said as she walked past.

I laughed and pulled myself back up. Skeeter arrived a moment later, and Rascal jumped and whined when he saw her. The robotic feline mimicked his behavior—probably a part of her programming—and they scampered back up the cargo ramp together.

As I rejoined Vrynn at the top of the ramp—her brow furrowed and arms folded across her chest—I had the sneaky suspicion that she was ready to get back in the fight. Personally, I wouldn't have minded a long nap on the couch, but I knew this was important to her.

We needed some sort of plan, though. "So, are there any other places on Mareesh where we could hide the *Starfire*?"

Vrynn's scowl softened a little, and she gave me a small smile. "I've been thinking about that, and I know of a cavern on the southern coast of Syr."

"I assume Syr is an island." A pretty safe assumption, considering Mareesh's geography.

Vrynn nodded. "It's the southern island. Where I grew up."

We walked through the cargo bay, heading back up to the flight deck as we continued the conversation.

"Perfect," I said. "But is it big enough for our ship?"

"It's definitely big enough," Vrynn replied. "But getting in might be a problem."

"Why?"

"The entrance is underwater."

I wanted to protest, but Vrynn continued.

"A person can squeeze in through a narrow crack in the wall, but something as big as a starship would have to use the underwater tunnel." Vrynn didn't seem perturbed at all by this, which was typical.

I leaned back in my chair and scratched my head. "Is the *Starfire* watertight? Won't we spring a leak if we tried to go underwater?"

"It's airtight against the vacuum of space," Vrynn said. "It should be able to handle a little water."

I chuckled. Of course, an optimist who grew up on a planet covered almost entirely in water would think it was no problem. I wondered if

Vrynn's optimism was unique to her or if it was a common trait in her culture. If we succeeded in freeing her people from occupation, I might get a chance to find out. Assuming our relationship ever got to the point that she'd want to introduce me to her family.

Gabe and Tera stood a few feet away, having a completely silent conversation. "Tera, can the *Starfire* go underwater?" I asked.

Her eyes briefly scanned back and forth. "Certainly. The hull is completely air and watertight."

"It will not go under water," Gabe said.

"What do you mean?" Tera sounded hurt that he would contradict her. "Of course it can go underwater."

Gabe shrugged. "It can. But I do not think it will."

No one knew exactly what that meant, so I turned back to Vrynn and said, "Assuming we can get the ship underwater, will the cavern be the best place to hide it?"

"I think so," she said.

I took a breath, already imagining thousands of pounds of water pressing against the flight deck glass. "Okay. I guess that's our plan."

Chapter Seven

After the next batch of ore was fully loaded, we jumped to Cypso using the standard intra-space drive because the Quake Drive power cells were still measuring low. Vrynn was sure they just needed a little more time to fully regenerate. I tried not to think about the possibility that they might never regenerate.

"So we're rich now?" I asked Vrynn when she returned from selling our cargo.

"Only halfway rich," she replied. "I bought enough supplies for a few more weeks on Mareesh just in case it takes that long to drive away the Barchee occupiers."

"Smart," I said. "I'm sure I'd be willing to make the sacrifice of eating Varusian hash a little while longer."

Vrynn wrinkled her nose but didn't take the bait.

With our newly stocked cargo bay, we made the jump to Mareesh. Not finding any convoys in orbit, we headed straight for the surface. Several minutes later, we were skimming just a few feet above Mareesh's tempestuous southern sea.

"There's Syr." Vrynn pointed at a growing speck on the horizon. "Slow down and stay low."

I slowed our speed but didn't drop any lower because I didn't want to use the *Starfire* as a surfboard. A submarine was bad enough. When we got close enough to make out details of the rocky cliff, I switched on the hover emitters and killed the throttle.

"If there's no entrance to the cave, how will we know where it is?" I asked, scanning the shoreline.

Vrynn stood and moved to the front of the flight deck, scrutinizing the coastline through the viewing windows. "I just have to find some landmarks I recognize." She waved her hand to the right. "I think it's that way."

I slid the ship sideways, staying parallel with the coast. Vrynn's expression changed from confusion to recognition and back several times. To me, everything seemed the same—foreboding cliffs of grayish rock mottled with splotches of blues and greens. Occasionally, a wave would crash against the cliff, sending a tower of water spraying up onto the land high above.

"There!" Vrynn pointed to an outcropping of rock that looked just like all the others. "You see those rocks in the water in the shape of a Shemra head?"

I squinted. "I don't know what a Shemra is, so I guess I don't."

Vrynn moved to my side and leaned down next to me, pointing toward a jagged rise. "That's where the above-ground entrance to the cavern is, just to the left of those rocks."

I tried to focus on my flying, but I couldn't help but notice her hip leaning against my arm and her hand resting gently on my shoulder. We'd been working closely together for several weeks now, but recently she seemed more and more comfortable with casual physical contact.

I shook my head to clear the distraction and gripped the control sticks. "Tera, are we ready to go under the water?"

"Sure." Her tone made it sound like she couldn't care less, but I knew better.

I reduced power to the hover emitters, and we settled on top of the water. I wasn't exactly sure what I had expected to happen next, but it definitely involved going underneath the surface. Instead, we simply bobbed up and down with the passing waves like a giant silver toy boat.

"I said the ship would not go under the water," Gabe said from the jump seat behind me. "It is too buoyant."

"How do we reduce our buoyancy?" I asked.

Tera shrugged. "The *Starfire's* a spaceship, not a submarine."

"Any ideas?" I asked Vrynn.

"We could try it again from higher up, with a steep dive," Vrynn said.

"You mean fly straight down at full speed at the water?" I asked. My tone must have indicated my skepticism.

"It's just a suggestion," Vrynn replied.

There had to be another way. I rubbed the stubble on my chin as I thought. "Can the hover emitter field be flipped?"

Tera's eyes scanned back and forth. "If we reverse the charge of the power flow into the emitters, that might reverse the field as well."

"Any danger in trying?" I asked.

"There's a very small chance it turns the space-time continuum inside out," she replied.

Leave it to Tera to make me regret being cautious.

"We can't stay here, bobbing up and down," Vrynn said. "Reversing the field is the best option."

I chuckled. "Okay, Tera, go ahead."

At first, nothing happened. Then, I added power to the emitters as if we were trying to take off, and the ship sank several feet into the water and stayed there, like some giant hand was pressing down on us. The waves sloshed up against the flight deck window. I had a brief moment of panic as I imagined a flood of water cracking through the super-glass.

As I increased the power even more, we descended further until finally we were completely submerged. It was amazing how quickly the noise of the waves lapping against the hull suddenly disappeared. We had transported ourselves into another world just a few dozen feet below the water's surface.

I'd been underwater plenty in my life, mostly at the community swimming pool. I'd even spent a week down on the Gulf Coast of Texas one summer after I graduated. Diving underwater there had felt like a small experience, with hazy greenish-tinted water teeming with tiny fish and little floaties everywhere.

This felt enormous and vast.

The deep-blue water around us was crystal clear—clear enough that I could see details on the seafloor hundreds of feet down. And yet, there was something about the water that felt like it had substance, almost the way gelatin flexes when it jiggles.

The water on Mareesh seemed to have flows and contours.

I'm not sure how long I sat there staring, but Vrynn finally waved her hand to get my attention. "We need to go that way." She pointed.

I gave her a sheepish smile and pushed the *Starfire* forward through the water. The water swirled and parted as it flowed around the ship. I scanned the submerged cliffside ahead of us, hoping it had a very large opening.

Tera pointed at the underwater cliff wall. "Is that the gap we're looking for?" she asked.

"That's it," Vrynn replied excitedly.

I guided the *Starfire* through a giant gap in the rocky face and into a shadowy underwater tunnel. The ship's external floodlights switched on, showing that the water was still impossibly blue.

We drifted along as the tube narrowed steadily. Maybe it was because I didn't feel confident maneuvering the *Starfire* in tight spaces yet, but this tunnel was giving me claustrophobia. I eased off on the thrust.

"Why'd you stop?" Vrynn asked.

"We're not going to fit," I replied, pointing out the front windows at the rock walls closing in on us.

"Oh, we'll fit," she said with confidence.

I shook my head and pulled up a video feed from the externally mounted cameras. "That's not much clearance on the sides," I said, trying to guess how tight of a squeeze it would be.

"I think it's enough," Vrynn replied, not sounding quite as sure as a moment ago.

I frowned. "What do you think, Tera? Will we fit?" I asked.

"What you should really be asking is whether the tunnel will hold if we run into it," my holographic friend replied.

"Yeah, that's not exactly helpful right now," I said.

Tera shrugged.

I scrutinized the narrowest part of the tunnel for several more seconds, still unsure.

"C'mon, Mitch. We can do it," Vrynn said. "The *Starfire* can withstand plasma rounds and exploding slugs. What's the worst that could happen?"

Tera started to reply, but I held up a hand. "Don't answer that." I grabbed the controls and took a deep breath. "Let's give it a try."

I pushed the ship forward, and the tunnel walls slid slowly by. After several seconds, we passed through the narrowest part, and I finally let myself breathe again.

Just then, an ominous scraping sound reverberated through the flight deck.

I glanced over at Tera, her eyes scanning back and forth.

"No structural damage," she said after a moment. "You might have ruined the paint job in that spot, though."

"I don't care that much about the appearance; I just don't want to spring a leak," I said.

"No guarantees," Tera replied with a smile. Apparently, she was trying to make a joke.

I guided the ship onward down the tunnel until we reached an opening in the ceiling.

"There's the cavern," Vrynn said, pointing to a shimmering patch of water above us.

I nodded and dialed back the power on the emitters. The ship rose slowly until we breached the surface.

The cavern was actually much larger than the small pool we were floating in. There was a wide expanse of rock sloping away from the water that would comfortably fit the *Starfire*. And narrow shafts of light streamed down into the space from cracks in the stone high above.

Turning to Vrynn, I asked, "If you only ever came in through a crack in the cavern, how did you know there was a tunnel leading out to the ocean?"

"My cousins and I would swim in this pool," she said. "And one of them once dared me to dive under the water to see if it connected to the outside." She smiled at the memory.

"But how did you know the *Starfire* would fit through?" I asked.

Vrynn shrugged. "Oh, I don't know. It seemed big enough."

I shook my head as visions of the *Starfire* wedged in an underwater tunnel filled my mind.

After hovering the ship out of the water and onto solid ground again, I asked Tera and Gabe to do a full internal systems check while Vrynn and I went outside to explore.

On our way to the cargo bay, Vrynn stopped at the fabrication lab. "We'll need a way to know when convoys are coming," Vrynn said as she grabbed a remote sensor module.

Out in the cavern, we checked all around the *Starfire* for any sign of damage from our underwater excursion. I didn't know if we would find any or not, but it didn't hurt to be thorough.

After that was done, Vrynn led me across the cavern. She pointed to a crevice higher up on the wall. "This is how we got in and out," she said as we began scaling what proved to be a series of rocks laid out almost like a giant staircase.

Half a minute later, she paused and looked out over the cavern at the pool of water. "I used to wonder what it would be like to bring a boy here." She turned her gaze to me, and with her on the rock above, our faces were nearly at the same height. "I never thought I'd bring an alien dirt man." Her mouth spread in a mischievous smile as she glanced at my lips.

My heart was beating so loud that I was sure it was echoing off the cavern walls. Just when I thought I might be brave enough to lean toward her, she turned and continued her climb up the rocks, and I was left to curse my hesitation.

After another minute of climbing and at least one narrow crevice that someone my size was never meant to go through, we finally reached the outside air and I got my first look at Vrynn's home island.

Despite the wind constantly whipping around us, the air didn't feel cold. It was thick with humidity and almost seemed to hold a warmth of its own. When we reached the top of the hill containing our cavern, Vrynn stopped and pointed at a valley below us.

"There's my hometown," she said, a sad smile playing across her lips.

Obviously, I couldn't see the entire island, but it seemed to be the remnants of a caldera formation just like Mardrys, except that it wasn't as tall on the sides or deep in the center. The valley was broad and green and dotted with towns. In fact, there were gray clusters of buildings as far into the distance as I could see.

The village below us looked like it was straight from a page out of a European travel guide. Homes and businesses sat next to each other in neat little rows that didn't appear to have any particular rhyme or reason. And the roads connecting the villages criss-crossed the valley like a spider web. But where a quaint European town might have had carts and oxen, these roads had large vehicles hovering along. And instead of smoke billowing from houses and factories, the roofs of the towns shimmered steel-blue, almost glowing with their own light.

We stood for several minutes in silence, looking out at the village below us. I wasn't sure exactly why I put my arm around Vrynn, but she quickly pulled herself closer to me.

Finally, I ventured to ask her, "Should we go see it?"

She shook her head against my chest. "Barchee occupiers are everywhere. We can't risk being followed or recognized." She turned and stared out at the ocean behind us. "Besides, we have a mission to do."

After lingering for another minute to place the sensor, we made our way back down the hill to the cavern entrance. After squeezing through the narrow passage a second time, I seriously considered tracking down some power tools to widen the crevice.

The first convoy to enter the atmosphere after we had set up camp on the south end of Syr came just as we were winding down for the night. I wasn't sure how many nighttime convoys Vrynn had faced before Gabe and I rejoined them, but this was my first.

As soon as Tera sounded the alert, we sprang into action. But despite our best efforts, it still took nearly seven minutes for us to submerge, navigate the narrow, underwater tunnel, put several miles distance between us and our hidden base for secrecy purposes, then pop out of the water to begin the pursuit.

I tracked the convoy's heading on the tactical console and aimed for the spot where we could intercept them. "What's this convoy look like?" I asked Tera as we flew upward.

"Two transports, four escorts," she replied.

That was pretty standard. This shouldn't be too difficult.

Suddenly, the twilight sky exploded around me.

"Mitch, we're too close to the plasma cannons on the Mardrys rim," Vrynn said.

I checked my tactical map and saw that, in my effort to intercept the incoming convoy, I'd flown right by the edge of the Mardrys caldera. I swerved away from the island, putting some distance between us and its defensive batteries. Now that I knew what I was looking at, I could just make out the faint glowing lines of the protective plasma grid spanning the caldera.

I tore my attention from that dangerous marvel of engineering and focused back on the convoy again. Two of the escorts peeled off to engage, and Vrynn gave them plenty to worry about with the plasma cannons.

Between the necessary change in course to avoid Mardrys and the weaving around to combat the escorts, by the time I had the convoy in our sights again, it had nearly reached the island.

I toggled to the weapons console and locked on two atmospheric missiles. They had barely registered locked on the transports when I mashed the trigger.

I watched the bright orange plumes of their rocket engines as they sailed toward their targets. Just before it found its mark, the missile destined for the lead transport was hit by the island's defensive batteries. The second missile fared better, striking the aft section of the second transport. But somehow, despite obvious damage to its airworthiness, the transport was still able to slice through the gap in the caldera wall and land at the Barchee airstrip, out of our reach.

"That's two transports that got through!" Vrynn exclaimed in dismay.

"We'll never get them all, Vrynn," I replied.

"The plan won't work unless we get them all," she said through gritted teeth.

"Let's just take care of the rest of the escorts," I said.

"Fine," Vrynn said as she lashed out at the nearest enemy fighter.

Somehow, Vrynn channeled her frustration into the plasma cannon, shooting clean through the closest craft and hitting the one behind it. There might also have been some screaming involved.

The other four escorts decided they would rather live to fight another day. By the time I had atmospheric missiles locked on the next target, they were all within the island's defenses. I didn't want to waste a perfectly good missile, so I banked away as we were forced to watch the last escorts land safely. Halfway back to Syr, I brought the *Starfire* down to the water and plunged us underneath.

After a few minutes of silent underwater travel, Vrynn turned toward me. "I don't think the cave is going to work."

That took me a little by surprise. "Why not?" I asked.

"Even with the sensor module on top of the island, we didn't have enough warning to stop the convoy," she said. "If we don't detect them until they enter the atmosphere, we'll never get out of the cavern and intercept them before they reach Mardrys."

My brows drew together. She had a good point. "But we can't just sit on the surface like last time, especially not Syr. We'd be sitting ducks."

The flight deck fell silent as we pondered our situation.

"What if we use one of the Mareesh satellites?" Tera asked.

"To hide behind?" I asked, not really understanding how that would help us.

Tera rolled her eyes. "No, to give us more warning so we can get out of the cavern in time."

"Hmm. That's not a bad idea," I said.

"It hardly matters," Vrynn said. "All the Mareesh infrastructure has been taken over by the Barchee occupiers."

A mischievous look crept across Tera's holographic face. "I didn't say we'd ask to use it."

Chapter Eight

It was easy enough to agree on which of the satellites we should steal back from the Barchee. Actually, there were only about a dozen satellites orbiting Mareesh. We chose the one with the worst view of Mardrys, figuring it would be the least likely to be constantly monitored.

"How do you sneak up on something that can see in every direction?" Gabe asked.

"You can't," I said. "But you can distract it."

"So that is why we are preparing to leave the *Starfire* while we are in orbit," he said. "To be a distraction."

"Actually, the *Starfire* is the distraction," I said. "We're the ones sneaking up on it."

"Why does it always have to be you and Gabe?" Tera asked with a pout. "Why can't Vrynn go with you on the dangerous missions and leave Gabe here with me?"

I wracked my brain for a good enough reason, but Gabe spoke first.

"I cannot pilot the ship," he said.

"I could teach you," Tera said excitedly. "It's really not that hard. We could even link your processors to the flight system so you wouldn't have to touch the controls at all." She glanced at the control sticks as if they were some sort of dead animal.

"I could stay on the ship, and Vrynn could go with Gabe, if you'd prefer that," I said to Tera.

She sighed. "I guess I'd rather have Vrynn with me. She's more fun than you are."

I chuckled. That was probably true.

We finished getting ready—which basically meant Gabe waited in the airlock for me to get my EVA suit on. His android body could handle the vacuum of space, but it felt oddly disconcerting to see him standing there, waiting to leave the ship, when he didn't have a spacesuit on. He wore a small jetpack that provided the same maneuverability features as my EVA suit. Plus, Tera had patched her direct link with Gabe into the ship's comm.

"Don't forget to pick us back up," I said to Vrynn.

She laughed playfully. "Are you kidding? Now that we've got the ship to ourselves again, Tera and I are going on a vacation."

Gabe's head swiveled toward Vrynn and then Tera.

"She's kidding, Gabe," Tera said.

He turned back to Vrynn. "It is strange that you would make a joke about something that sounds so similar to our experience of a few days ago. Especially considering how unsettling it was for both of us, and emotionally scarring for Mitch."

Vrynn's brow went up. "Emotionally scarring?"

"I'm not emotionally scarred," I said to Vrynn and Gabe.

Vrynn pretended not to be convinced. "So it's too soon?"

"No one would blame you," Tera added.

"Listen, everyone needs to know that I trust Vrynn." I said it like an announcement. "And the fact that I'm willing to let her take control of the ship again should prove it." I leaned closer to Vrynn. "But just know that my air will run out in about ten hours," I said quietly.

"I'll only leave you stranded for half that," she said, adding a very emphatic attempt to close one eye.

I smiled. At least she was only using one eye in her winks now.

Vrynn went back up to the flight deck to set our final heading. Tera stayed down near the airlock to see us off.

"Get ready," Vrynn said over the internal comm.

"We're cycling into the airlock now," I replied.

Gabe and Tera gave each other a very dramatic goodbye through the airlock window. I covered my grin at their sappy antics.

With the airlock cycle complete, we floated out and positioned ourselves on nearby hand grips. That was when I turned my attention away from the ship and to the blackness of space surrounding us.

It was breathtaking.

I'd orbited dozens of planets and traveled hundreds of light-years. I'd even been outside the starship with only an EVA suit for protection.

But it never got old.

I gaped at the immensity of the space around me. Stars like pinpricks of light dotted the blackness. Below us—or what my brain wanted to call "below"—was the giant orb of Mareesh. It looked like a vast, cloud-speckled, blue carpet, soft enough to just descend onto and take a nap. In the distance, Mareesh's single moon rose over the curved horizon.

I suddenly felt incredibly small.

"We're on a perfect collision course with the satellite," Vrynn said over the comm. "All you have to do is let go."

Her voice stirred me from my thoughts. "I'd rather you not use the phrase 'collision course' when I'm outside the ship."

I heard her soft laugh. "What? You'd rather miss the satellite entirely?"

I shook my head, even knowing she couldn't see it. Glancing down at the handgrip, I forced myself to let go.

Nothing happened.

"We have released the ship," Gabe said over the comm without actually moving his mouth.

"Acknowledged," Tera replied.

The *Starfire's* thrusters activated as they pushed away from us, and Gabe and I were left floating alone in orbit—still moving several hundred miles per hour, I assumed.

Vrynn maneuvered the *Starfire* ahead of us in orbit, slowing once they had lined up in front of the satellite. A moment later, the plasma cannons pivoted toward it. Those weapons had gotten my attention when we were in the small scout. Hopefully, they had the same effect on the operators watching the feed, assuming any live operators were actually paying attention.

Fortunately, the satellite wasn't armed because they might be tempted to take a shot at the *Starfire* for such an aggressive action.

Suddenly, a plasma round erupted from the satellite and hit the *Starfire* broadside.

"It's firing at you," I called out through the comm.

"Deflectors are holding at ninety-three percent," Tera replied.

I focused on our target. The next step was critical to the mission—and my physical safety. We were now only a few hundred feet from the satellite, and I prepared my retro burn.

A second plasma round shot out of the satellite, aimed at the *Starfire*.

"That one dropped us to eighty-nine," Tera said.

"Maybe we should back up a little bit," Vrynn said.

The *Starfire* shifted position, putting some distance between it and the satellite.

That turned out to be a bad idea.

I started firing my thrusters to slow my relative speed, and Gabe matched the maneuver, keeping right at my side. A moment later, something on the satellite—which was growing larger by the second—shifted toward us.

It must have decided that we were closer than the *Starfire*, so we were the bigger threat.

It wasn't wrong.

But even at our current speed, we wouldn't hit it for another ten or twenty seconds.

I realized a split-second too late that we were about to be blown into a million pieces. Fortunately, my buddy Gabe's reactions were faster. At the exact moment that the satellite's cannon fired, he pushed me sideways—hard. And with his android strength, this wasn't human-level hard, this was altering-orbital-trajectories hard. We immediately flew apart—thanks Sir Isaac Newton—and the plasma round streaked between us. I couldn't feel any heat due to the vacuum of space, but the white fabric of my EVA suit did look a little singed.

"Gabe!" Tera screamed through the comm.

"I am still unharmed," he replied calmly.

As I struggled with the built-in jetpack controls in an attempt to right myself, Vrynn's concerned voice came over the comm.

"You'll miss the satellite, Mitch," Vrynn said. "Get back on course."

"That's what I'm trying to do," I replied.

After a few uncontrolled spins, I was able to do a few controlled spins. Meanwhile, Gabe had already started jetting back toward the satellite. His head start put him closer to the defensive cannon, and it swiveled toward him. I pressed hard on my controls, willing my bulky EVA suit to fly faster. Right when I thought the satellite would fire on Gabe, the cannon stopped moving and twisted back toward me. I eased off the throttle a bit, hoping that the cannon wouldn't fire on me. Gabe saw the situation and sped up his approach.

We quickly fell into a rhythm of back and forth, closer and farther, tricking the auto cannon on the satellite to swivel toward me and then, at the last second, to swivel toward Gabe.

When we finally made contact with the satellite, it was such a bone-jarring impact that I missed the handgrip and bounced off the side. Gabe quickly scrambled around and grabbed my arm before I floated back out to space.

"Nice work, guys," Vrynn said.

I breathed a sigh of relief. "You saved me twice," I said to Gabe. "Good thing I didn't bring Vrynn out here with me."

"I heard that," Vrynn replied.

We set to work tapping into the satellite's feed with our small transmitter. It wasn't easy with the auto-cannon continually taking shots at the *Starfire*. Once the transmitter was installed, we moved around to face our ship.

"Now what do we do?" I asked Gabe. "As soon as we push off, the cannon will target us. And I don't think I'm coordinated enough to pull off the same trick twice."

Gabe tilted his head, considering me. Then he moved over near the auto-cannon mount. Reaching behind the cannon barrel, he grabbed a plasma line and yanked it off the back.

"Oh, we should have done that earlier," I said.

Gabe nodded. "That is what you call hindsight, correct?"

"Yeah, buddy," I answered.

"So next time we are required to float up to an armed satellite, we will know to disable the plasma cannon first," Gabe said.

"Yep," I replied with a laugh. "Next time."

The trip back down to our cavern was uneventful.

So were the next five hours waiting.

We were sitting in the flight deck, watching for any sign that the satellite feed had picked up a convoy, when I turned to Vrynn. "Do you think this is working?"

"It's hard to know until we can detect a convoy," she replied.

"No, not the hacking-the-satellite plan; I think that's a great idea. I'm talking about the overall plan to destroy the convoys. Even if we succeed, will that liberate your people?"

Vrynn bit her lip, suddenly looking much less optimistic. "Really, I'm not sure. I guess if we could stop every single transport, the occupiers wouldn't have any supplies, right?"

I gave her a half-hearted shrug. "Maybe," I said. "Or maybe they'll just start taking supplies from your people."

Her shoulders sagged, an uncharacteristic expression of defeat on her face. "I don't know what to do then."

"Maybe we should start planning for a ground fight," I replied.

Vrynn shook her head. "There's no way we can fight them on the ground. Their advantage is too—"

"Convoy coming out of intra-space," Tera announced.

Vrynn and I both sat up straight then sprang into action. We had the ship's systems running and the hover emitters at full power in under a minute. As we glided through the water, Vrynn studied the sensor information we'd captured.

"This is a big convoy, Mitch," she said. "Five transports and ten escorts."

I let out a long whistle. "That's the most freighters they've sent at once."

Forcing myself to wait the last few seconds before surfacing felt like torture. I didn't know exactly how we would take on a convoy this size, but we'd taken on ten fighters at once before. Plus, this time, if we succeeded, we'd score five transports.

We finally hit the surface, and I pointed the *Starfire* toward the convoy, ready to blast us into action. Then an idea occurred to me.

"Does the sensor feed have good enough resolution that we could put a portal aperture in front of one of the convoy ships?" I asked Tera.

Tera's eyes stared off at nothing for a moment. "Of course. We have their location and speed to within a few meters."

"What do you have in mind?" Vrynn asked.

"Remember when we lost one of the transports because they went through the same portal we came out of?"

"Yeah?" she replied slowly.

"We could do that again on purpose. Pick off the escorts one at a time."

A wide smile spread across Vrynn's face. "I love it."

"Tera, track the trailing escort," I said. "Put an aperture right in front of it. Close enough that it won't miss."

"I'll try," Tera said.

The *Starfire* was still hovering just above the water, several miles from the coast of Syr. A moment later, a portal aperture opened in front of us, then two seconds later, it disappeared, and a Barchee fighter was in its place, still flying at full speed directly away from us.

"Fire, Vrynn," I said.

Despite hoping it would work, we were both a little surprised when it did. By the time she started firing, Vrynn's plasma rounds weren't as effective as they needed to be.

"I got it," I said as I fired an atmospheric missile. A few seconds later, it found its mark and the enemy ship exploded.

"Thanks," Vrynn said, "I'll be ready next time."

I nodded, and we both gripped our controls, weapons activated. "Do it again, Tera. The next escort from the back."

The portal opened and closed, and Vrynn unleashed a barrage of plasma fire. The rounds hit the second kidnapped escort square on the left side, tearing off its wing and causing it to spin into the water.

"Nice," I said with a nod. "Keep them coming as fast as possible, Tera."

We repeated the exercise four more times before Tera said, "The last four escorts aren't flying straight anymore; they're zigzagging randomly."

"They must be onto us," I said.

"I can't catch them with a small portal. Should I use a larger one?" she asked.

"No, that will take too much power. I think we're ready to go after the rest." I pushed the *Starfire* forward into full-speed flight. "Target the aperture for standard rear attack."

The Quake Drive portal opened in front of us, and I could see the rest of the convoy just ahead. As soon as we flew through, Vrynn targeted the engine nozzles of the closest transport. I fired several slugs from the rail gun in the path of the next freighter, knowing that at least one of them would find their mark at this range.

"After that jump, the Quake Drive power level is—" Tera stopped suddenly. "Fighters launching from the surface," she said. "Ten Barchee Heavies."

Vrynn and I shared an unspoken look. I wasn't exactly sure what she was thinking—I rarely was—but this time, I figured we were on the same page. "We have to stop the transports before the heavies get here."

My co-pilot leaned forward, adding intensity to every shot she fired.

"More ships coming out of intra-space," Tera announced. She frowned. "They're reading as Kochelian Raiders. Six of them—no wait, eight. Ten. They'll reach us in three minutes."

"Kochelian Raiders?" I glanced at Vrynn. "Are those Nexus-affiliated?"

She shrugged. "Are they running with transponders?"

"Yes. Their transponders are operating, and they are broadcasting a message saying they're aiding an ally in distress from pirates."

My eyes bugged out. "They think we're pirates?" That was both cool and scary at the same time. I knew what people on Earth did to pirates. The Bonara Cluster probably wasn't much different.

I pushed the *Starfire* forward, bearing down on the next transport in the convoy as Vrynn unleashed a firestorm.

"We might not get them all," I said to Vrynn.

"Don't give up yet. We've still got time," she shot back.

We'd taken out three transports when I caught sight of the first heavies from the surface coming into weapons' range. The alarm for incoming fire went off on my console.

"Tera, are the defensive lasers online?"

"Yes," she replied. I could almost hear the "duh" in her tone.

I increased the throttle, zeroing in on the next transport while dodging incoming fire.

"Another ship is entering the atmosphere," Tera announced.

"Oh, just one?" I said. "That's hardly worth mentioning."

"It's a Vezor-Class runabout," she said.

It felt like my heart had stopped. "Are you sure?"

Tera nodded.

"But that was the ship that . . ." Vrynn's skin turned even more pale-blue.

"Gralik," I finished for her.

"Is it really Gralik's ship?" Vrynn asked.

Tera shrugged. "I would normally say yes, but the ship's transponder says it's a light cruiser registered to the Mareesh government."

"It can't be Gralik, then," Vrynn said. "Why would he be flying a Mareesh government ship?"

"I'm telling you," Tera said. "Except for the transponder signal, this is the exact same ship that attacked us on Earth. The one with the soldiers that killed Gabe."

"It doesn't matter. We have to leave now," I said.

Tera said, "But Mitch, the power cells are—"

Vrynn interrupted. "Not yet. Just let me get this next freighter." Vrynn turned her attention back to blasting the freighter we were hiding behind. After a few seconds of sustained fire, it began losing altitude.

So much for our cover.

The warnings on my console blared to life again, and I swerved away from an incoming missile just in time. It exploded in the air behind us, rattling the bulkheads.

"Seriously. You need to know that the power levels—" Tera stopped mid sentence. "The runabout has altered course to intercept us."

"That's got to be Gralik," I said. "We need to get out of here while we still can. Tera, set an escape portal."

Tera shook her head. "Mitch, the drive—"

"Wait!" Vrynn called. "Just a little longer. We can still get the last one."

Incoming fire and imminent impact warnings blared incessantly. The sky was filled with explosions and enemy fighters. I rapidly fired atmospheric missiles as soon as they would lock on to the next target. Plasma rounds from the cannons were a blur.

A spread of slugs streaked out of the upper atmosphere toward us. The runabout—Gralik—had joined the fray.

Our laser defenses took out some of them, but several exploded near us.

"Rear deflectors at sixty percent. Lateral deflectors at seventy-two percent. Quake Drive power cells at eighteen percent." Tera snuck the last part in as if it had something to do with the fight.

"Vrynn, we've missed transports before. It's okay if this one gets through," I said.

"No. I can tell they're getting desperate," she said. "That means the plan is working. We can't let any more through."

Another atmospheric missile, fired from a nearby heavy, streaked straight for us.

"Vrynn!" I pointed at the incoming threat.

Vrynn tore her attention from the last transport to target the missile. Her rounds found their mark at the last second. Remnants of the exploding missile smashed violently into our front view port.

The fact that Vrynn wanted to stay in the fight in the middle of this onslaught made me wonder if she was still thinking straight.

My console blared another impact warning, and I jerked hard on the control stick. A slug exploded underneath us, sending bone-jolting reverberations through the hull.

"Damage?" I asked.

"No hull breaches," Tera replied. "But the power regulation system was damaged by that last impact."

"That's it. We're out of here." I pulled back on the stick. "Tera, activate the Quake Drive."

"We can't jump far," she replied.

"What?!" Vrynn and I exclaimed almost simultaneously.

"I was trying to tell you earlier," Tera complained.

Streaks of plasma rounds zipped past us, and I sent the ship into a corkscrew as we pulled away from the last transport.

"All the escorts we kidnapped," Tera said, as if it should be obvious. "The Quake Drive power cells are so low, we probably only have enough for one short jump."

"Then let's do that," I said through gritted teeth.

Another missile streaked toward us, and I rolled the *Starfire* to avoid the impact. It blew up a few feet from the hull, sending us spinning.

"Actually, not anymore. That last explosion created a power surge that drained what little we had left in the cells," Tera said.

My eyes probably looked like saucers. "We can't portal jump at all?"

"Nope," Tera replied. "And I'm still really mad that you brought Gabe along, and he's going to get killed with the rest of us."

"No one's getting killed, Tera," Vrynn declared. "But we should probably get out of here, Mitch."

"You think?!" I barked, shaking my head in frustration as I pulled the *Starfire* into a steep climb, aiming away from the approaching runabout as Vrynn made that craft the focus of her plasma cannons.

"Tera, as soon as we're clear of the atmosphere, engage the intra-space drive," I said.

"Destination?" Tera asked as another explosion flashed next to us.

"Three-point jump. Someplace relatively nearby that we haven't used before," I replied. "We eventually want to get back to Thetis Max."

"Here's your waypoint," Tera replied as a blinking square appeared on my holographic display. "Twenty seconds to clear the atmosphere."

I pointed us directly at the waypoint for our first jump. The throttle was already at maximum, so I switched my controls to weapons, splitting off the slightly less powerful dorsal plasma cannons from Vrynn's control.

Together, we carved a path through the dome of Kochelian Raiders as we punched our way out of the atmosphere. I spared two more atmospheric missiles for Gralik's runabout, just to keep him off our tail.

The *Starfire's* superior climbing power made it hard for our enemies to keep up.

"Should we switch controls?" Vrynn asked as we approached the atmospheric boundary.

I knew it was just a habit, but I looked forward to the day when she didn't think my zero-G abilities were so horrible that we needed to switch in the middle of a firefight. I shook my head. We were about to jump anyway.

Several raiders were following close behind us, firing. But they were too late.

A few seconds later, the star-speckled sky around us faded to grayish-brown swirls.

We'd made it.

"I don't understand what happened with the power cells," Vrynn said as she twisted in her seat to more fully face Tera. "We only opened the portal a few times."

"Six times to kidnap the escorts," Tera said. "And once to bring us to the convoy."

Vrynn huffed in frustration. "Fine, exactly seven portals. Shouldn't the power cells be able to handle that? They regenerate themselves, don't they?"

"The power cells hadn't fully recovered, and we knew this was a possibility," I said, still seething at the narrowness of our escape.

Vrynn folded her arms across her chest. "*I* never thought it was a possibility," she said with a huff.

"That's because you never consider how things can go wrong," I shot back.

Vrynn tilted her head and gave me a deadpan glare. "There's no way this ship was designed to only make a few portal jumps."

"We've done more than a few," I said. Vrynn opened her mouth to argue, but I held up a hand. "Listen, we'll figure out what's going on with the power cells," I said. "We're all on the same team here."

Vrynn's expression softened. "Sorry, Mitch."

I nodded in acknowledgment, but didn't say anything.

She lightly touched my arm, probably trying to calm my annoyance with her. "It just feels like we're so close to winning," she said softly.

I let out a sharp, frustrated breath. "And we will. But we have to be smart about it."

Her lips lifted in a small smile. "Look who's being optimistic now."

"I know. You're a bad influence on me," I muttered.

We sat in silence for a minute or two, enjoying the respite from combat.

"Coming out of intra-space in five seconds," Tera announced.

The browns and grays faded away as we reappeared in normal space. Half a second later, the incoming threat alarm blared.

"Two Kochelian Raiders. Three kilometers away," Tera said.

I pushed the stick forward and to the side in an attempt to bank away from the enemy ships. Then my brain caught up to my instincts, reminding me that we were in orbit and my normal flying skills wouldn't work here.

Rather than trying to force myself to think in zero-G, I quickly said to Vrynn, "Switch with me."

After a few well-practiced swipes on the consoles, I had full command of the weapons system, and Vrynn had the ship vectoring away from the incoming slugs. I activated the laser battery and targeted one of the raiders. Then I fired several volleys from the plasma cannons at the other. They split formation, not looking nearly as graceful as they did in the atmosphere. It was nice to think I wasn't the only pilot who was all thumbs in zero-G.

My shots missed the second ship, and it vectored to put some distance between us. I shifted my attention back to the first ship and wondered if the laser had done its job faster than I expected. A field of metal and debris floated where the raider had been. As I looked closer, I realized that the ship was still there, hiding behind an anti-laser scattering field.

"Another ship coming out of intra-space," Tera said. "It's the runabout."

"Still broadcasting that it's a Mareesh government ship?" I asked.

"Same transponder signal," Tera replied. "But I swear, Mitch, that's Gralik's ship. It even has the same hull damage."

"I believe you." I was already convinced it was Gralik—more so now that it had followed us. I wondered how long he would keep up the charade.

I didn't have time to ponder on that question because another raider just arrived and maneuvered into position to cut off our escape. I fired the cannons at the second raider's scattering field, hoping to either disperse or destroy it. The rounds passed through the metal debris and scored several hits on the vessel itself. The hiding ship boosted toward us just as the other raider moved in.

"A fourth raider just arrived," Tera said. "Mitch, they definitely tracked our intra-space vector. They're going to keep coming."

"We can't stay here." I scanned the orbit around this unfamiliar planet we'd jumped to. A small moon caught my attention. "Head for that moon."

"What do you have in mind?" Vrynn asked as she used the thrusters to angle the ship.

"If we can get around it with enough distance between us and the raiders, we can hide from their tracking when we make another jump." I pivoted the cannons aft and fired on the raider coming up behind us.

Vrynn applied full thrust, and we accelerated toward the small moon. One of the raiders moved to cut off our escape, so I spewed out a fountain of plasma rounds toward it. If we hadn't been in imminent danger of being blown up, I might have stopped to enjoy the beauty of the spectacle.

The incoming fire alarm blared as more slugs flew toward us. I lined up the cannons and shot at anything close enough to be a threat. The laser batteries took out the few that I missed.

The four Kochelian Raiders formed up in a loose diamond shape behind us, but they'd stopped firing slugs. I scanned the tactical console and the video feeds.

"Where's the runabout?" I asked.

Vrynn scrutinized her display and shrugged. "I've lost it."

"The runabout made an intra-space jump," Tera said.

"It ran away?" I asked. That didn't seem like Gralik, especially when we were outnumbered five to one.

"It didn't run away," Tera added. "The intra-space jump was pointed at—"

"Look!" Vrynn interrupted, pointing out the front flight deck windows.

The runabout had materialized just ahead of us, very near the moon we were trying to reach. "He must have used the moon as the destination anchor of the jump," Vrynn said.

"Smart," I muttered.

I fired three rail gun slugs directly at it, one right after the other, just as Vrynn angled the ship on a new trajectory, vectoring us away from the runabout and toward the horizon of the moon.

Somehow, Gralik's ship managed to dodge the spread of slugs, and it fired a full engine burn to intercept us. The raiders were still closing from behind, and they adjusted direction to match our position.

We were fully committed to this plan now. Of course, the look of determination on Vrynn's face told me she had no intention of backing out anyway.

The runabout fired a salvo of plasma rounds, none of them close enough to hit the ship, but Vrynn was forced to adjust our heading to miss them. I continued to fire on as many enemy ships as I could while the small moon continued to grow in the front window.

The runabout obviously wanted to cut off our escape around the moon, but with our engines burning at full power, we came out ahead. Once it had reached full orbital speed, the runabout was only a few hundred yards behind us. I poured out a steady stream of plasma straight at the enemy ship, forcing it to dodge several times.

"We can't hide from the runabout, it's too close," Vrynn said.

"How far ahead do we need to be for the moon to hide us?" I asked.

"At this altitude from the surface, we need to be seven kilometers ahead for the moon's horizon to hide us," Tera replied.

"Can we get that far ahead?" I asked as I continued firing.

Vrynn shook her head. "It would take an orbit or two. And I bet those raiders will be waiting for us on the other side."

I racked my brain for some way out of this chase. "Take us closer to the surface," I told Vrynn.

"Closer? But that . . ." Her brows lifted as she recognized what I was suggesting.

"Based on the runabout's current distance, how low do we need to fly to hide behind the horizon?" I asked Tera.

Tera's eyes scanned back and forth. "At sixty-five meters, the current gap between our ships would be enough to allow us to slip over the horizon. Assuming the runabout follows us down to a lower orbit."

"Oh, he will." I grinned. "He'll have to, if he wants to keep up."

Vrynn understood the plan perfectly. She nosed the ship down and fired the engines on full again. The drop in altitude and the additional thrust increased our speed. Of course, it was terrifying to be hurtling downward toward the gray, rocky terrain below. It didn't look too different from Earth's moon, except that the surface was pocked with even more craters, and the rocks had a slightly rust color to them.

As we approached the moon's surface, skimming impossibly low over boulders and craters, Vrynn inverted the *Starfire* and continued the engine burn, giving us enough speed to slingshot around the small gravity well.

The runabout was obviously becoming more desperate and fired wildly in our general direction. A few of the rounds hit the aft deflector emitters, but the ship held together.

Screaming past the moon's jagged surface at such a low altitude made my gut feel like lead, so I focused my attention on the rear video feed. As we sped lower, coming so dangerously close to the ground that it could barely be called orbit anymore, our line of sight to the runabout gradually sank closer and closer to the horizon of the moon.

"Program the next jump point," I said to Tera. "But don't aim for it yet," I added to Vrynn.

I watched the video feed as the upper edge of the runabout slowly disappeared behind the horizon.

"And . . . now," I said, as the last of the enemy ship was obscured.

Vrynn angled the ship to line up our heading, and a second later, we faded into intra-space.

My sigh of relief filled the small flight deck. Vrynn's echoed mine, but somehow she added even more emotion to it.

By the time we had completed our jump a few minutes later, Tera already had the next jump coordinates programmed in. Vrynn rotated the ship, and we made the final jump to Thetis Max, spending only six seconds in normal space. I felt quite proud of how efficient we'd become at the multi-point intra-space jump. Our enemies never had a chance to even guess where we'd gone.

But it didn't do anything to alleviate the sense of failure at our latest catastrophe.

When we came out of intra-space in orbit above Thetis Max, Vrynn slumped back in her seat. "All that work, and we're back where we started," she muttered.

By the time I had maneuvered the *Starfire* back into the hangar of the mining facility, Vrynn had already left the flight deck. I found her a few minutes later, down in the engineering room.

"What's it reading?" I asked as I approached her side.

"Nine percent," she replied. "It was eleven when I first came down."

I blew out a breath. "Well, that's not good."

Vrynn considered for a moment before saying, "Maybe there's always some natural fluctuation in the readings."

I shrugged, but it was only half-hearted. We were about to be without our greatest weapon.

A moment later, the power gauge dipped to eight percent.

"Tera?" I called out, glancing at the camera above our heads.

"Yes?" she asked as her hologram transferred to the engineering room.

"Are any other systems drawing power from the Quake Drive cells?" I asked.

"The drive itself consumes a small amount of energy," she replied.

"If we disconnect the cells from the drive, would that keep them from dropping any more?" I asked.

Tera shook her head. "I don't think so. The only thing keeping the level from dropping more is that they're still hooked up to the plasma converter."

I rubbed the back of my neck as I stared down at this amazing, and yet aggravating, piece of advanced alien tech.

Then an idea occurred to me. "Hang on. What's the current power input to the cells?"

"It's less than one tenth the normal flow," Tera said.

I frowned at that information. "The cells need to recharge. Why isn't it feeding the full amount?"

"It would seem that the system automatically reduces the charging input when the cells are in distress," Tera replied.

"What would happen if you increased the recharge flow?" Vrynn asked.

Tera shrugged. "It might bring the power cells back to full charge. Or it might blow them up."

"Nothing like living on the extremes," I said.

"Actually, the computer system has calculated eleven other results with a probability of greater than half a percent. Do you want to hear them?" Tera asked.

"Not really," I replied.

"Let's increase the recharge flow to the cells, and see if they recover," Vrynn suggested.

She and Tera both looked over at me. I blew out a breath. "Yeah, I guess it's worth a try. Increase the recharge input to half."

We watched the readout, but nothing happened with the cells.

"Full recharge rate?" Vrynn asked.

"Go ahead," I said, and Tera adjusted the input.

We stood watching the readout for several more minutes. After about ten minutes, Tera decided she didn't need to be there to monitor the levels, so she disappeared, leaving Vrynn and me staring at the display, holding our breaths that it didn't drop again.

After another ten minutes, with the reading still at eight percent, I decided it was safe to leave the system running. I wandered over to the back of the cargo bay and greeted Rascal, figuring he might enjoy a little time outside the ship, even if it was just our old mining facility. Skeeter quickly appeared and joined us.

I opened the cargo bay door and let them run free while I stood there staring at the rows of derelict spacecraft crammed into the back of the hangar. Vrynn was right. This really did feel like we were right back where we started.

Leaving the cargo door open for Rascal and Skeeter's return, I walked back to the engineering room. "I need something to eat. Do you want anything?" I asked Vrynn.

She shook her head, eyes still riveted to the power level.

I shrugged and made my way up to the kitchen to grab a bite. I wasn't actually sure the last time I'd stopped to have a real meal.

Halfway through my second package of Caridyan tarts, Vrynn came up the ladder to the kitchen area.

"Any change in the power level?" I asked.

"No," she said as she plopped into the chair next to me.

"We have to face the reality that it might not ever recover," I said.

"But at least the cells have stabilized. Maybe they'll start recharging again soon."

I slowly shook my head, too exhausted to get into an argument about how unrealistic I thought that was. I stared across the room, eyes unfocused. "This definitely changes things," I said.

Vrynn's spine straightened, her gaze jerking back to me. "Why? We're still more powerful than any other ship in the cluster."

"Sure, but we're not invincible. You think we can continue hitting the convoys like we've been doing?"

"I don't see why not. They haven't been able to stop us yet." Vrynn's voice dripped with defiance.

I held out a hand and ticked off my fingers. "First off, we've been using the Quake Drive as a major part of our strategy. If that's gone, what have we got?" She started to say something, but I continued with my list. "Second, without the Quake Drive, we're at much greater risk of being discovered. Sure, we can go underwater, but unless we start travelling farther and farther submerged, it won't take them long to figure out the general location of our cavern." Vrynn begrudgingly nodded. I touched another finger. "And third, without the Quake Drive, we don't have our emergency escape. We've taken some serious risks in combat because we knew we could just portal jump out of danger. That's gone now."

Vrynn fixed me with a determined gaze. "So you want to give up?"

I let out a frustrated breath. "That's not what I'm saying. I'm just saying that this changes things, and we might need to reevaluate our strategy."

Vrynn stood and walked to the ladder. She paused and turned back to me. "I'm not willing to give up that easily," she said before sliding down to the lower deck, presumably to stare at the power cell readout some more.

I shook my head at her stubbornness then grabbed another meal pack. This one had a picture of a pink fruit with blood red juices oozing out. I tried to remind myself that a juicy peach or a rich melon would probably look gross to an alien who'd never seen one before.

As I ate the odd-tasting, yet strangely satisfying fruit, I could hear Vrynn and Tera talking on the lower deck. My brow furrowed. It'd be just my luck they were down there planning some sort of mutiny. The chuckle died on my lips when I realized that wasn't as far-fetched as it had been a few weeks earlier. Vrynn knew that I wanted to help her liberate Mareesh, didn't she? Hopefully, they were just talking about ways to get the Quake Drive's power cells functional again.

A moment later, Tera appeared next to me.

"What's up, Tera?" I asked.

She lifted her holographic shoulders and glanced toward the ladder from the lower deck. A few seconds later, Gabe's head came into view as he made his way to the top. Then I heard Vrynn's voice from below him on the ladder. "Could you speed things up a little, Gabe? We're sort of in a hurry here."

The three of them stood in front of my table. I was still fairly certain it wasn't a mutiny, unless it was the most polite mutiny ever.

Vrynn squared her petite shoulders. "We need to go back to Mela Suphoria," she declared.

That was a surprise. The last time we'd been on Mela Suphoria, we'd purposely destroyed the Mark 7 factory where the *Starfire* had been manufactured to keep the dozens of half-completed ships from falling into Gralik's hands.

"Really?" I asked. "What's on Mela Suphoria?"

Gabe spoke up. "Mela Suphoria is the former home of the—" The simultaneous glares he got from Vrynn and Tera cut him off. "But I do not think that is what you were asking, was it?"

I smiled at him. Good old Gabe.

"Tell him what you told me, Tera," Vrynn said.

Tera simulated taking a deep breath to steel her courage. "There might not have been any working Quake Drives in the Mark 7 factory on Mela Suphoria, but it's possible that there were power cells somewhere among all the inventory."

That sounded a little too good—or maybe optimistic—to be true. "How could that be? Wouldn't we have seen them?"

Vrynn jumped in. "We weren't looking for power cells at the time. We were looking for a fully intact Quake Drive, and we only had a vague idea what that even was. Now that we have one—and we know exactly what the power cells look like—there's a chance we could find replacement cells."

"Under normal circumstances, I might agree with that," I said. "But you remember the part where we blew up the factory?"

Vrynn glared at me. "Obviously. But something as small as a power cell might have survived, especially if they were stored away from the main factory building."

I considered my three crew mates for several moments. "And this is what all three of you want to do?"

Vrynn and Tera both nodded. Gabe tilted his head. "I agree with whatever they choose. I am simply glad to be fully functional."

I chuckled. "Then I guess we're headed back to the ghost planet."

Chapter Nine

It was strange to travel to Mela Suphoria without the mystique of searching for a lost planet with ancient advanced technology. Though the blaring message from the orbital quarantine buoy wasn't a fun thing to repeat, at least we knew how to mute it faster this time.

With only a few zero-G course corrections needed, I brought us out of orbit on the opposite side of the continent from the battered remnants of Maniphra City, flying low over the alien terrain.

"Why are we flying so low?" Vrynn asked. "We're still a long way from the factory."

I lifted a shoulder. "I didn't want to come blazing out of the sky directly above the facility. Last time we were there, it was crawling with Nexus soldiers."

Vrynn tapped a finger to her chin. "Not a bad idea. Gralik might have left a guard there, like on Ludros Beta Five."

"Anything on the scanners?" I asked Tera as we approached the Mark 7 factory. Maybe it was my own fault for assuming there would be a welcoming party, but I was feeling a little jumpy.

She rolled her eyes. "I can't even detect the production facility from this distance, much less whether there are any Nexus forces waiting for us. The best thing we can do is . . . wait a minute."

"The best thing we can do is wait a minute?" I repeated. "That's an interesting plan."

I knew Tera was checking something, but I couldn't help making a joke about her timing. Vrynn simply shook her head at my attempted humor.

"My link to the plant's sensor net just reconnected," Tera said, looking genuinely surprised.

"Excellent. What can you see?" I asked.

"There's nothing on the sensors right now," Tera replied, eyes scanning the air. "But the logs show a pair of fighters landed at the facility yesterday."

That was serious. "If those were Nexus ships, we might need to change our plans."

Vrynn's brow furrowed. "Why?"

"Because that would mean there must be something still intact in the facility. Something they want." I glanced down at my tactical console, preparing myself for a strafing run on the old factory. "We have to destroy whatever's left."

Vrynn grabbed my arm. "Mitch, we can't."

"Why not? If there's anything left that Nexus cares about, we should destroy it."

"Because the power cells for the Quake Drive might be down there," Vrynn replied. "Besides, I can't imagine there are any Mark 7s left. We blew up everything but Dack's ship."

I stared out the front window at the terrain ahead of us. At our current speed, the facility would come over the horizon in less than a minute. I needed to decide if we were going to attack or not.

Finally, I blew out a breath. "Fine. Maybe we can sneak in and get the power cells first."

Vrynn smiled at me. She left her hand on my arm a few seconds longer.

"But we still might have to destroy it," I added.

She scowled and pulled her hand away, making me regret voicing my last comment despite it being true.

I held the *Starfire* close to the canopy of trees until we could just see the top of the factory buildings then switched to hover mode. "Can our sensors detect if those ships are still there?"

A projection of the facility appeared above my console. It showed several shaded spots where our sensors couldn't see.

"I'm surprised any of the main hangar building is even still standing," Vrynn said. "The damage isn't as bad as I expected."

I turned to my co-pilot. "Yeah, but if Nexus forces are here, having anything left of the original technology is really bad." I leaned in to scrutinize the projection. "Can we see more in this area?" I pointed at the staging area in front of the main hangar, which didn't show any data.

"Not without getting closer," Tera replied.

"Someone could fly the scout ship over," Gabe said.

Vrynn shook her head. "It might be smaller than the *Starfire*, but the scout is still too big to go unnoticed."

"We could always attach a jetpack to Skeeter and launch her over the facility," I suggested.

"You are not launching my pet," Tera said flatly.

"How could you even suggest such a thing?" Vrynn asked. "How would you like it if we lobbed Rascal at them?"

"That's an interesting idea," I said, rubbing my chin.

The others all glared at me.

I held up my hands. "I was only joking."

We hovered there above the trees, just out of range of the facility, for several minutes, considering our options.

"I still think we should fly over the factory and blow everything up," I said.

Vrynn frowned at me like I was a small child who didn't understand a simple concept. "I've told you. We can't blow up the facility. We can't risk destroying the power cells."

I shrugged. "You're a pretty good shot. Only blow up the Nexus ships."

"Even I'm not that optimistic," Vrynn said ruefully. "No. We have to sneak in and find the power cells first. We'll worry about blowing things up later."

I considered her plan, then finally nodded grudgingly and maneuvered the *Starfire* to a clearing in the trees below us. The powerful ship settled onto the ground with a thud.

"Looks like we'll be walking from here," I said.

We didn't have much in the way of weapons, not counting what was permanently mounted on the *Starfire*, but we had a few blasters and a plasma rifle we'd picked up at some point. We decided to take all of them.

Obviously, Tera couldn't come with us, but she connected to Skeeter in case we needed more precise control of the robotic feline—and so she could "see" what was happening. Rascal was excited to get out of the ship, not that I would have left him behind in a situation like this anyway. Gabe came along, too, despite his new romantic attachment algorithm causing a fair bit of distress at being away from Tera.

"I am not authorized to operate a lethal weapon," Gabe protested when Vrynn and I collected our blasters.

"Then just grab something that you could use in an emergency," I said.

Tera waved goodbye as we tromped down the cargo ramp and into the dense forest. It was hard to know what Mela Suphoria might have originally been like—we found hints here and there—but the surface was currently teeming with plant and animal life.

Vrynn plunged forward into the forest, leading our little group in the general direction of the manufacturing facility. A few minutes into our trek, we found a wider path with fewer scratchy branches. We had only gone a few dozen feet along the path when Vrynn stopped and held up a hand.

I glanced around. "What is it?" I whispered.

"I thought I heard something," she said.

I opened my mouth to tell her that it was a jungle—and jungles tended to be fairly noisy—when I heard, or rather felt, a distant rumble. I instinctively crouched down. Another rumble came through the ground, feeling much closer this time. I glanced at my feet, really examining the trail for the first time. The dirt had hundreds of faint paw imprints—of giant beasts.

What we had thought was a convenient path through the jungle must have been created by animals traveling back and forth. And one of them was coming our way.

"Hide," I hissed, grabbing Vrynn's arm and pulling her into the nearby brush. I motioned for Gabe and Skeeter to join us. Rascal instinctively came to my side, too.

We huddled behind a dense patch of bushes as the rumbling grew louder. When it sounded like the creature was nearly on top of us, I peeked through an opening in the leaves. It was the purple, spider-like beast we'd encountered in the city. Well, not the exact animal. That one had been killed by a band of ancient natives.

I held my breath as the creature lumbered past. Maybe it was the perspective—lying on the ground under a bush—but this animal seemed much larger than the one we'd fought a few weeks earlier.

"Are you sure we shouldn't just strafe the facility and be done with it?" I asked Vrynn as the beast's thudding footsteps receded.

Before she had a chance to answer, a soft patter passed just in front of our hiding place. It was accompanied a moment later by a small, screeching roar. Rascal whined and strained against my hold on him.

"Shh, Rascal. We're trying to stay hidden." I whispered to my faithful companion.

He whined in response, which actually sounded more like a prolonged chirp, but didn't move.

A moment later, a mini-version of the giant purple monster stuck its head through the foliage. I nearly fell backward in surprise—not to mention the traumatic flashback. But despite my earlier, near-fatal encounter with a larger member of the species, I couldn't help but think that this little guy was actually quite cute.

He was slightly smaller than Rascal, with clumsy, awkward movements. This was definitely the baby model. Rascal took a tentative step forward, sniffing the air in front of the small purple monster. His whole body started to jiggle back and forth, and I could tell exactly what my large friend was thinking.

It was time to play.

Skeeter—never one to miss an opportunity to interact with biological animals—padded over to Rascal and copied his movements.

Even though I knew we were right in the middle of a mission to get what we needed to save Vrynn's planet, I was tempted to let Rascal and Skeeter have fun for a little while. Maybe they could just stay in this hidden hollow behind the bushes with their new friend while we went in to steal the power cells.

Then reality hit me.

If this little creature was the baby, that meant the giant that had just gone by was the mother. If large creatures on Mela Suphoria were anything like mama bears on Earth, we were in serious trouble.

"We have to get out of here," I whispered to Vrynn. "If that monster finds us with her baby, it will kill us."

She nodded in eager agreement as I pulled Rascal back through the overgrowth. Skeeter followed, but fortunately, the small beast didn't, though it did look on with curiosity.

We'd put a dozen feet or so between us and the baby monster when an ear-splitting roar confirmed our suspicions. The mother didn't sound happy that her offspring wasn't following close behind. For a moment, I thought the baby might decide to follow us instead, but a second roar convinced the little guy to race after his mother.

A sigh of relief froze in my chest when the rumbling sound of more giant beasts shook the ground. I pulled Vrynn and Gabe farther away from the worn trail—which I was certain now was not people-made—with Rascal and Skeeter right behind us.

"I knew that path was too good to be true," I whispered to Vrynn.

She simply nodded in response as we pressed through the forest toward the facility. Occasionally, we caught glimpses of flashes of purple through the foliage. It had to be an entire herd of those spider monsters passing by. Not the best timing for our infiltration mission.

A few minutes later, we reached a small clearing. Across the open area, a tall fence stretched in both directions, disappearing into the trees on both sides.

"What's this fence doing here?" I asked.

"It may have been constructed to keep out wild animals," Gabe offered.

I frowned. "Yeah, but I just don't remember the facility having an outside fence."

"Mitch, we never walked into the facility," Vrynn said with a laugh. "We always flew over the fence."

I wasn't happy about this new development, but there wasn't really much that could be done.

"Tera, can you still hear me?" I said into the comm as we hurried across the clearing.

"Yeah, of course," she said.

"Skeeter has a bunch of attachments that she can use for different projects, right?" I said.

"Sure."

"Could one of them cut through the security fence surrounding the compound?" I flinched as a purple monster from the passing herd roared nearby, setting my nerves on edge.

"Probably," Tera said. "But she doesn't have that tool with her."

I palmed my forehead. "She'll have to go back to the ship, won't she?" I asked. The sinking feeling in my stomach already told me the answer.

"Yeah. And you'll have to send someone with her because I don't have any physical hands to attach the tool," she said, sounding defensive at being forced to mention it.

The tromping of the wild, purple creatures grew louder, and our little group hunkered down closer to the fence. Maybe the giant spider monster herd wasn't traveling anywhere in particular. Maybe they were just meandering around the forest searching for hapless biologicals trapped against the security fence.

That was a discouraging thought.

There was no way we could all sneak through the herd, get the attachment, and sneak back to the fence without being seen—and possibly eaten—by the giant beasts. And I definitely didn't want to split up.

"Would it help that I have the plasma torch from the cargo bay?" Gabe asked, holding up the hand-held cutting device.

"Actually, yes, Gabe, that's perfect. Just cut a hole right here so we can get through before we get eaten." I pointed at the fence.

Gabe knelt next to the metal chains and began furiously cutting away.

Another roar split the silence, and Vrynn and I shared a nervous look. I glanced back at the tops of the nearby trees and could see the canopy shaking.

Something large was moving through the forest. And it was heading in our general direction. Maybe these giant, furry spider-monsters' superpower was their ability to sense fear.

I turned my attention back to the fence. "How's it going, Gabe?" I tried to keep my voice level, but anxiety made it sound like I was a ninth-grader again. I leaned down to watch his progress.

"I have nearly finished cutting through the first layer of the fence," he replied.

"How many layers are there?" I scrutinized the material in his hands. It was nothing like the ubiquitous chain-link construction on Earth. This fence looked like a layer of coarse chain mail followed by a layer of something that might have been metallic fabric in a weird, futuristic, sci-fi B-movie. I shook my head when I realized that my life had sorta become a weird, futuristic, sci-fi B-movie.

Vrynn peered over my shoulder. "How much longer?"

As if having Vrynn standing over me wasn't enough pressure, another roar from the nearby monsters echoed through the trees around us.

"Hurry, Gabe." I knew he was already using the cutting torch at peak efficiency, but I couldn't help myself.

The shaking of the forest canopy was getting closer, close enough that I could hear the whipping leaves and cracking branches. I was about to tell Gabe to hurry again—I wasn't particularly worried about making him anxious—when he suddenly stood.

"Finished," he announced, stepping back to admire the perfect, four-foot high, arch-shaped hole he'd made in the fence.

"C'mon," I said to Vrynn as I dragged Gabe through the hole and to the protection of a nearby shed.

We leaned against the cold surface of the shed's outside wall and caught our breath. The trees across the small clearing parted and a medium-sized purple monster emerged. We all stood perfectly still—no small feat for Vrynn, Rascal, and me, considering our exertion. The creature scanned the open area, sniffed the air, and moved on through the trees.

As soon as it was out of sight, I finally allowed myself to breathe. "That was too close."

"Another perfectly timed escape," Vrynn said with a nod. "Now let's go find the power cells."

I turned to Gabe. "Stay here with Skeeter and Rascal. I'll let you know if we need help."

Gabe nodded his agreement and took up position by a broad tree trunk next to the shed. Vrynn and I hurried toward the next cluster of buildings. We stopped at the last building before a wide-open space, and Vrynn peeked around the corner.

"Are we sure the power cells would be in the main hangar?" she asked.

"No. In fact, I doubt there's anything left in that building at all," I said when I caught a glimpse of what was left of the ruined structure that had once housed the main production line. "I can't even imagine what Nexus soldiers are still doing here. None of the Mark 7s are left. What else could they want?"

Vrynn shook her head as if that question was an annoyance. "It doesn't matter. Let's just find the power cells and get back to Mareesh. They've probably snuck five or six convoys past since we've been out of commission."

I had to admire her singularity of focus.

A moment later, Vrynn streaked across the empty space and hid against the wall of a broad building that had been used for storage the last time we checked. When she saw that I was still hiding behind the last shed, she impatiently waved me forward. I forced myself to take a few calming breaths, then checked for guards before sprinting across the wide gap.

I slammed into the wall next to her, chest heaving. "You could give me some warning next time," I huffed.

Patting my arm, she said. "You did fine."

She checked around the corner then motioned me to the nearby door that we carefully pushed open. After slipping inside, I pulled a flashlight from my pocket and used it to sweep the room. With the exception of a few pairs of footprints in the layer of dust, most of the stuff in this building was untouched.

Vrynn walked to a nearby shelf and examined a piece of equipment while I picked up a small tool that looked like a pair of pliers—albeit alien pliers.

"Too bad we can't tell what Nexus is interested in here at the plant," I said as I glanced around. Everything on Mela Suphoria was advanced—though ancient and deteriorating—technology, even to the most modern planets in the Bonara Cluster. If Nexus figured out a way to salvage that tech, especially the ability to manufacture devastatingly powerful ships like the *Starfire*, any efforts to oppose them would be useless.

"They obviously didn't care about anything in this building," Vrynn said, making her way back to the entrance. "Let's go."

I followed Vrynn across a narrow gap between the outbuildings to the next storage structure, where we found a similar scene. Nothing of interest to Nexus. Nothing useful to us.

We searched two more buildings without success, until we crept up to another, larger building, closer to the main assembly hangar, and peeked in through the windows. At least a dozen people were hunched over a cluster of tables in the center, not soldiers, more like the technicians we'd come across in Gralik's headquarters on Zerlon. They wore gray jumpsuits and seemed very intent on their work. Based on the piles of dusty boxes on one side of the group, and the piles of parts on the other side, they appeared to be taking an inventory of the warehouse's contents.

A stack of modules in the corner caught my eye. "Power cells." I tilted my head toward them. "But how do we get past the technicians?"

"We can do it," Vrynn said with an aggravating smile.

I shook my head. "There's absolutely no way we'll get in there without being seen," I said emphatically. "But I could always blow up another building. That might be enough of a distraction to get them all out."

Vrynn scowled. Apparently, it was too soon to make that joke.

"I bet Gabe, or better yet, Skeeter, could sneak in." I activated my comm. "Gabe, we might need your help. Or possibly Skeeter's. Do you think you two can sneak closer to our position?"

"I believe Skeeter and I both possess the physical ability," Gabe replied. "But it would not be advisable at this moment."

"Why not?" I asked. If this was another one of those "can I, may I" arguments, I would strangle Gabe the next time I saw him, android body or not.

"Because if I stop restraining Rascal, I predict that he will race out through the hole in the fence to play with the small purple creature we encountered earlier."

My eyes went wide. "The baby monster found you?"

"That is an apt description, yes," Gabe replied.

I scrubbed a hand across my face. This was going from bad to worse. "Okay, we'll come to you."

Vrynn and I snuck through the scattered outbuildings back to Gabe's position by the hole in the fence. Sure enough, the little monster was inside the security perimeter. By the time we arrived, Rascal and Skeeter had made friends with the little guy and were bounding around, nipping at each other and running circles around our group.

"Okay, I'll take Rascal back out into the forest and try to get rid of the little beast." I smiled at Vrynn and Gabe and added, "The purple one, not Rascal. You two sneak back to the warehouse and see if Skeeter can get in and out with a few of those power cells."

A roar sounded from the forest across the clearing.

"There is a high probability that the mother creature is searching for her young," Gabe said, scrutinizing the nearby tree line.

"Great," I muttered. My job just got a whole lot harder.

Vrynn grabbed my arm. "Wait, this is perfect," she said, her blue eyes sparkling with hope.

I stared at her, dumbfounded that she could be so optimistic at a time like this. Unless, of course, it had been her plan all along to lure me here to my death so she could steal my starship.

"You said you needed a distraction to get the technicians out of the warehouse . . ." Vrynn trailed off as she motioned theatrically from the baby monster toward the rest of the facility several times.

"Are you serious?" I asked.

"I mean, it might be a little messy," she said with a mischievous smirk. "But it'll do the job."

"You want to intentionally lead that giant purple beast into the compound, and then . . ."

"And then we go get the power cells," Vrynn said, skipping over the messy part.

I frowned at her, unsure that the plan would go as well as she expected.

The next—much closer—roar from the forest convinced me to give her idea a try.

I handed Gabe a spare Rascal-treat. "Take this and run to the center of the compound. Rascal will follow you. Don't get killed, and don't lose Rascal."

Gabe nodded and started off. He had Rascal's attention immediately—even a new friend couldn't compete with his favorite snack.

I grabbed Vrynn's hand and pulled her over to the nearest shed. "Let's just hope this works," I whispered as we settled in to watch the show—or rather, the parade.

Gabe was in the lead, with Skeeter close by his side. Next came Rascal—nipping at Gabe for the treat—and then the little purple monster. Technically, there was one more entry in this crazy procession, but the mama bear had yet to arrive.

Suddenly, I heard a shout. "Drop your weapons!" A Nexus soldier stood a few dozen feet away, his rifle aiming straight at us. Vrynn set her rifle on the ground, and I tossed my blaster down next to it.

The mama monster's timing couldn't have been better. She burst through the trees into the clearing, baring giant teeth, and bellowed loudly. I'd never seen any animal of that size—on Earth or otherwise—move so quickly. Though twice as tall as an elephant, she crossed the forty-foot clearing in just a few seconds. Without missing a beat—or even slowing—she leveled the security fence.

The Nexus soldier must have decided that the rampaging purple monster was a bigger threat—which she was—and opened fire with his plasma rifle. Unfortunately for him, he had unknowingly stepped into the path of our makeshift parade, making him the only thing that now stood between the mother monster and her baby. The purple creature knocked him aside like a bowling pin.

As Gabe and the rest of his entourage marched farther into the Mark 7 facility, the mother creature picked up the pace until she was at a full sprint. Gabe disappeared among the trees and outbuildings with the three playful animals in tow, and the mother bellowed her disapproval. That was when we got our first indication that the Nexus forces had noticed something was going on. Sporadic rifle fire echoed among the buildings.

"I really hope they're not shooting at Gabe," I said as I retrieved my blaster.

"They'll be fine." Vrynn grabbed her plasma rifle and my hand. "C'mon. That's our cue."

Skirting the tussle the giant mama was having with the Nexus soldiers, we snuck past the abandoned outbuildings until we reached the warehouse where the power cells were stored. Fortunately, the mayhem caused by a nineteen-foot tall, rampaging purple beast was enough of a distraction that none of the fleeing technicians or soldiers really paid much attention to us.

Vrynn leaned up on her tiptoes, checking through the window. "It's empty," she said. "They must have made a run for it."

"Can't say I blame them," I muttered.

Just before turning the corner, a Nexus soldier appeared in front of us. He seemed as shocked to see us as we were to see him. I fired my blaster before I'd really had a chance to aim, but my shot caught his shoulder at the same time Vrynn hit him in the stomach with the butt of her rifle.

"Sorry," I said, eyes wide. "That was too close."

Vrynn shrugged. "It got the job done."

We snuck over to the door and ducked into the building. I went immediately to the stack of Quake Drive power cells in the corner. "How will we know which ones are still any good?" I asked.

"We don't have time to figure it out. Just grab them all," Vrynn said.

I hefted one, and it must have weighed at least fifty pounds. I considered the rest of the stack. "I don't think we'll get out of here with more than three or four."

Vrynn grabbed one, and I was secretly satisfied to see that she had underestimated its weight, too. She shifted the power cell to one hand and grabbed a second one. "Okay, we'll each carry two."

I reached for two power cells, preparing to lift them off the pile. Each module was only about the size of a modest briefcase, but they weighed as much as an anvil salesman's check-on luggage. How were we supposed to make it all the way back to the ship like this? Not only would we look incredibly conspicuous, but we would be sitting ducks if anyone tried to stop us.

Of course, it was a little late to voice that concern, as Vrynn was already out the door and halfway around the corner. I waddled after her, doing my best to keep up. I couldn't figure out how she was so effortlessly carrying the same amount and only weighed half as much as I did.

We were halfway back to the outer fence, and I was feeling pretty good about our chances, when one particular shout rose above the din of confusion.

"Intruders!"

I glanced over my shoulder to see an older man dressed in a technician uniform pointing our direction. Nearby soldiers took aim and fired. Plasma rounds streaked by, the heat waves warming my face.

I glanced ahead at Vrynn for any sign of slowing. Apparently, she thought her optimism had an effect on weapons fire, too.

That meant it was up to me.

Without slowing my pace, I dropped one of the power cells and pulled the blaster from my belt. I wasn't a particularly great shot under normal circumstances, but while running for my life with a fifty-pound power module in one hand, my aim was terrible.

But even a blind dog finds a bone sometimes.

One of my shots hit the building next to the soldiers firing at us. The explosion showered them in bricks and debris, giving us the few precious seconds we needed to run over the security fence the purple mama beast had smashed. Without the second power cell, my pace increased, and I easily caught up to Vrynn. When I came even with her, she stared down at my one power module.

"Where did the other one go?" she asked with a frown.

I waved the blaster at her. "Needed a free hand . . . so I could shoot." I was getting seriously winded, and talking wasn't helping the situation.

"Now we only have three," she said, annoyed.

"Would you like me . . . to go back and . . . get the one I dropped?"

She gave me a deadpan look, and we both kept running.

Across the clearing, Gabe was waiting patiently for us at the edge of the forest.

"Skeeter and Rascal?" I asked when we got close enough that he could hear me.

"Yes. They are both here." He pointed behind him. "Did I perform up to expectations?" he asked.

I nodded as emphatically as I could. "You were awesome."

Soldiers fired on us from the compound's broken perimeter, and we ducked behind the trees. Vrynn dropped one of her power cells and pulled the plasma rifle off her back to return fire. I took a few shots with my blaster, then tucked it back in my belt and picked up Vrynn's power cell.

Just because we were in a firefight on an abandoned alien planet didn't mean I couldn't at least attempt to be chivalrous.

A moment later, a pair of furry purple spider monsters erupted from the forest, roaring loudly as they tromped across the clearing. The soldiers at the demolished security fence made the mistake of firing on the creatures who then decided it was time to play "smash the little men with guns."

We took off through the trees, ducking the sporadic weapons fire that followed us, and doing our best to avoid the herd's well-worn path. We weren't nearly as stealthy on the return trip to the *Starfire*, but it hardly mattered. By the time we reached the relative safety of the ship, no one was following us.

Tera stood at the top of the ramp, arms out to hug Gabe, who trailed behind me.

"Tera . . . let's . . . take off," I said.

"I'm a little busy," she replied amidst the embrace.

"Are you unable to activate the lift-off sequence while we are touching?" Gabe asked, sounding honestly concerned. "If the computing requirements of our interface are too much, I can cease embracing you for a moment until you—"

Her scowl cut him off, and I felt the ship's engines rumble to life as the loading ramp began to close.

I noticed she didn't let go of him, though.

Chapter Ten

The fifteen minutes we were forced to wait until the ship came out of intra-space near Thetis Max were long and boring. Tera had informed us that we couldn't replace the Quake drive cells while the standard intra-space drive was drawing power from the core. Something about a painful death from plasma burns.

When the jump finally ended, Vrynn immediately pulled one of the old cells from the power stack and replaced it with a recently stolen one.

"What's the reading on this cell?" Vrynn asked Tera.

Tera's eyes scanned as the system checked. "Seventy-two percent," she replied.

"Will it last longer than the worn-out ones did?" Vrynn pressed.

Tera just sort of shrugged. "We don't have much to go on, but these might last longer if we aren't as rough on them."

Vrynn absently nodded her understanding as she pulled another dead cell out, replacing it with a new one. The other two tested about the same.

"Okay, let's go," Vrynn said as she ran from the engineering room toward the ladder.

I followed after her—something that was becoming a regular occurrence, it seemed—wondering why we didn't just let Tera land and park the ship in the hangar. By the time I caught up with Vrynn on the flight deck, she was giving Tera intra-space jump instructions.

"We're already going back to Mareesh?" I asked, a little out of breath.

Vrynn gripped the flight sticks. "Uh, yeah. We have to stop the convoys."

Despite knowing she was probably right about the convoys, I wasn't sure I was ready to jump right back into the action. "The mining bots probably have another load of ore for us in the hangar," I said. "Don't you want to pick that up first? That would give us a little buffer in our supplies."

It must have cost Vrynn a great deal to agree with my suggestion. At least, that's what her expression told me.

After landing on Thetis Max, I found Slate and asked him to load the cargo. Then I crashed on the couch in the *Starfire's* living area.

What felt like only a few minutes later, Vrynn tapped me on the shoulder. I squinted up at her face looming over me.

"Mitch, we need to get going," she said.

There were worse things than being woken up by that beautiful face.

I sighed and heaved myself into a sitting position. "Everything's loaded already?"

"Just about," Vrynn answered cheerfully.

I stumbled over to the kitchen and grabbed a drink pouch then made my way to the flight deck and plopped into the pilot's seat.

"I haven't really had time to come up with a new plan of attack," I mumbled.

"No problem," Vrynn shot back. "Let's just get back to Mareesh and stop the convoys."

That sounded a lot like the old plan.

I was too groggy to offer any good objection, so away we went. Traveling through intra-space did have its advantages. After a ten-minute jump, I was certainly feeling more alert than I would have if we had portal jumped right into the action.

As soon as we passed through the stratosphere, my tactical display lit up.

"There's a convoy already heading for Mardrys," I said.

"Increase speed," Vrynn said. "I think we can catch them."

I wasn't as hopeful, but I pushed the throttle forward anyway. "Tell us about the convoy, Tera."

"Four transports. Fifteen fighter escorts," she replied.

I whistled. "Wow. That's a big convoy." I leaned over the console, scrutinizing their formation.

"Could we portal jump past these ones?" Vrynn gestured at the half dozen ships clustered in the middle, closest to the transports.

I shook my head. "Look at how they arranged these ships." I pointed to the fighters she had indicated. "They're not leaving any spots open. They're all in perfect position to fire on a ship that suddenly comes through a portal."

"What if we kidnap them again?" Vrynn asked.

I frowned. "You mean do the same thing that destroyed the other power cells?"

"What if we swing wide and flank these ships on the outside?" Vrynn asked, pointing again.

"By the time we make it around them, the convoy will have landed."

"We have to do something!" She held a hand out to the approaching ships.

Before I could respond, Tera interrupted. "There is a flight lifting off from the Mardrys spaceport," she announced. "Eight ships. They've set an intercept course for us." She paused for a second. "And ten more ships just came out of intra-space. They're directly above us; entering the atmosphere in less than a minute."

"Can you identify them?" I asked.

"Varusian Interceptors," Tera said.

"Which ones?" I asked.

"All of them," she replied.

Her pronouncement sent a chill down my spine.

It was one thing to go up against inferior Barchee ships or fighters from far-flung systems who might not know who we were. But ships from Varus Prime, the capital planet of the Bonara Cluster, could mean only one of two things. Either they were here on official Bonara Defense Force business. Or they were loyal to Gralik and operating as Nexus.

"Oh, and no active transponder signals," Tera added a moment later.

I locked eyes with Vrynn. Her usually pale skin was even whiter than normal.

Nexus ships.

They knew who we were, and they were here on Gralik's orders.

"Is there any way we could get to the convoy?" Vrynn asked. Her pleading tone told me she already knew the answer.

"Those interceptors aren't here to protect the convoy," I said grimly. "They're coming after us."

Before Vrynn and I could even discuss a new plan of attack, Tera piped in. "I hate to be the bearer of bad news . . . again. But we have an incoming message."

"Who is it?" I asked.

"Gralik," Tera replied. "And coincidentally, there is a Vezor-class runabout lifting off from Mardrys. I knew that was Gralik's ship," she muttered.

"Okay, let's see it," I said.

A moment later, the main holographic display flickered to life, and Gralik's upper body loomed in front of me, a sneer on his annoying face.

"You two have been a rock under my eyelid, do you know that?" he said. "I should have killed you when I had the chance. I would do it now, except that you have something that belongs to me."

"You'll understand if we don't agree with you on that," I replied with a wry smile. "Both on the timing of killing us and on the claim to our ship."

"My ship!" he screamed over me. A moment later, he sat back, seeming to collect himself. "But I'm willing to forgo killing you if you turn the ship over to me."

I glanced over at Vrynn to see her reaction. Her hands squeezed tightly around the control sticks, as if they would shoot Gralik of their own accord.

I knew how she felt about Gralik's offer.

"I'm sorry, but we aren't in a position to accept your offer at this time." I moved to cut the connection.

"We have you trapped!" he yelled. "If you don't give me the ship, I'll take it anyway, and then I will definitely kill you!"

With an immense amount of pleasure—probably more than was reasonable, considering the situation—I gave him my most cheeky smile and cut the comm. Gralik's hologram vanished mid scream, his obnoxious face contorted in rage.

I glanced over at Vrynn, and for a split second, I saw the gravity of our situation on her face. My feelings of delight at needling Gralik suddenly vanished.

We were in the fight of our lives.

Vrynn's expression hardened. "Let's take out as many of these rot-piles as we can." That one didn't need any translation.

Though we didn't always see eye to eye on our plans, at that moment, I couldn't have agreed more with my impetuous co-pilot.

I banked the *Starfire* hard to the right, turning away from the rising interceptors. They shifted as a single unit to match our course—Gralik's ship hanging slightly back—while still closing on us. I inverted the turn and pulled back hard on the controls until we were heading toward the upper atmosphere. But the ten interceptors above us had already spread out and were matching our moves, too.

"A net above us and a net below us," Vrynn muttered.

Focusing on the ship closest to us, I steered toward it, hoping we could engage a few and break our way out. Almost immediately, that ship slowed, hanging back, keeping a constant distance from us. I turned toward the next closest ship, and the same thing happened. They were still closing in on us, but none of the ships would engage us individually.

They were waiting to engage us all at once.

Suddenly, the sky in front of us erupted in bright orange and yellow plasma rounds coming from all ten ships. The feed from the rear video showed the same.

"Defensive lasers!" I yelled at Tera. "Vrynn, do what you can."

"The cannons aren't designed to take out other plasma rounds," she said as she unleashed a withering barrage toward the ships ahead of us.

"Then fire off some atmospheric missiles," I said. "We've got about a dozen left."

"But the targeting—"

"Don't worry about locking on. Just fire," I replied.

I weaved and banked as I attempted to dodge the incoming rounds, but several still impacted the hull.

"Forward deflector array at eighty-five percent," Tera announced.

A pair of missiles streaked away as more rounds slammed into us.

"Rear array down to seventy," Tera said right before another impact. "No, sixty-two percent."

"We have to get out of here!" Vrynn yelled as she continued firing on the closest interceptors, which was difficult because they kept shifting farther away from us as we tried to engage them.

"What do you think I'm trying to do?" I said through gritted teeth, banking hard to avoid an incoming barrage.

I pointed the *Starfire* directly at Gralik's runabout, lurking behind the web of interceptors that was closing on us. Apparently, he thought he was safe hanging back out of the fight. I knew there was no way to get to him, but I also figured that none of the interceptors would want to jump in the path of my railgun slugs.

Squeezing the trigger, I fired off round after round straight ahead. I'd like to say I intentionally created a perfect spread pattern that would prevent Gralik from dodging all of them, but that was mostly due to the impacts of plasma rounds against our hull. Most of my shots missed, but one exploded close enough to the runabout to send it wobbling off course.

A moment later, another plasma round hit us broad-side, right behind the flight deck windows, and the *Starfire* careened to the side, nearly knocking us both from our seats.

I tightened my grip on the controls again, only to find them sluggish. "Tera, what happened?" I yelled as I fought to stabilize us.

"That last shot disrupted the primary flight control," Tera cried. "Several of the connections are knocked out, and there's nothing I can do until someone goes down and physically fixes the wires."

The ship continued its downward corkscrew.

"Mitch!" Vrynn yelled, uncharacteristic terror filling her voice.

I struggled with the controls, surprised that this powerful starship that had gotten us through every battle was suddenly so intent on dragging us down to the cold ocean below.

It felt like we were flying through molasses, and every time I thought I had a way to recover, the control systems refused to make it happen.

We were going to crash. There was no way to avoid it.

Almost.

In a split-second decision, I did the only thing I could think of to save the ship. I reached down and mashed the button to activate the hover emitters. My stomach lurched as the emitters strained against our freefall, finally bringing us to a stop in midair.

The flight deck turned eerily quiet except for the sound of blood pounding in my ears. I could hear Vrynn's ragged breathing beside me, and somewhere on the lower deck, Rascal whined his displeasure.

As my panic subsided, I took stock of the situation. We were still several thousand feet above the ocean, but that was the only good news. The tactical display said there were fourteen Varusian Interceptors and one Vezor-class runabout, which didn't really match up with my mental kill-count, but it had been a hectic battle. The interceptors kept their distance, flying around us like they were in orbit of the *Starfire*, while the runabout moved closer toward us, bringing the two ships face to face.

The silence was broken by a series of beeps and then Tera's soft voice. "Incoming transmission."

I felt too tired to argue. "Go ahead," I said.

The only silver lining in the whole situation was seeing how upset Gralik was when he appeared on our display. He looked like he'd just survived a very close call with an exploding railgun slug. Too bad my aim hadn't been a little better.

"Surrender my ship immediately, or—"

I waved my hand in the air. "Or you'll kill us, yeah, yeah, we know."

"No," Gralik snapped. "After that last stunt, I'm going to kill you either way. But if you turn over the ship now, I'll make it quick and painless."

"We would rather die long and painful deaths than ever give you this ship," Vrynn spat.

I wasn't surprised at all by Vrynn's answer to his offer. Though I wasn't excited about the prospect of death—especially not a long and painful one—meeting my end with Vrynn by my side fighting for her homeworld wasn't a bad way to go.

"Nexus ships moving in," Tera announced.

I considered the beautiful, impetuous, alien woman at my side. My brave co-pilot through it all. She had so much that attracted me to her—her optimism, her tenacity, her strength in the face of opposition. I only wished she knew how much more I'd begun to care for her. More than care for her. At some point in the last few weeks, I'd fallen completely in love with her.

I swallowed hard. "Vrynn, I . . ." The lump in my throat choked off my voice.

Reaching across the gap between our seats, Vrynn placed her small hand in mine. She nodded, as if to tell me she already knew what I wanted to say. The longing in her deep blue eyes was the most beautiful and heartbreaking thing I'd ever seen.

The moment stretched on, and I wasn't going to be the one to break it.

Unfortunately, it was broken by a grating voice over the comm.

"Do you surrender?" Gralik demanded, pulling me back to our impending doom.

We were about to die.

That thought felt like a ton of bricks in my gut, as if someone had turned the hover emitters on full-rise.

My brain seized on the thought of the hover emitters.

That was it.

I swiped a finger across the console to cut the comm link.

"Prepare a portal jump," I said to Tera.

"We can't portal jump if we can't move forward through the portal," Tera said, sounding confused at my sudden enthusiasm.

"Our flight systems are all dead; we can't make the ship fly forward," Vrynn added.

"Who says anything about flying forward?" I replied.

A moment later, Vrynn's expression morphed from confusion to understanding. We both straightened in our pilot seats, ready for action.

"Tera, activate the Quake drive and open a portal right under the ship," I said. "Set the destination somewhere on the other side of Mareesh."

"But if we can't—" Tera stopped mid reply. "Oh. That's smart." Her eyes scanned back and forth, then she nodded. "Portal open."

An alarm blared.

"Missiles!" Vrynn cried.

I glanced at my console. More than half the interceptors had fired atmospheric missiles, some of them more than one. Apparently, even though Gralik really wanted the *Starfire*, he definitely didn't want us getting away with it.

I cut power to the hover emitters, and my stomach jumped into my throat as we dropped out of the sky.

In our freefall, the laser batteries activated, attempting to neutralize the incoming threats. Two of the missiles were close enough to worry about. The laser defenses targeted one, and Vrynn shot at the other.

It was probably only three or four seconds, but it felt like an eternity. It was so long that I nearly turned to ask Tera how far below us she had opened the portal.

One of the missiles broke apart—thanks to Vrynn—but the laser defenses wouldn't have time to disable the other. I could see the edge of the portal; we were so close to getting away.

We crossed through the aperture, and the second missile blew up just as I yelled, "Close the portal!"

The explosion rocked the *Starfire*, sending it into a spin. Vrynn and I were thrown from our seats by the rotation. Shrapnel pinged against the hull and then suddenly stopped. I crawled back toward my seat, fighting the force of our spin, and reached for the hover emitter controls. I fumbled across the control console until I found the right button. A second later, the emitters came back online with a jolt and pushed us down against the deck.

When the ship finally came to a stop, I said to Vrynn, "That was close."

"Way too close," she said.

"Are we actually on the other side of Mareesh?" I asked Tera.

"The sensors say that we are," she said.

"Well, they'll find us if we stay in the air," I said.

Assuming the flight control systems hadn't magically fixed themselves during our death-defying drop, I used the only tool I had available. I slowly reduced power to the hover emitters, and the ship descended to the ocean's surface. Then, we inverted the emitter field and pushed ourselves underwater.

With some help from Vrynn and Gabe, we got the flight control systems connected and operational again. I instructed Tera to take us back to the cavern, but I insisted on going up to the flight deck and sitting in my chair anyway.

I stared absently out the window as the water quietly swirled around us, lost in my thoughts. We had never come up against that sort of strategy from Nexus. It was probably because they could never predict where we would be, so they could never gather that many ships against us.

But they knew where we were now, and that meant everything had changed.

"We'll need to wait a day or two before we attack another convoy," Vrynn finally said.

Her tone was so calm and nonchalant that I couldn't help but gape at her.

"How can you say that?" I asked in disbelief.

Vrynn lifted a shoulder. "I mean, it wouldn't be safe to come out against the convoys any sooner than that." Her expression brightened a little. "Unless you think we should."

How could her conclusion from our battle with the interceptors be so completely opposite of mine?

"Vrynn, Nexus definitely knows we're here now. Did you see the way they came after us? They don't care about the convoys; they only want the *Starfire*. We can't ever put ourselves in that situation again."

Vrynn frowned. "We got away, didn't we?"

I shook my head. "Barely." I realized there was no way to ease her into the reality that she needed to face. I just had to say it bluntly. I turned my body to face her directly. "If we go against that many Nexus interceptors again, we'll lose the *Starfire*. Gralik's traps aren't affected by your optimism." The last part was probably unnecessarily mean, but it was true.

Vrynn's eyes grew round, the pain evident on her face. Then she turned away, her posture deflated.

A few minutes later, Vrynn got up and walked out of the flight deck. I had hurt her with that comment, but I didn't know what to do about it. Or even if I *should* do anything about it. Part of me knew that I should probably go after her, but I decided I needed the solitude to consider what our next plan of action would be. Besides, if I went to find Vrynn, I would probably just say something insensitive or stupid.

I sat in the pilot seat, pondering our situation. The plan to attack the convoys was a good one, and it would eventually work if we only had enough time.

The problem was Gralik. His sudden appearance complicated things. I knew he had been involved in the battle that brought Mareesh under Barchee occupation, but I had no idea he stuck around. Why would the Bonara Defense Force leave him here all these years? Didn't he have other duties or assignments somewhere else?

If only there was some way to get BDF command to reassign him to another planet. The *Starfire* was powerful enough to prevail against the Barchee.

It was unfortunate that I didn't have any friends in high places here in the Bonara Cluster. Who was I kidding? I didn't even have any friends in high places back on Earth.

I suddenly remembered my interaction with Shariamy Razome on Ludros Beta Five. I reached into the pocket of my flight jacket and pulled out the tiny, coin-sized encryption disk. What had Shariamy said about being the cousin of a chancellor or something? Was that high up enough in the Bonaran government to help us get rid of Gralik?

It was worth a try.

With Tera's help, I activated the comm system and scanned the encryption disk.

"Do you want to communicate with intra-space or standard space?" Tera asked.

"What's the difference in response time between the two?" I asked.

"An intra-space signal could be as fast as a few seconds, depending on the intra-space dimensional plane," Tera said.

"And the standard space signal?"

"About eight and a half years," Tera said flatly.

"Why would you even offer me that option?"

My teenage friend shrugged. "You've gotten annoyed before when I haven't told you things. I'm just making sure you know."

I sighed. "Let's do the intra-space one."

A few moments later, the holographic display above my console activated.

"According to the response time-stamp, you'll have about a five or six-second lag on this connection," Tera said.

A projection of Shariamy appeared on the display.

"Hi, Shariamy," I said with a wave. "This is Mitch Foster. You remember me from the spaceport? My friend and I helped you fix your intra-space drive. Or at least, we installed your new plasma injector module." Remembering that it would be a five-second delay before she would respond, I forced myself to stop speaking so she could jump in.

Several seconds passed, probably more than five, when she finally reacted. "Yes, hello Mitch Foster. Thank you for calling Shariamy Razome."

She was speaking in third person. That was weird. "You're Shariamy Razome," I said. It was supposed to be a statement, but it came out more like a question. I cringed internally for wasting another five or six seconds on something that should have been obvious.

"No, but thank you for calling Shariamy Razome," she replied.

I frowned. Was this some sort of joke?

"I think it's a holographic stand-in," Tera whispered. "Sort of like me, but not as advanced."

"Ah, got it. Thanks," I whispered back. Turning my attention to the Shariamy doppelganger, I said. "I need to speak to Shariamy, please."

Six seconds later, the holographic assistant replied, "I'm sorry, but Shariamy is currently busy with very important government negotiations. If you would like to transmit a message, that information will be forwarded to Shariamy, and she will reply at her earliest convenience."

So much for getting a quick resolution to the problem. It seemed that a message left with Shariamy's quirky assistant was probably the best I was going to get at the moment. In the vaguest terms possible—I wasn't sure how Shariamy felt about destructive sabotage against oppressive governments—I explained that it would be an incredible favor to us if she could get the BDF to recall Gralik from Mareesh.

"Have you completed your message to Shariamy?" her virtual assistant asked.

"Yes." I found myself being more and more concise because of the transmission lag.

"Thank you for calling Shariamy. She will contact you as soon as she can."

The connection terminated, and I was left staring at the empty space where the projection had been. "Well, that felt like a waste of time."

Tera shrugged.

With the message to Shariamy on its way, I did my best to turn my thoughts back to our predicament. We couldn't use the *Starfire* the same way anymore, that much was clear to me. Attacking convoys was simply too predictable, and even if we did have unlimited use of the Quake Drive—which we definitely didn't—it was only a matter of time before Nexus ships would eventually score an incapacitating shot on us.

But the cavern on the south end of Syr was still a great place to hide ourselves and the ship. My mind turned to the island and the little towns I'd only seen from the hilltop. Those towns had people in them. And those people would certainly want to fight back against the Barchee occupation.

Could we stage a ground offensive from Syr? With nothing but regular citizens?

I remembered Vrynn telling me about the original Barchee invasion. She'd mentioned a Mareesh military, hadn't she? Maybe some remnants of the army had survived, and we could enlist their help.

But first, I needed Vrynn to be on board with the idea.

I stood from the pilot's seat and exited the flight deck. Vrynn wasn't in the living area, so I slid down the ladder and checked the engineering room and fabrication lab. She wasn't in either. Next, I checked the cargo bay.

"How may this unit be of service to you?" HelperBot asked when it saw me poking around the storage shelves.

"Have you seen Vrynn?" I asked.

"Please point this unit in the direction of Vrynn."

"No, I don't know where Vrynn is. That's why I'm asking you." I glanced behind the next row of cargo.

"This unit does not have the location of Vrynn."

I shook my head wryly. No big surprise there. "Tera?" I called out to the ceiling.

Tera shimmered into view next to me. "Yes?"

"Do you know where Vrynn is?"

"When a girl is mad at a guy, her friends aren't supposed to tell that guy where she is," Tera replied, going full junior high mode on me. "Unless, of course, the girl wants her friends to tell the guy."

"Grrr." I clenched my fists. "I'm not the one she should be mad at. I'm just trying to help her face reality."

Tera shrugged in a way that said I might be right, but she still wasn't going to tell me.

I stared back at her. "You know, this feels like a double standard. When I was down here a few weeks ago, ready to give up, you told Vrynn where I was so she could cheer me up."

"That was different."

"Different how?" I asked.

She shrugged again in that aggravating way.

I pinched the bridge of my nose. I couldn't believe I was being sucked into an argument with a virtual teenager. I held up a hand. "You know what? It's fine. This is a small ship, and I've got plenty of time. I'll find her eventually." I walked out of the cargo bay and turned toward the ladder.

The only place left to check was her quarters.

On the upper deck, I paused outside Vrynn's room. I considered leaving her alone with her melancholy, but she had always been willing to cheer me up. I needed to return the favor.

I took a deep breath and knocked lightly on her door. "Vrynn, it's Mitch. Do you want to talk?"

A few seconds later, the door slid open. This beautiful, resilient, alien woman, who had battled enemy soldiers, taken on rogue robots, and shot her way through veritable armadas of spacecraft, stood in front of me looking beaten down. She wiped at her tear-stained cheeks, tinted blue from crying.

I had intended to say something deep and profound, or maybe something sensitive and caring. Whatever I had intended to say never made it to my lips. When I saw Vrynn's distress, my hands instinctively reached for her, and she flung herself into my arms, burying her face against my chest.

I held her there as she cried, caressing her long hair. "We'll figure this out," I said softly. "There has to be a way to beat them."

"Now look who's being optimistic," she murmured into my chest.

"Hey, I've seen the fire you've got inside," I replied. "You could take on Nexus single-handedly."

She responded with a watery laugh. "And get myself killed in the process."

I shrugged. "Probably. That's why I'm trying to come up with a better way. Because I don't want to lose you."

I held her there for another minute or two, just waiting for her to be ready.

Finally, she pulled back and stared up at me. "Thanks, Mitch," she said, wiping the tears from those beautiful, cobalt eyes. A moment later, her expression turned mischievous. "So you're saying you can't live without me?"

I smiled. "Yeah, pretty much."

She continued gazing up at me, an inscrutable expression on her face. Though I had no idea what she was thinking, I wasn't about to break our embrace.

Finally, Vrynn stepped back and took a deep, cleansing breath. "We need to come up with a new plan." She slipped past me into the hall and strode to the living area. "If we can't use the Quake Drive, where does that leave us?"

"What if we enlist your people to help?" I asked.

Vrynn glanced back at me with a harsh scowl. "You mean, gather a rebellion and lead them against the enemy in wave after wave of suicide missions until there's no population left for the Barchee to occupy?"

"Well, anything sounds bad when you say it that way," I complained.

"Don't you think we tried to fight them? Don't you think we did everything we could to beat them back?" Some of Vrynn's anger faded as she considered me. "You have no idea what it was like. Gralik and his forces were too strong. My people were slaughtered."

"But they didn't have us," I replied. "Or the *Starfire*."

"We don't even have the *Starfire*," she shot back.

I put a hand on her arm, hoping to calm her. "It's true; we can't use the ship like before, but at least we still have the ship."

Vrynn's brow furrowed.

"We just need to be strategic," I said. "We can't go rushing into situations where we're outnumbered. We have to pick our battles."

As I spoke, I could see the excitement returning to Vrynn's expression.

"Yeah, we'll gather my people to fight again," she said, "but this time, the Barchee will be no match for the *Starfire*." The wheels were already spinning in her brain. "I think this could work."

We stood there, both lost in thought for a few minutes before she spoke again.

"You know, I still have extended family on Syr," she said. "If we're there gathering an army, my cousins will want to meet you."

The obvious implication hung in the air.

I took Vrynn's hands into mine. "I'd love to meet your family," I said, with more confidence than I felt.

A sly grin spread across her lips. "You're feeling brave?"

Was meeting a Mareesh extended family really that scary? I'd never even done it on Earth, so I had no idea. I took a breath and chuckled nervously. "Sure. I think so."

Chapter Eleven

T he next morning, after squeezing through the narrow crevices out of our hidden cavern, Vrynn and I set off down the hill toward Neevra, her hometown. In an effort to not over-complicate our first encounter with Vrynn's people, we had decided to leave Gabe, Skeeter, and Rascal behind. The Mareesh had technology, but it wasn't as openly displayed as in other cultures. It certainly wasn't flaunted, like marching down the main street with a robotic feline and an android. And according to Vrynn, the small island of Syr didn't have any animals larger than a puppy. They would not react well to a bear-sized beast invading their town.

While we walked down the side of the mountain toward the broad valley dotted with towns, I admired the lush green vegetation. I couldn't exactly call it grass because it was so different from what I was used to on Earth—more of a combination of broad leaves and puffy green flowers. But it was still breath-taking.

Then a thought suddenly occurred to me. "Are you considered optimistic in your culture? Or is everyone as hopeful as you are?"

Vrynn laughed out loud. It was a nice sound to hear. "The people of Mareesh are naturally optimistic. What do you expect from people who settled a planet like this?" She turned thoughtful. "But even in my culture, I'm considered optimistic. The phrase in Mareesh is 'sky eyes'."

I smiled at her. "Your eyes do look like the sky to me." I glanced up at the bluish-gray of the Mareesh sky. "Well, maybe not the color of the sky here, but back on Earth, the sky can be deep blue on a clear day."

Her cheeks colored an adorable light blue—just like a blush. "I'm glad you have beautiful sights on Dirt. I would be sad if it was as ugly as the name," she said with an impish grin. "But actually, the phrase 'sky eyes' is meant to describe someone who is always thinking of the best possible outcome."

I ignored the jab. "That sounds like you," I said with a smile.

We enjoyed the rest of the walk in comfortable contemplation, but as we got closer to her village, Vrynn became more and more nervous. She kept fidgeting with her hair and re-adjusting the small pack on her shoulder. Just when it seemed like she would wrap her hair into a frazzled knot, I reached up and took her hand.

"It's going to be fine," I said.

"I know," she replied. "I'm sure I'll have no problem convincing my cousins that it wasn't a huge mistake to get involved with a guy from a planet called Dirt,"—Vrynn shot me a sidelong glance with a brief flutter of one eye that almost counted as a wink—"and that they should drop everything and join the uprising against the occupiers."

"Well, thanks for the vote of confidence." I squeezed her hand and returned her wink.

As we entered Neevra, we passed a guard station next to the road. At first, I assumed we would be stopped and searched by a Barchee soldier. But the guard appeared to be lounging, or perhaps sleeping; it was hard to tell through the semi-reflective glass.

From a distance, Vrynn's hometown had seemed like a quaint European village sitting on the side of a gentle green hill. Up close, that impression was reinforced by the tightly packed homes and businesses threaded through with narrow streets and walkways.

The people passing by seemed polite, though not incredibly friendly or open. Most of them looked like Vrynn—fair skin with blue rather than pink or olive tints, and blond hair with blue streaks. As I watched the various townspeople moving along the streets, I realized that Mareesh hair must become more and more blue as they age because all the old people I saw had full heads of dark blue hair.

Vrynn received no more than a cursory glance from most, while I got my fair share of double-takes. Probably because I stuck out like a sore thumb. At least the Mareesh people weren't openly hostile to outsiders.

As we continued down the main street, I did my best not to gape at everything I saw. Dozens of short, narrow vehicles zipped past us in both directions. They resembled cars that had been squeezed through a metal compactor, or like a motor scooter that had been given a protective shell. There were other, larger vehicles with outward-facing seats that would slow down long enough for a pedestrian to quickly hop on or off. But none of the vehicles, big or small, made any noise besides a faint buzz like a high-voltage transformer.

"Why are the roads shimmering?" I asked, pointing at the waves rippling off the gray-colored street.

"The quasarium conduits are transferring energy to the vehicles," Vrynn said matter-of-factly.

My brow knit. That might have been a good explanation to someone who had seen this type of street before, but I was completely baffled.

Vrynn smiled patiently. "The vehicles drive over the street, and it transfers power to them as they go."

"Yeah, I got that part, sort of like the power cable to a trolley car," I said. "But what was the quasar part?"

"Quasarium," Vrynn corrected. "There are conduits running down to the quasarium deposits deep under the island. That's where we get power to run everything."

I nodded. That was enough for me to grasp the general concept.

The houses, which had seemed small and primitive from a distance, were precisely constructed of a smooth reflective substance that I would have thought was some sort of marble except that it also seemed to have metallic characteristics. The colors of the buildings ranged from light gray to pearlescent white. The roofs were a dark metal alloy that reflected steel blue.

The scattered blues and whites actually reminded me of pictures I'd seen of Santorini.

At first, I didn't see windows in any of the buildings, but then I noticed that portions of the walls would turn transparent as I passed. There weren't distinct, inset glass windows. It was as if the molecules of the material had been altered so that they were transparent in only certain directions. It was fascinating.

We rounded a corner, and I got my first glimpse of what I assume were Barchee. At the small sidewalk shop ahead of us stood two soldiers, plasma rifles casually slung over their shoulders. They didn't seem overly concerned about us or any of the other people around us; they were far more intent on the food the shop's proprietor had just handed them.

My initial impression was that they didn't look that different from the Mareesh I'd seen, not surprising considering their recent common ancestry.

The Barchee soldiers were about the same build as the Mareesh men we'd passed—a little shorter than me, but very broadly built. The main difference I could see between the Mareesh and the Barchee was in the tint of the skin. Where the Mareesh skin tone was fair with a blue tint that tended toward water or ice, the Barchee skin tone—at least in these two men—was slightly darker and more on the aqua side. Like the difference between the cold blue of an ice cave and the greenish-blue of a shallow Caribbean lagoon. It was subtle, but distinctive.

Vrynn stiffened when she saw them and pulled me across the street, probably wanting to avoid a face-to-face meeting with Barchee soldiers so soon.

"My cousins live down this way," Vrynn said, pointing to the next street. "Or, at least, they used to."

We continued along, passing more houses and several businesses. It was nothing like the showy, audacious market on New Talpreus or the run-down shops on Rulioa IV. These businesses—if that's really what they were—had simple signs hanging above their doors or etched into their walls. Given that I couldn't read the Mareesh language, it was Greek to me.

"Will your cousins be glad to see you?" I asked, searching for something that might lighten Vrynn's mood.

"They will be pleased to see that I'm alive," she replied shortly.

We walked a block or two in silence, passing another pair of Barchee soldiers who ambled along the other side of the street. I avoided eye contact with them, just in case.

Since arriving in Neevra, Vrynn seemed tense and guarded. Her eyes darted down side streets, and she frequently glanced over her shoulder. I hadn't expected her to be the nervous one; that role had always fallen to me. But being back in her hometown had brought out a side of her

I hadn't seen before. Maybe if I'd experienced the same struggle and sorrow she'd gone through, I might not have been so comfortable with being back in this town either.

"Here it is," Vrynn said as she stopped and faced a smooth, ivory door. She took a breath, raised her hand, and knocked.

Several seconds later, a young man opened the door. Unlike Vrynn's thin, graceful frame, he was more on the stocky side, with broad shoulders and a wide, happy-looking face. He was about half a head shorter than me, still a little taller than Vrynn, though.

He barely glanced at Vrynn before fixing me with a glare. "Can I help you?" he asked.

Vrynn cleared her throat. "Mosai."

He did a double take. "Vrynn?" he asked incredulously.

Vrynn smiled. "How are you, Mo?"

He stepped forward and pulled Vrynn into a rough hug. "Vrynn! I can't believe you're alive!" He dragged her into the house and yelled, "Bryneen! Come see who it is!"

As he attempted to close the door behind them—ready to leave me standing alone out on the doorstep—Vrynn stopped short and held the door. "Mosai, this is my friend Mitch." She grabbed my hand and pulled me forward.

Mosai scowled at me. "Why are you with my cousin?"

Though a little taken aback by his bluntness, I did my best to recover. "I'm her friend. I'm helping her."

Mosai opened his mouth to say something when he was roughly shoved aside by a young woman who could have been Vrynn's body double, only a little younger and not quite as strikingly beautiful.

"Vrynn!" she yelled, nearly bowling her unsuspecting cousin over with a huge hug.

Apparently, energetic embraces ran in the family.

"Bryneen!" Vrynn cried. "You've grown up. The last time I saw you, you were barely hip deep." She held a hand up to indicate the height she remembered.

"I can't believe you're—" Vrynn's cousin noticed me for the first time. But unlike Mosai's immediate skepticism and borderline hostility, this girl ogled me up and down like she was considering a car purchase or appraising a slab of meat. She muttered something that my chip translated as "mountain high."

Vrynn giggled. "Bryneen, this is Mitch." She touched me on the arm. "Mitch, this is my cousin Bryneen."

Was there a specific greeting in Mareesh culture that I was meant to do?

Before I could worry too much about customs, Bryneen moved forward and wrapped her arms around my middle. "You're tall," she said as she gazed up at me. "And you have very red cheeks."

I couldn't help but chuckle nervously as I felt my face heat.

"That's enough, Bryn," Mosai said, pulling her away from me.

I rubbed the back of my neck, glancing around for some distraction from my embarrassment. Vrynn smirked mischievously, which was no help at all.

Mosai positioned himself in front of me, wide stance, hands on his hips. "I feel obligated to tell you that as one of Vrynn's closest relatives, I stand as her barrier," he nodded toward Vrynn. My translator hiccupped and added "guardian," then "protector." I got the general idea. "Are you intending to entangle yourself with my cousin?"

If I didn't already feel awkward enough with this whole situation, Mosai's sudden demand only added to it. "Uh . . . I'm not sure if I . . . understand . . ." I looked at Vrynn, but she only giggled. It made me wish that my embedded chip had the ability to re-explain things when I got flustered.

Finally, Vrynn stepped up next to me, her hand threading through my arm. "Don't worry about Mosai, Mitch. Normally, it would be my father's or uncle's job to stand as my protector. But since I don't have . . ." She trailed off, and I knew why.

She had told me her family had been killed in the original Barchee invasion. I could only assume that meant her father.

The four of us stood in silence for several moments before Bryneen eventually pulled us forward. "Don't stand by the door like strangers. Come in."

Bryneen led us through their home, which was made of the same white material as the exterior. The light from outside seemed to pass through the stone as if the entire structure was a skylight. And yet, it wasn't too bright, just a gentle, ambient glow everywhere.

Vrynn's cousin led us to a set of strange couches—at least, I thought they were couches. The irregularly shaped seats—not round, but not rectangular—were arranged in a circle in the middle of the main room. Despite the unpleasantly lumpy appearance, they were surprisingly comfortable to sit in. After a moment, I realized that the furniture was probably meant to mimic undulating ocean waves. That made sense, given what the planet Mareesh was like.

"Tell us what has happened to you," Bryneen insisted once we were settled. "We thought you were dead."

Vrynn took a deep breath. I knew she didn't relish the idea of recounting her experience during the Barchee invasion. "After we lost the Battle of Mardrys, I hid in a blown-out warehouse near the spaceport," Vrynn said. "I probably should have let you know that I was alive. But I was so angry at the occupiers that I knew I couldn't stay. I had to do something."

"What did you do?" Mosai asked, glancing suspiciously at me, as if I had anything to do with it.

"I stowed away on a cargo transport bound for the Ludros Alpha system," Vrynn said. "I spent the next cycle doing everything I could to sabotage the occupation."

"What could you possibly do from Ludros?" Bryneen asked.

Vrynn shrugged. "Not much, really. I watched for shipments bound for Barchee, and I tried to destroy them."

"You destroyed ships on their way to Barchee?" Mosai asked incredulously.

Vrynn's cheeks tinted blue. "No. I was just a stupid girl hiding in the slums near the spaceport. All I could do was make cracks in the containers or throw rodents in the food boxes. I doubt it made much difference."

"I bet someone on Barchee had a bad day when they found a rat in their food," I quipped. Vrynn smiled at me and squeezed my hand.

Mosai narrowed his eyes at me. "And when did you meet the big outsider?" He tilted his head toward me.

"Spaceport security caught me trying to sabotage the fuel system of a transport bound for Barchee. They took me to a holding cell where they said the police would come to deal with me."

"And what happened?" Bryneen asked.

"A man in an official uniform showed up and took me away," Vrynn replied. "But instead of taking me to the police. He dropped me off in a dark alley where two operatives met me."

Mosai must have forgotten his annoyance with me. "Operatives of what?" he asked.

"They said they had noticed my efforts to fight the Barchee occupation, and they wanted to put that energy to better use. They recruited me to the Resistance."

Bryneen's eyes popped wide. "You joined the Resistance? Is that why you never came back?"

Vrynn nodded slowly.

Mosai scowled at me again. "And is this one of the mercenaries who corrupted you?"

Vrynn laughed. "No. Mitch is just a regular guy who stumbled on the starship we needed."

"He doesn't look very regular," Mosai said.

"Hey. I'm sitting right here," I said playfully.

Vrynn gave me one of her adorable, overdone winks, obviously compensating for her too-subtle previous attempt. She turned back to Bryneen and Mosai. "No. Mitch and I met entirely by accident. He's not even from the Bonara Cluster."

Mosai nodded slowly, as if this news confirmed his suspicions. Bryneen, on the other hand, reacted like I was suddenly the most exotic, interesting thing she'd ever seen.

Vrynn told the story of how she had been sent to a rendezvous point to wait for the delivery of a top-secret starship, but that she'd waited for weeks and no delivery had come. "When he finally got there—five weeks late—I was so excited to see someone, that it took me a while to realize he wasn't with the Resistance," Vrynn said.

"I wasn't late; I wasn't even supposed to be there," I declared. "And if I recall correctly, when you did realize I wasn't with the Resistance, you pulled your blaster on me and threatened to shoot me and steal my ship."

"It was supposed to be *my* ship," Vrynn corrected.

I squeezed her hand again, knowing we had come to a sort of truce on that one. Hearing Vrynn recount our initial meeting made me realize how fortunate I was to have met her at all. I shifted myself closer to her.

Mosai scowled. Bryneen sighed.

"Are all men from your planet like you?" Bryneen asked.

The collar of my flight suit suddenly felt very tight. "Uh, what do you mean?"

"Are they all tall and strong and handsome?" Her words came out a little breathless.

"Bryneen," Vrynn said, her tone a clear warning to her cousin.

Bryneen straightened, attempting to not look besotted with me.

I decided to try and smooth things over. "Actually, there are hundreds of men on Earth, probably even thousands, that are taller, stronger, and more handsome than I am." Hopefully I was selling Bryneen on the idea that I was definitely a small fish.

She simply shook her head. "Unbelievable."

Vrynn gave a satisfied little laugh and threaded her arm through mine.

I was eager to change the subject. "So, are you two cousins as well?" I waved a hand between Bryneen and Mosai.

"Siblings," Bryneen replied, still gazing at me a little starry-eyed.

"Do you have any other family around?" I asked, trying to make small talk.

I could feel Vrynn tense at my side.

"Their father, my uncle, was also killed during the Barchee invasion." A somber mood accompanied Vrynn's words.

So much for small talk.

After a few seconds of silence, Vrynn took a deep breath and leaned toward her cousins. "That's why we're here. We've come back to fight the Barchee."

Mosai's expression shifted to one of surprise. "What? Why?"

Vrynn's brow knit in confusion. "Because our towns are being occupied and our people oppressed."

"You've been gone a long time," Mosai said as he relaxed back in his seat.

"Barely eight years," she shot back.

"Yeah, and things have changed," Mosai said, waving a hand toward the street outside. "Look around. We're not slaves here. The Barchee treat us well. No one wants to fight anymore, especially not our planet-cousins."

"Planet-cousins?" Vrynn sounded as perplexed as I was.

"The Barchee," Bryneen answered. "They aren't some alien force coming down to destroy us. They're our people."

"Exactly," Mosai added. "And why would we fight our own people?"

Vrynn gaped at them, shifting her gaze from one to the other, then back. "They're not our people. They're our enemy!"

Mosai folded his arms. "You don't understand," he declared emphatically.

"I understand they killed my parents!" Vrynn yelled at him. "They killed my brother and your father and your sister!" She was on her feet now, fists clenched at her sides.

Her cousin jumped from his seat, too. "No one knows what really happened, Vrynn. The Battle of Mardrys was a horrible mistake."

Vrynn jerked back as if she'd been slapped. Her eyes narrowed. "How could you say that?" she whispered.

Holding her hands out toward Vrynn and Mosai, Bryneen yelled, "Please stop fighting. It won't change anything."

Vrynn and Mosai glared at each other, chests heaving with emotion. After a few moments, they both sat.

Bryneen gave Vrynn a pleading look. "But, truly, Vrynn, we are fine here now. We're safe. The war is over. Governor Gralik brought peace to the islands."

My jaw dropped. "Governor Gralik?!"

Bryneen appeared taken aback at my outburst. She nodded firmly. "Gralik stopped the war with the Barchee."

"Oh, really?" Vrynn interjected. "Then why are the Barchee still here?".

"To protect us," Bryneen said without missing a beat.

"From what?" Vrynn shot back.

Bryneen didn't seem to have an answer to that question. She just stared defiantly back at us. Vrynn turned to Mosai for an explanation. He shrugged but didn't reply.

I was dumbfounded. Speechless. How could Bryneen not know what was happening on her planet? From the fire in Vrynn's eyes, I could tell she felt the same.

Then another thought occurred to me. "Hang on. How can Gralik be the governor of a planet? He's in the BDF, commander of the Vanguard Dragoons, plus he has a base on Zerlon. When would he ever be on Mareesh?"

"He's not here all the time," Bryneen replied defensively. "He does have other duties that take him away sometimes."

I hadn't heard Gralik spoken of so favorably since my meeting with Sergeant Zondy and Corporal Kyuli on Varus Prime. But it was all the more surprising to hear it from someone who should hate the man as much as Vrynn did.

"Bryn, I need to tell you something that might be hard to hear." Vrynn scooted to the edge of her seat and reached for Bryneen's hand. "Everything you know about Gralik is wrong," she said in a calm, patient voice. "He didn't stop the Battle of Mardrys. Gralik is the one who betrayed our people. He was sent by the BDF to fight the Barchee, but instead, he helped them take over our islands."

"That's not what happened," Bryneen replied. "Gralik saved us. That's why they made him our governor. Right, Mosai?"

Uncertainty flashed across Mosai's face, replaced a moment later by stubborn determination. Ignoring his sister, he said to Vrynn, "At least the war is over. No one is dying anymore."

"That's not the same thing as being free," Vrynn answered.

"Sometimes it's better to be alive," Mosai shot back.

Vrynn scowled at her cousin. "What happened to you?" she asked. "What happened to the warrior who fought at my side to defend our islands from the Barchee?" She sounded more sad than angry.

Mosai's expression spoke of slowly awakening memories that had faded over the years. "That was a long time ago, Vrynn," he whispered.

Vrynn's gaze drifted away, her eyes unfocused. "I remember like it was yesterday."

In the silence that followed, Bryneen looked from Mosai to Vrynn, then back. Her brow furrowed as she scrutinized her brother. "Mosai?" Bryneen waited until she had her brother's attention. "You didn't answer my question. Is Vrynn right about Gralik?"

The truth—and his knowledge of it—were obvious in Mosai's pained expression.

"You mean it's true?!" Bryneen exclaimed.

Mosai held a hand out to his sister. "You have to understand that those who survived the battle, those of us who stayed behind"—he shot Vrynn a withering glare—"had to learn to face reality. We adapted. We changed the way we felt about the Barchee, and we taught the children to think the same way." He indicated Bryneen. "Otherwise, the hatred and resentment would have consumed us."

Bryneen blinked several times, as if trying to process what she was hearing. Then her eyes lost focus, and she stared at nothing for several seconds.

Vrynn reached over and grabbed Bryneen's hand. "I'm so sorry, Bryn," she said, her eyes welling up with tears. "I'm so sorry for the way things turned out. I'm sorry I left you behind. That I abandoned our people." She exhaled a shaky breath. "But I'm here now, and I want to fix it," Vrynn added, eyes fixed firmly on her young cousin.

A moment later, Bryneen pulled Vrynn into a hug. "I'm so glad you came back," she whispered.

The cousins held the embrace for a long while, until they finally sat back down, each wiping tears away from blue-stained cheeks.

"Just know that this doesn't change anything," Mosai declared emphatically. He glanced at Bryneen as he considered his next words. "We can help you look for people crazy enough to join your little rebellion, but that's it. We're not getting involved beyond that."

Bryneen wheeled on her brother. "What are you talking about? This changes everything. I just found out that my people aren't free. I plan to do something about it!" she declared with fiery intensity.

"No," Mosai said firmly. "We aren't going to fight." He turned his attention back to us. "That's all I can offer you. If you're not willing to accept that, then you're on your own. Maybe you can go find the rogue ship that's been attacking the supply convoys and join up with them."

I barked out a short laugh before I could stop myself.

Vrynn fought a smile. "That won't add any more strength to our cause," she told her cousins, "because that's us."

"You're the ones attacking the Barchee transports?" Bryneen asked incredulously. She almost sounded a little inspired by it.

Vrynn nodded.

Mosai shot to his feet. "This is really bad."

"Why?" Vrynn asked. "You knew we were here to fight the occupation."

"Yeah, but not like that." Mosai stepped toward us. "Governor Gralik's last daily broadcast said that when that starship is caught, they—and anyone who has helped them—will be executed."

My stomach sank at that news. Gralik's feelings toward us weren't exactly a huge surprise, but he'd taken it a step further. That threat would turn the entire population of Mareesh against us before we'd even organized our uprising.

"Do you realize the trouble we could all be in if the Barchee soldiers find out you're here?" Mosai asked, running a hand through his hair.

"I thought you said they protect you," Vrynn said. "That you don't fight any more." Her tone was thick with contempt.

"Yeah, but only if you follow their rules." Mosai nodded wildly, as if the situation should be obvious to us. "Vrynn, you can stay; you're less likely to draw attention. But he has to leave right now." He tilted his head in my direction.

I had to admit, there was a certain logic to Mosai's crazy rant. And for my part, I'd certainly feel much safer back in the cavern with the *Starfire*.

"Mosai, wait." Bryneen said.

Mosai stopped and turned to his sister.

"Vrynn was right. We're scared of the Barchee,"—Bryneen indicated his frantic behavior—"and that's not freedom. If everything she said is true, then we have to fight to get our freedom back."

Mosai leaned toward her. "Bryn, this is crazy talk," he said harshly. "We're not going to change anything by causing trouble. The only thing that's going to happen is we'll end up getting ourselves killed."

"Like Papa." Bryneen's voice cracked on the word, but the determination in her deep blue eyes burned bright.

"Bryn, no. Don't do this," he pleaded with her.

Bryneen squared her shoulders, her back straight and proud. "Papa fought and died for us to live free. Are we going to drop that in the water?"

Some of Mosai's bravado faded. "I'm supposed to keep you safe," he whispered. "I promised Papa I would."

Bryneen fixed her gaze on him. "I'm not a little girl anymore, Mosai. I'm old enough to make my own choices. Besides,"—she gave a small shrug—"if we fight for our freedom and meet the same fate as Papa, we'll be with him and Mama in the Afternow. Would that really be so bad?"

Mosai's expression slowly morphed from disapproval to resignation. He shook his head. "I suppose not." He pulled his sister into an embrace. "I think Mama and Papa would be proud of the woman you've become."

After a moment, Bryneen turned to her cousin. "Thank you, Vrynn," she said, her chin still resting on Mosai's shoulder.

Vrynn rushed forward and joined the family hug. I stood there awkwardly, wondering if I should look away or join the circle. They broke their embrace and Mosai turned his attention to me.

"Just because we're ready to get our freedom back, doesn't mean we should just dive into this head-first." Mosai gave me a withering glare, as if the whole Barchee occupation was somehow my fault. "There's only four of us. We can't take on an entire army."

Vrynn smiled at him. "Yeah, but I know there are others who will want to fight back," she said. "We just have to find them."

For the next several hours, we traipsed through town, visiting friends of Mosai and Bryneen. I noticed Barchee soldiers patrolling the streets, but they didn't appear overly hostile. Vrynn couldn't believe we were just walking past them without trying to hide.

"If you don't act suspicious," Bryneen said, "they won't have any reason to pay attention to you."

"It's hard not to act suspicious when armed alien guards are patrolling the streets of my hometown," Vrynn muttered.

On our excursion, I also caught glimpses of a few people who definitely weren't Barchee or Mareesh. That made sense in a space-faring society. It also explained why I hadn't been immediately apprehended and thrown in jail. The town must have received enough off-world visitors that my presence was a curiosity but not an oddity.

As we visited Mosai and Bryneen's friends and extended family, we were primarily met with subdued indifference. Most didn't understand our reasons for wanting to fight the occupation. And those that did remember what true freedom was like seemed content to tolerate the current situation rather than make waves. A very few went as far as offering tentative support—assuming they didn't have to be the first ones to fight.

Rather a disappointing insurrection so far.

As we walked the outskirts of the town, Vrynn turned to Mosai. "What about Natheem and Hustan? I can't imagine they've given up the fight; they were some of the bravest soldiers in the regiment."

Mosai shook his head. "Yeah. And their bravery got them rounded up and thrown in the Barchee prison on Mardrys."

"I heard Natheem had been released, but I think Hustan is still in," Bryneen said.

Mosai simply shrugged.

"And Sharlee?" Vrynn asked.

Bryneen gave a small sigh. "She was always lovesick for Hustan, saying she couldn't live if he wasn't free. She went to Mardrys to break him out, but we haven't seen either of them since."

We continued along the wide, outer road, as the rest of the group brainstormed what could be done to start an insurrection. I didn't have much to contribute, so I simply admired the gorgeous emerald-green landscape around us. It reminded me of pictures I'd seen of Ireland, all green meadows, mossy rocks, and windswept beauty.

"We really need Chief Commander Raveel," Vrynn said. "He would know what to do."

"But Raveel is dead," Mosai said.

"Actually," Bryneen began. "There are rumors that—"

Mosai cut her off. "They're just rumors. None of the Mareesh leaders survived the Battle of Mardrys."

Bryneen scowled at her brother, but said nothing.

"Then we need the highest ranking officer who survived," Vrynn said. "What was the name of that batty old lieutenant who was always hanging around the commanders? The one who thought she could use a disguise to infiltrate the Barchee forces?"

"You mean Keelsa?" Mosai laughed. "Oh, she's still around. But if you thought she was a little crazy before, the occupation has made it much worse."

Vrynn's hopeful expression faded.

We walked along the edge of a fenced field with some kind of grain growing in it. The town of Neevra sat a little higher in the valley than the others, and the view was amazing. Narrow gray roads wound like ribbons across green cropland. Some of the towns appeared a little larger than Neevra, but there were others even smaller. Vehicles, large and small, flowed smoothly along the roads like blood through veins.

Vrynn stopped walking and blew out a long breath. "Do we have any other options?"

"It's not too late to pretend none of this ever happened and go back to our peaceful lives," Mosai offered hopefully.

Bryneen elbowed him.

Vrynn glanced around and lowered her voice. "Clearly, we can't start an uprising with only the four of us," she said with quiet determination. "Maybe Keelsa knows people who would be willing to join the effort."

"It's a train ride to the other side of Syr." Mosai's tone sounded like he was trying to talk us out of it. "Plus, I'm telling you, she's crazy."

"Crazy never bothered us, right?" Vrynn gave me a nearly passable wink. "We might be a little crazy ourselves."

For my translator chip to use the word "train" to describe the vehicle we rode across the island would be like calling a giant roller coaster a nice little trolley. The passenger enclosure was shaped like a bullet, but with a strange plasma emitter at the tip. When we started moving, there was almost no rocking or bumping.

I leaned over to Mosai. "Is it magnetic levitation?"

His brow furrowed as his chip translated my words. Finally, his expression cleared, and he gave me a look one might give to a child who was just learning about basic science.

"It's actually a gravitational inversion field," Mosai explained. "The gravity well created at the front of the train pulls the car, and the surrounding air, forward along the power line."

Maybe a different topic wouldn't make me seem so clueless. "What are the chances this Keelsa person will actually be able to help us?" I asked.

Mosai cleared his throat and puffed out his chest slightly. "Keelsa was never all that high up within the Steadfast Army of the Mareesh Islands."

A short laugh escaped my mouth when the phrase "Steadfast Army of the Mareesh Islands" came out at high speed, crunched into less than a second. I'd experienced changes in speaking speed as my chip tried to fit long, translated phrases into the space of fewer, originally spoken words, but nothing this extreme.

"What's so funny?" Mosai asked, scowling at me.

I shook my head. "It's nothing. Just that 'Steadfast Army of the Mareesh Islands' must be much shorter in Mareesh."

His expression relaxed a little. "I would have thought you were mocking our army, except that I've never heard anyone say its name so slowly." He eyed me for another second before continuing. "Anyway, Keelsa was a mid-level lieutenant in our regiment, and one of the few who avoided prison. She might be aware of efforts to fight the occupation. Assuming she's still sane," he added under his breath.

After a short, four-minute trip—flashing by at least five other small towns, their white buildings gleaming in the sunlight—we reached Leenai on the opposite side of the island. To me, it looked just like Neevra, except some of the houses were larger, and the streets were busier. Mosai and Bryneen led us to the outskirts of town, beyond most of the buildings, where there were only footpaths and rocks.

"Are we sure this is the one?" I asked when they stopped in front of a shack on the verge of falling apart.

"I told you this might not be worth the effort," Mosai said as he tapped on the front door.

Several seconds later, a woman opened it an inch or two and peered at us through the crack like a paranoid hermit. Apparently we didn't look too threatening because she pulled the door farther open. Her hair was mostly blue with platinum streaks, but it was much shorter than Vrynn's or Bryneen's and probably hadn't been brushed in months. She had pale skin and bright blue eyes.

"Do you have my garbage?" she asked in a slightly deranged voice.

Mosai might have been right about her waning sanity.

"Keelsa. It's me. Mosai." He placed a hand softly against his chest.

It took a moment, but the woman finally reacted. "You know Keelsa?" she asked, suddenly very animated.

"Yes, we do," Mosai said. "We're friends of hers. Can we come in and visit?"

She nodded emphatically and threw the door open wide. "Yes, friends of Keelsa come here. Yes, come in, come in. You can wait until she gets back."

"Is that not Keelsa?" I whispered to Vrynn as we stepped over the threshold into the house.

"It is," she replied. "I just don't remember her being this crazy."

"Come sit on the piles of things," Keelsa said, motioning to several pieces of worn furniture.

We settled in, most of us staring at Keelsa as she fiddled with her ratty blue hair. She glanced back and forth from Vrynn's cousins to us.

"So, why have you come to visit Keelsa? If I may ask," Keelsa said.

Vrynn leaned forward, gazing intently at her. "We need your help. We're fighting the Barchee, but we can't do it with only four."

Keelsa let loose a rather eerie cackle. "Many people come to visit Keelsa, hoping she will start a fight with the occupiers." She glanced at the four of us in turn. "They are always disappointed."

"Well, at least we tried," I said as I put my hands on my knees, preparing to stand.

Vrynn grabbed my arm to stop me. She returned her attention to Keelsa. "Please, we need your help. We know there are others who would be willing to fight the Barchee, but we don't know how to safely find them."

As Vrynn spoke, Keelsa's nervous movements became more pronounced. Her wild eyes darted back and forth, then focused directly on Vrynn. "You must find the others," she whispered.

"The others?" Mosai asked.

"Keelsa's friends," Keelsa said, searching the room. "But I shouldn't say anything more. Keelsa wouldn't like it."

"You mean the other fighters?" Bryneen prompted.

Keelsa nodded vigorously, as if she really couldn't say anything else.

"Are they around here?" Bryneen asked.

Keelsa shook her head.

"All the fighters are in prison," Mosai muttered to his sister.

Keelsa broke her temporary silence. "Not all. Not Natheem. Not Bleesha."

Mosai shrugged. "Maybe Natheem did get out," he whispered to us with a conspiratorial smile.

"Find them! Find Natheem!" Keelsa bellowed.

We all flinched at Keelsa's sudden outburst, and my heart nearly jumped out of my chest.

Vrynn recovered first. "Where?"

Keelsa's voice suddenly dropped to almost a whisper. "Near the five crossings. Where the final barricades fell. You'll find him when high tide comes to the streets."

What was Keelsa talking about? Were there enough non-crazy thoughts in her head that she could actually be giving us a clue?

"The ocean doesn't come inside the city of Mardrys. How could there be a high tide?" Mosai asked.

Keelsa stood abruptly. "Find Keelsa's friends. That's all I can say."

The four of us instinctively rose when she did, and by unspoken agreement, quickly shuffled to the door and left the house.

Standing out on the wide road, Mosai summed up the experience. "That was the strangest thing I've ever seen. I had no idea someone could get that crazy."

"Are you sure she's crazy?" Bryneen asked. "She did mention Natheem."

"She might not even know the occupation is still going on, much less whether Natheem is still in prison or not." Mosai turned thoughtful. "Of course, Natheem was in the regiment with us. If he is out of prison, he would be a good person to make contact with."

Bryneen lifted a shoulder. "We could do worse."

"Maybe Keelsa was trying to give us a clue through her madness," Vrynn said as we walked away from Keelsa's home. "If we can find Natheem, maybe we'll find others who'll be willing to join the fight."

Bryneen nodded enthusiastically. "We're with you."

"Obviously, I'm in," I said.

Mosai heaved a long sigh. "Yeah, I guess we might as well."

"Great." Vrynn smiled. "Now, how do we figure out what her clues meant?"

Chapter Twelve

Our time with Mosai and Bryneen had taken the entire day and most of my energy. By the time we made the trip back to Neevra and the walk to the cavern, I was completely exhausted. But there was one more thing I'd needed to do. Before saying goodnight to Tera and Gabe and falling into my bed, I sent off a quick message to Shariamy asking for some sort of explanation as to why Gralik had been appointed governor of Mareesh.

The next morning, Vrynn and I set off for Neevra again, this time dressed in simple Mareesh clothing Bryneen had given us. We met her cousins at the train terminus in the center of town and boarded the rapid transport bound for Mardrys. Vrynn and Mosai were absolutely certain that the clue from Keelsa referred to a location in the capital city, where the final skirmish in the Battle of Mardrys had taken place.

I stared out the window as we rocketed along the countryside. About twenty minutes into our trip, the rocky greenery suddenly changed to water as we left the northern tip of Vrynn's home island. Not being able to see the front of the train, or anything beneath us, I assumed we were riding on some sort of track above the water. Obviously, the train didn't actually need to touch anything—what with the inverted gravity field or whatever—but I assumed the train needed something to guide it and transfer power to it.

The view from my window was spectacular as we sped along forty feet above the water. Waves tumbled and crashed against nearby rock formations. Pretty soon, the rock clusters became fewer and farther between and all I could see was a wide expanse of ocean, its waves towering at least ten feet high and blue-capped.

As the slopes of the central island of Mardrys, home of the capital city, came into view, I leaned against the window to get a better look. It looked like a giant volcano that had had its top chopped off. I'd already seen the rest of Mardrys from the air, including the plasma grid that covered the opening of the caldera and protected the city. But it was interesting to see the island up close from this perspective.

I caught a glimpse of the front of the train as we rounded a gentle bend.

There was indeed a bridge with regular vehicles traveling back and forth between the islands. But the train didn't touch the bridge. It wasn't even close. We floated along through the air more than a dozen feet above the regular cars and trucks. I blinked to make sure I wasn't hallucinating. Apparently, the gravity vortex field thingy was more advanced than my brain was ready for. I decided not to look too closely or wonder what would happen if we suddenly lost power, focusing my attention on our destination instead. Up ahead, there was a giant hole carved into the side of the rocky caldera wall.

A minute later, the train was swallowed by the short tunnel, and the cabin was temporarily plunged into darkness for several seconds before bursting out of the tunnel into the interior of the Mardrys caldera.

Hundreds—actually thousands—of buildings of various shapes and sizes crowded the basin of the bowl-shaped island. And they didn't only cover the floor of the caldera. Some were perched higher up, on the sloping side walls.

From watching convoy transports and escorts disappear through the gap in the side of the mountain, I knew the general location of the spaceport. I craned my neck to see the other side of the island, hoping to catch a glimpse of the Barchee military base from inside the Mardrys caldera.

A narrow crack in the caldera wall, much larger than the tunnel we had just passed through, marked the location of the spaceport landing strip. I couldn't really see the runway, but I could see the buildings around it, noticeably different from the regular civilian buildings because of their larger size and boring, rectangular shapes.

Another geographical feature of the capital city quickly caught my attention. Very close to the spaceport military base, a round plateau shape rose from the valley floor. On top of the small hill, there was a beautiful building made of the same pearlescent white material I'd seen before. It had three terraced levels, almost like a wedding cake, and even from this distance, I could see waterfalls and fountains accentuating the design.

"What's that?" I asked Vrynn.

She leaned over to see what I was looking at. "That's the capitol building. The Mareesh government was run from there." She turned away, her expression somber. "The occupiers use it now."

I tried to imagine what I would feel like if my nation's capital had been taken over by enemies and I was forced to submit to their government. It was difficult to fathom.

The train's path brought us lower toward the caldera floor into a canyon of buildings. Unlike the one- and two-story homes and stores of Neevra or Leenai, tall, sleek buildings crowded together in the center of the capital city, their gleaming white surfaces shining brilliantly in the sunlight.

The train's speed slowed, and a voice announced, "Mardrys City."

The occupants of the train stood as it slowed to a stop.

I followed Vrynn and her cousins, filing out with the other passengers. We moved across the platform and out onto the city street, then Mosai pulled us down a nearby lane, heading in the general direction of where I thought the spaceport was.

He turned right and left, ducking under low archways and sliding through narrow alleys. Finally, Mosai stopped at a narrow intersection. "This is where we made our final stand."

Except for Mosai's assertion about its historical significance, I wouldn't have thought twice about this intersection. It looked no different than any other.

"Look at this," Bryneen said, pointing to the faded wall of a nearby alley. The faint line of a high-water mark was barely visible about ankle high.

We walked into the alley, watching the water line rise along the wall as the road sloped gently downward. The line reached a lone, nondescript door and stopped. I looked up and down the alley, trying to figure out what could be inside the building on the other side of the door. To me, it looked like a warehouse or some kind of processing facility.

Mosai glanced over his shoulder at the group, shrugged, and rapped smartly on the door. A second later, a mean-looking guy opened the door, scowling at us. I waited for someone to explain who we were. But before we had the chance, the large man lunged into the alley and grabbed Mosai.

I stepped forward to intervene, but the sound of muffled laughter stopped me.

"Natheem, you're crushing me," Mosai said with a wheeze.

The large man, Natheem, pulled back. "You know I can't hold back when I'm happy." He was nearly my height, the tallest Mareesh I'd seen so far, and built like a linebacker. He set Mosai back down and patted his shoulders. "It's so good to see you, Mosai."

"When did you get out of prison?" Mosai asked as Bryneen moved forward to hug Natheem. Maybe he was a friend of the family.

"About four years ago." At the expressions of surprise from Mosai and Bryneen, he added. "I decided to stay in Mardrys because I thought I could do more good here."

"Well, we're just glad you're out," Bryneen said. "Even if you didn't drop in for a visit," she added under her breath.

Natheem chuckled. "So are the Barchee. They got tired of my appetite"—he patted his ample middle—"and decided I wasn't enough of a threat to keep feeding."

Natheem laughed, and Mosai and Bryneen joined in. Until that moment, I hadn't noticed that Vrynn had been hiding behind me. She stepped into the open, putting her hand in mine, and Natheem's laughter died almost immediately.

The large man blinked several times. "Vrynn?"

"Hi Natheem," she replied.

He stared at her as if she was a ghost. He must have caught sight of our clasped hands because his face turned somber. He scrutinized me, his expression something like resignation or possibly loathing; it was hard to read.

Whatever it was, he clamped it down and stepped backward, throwing the door open wide. "Come inside. We should talk."

We moved past him into a large open space, scattered with piles of equipment and trash. There were several vehicles on the opposite side, and a handful of Mareesh dressed in grimy clothes. Maybe Natheem ran a hole-in-the-wall chop shop.

"What was that about?" I whispered to Vrynn.

She glanced over her shoulder at Natheem. "We used to splash together, and I think he's mad that I left without telling him."

I frowned, hoping my translator chip would help out, but it didn't. "Splashed together?" I asked, considering the large Mareesh man moving toward us.

Seeing the obvious confusion on my face, Vrynn smiled. "It means we liked each other when we were young."

I felt a sudden rush of jealousy as I imagined Vrynn and Natheem frolicking together in the surf on some beautiful tropical island.

Vrynn brought me back from my thoughts by saying, "Don't you have a phrase on Dirt for when you like each other as kids?"

I shrugged, hoping my feelings didn't show on my face. "Yeah. We would say you were crushing on each other."

"Crushing?" Vrynn scowled at the word. "That sounds terrifying. What is it with your people and rocks and dirt?"

I opened my mouth to say that her culture was just as bad with water references, but Natheem joined us, his arms folded across his chest, curiosity evident in his expression.

Vrynn jumped right in. "We need help, Natheem," she said. "We're hoping you know people who want to fight the occupation."

Natheem scratched at the back of his neck. "I spent four years in prison for fighting the Barchee. And now, after four years of freedom, you think I want to risk going back?"

Vrynn stared at him. "I bet you'd fight for our freedom again if you wanted it badly enough."

Natheem let out a short laugh that indicated she'd guessed right. "Yeah, that's true," he said. Then his expression turned more serious. "But what makes you think things are any different than they were eight years ago?" The phrase "eight years ago" was clearly a barb directed at Vrynn.

Like so many other things, Vrynn didn't let it faze her. "We have a buried tool now." A second later my translator clarified, "... secret weapon." Vrynn tilted her head over her shoulder, in the direction that I assumed was back toward the island of Syr where the *Starfire* was still hidden.

Natheem turned his attention to me, eyeing me up and down. "This is your buried tool?" he asked incredulously.

Vrynn's cheeks colored. "No. Well, yes." She squeezed my hand tighter. "He's part of it. This is Mitch. He found a starship on his planet that is powerful enough to help us win our war against the occupiers."

Natheem eyed me again. "Well, he's tall; that might be an asset when peeking over walls. At least, that's what they always told me." He elbowed Mosai as if he'd just told a hilarious joke. He turned to me. "So, Buried Tool, are you ready to subvert the occupiers?"

I didn't want Vrynn's childhood boyfriend thinking he could scare me. I puffed out my chest. "Yeah, I'm ready. In fact, while you've been sitting around down here, I've been fighting the Barchee up there." I nodded toward the sky.

Natheem huffed as if he wasn't impressed. "Shipments from Barchee are coming in more regularly again," he said, completely oblivious to the connection between our recent change in tactics and the resumption of convoy activity. Vrynn and I shared a knowing look. "We've got spies watching for trucks from the spaceport. Maybe you could help us hijack one."

"Let's do it," Vrynn said enthusiastically.

"Hang on. Do we have a plan?" I asked. "Have you ever hijacked one of these shipments?"

Natheem and Mosai stared at me for a few seconds, then Natheem leaned over and whispered something to Mosai. He snickered, and I could feel my cheeks heat.

"Don't worry Buried Tool," Natheem said, "We hijack a truck every day. All you have to do is drive, then jump, then drive some more."

That sounded easy enough. "Fine, I can help you hijack a truck," I said, attempting to project more bravado than I actually felt. "When do we leave?"

"Five minutes ago," declared a woman's voice from behind us.

We all turned as the door slammed open, a medium-sized silhouette framed in the opening. The person stepped forward and I couldn't believe my eyes.

"Keelsa?" Vrynn said as the woman approached our group.

She simply nodded. Her hair was still wild, but her eyes held a clarity that told me she had complete control of her faculties. Her gait was labored, but steady.

"What's going on here?" Mosai asked, confusion obvious on his face.

"She was pretending," Bryneen muttered to herself.

Mosai's brow furrowed. "Pretending?"

"Pretending to be crazy so they wouldn't lock her up," Bryneen said.

Keelsa smiled at her. "Prison might be fun,"—she cast a glance at Natheem, who shrugged awkwardly—"but I can do much more damage out here, in the free air." She held her hands out above her head.

"But why pretend with us?" Vrynn asked. "We're your allies. We want to help you."

Keelsa considered Vrynn. "Oh, I've had plenty of supposed allies come to me since the occupation began. Some pretending to be friends but really spying for the enemy. Others wanting to help but lacking determination." She pounded a fisted hand against the other. "I had to know you were truly willing to fight."

"I could still be a spy," I pointed out, though that probably wasn't incredibly helpful at the moment.

Keelsa gave me a wry smile. "Maybe you are. But I doubt it. You're with Vrynn, and she's fresh water." My chip tweaked it to "good people." She tilted her head toward Mosai. "And I'm glad this one has finally decided to rejoin the fight."

"The war was over," Mosai complained. "We lost."

"If the Barchee are still here, High Tide will push them back," Keelsa raised a fist above her head. Natheem copied the gesture.

Apparently, High Tide was the name of the rebel group, not the oceanic event.

"But enough of all that. We're behind schedule. Natheem." Keelsa turned her attention to the broad man. "Prepare for the hijacking."

Natheem stiffened to attention. "Yes, ma'am," he said with a smile. He ran over to the small group of what I now understood to be freedom fighters gathered around a collection of trucks and light attack vehicles, or the Mareesh versions of them, anyway.

Keelsa returned her attention to us. "The occupiers take one of four routes from the spaceport to the depot. Usually we can only cover three, but with you here, we can do all four."

Vrynn nodded. She seemed ready and eager to spring into action. "Just tell us what to do."

"One person drives the vehicle, bringing it close enough to the supply truck for the others to jump on board." Keelsa gestured excitedly with her hands, showing us the maneuver. "Overpower the driver, commandeer the truck, and then we've got them." She clapped her hands together with a whoop.

"And then what?" Bryneen asked.

Keelsa gave her a patronizing smile. "We keep the supplies, of course. Or we give them to the people." She flailed her arms, miming throwing things. "We'll worry about that later."

This woman must also be one of the "sky eyes" people that Vrynn mentioned. Her method of planning reminded me a lot of Vrynn's style.

"Now, go get them," Keelsa said. "And stay in radio contact. That's important in case you are on the route of the supply truck."

Vrynn nodded and started toward the waiting vehicles, immediately taking the driver's spot on the last empty one. I jumped into the seat next to her, and Mosai and Bryneen hopped into the back.

I examined the interior of the car. It wasn't too different from cars on Earth, except that it appeared to have been built for utility rather than comfort. The seats were hard, and the sides were open—no doors at all.

"First time in a Veechu?" Mosai asked.

I frowned. "What's a Veechu?"

"It's a deep-sea predator," he replied. "The military named their rough utility vehicle after it. Don't you have army vehicles on Dirt?"

"Yeah, but they're named after their own acronyms," I said with a chuckle.

As the other teams prepared, I leaned over to Vrynn. "So, I'm curious; how serious was this 'splashing around' between you and Natheem?" I tried to keep my tone casual, as if I didn't really care what her answer was.

She gave me a mischievous smirk, probably to make me think it had been more serious than it really was. At least, that's what I hoped it meant.

A moment later, the warehouse doors opened, and Vrynn gunned the motor to keep up with the other teams. We all grabbed hand grips as the vehicle rounded the first corner at excessively high speed. The route we had been assigned was the highest road that looped around inside of the caldera wall. Vrynn drove to our assigned spot and steered the car onto a narrow pull off adjacent to the road.

We had been waiting for about ten minutes when the call came over the radio.

"Team two has the lucky route today." Keelsa made it sound like she was announcing the winning lottery number. "All other teams return to base."

Vrynn's shoulders sagged with the news, and I patted her arm. "We'll get our chance soon enough."

Vrynn sighed and nodded, pulling us onto the main road, heading back toward the Barchee base. We hadn't gone more than half a mile when Vrynn stiffened at the controls. "There's another one."

I glanced at the road ahead of us and saw a large lumbering vehicle matching the images Keelsa had shown us. "Are we sure that's a Barchee transport truck?"

"It sure looks like one," Bryneen said, squinting out the front windshield.

The truck trundled past us, two soldiers—a driver and a guard—sitting in the cab. "Barchee soldiers!" Mosai yelled. "It is a supply truck!"

Vrynn slammed the controls to the side, sending our Veechu into a half spin. Then she mashed the throttle forward, leaving skid marks on the road behind us. We'd gone from empty-handed to hot-pursuit in ten seconds flat.

I clung on for dear life as we careened around a hair-pin turn. The driver of the truck must have seen our U-turn because he immediately poured on the speed, at least, as much speed as a wide, heavy-laden truck could manage.

Vrynn quickly closed the distance, maneuvering so that the driver side was closest to the back of the truck.

"It would be easier for us to jump on the truck if you pull up to the other side," I said.

She gave me a devious, side-long glance. "This stick is to steer. This lever is the throttle," Vrynn said to me in all seriousness.

"What?!" I asked in disbelief.

She veered to avoid colliding with the zigzagging truck, then she huffed her frustration. "This stick is—"

"I heard you," I yelled over the wind coming in through the open sides. "I just can't believe you're giving me my first Veechu driving lesson right before you're about to jump out."

"Do you want me to wait until after I jump out to give you the instructions?" Vrynn shot me an impish grin.

A soldier in the supply truck stuck his head out the passenger side window and took aim at us with his plasma rifle. He fired several rounds, and Vrynn swerved to avoid getting hit. The truck weaved to the other side of the road, cutting off the soldier's line of fire.

"We could let Mosai or Bryneen drive," I said, tilting my head toward the back seat.

"Mosai's a maniac driver," Vrynn said.

"I am not!" Mosai yelled from the back seat.

"Besides, we don't have time," Vrynn said. "You're up here, they're back there. Now take the controls."

I huffed in frustration and reluctantly grabbed the stick. She immediately crouched on the edge of the seat and motioned for me to bring us closer. I was still in the uncomfortable position of trying to drive from the passenger seat, but I leaned over and pushed the throttle up slightly. The Veechu responded nicely, and we pulled even with the truck again.

I was about to tell Vrynn that I'd give her a countdown when she suddenly leapt onto the back corner of the truck. She made it look as easy as hopping between two steps on a footpath. I slid over into the driver's seat to make things less awkward.

The truck swerved to the side, and Vrynn lost grip with one of her hands.

"Vrynn!" I pulled closer to the truck, hoping Vrynn could push off the edge of the Veechu, but nothing on our vehicle was close enough to do her any good.

Plasma rounds streaked by again. A pair glanced off the front hood and punched through the windshield, leaving two holes right where I had been sitting. I swerved to get out of his line of fire again, leaving Vrynn dangling awkwardly from the back of the truck.

"Mosai, get up here!" I yelled over my shoulder.

He jumped into the front seat next to me, and I let him grab the controls as I positioned myself to lean farther out to help Vrynn. The truck hit a bump in the road, jostling Vrynn into an even more precarious position.

Without thinking about the consequences, I jumped across the narrow gap and grabbed the side of the truck. With one hand holding onto the truck for dear life, I reached down for Vrynn, dangling from the back edge. She gripped my hand, and I pulled her into a safer position.

"Thanks," she yelled above the sound of the wind rushing past.

She climbed the rest of the way up, and I followed after her, pulling myself over the edge to the relative safety of the top of the truck. Crouching low, we inched our way toward the front. Halfway there, we went over another bump, and I lost my footing. I dropped to my knees, hitting the roof pretty hard.

My impact must have alerted the driver because he suddenly started swerving back and forth again. Vrynn dropped to her stomach, and we both clung to the top as the truck weaved all over the road.

"We have to get off the roof," I yelled at Vrynn.

"You take the driver side," Vrynn indicated with a nod of her head. "I'll take the passenger side."

Together, we slid forward until we had nearly reached the front of the truck. Peeking over the edge, I tried to figure out how I was going to get inside the cab. There wasn't really a running board to land on. In fact, there didn't appear to be any place I could stand or grab. Apparently, the Barchee hadn't really built their transport vehicles with a good hijacking in mind.

The seam of the door was far too narrow to grab, and the door handle was streamlined, so no help there either. I glanced over my shoulder to see if Vrynn was having any better luck. My stomach leapt into my throat when I only saw her legs still on the roof. Everything from the waist up was hanging off the edge.

I scampered to her side and grabbed her legs just before she went over the edge.

"Are you crazy? What are you doing?" I yelled.

"Opening the door," she shouted back.

That part was obvious; I just didn't understand why she hadn't asked for help first. "Be careful," I called.

But before Vrynn could do anything, the guard leaned out the door and fired his plasma rifle at the Veechu again. I heard Bryneen scream as the Veechu gushed out some sort of green liquid from the front. They fell behind as the vehicle lost power.

Vrynn and I were on our own now.

I instinctively pulled Vrynn upward to get her away from the soldier. But she must have decided it was a good time to start a fight with the guy. As they grappled for control of the plasma rifle, the weapon erupted, sending plasma bolts into nearby buildings, the side of the truck itself, and past my head.

It was all I could do to keep Vrynn from falling as she pulled and tugged against the guard and his rifle. I could feel my fingers losing grip on her legs. "Vrynn!" I yelled. "You're slipping."

The guard looked up at me, bewildered. As if it wasn't enough of a surprise that an elfish woman was floating upside down outside his door, he was shocked that I was on top, holding her by the legs.

Vrynn took advantage of his momentary lapse and punched him in the throat, sending him off balance. She grabbed his shoulders and pulled, flinging him out of the cab.

"A little lower," Vrynn called up to me.

The truck swerved again, throwing us off balance, but Vrynn was able to grab the door jamb and hold on.

"Let go now," Vrynn yelled.

I released her legs, and she flipped down into a crouch against the seat just as blaster rounds struck the open door. Vrynn ducked low, trying to stay out of sight of the driver, who was now shooting and driving at the same time. She wouldn't be safe there for long. And she couldn't jump into the cab without risking being shot.

I pulled out my own blaster and fired blindly into the cab through the open door. The truck swerved dangerously toward the edge of the winding road, then several rounds struck the opening near my hand.

"I can't see the driver well enough to shoot him," I called down to Vrynn.

"That's okay," she answered. "If you kill the driver, and I don't get to the controls fast enough, we'll drive off the cliff."

"Hang on. I have an idea," I yelled.

From her perch, crouched against the cab's seat, Vrynn yelled back at me. "I'm not going anywhere at the moment."

I hastily slid across the roof to the other side of the truck and leaned over the edge, firing several shots at the window. It exploded in a shower of glass pellets. Gripping the edge of the roof with one hand, I leaned farther over, hoping to get a shot at the driver's leg or arm or something.

I was greeted by the business end of the driver's blaster.

I pulled my head back just as a pair of rounds burned by. I might have even been a little too slow because I could have sworn I smelled singed hair. A second later, I heard a loud thud, and the truck lurched to the side. I risked another peek into the cab and saw Vrynn wrestling with the driver. He had her pinned against the seat—though she was landing a fair number of blows on his face and ribs. The blaster lay on the floor at her feet.

Flipping around feet-first, I swung myself into the cab. My momentum carried me far enough that my boot caught the driver in the side of the head, knocking him across the seat. Now freed, Vrynn stretched down and grabbed the blaster and trained it on the incapacitated driver.

I grabbed the control stick and steered us away from a looming building just in time.

"That was perfect," she said. "You and I are an amazing team."

My laugh was only slightly sarcastic. "Obviously."

Vrynn leaned over and pulled the side door shut. She got the unconscious driver's head to move out of the way on the second try. "Where are Mosai and Bryneen?" she asked.

"Still behind us, I think," I said. "The Veechu was hit with a plasma round, and something green was coming out of the front."

"Should we wait for them to catch up?" Vrynn asked. "The Veechu has the radio, and I don't know where we're supposed to take the truck after we hijack it."

I glanced at her. "If we stop, the Barchee are more likely to catch us. Let's just take it back to the warehouse."

"I don't know the way back to the warehouse, do you?"

I shook my head. "Not really. But we have to drive somewhere," I said as I dodged another rocky outcropping. "We're bound to attract the wrong kind of attention at some point."

"What if we drive the truck back to Syr?" Vrynn asked.

"To Mosai and Bryneen's house?"

Vrynn shook her head. "No, just to one of the other towns. Keelsa said if we hijacked one of the trucks, we should give the supplies to the people."

"Better than driving it into the ocean," I said with a shrug. "Should we switch drivers?" I asked her. I'd never even considered changing drivers in a moving vehicle, but I'd done it twice in the last ten minutes. Plus, no one was shooting at us anymore, so it would definitely be easier this time.

"No, you drive; I'll watch for Barchee forces."

"But I can't read your language. How will I know which sign is giving directions to Syr?"

She tilted her head in confusion. "A sign giving directions?"

"Yeah. You know, the markers on the side of the road that tell us where to go."

Vrynn's brow furrowed. "We just barely decided we want to go to Syr. How could someone have written directions for us already?"

I chuckled. "They wouldn't write directions for us specifically. They would write the directions of how to get to Syr."

"Everyone knows how to get to Syr. It's that way." Vrynn pointed toward the southern island.

"Yeah, but for people who aren't from here, who don't know how to get there . . . actually, nevermind. Just tell me which way to drive."

Vrynn nodded her agreement.

After turning down from the upper loop road, we skirted around the hill with the capitol building and back toward the center of the city. Then Vrynn guided me to the highway heading south through the tunnel. Once we were on the bridge, I let myself relax a little bit. "I wonder how Bryneen and Mosai will get back home."

Vrynn shrugged. "This wouldn't be their first time to Mardrys and back. They'll find a way."

About twenty minutes later, we reached the northern coast of Syr.

"Turn right," Vrynn instructed. "That'll take us to Burnee."

I chuckled. "Bernie. That's a great name for a town."

Vrynn gave me a puzzled look, but didn't say anything.

Once we reached Burnee, Vrynn directed me toward the center of town. It wasn't exactly like the classic small-town plaza on Earth, but close enough. A series of terraced platforms, with trees perched inside each, surrounded a large, central gathering area. We had attracted a fair amount of attention trundling through Burnee's small streets, so by the time I brought the cargo truck to a stop in the square, the citizens were gravitating toward us, observing with curiosity.

Vrynn and I jumped out and pulled open the door to the cargo space. If the villagers were surprised to see two regular-looking civilians—well, one regular-looking Mareesh and a tall, ugly alien—they were even more surprised when we started handing out supplies.

I stood up in the bed of the truck, lifting crates and bags down to Vrynn, who handed them to the dozens of townspeople flocking around us. As the crowd increased, several men jumped into the truck to help, happy to lend their muscle to the distribution of our ill-gotten Barchee supplies. I was quickly pushed out of the way by their exuberant efforts, but that was fine. We'd done our jobs.

Jumping down from the truck bed, I found Vrynn in the throng of grateful villagers. I pulled her away from a small group of older Mareesh women who seemed intent on smothering her with their gratitude.

"I think they can take care of the rest, don't you?" I asked Vrynn as we attempted to extricate ourselves from the press.

Vrynn turned a broad grin toward me. "We did a good thing today, didn't we?"

I smiled and nodded, considering the results of our handiwork. If the frenzy in front of us was any indication, what we'd done was monumental.

We'd been standing there on the edge of the square for several minutes when a pair of large hands grabbed us by the shoulders, pulling us into the shadows.

"What did you do?" a voice asked.

Natheem stood in front of us, looking extremely annoyed and slightly worried at the same time, though I couldn't understand why.

"There was another truck," Vrynn explained exuberantly. "We hijacked it!"

"I can see that." Natheem scowled at the crowd. "But I don't think this is what Keelsa had in mind."

"What do you mean?" I asked. "We stopped the supplies from reaching the Barchee forces, and we helped people at the same time."

"What do you normally do with the hijacked trucks?" Vrynn asked.

He sighed. "We unload some of the supplies, and then we leave the truck abandoned in Mardrys."

"That's sort of what we're doing here," I pointed out.

"Not really." Natheem scrubbed a hand across his face, surveying the chaotic scene with evident frustration. "This really messes things up. The occupiers will certainly retaliate."

Vrynn tilted her head at Natheem. "Good. It's about time we started a fight. Isn't that the point?"

Natheem blew out a breath. "You've been gone a long time, Vrynn. I wouldn't expect you to understand."

As Vrynn started to object, cries of dismay rose from the far corner of the square. A handful of armed Barchee soldiers were struggling toward the supply truck, pulling citizens out of the way and stunning them as they went.

Vrynn stepped back toward the crowd. "We have to help."

Natheem and I both grabbed her by the arms.

"The three of us are no match for Barchee soldiers," I said.

Vrynn struggled against my grip. "We could at least try."

"They're heavily armed," Natheem added. "Unless you plan to start a firefight in the middle of the square, we need to leave it alone."

Vrynn's struggling ebbed, and she allowed us to pull her away from the square. "What about the villagers?" she asked sadly.

"They'll be okay," Natheem replied. "They haven't actually done anything wrong."

We ran down a side alley until we reached a broader road. There were townspeople everywhere, some running toward the square, others trying to get as far away from it as possible. And there were soldiers, too—more than had initially arrived in the square—grabbing everyone in reach and yelling at the rest to stop. Farther up the street, a dozen Barchee soldiers in riot gear appeared, herding the fleeing citizens.

Natheem surveyed the situation as the chaos of the crowd increased. "They'll want to punish the ones responsible for bringing the truck here," he said, pointing down the road at the approaching soldiers. "This is what happens if you upset the occupiers." He pushed Vrynn and me down another alley. "You two can't get caught here. Get out of Burnee. Walk to the next town and get yourselves back to Neevra."

Vrynn started to object, but Natheem had already turned and disappeared into the crowd. I pulled her deeper into the alley. "Let's get out of here. We can't win this fight."

We wound through the narrow streets until the buildings began to thin. Joining a sparse stream of Mareesh villagers fleeing the small town, we trudged across the valley between wide green fields. In the distance, I could see other roads similarly filled with escaping refugees.

In the next town, we boarded the train back to Neevra.

As we settled into seats for the short ride, Vrynn turned to me. "Did you get the feeling that Natheem seemed more intent on placating the occupiers than actually fighting them?"

"It did seem like that. But maybe he's right. Maybe we don't actually understand how things work."

Vrynn scowled. "If you mean that the fight against the occupiers is going to cause problems for everyone, then I understand perfectly. That's what it's going to take."

We rode on in silence for another minute or two before Vrynn spoke again.

"Also, I don't think High Tide is actually trying very hard to fight the Barchee."

I waited a moment as her declaration sank in. "So, what should we do?"

Vrynn's expression hardened. "We'll have to start our own rebellion."

Chapter Thirteen

The next morning, I sat having breakfast in the *Starfire's* kitchen area, when Vrynn walked in and started making herself some food.

"Tera just told me she picked up some increased Barchee comm chatter this morning," I said through a mouthful. "It sounds like they're moving additional soldiers to Syr, particularly the town of Burnee."

"They must be upset about the hijacking," Vrynn said as she continued her meal preparations.

"Probably so," I said. "I really hope Mosai and Bryneen made it back okay."

Vrynn sat down next to me with her breakfast meal, a bright purple fruit cut in half and sprinkled with something that might have been salt. "They're resourceful," she said. "Plus, they've been on their own for several years now. I'm sure they'll be fine."

We hadn't talked much about the unsuccessful ending to our hijacking effort the day before, but I could tell it was eating at Vrynn.

A few minutes later, Tera and Gabe joined us at the table, even though Gabe didn't need to eat and Tera didn't need to sit. But it was sorta like a crew meeting, so it was good to have them there.

"We need to do more," Vrynn finally said.

"More convoy attacks?" I asked.

"No. Although, that might not be a bad idea if there's time." Vrynn's expression was determined. "We need to make more of an impact."

"If your goal is to annoy Gralik, then the truck hijacking yesterday was pretty effective," Tera offered.

"Why do you say that?" I asked.

"His daily broadcast last night was a mess," Tera answered with a smile. "I'd say you definitely got under his skin."

I chuckled. "I'd love to see that."

"I have the recording if you want to watch it later," Tera said.

"Upsetting Gralik is great, but we need to do more." Vrynn pounded her palm on the table, making my mostly empty bowl of hash jump.

"What did you have in mind?" I asked.

Vrynn stood and started pacing the adjacent living area. "If we're going to make a difference, we have to hit them where it hurts."

"Is it not effective when you steal their food?" Gabe asked. He turned to Tera. "If I were a biological, I would be very upset if someone stole my food."

"I would have thought the same thing," Vrynn said. "But it hasn't worked. So we have to ask ourselves what the Barchee want. Why are they here on Mareesh?"

"Why are any of us here?" Gabe said. "I have devoted considerable algorithmic resources to—"

Tera patted Gabe's hand. "It's not philosophy time, Gabe."

"Oh." Gabe fell silent.

"Hang on. I see where you're going with this," I said to Vrynn. "You once told me the Barchee only came here because of some super-important natural resource your people discovered."

"Exactly. They're here for the Quasarium," she replied.

"Quasarium," I repeated. "That's the stuff that powers the roads and trains, right?"

She nodded.

"But what's so special about it?" I asked.

"Quasarium is a crystalline mineral with high natural energy storage and output characteristics. It has been synthetically produced in laboratories in small quantities, but is found in larger amounts in undersea pockets and magma deposits on Mareesh," Gabe volunteered. When we all turned to stare at him in surprise, he added, "I have taken an interest in advanced chemistry."

"Huh. Well, the real Gabe did always enjoy chemistry," I said. I turned back to Vrynn. "So how does quasarium fit with our new plan?"

"If they can't have our quasarium, they won't want to stay," Vrynn said matter-of-factly.

"But if that's the whole reason they came, don't you think taking the quasarium back will be a little tough?" I asked.

Vrynn shrugged. "I'm sure we'll figure out a way."

"Well, whatever you do, can it please not involve leaving us in this dank cavern for hours on end?" Tera asked.

I frowned at my holographic friend. "You can't actually feel the humidity, can you?"

She rounded on me. "Just because I have sensors instead of skin doesn't mean I can't feel that it's humid. Besides, this cave is boring."

"How can you be bored?" I asked. "I can't imagine you were programmed with a bored algorithm."

"No. But when we were sitting around all day yesterday with nothing to do, Gabe helped me create one."

I laughed out loud. "You were sitting around with nothing to do, so you wrote yourself a subroutine so you could experience boredom?"

"Exactly," Tera said.

"And what would happen if you disable it?" I asked.

"Then I would just be sitting around with nothing to do again," Tera replied.

"So you'd be bored?" I prompted.

Tera rolled her eyes. "No. Obviously, I couldn't be bored if the subroutine was disabled," she explained in a not-very-patient tone.

I grinned. "But if you don't have anything to do, wouldn't you—"

Vrynn glared at me. "Mitch, before you break something, maybe we should get back to planning."

"Sure. As long as someone appreciates the logical paradox." I winked at her.

Vrynn shook her head in mild exasperation. "You're hilarious. But you're about to send them into an infinite loop." She indicated Tera and Gabe, sitting across the table.

Tera's eyes scanned back and forth as if computing something, and Gabe kept tilting his head to one side and then the other, not looking at anything in particular. I was about to interrupt their computational death spiral when Tera snapped out of it.

"We have visitors," she said.

Vrynn and I both stood and moved toward nearby portals. "Where?" I asked.

"Not in the cavern," Tera replied, which calmed my mind slightly. "The sensors you left on top of the hill are picking up three individuals walking along the path toward the crevice."

"Who is it?" Vrynn asked.

"Even if the sensors were sensitive enough to tell what the person looked like, I haven't been out of this cavern, so I wouldn't know who they are." She said the last part with a fair bit of annoyance.

"We need to go up there," Vrynn said.

"Maybe they won't find us," I said. "We're pretty well hidden. Does anyone else know about the cavern?"

"Mosai and Bryneen definitely do," Vrynn answered. "So do half the younger adults in town who went to school with us."

I stared at her, dumbfounded. "You've got a one-of-a-kind starship that could literally obliterate small armadas of ships, and you decide to hide it in a cave that dozens of people know about?"

"It's not like we had that many options," she shot back. "Besides, Tera would never let them steal it."

Tera's expression told me she might consider it in order to get out of the cavern every once in a while.

Gabe suddenly made a sound that might have been a laugh. "I get it."

"Get what?" I asked.

"The thing you were asking about the boredom subroutine and not having anything to do," he replied. "That is a very funny joke."

I chuckled. "Thanks, Gabe. We'll be back soon," I said as I grabbed my blaster.

Tera rolled her eyes. "Fine. Another day for us in the sad cave," she said, sounding depressed.

Gabe considered her. "If you really are feeling dissatisfied with the time we are left alone in the *Starfire*, I would be happy to increase the level of attention I give you. We could even discuss our relationship and future plans together."

Tera's face broke into a smile, and she threw her arms around Gabe's neck.

I shook my head. How was it that Gabe could say something that awkward and still have it work? Maybe I needed to start taking relationship lessons from my android friend. "Be good while we're gone," I called over my shoulder as Vrynn grabbed her weapon and met me at the ladder.

"We will," they both replied.

We hurried to the lower deck and out through the cargo bay. Halfway across the cave, I glanced back at the flight deck windows. "Should we really be leaving those teenage lovebirds alone together? Their real parents would've had a fit."

Vrynn laughed. "Weren't the real Gabe and Tera grown and married?"

"Yeah."

"So it's fine," she said.

I shook my head. What a strange life I led.

Out on the hill above the cavern, we saw three figures walking along the trail toward us. At about forty or fifty feet away, one of them started to look familiar.

"Mosai!" Vrynn exclaimed as she broke into a run. I jogged to catch up. "I'm glad to see you in one piece," she said, wrapping him in a hug. "Is Bryneen safe?"

Mosai nodded. "She's fine."

"We waited at your home as long as we could last night," I said, feeling apologetic. "When the soldiers started going door to door searching for us, we decided we had to get out."

"The same thing happened in Mardrys," Mosai said. "By the time Bryneen and I finally got the damaged Veechu back to the warehouse, there were soldiers everywhere."

"How did you get away?" Vrynn asked.

Mosai thumbed over his shoulder, and I turned my attention to his companions for the first time. They appeared to be a couple—assuming that holding hands to show romantic affection was a universal constant. The guy was Mosai's height, but much leaner, with tousled hair and an impish smirk. The woman was Vrynn's age, but with her platinum hair in a tight braid down the back of her neck. She had an austere, almost tenacious demeanor.

"Hustan and Sharlee found us," Mosai said.

Vrynn gaped at the couple. "Hustan? Sharlee? Is it really you?" She sounded completely surprised. "I didn't even recognize you. You've both grown so much since I last saw you." Vrynn took a few steps and threw her arms around them. She turned to Hustan. "Did you get released from prison, too? Like Natheem."

Hustan's expression turned chagrined. "Not so much. Natheem was released on good behavior. That's never really been my thing." He took Sharlee's hand again. "A few years back, Shar figured out how to get inside the Barchee prison. She broke me out one night. We've been hiding out on Nildyr ever since."

"She did the same with us," Mosai added. "Sharlee pulled us out of the chaos of the Barchee patrols and whisked us away on the train to Nildyr."

I turned to Vrynn. "What's Nildyr?"

"That's the north island," she replied. "It's not very populated. It's mostly for solitude and recreation."

I grinned. "I wouldn't mind seeing that, once this is all over."

Vrynn tucked herself in close to me. Hustan's brow went up, and Sharlee's mouth spread in a knowing smirk. Mosai scowled at us, but didn't seem as annoyed as he had before. He glanced nervously around the wide hillside. "We need to get out of the open. Can we go to the cave?" he asked Vrynn.

She nodded, motioning them to follow, and we led the group up the hill toward the path leading to the cavern.

"High Tide is actually a sham," Sharlee announced, picking up the conversation where we'd left off.

"We came to that same conclusion last night," I said.

"Are they in league with the Barchee?" Vrynn asked.

Hustan shook his head. "No. I think their efforts are sincere. But they're so inept, especially Keelsa, that the Barchee tolerate them."

"Why do the Barchee put up with a daily supply hijacking?" I wondered aloud. "Wouldn't they have hunted High Tide down and put a stop to it a long time ago?"

"The occupiers are probably glad," Sharlee said with a wry laugh.

"Glad that there's a rebel organization in the capital city?" I asked, incredulous.

"Glad that the most serious threat to their power is only a minor annoyance," she replied.

"But after what happened yesterday, their patience might not last much longer," Mosai said.

The group trudged along in silence, considering his prediction.

"It hardly matters. The last real effort of open rebellion died with Raveel," Hustan said bitterly.

Sharlee's head whipped toward him, her eyes fierce. "I told you. He's not dead."

Hustan simply shook his head. They'd obviously had this disagreement before.

"Who's Raveel again?" I asked Vrynn.

Mosai answered first. "He was the leader of the Mareesh army." He turned his attention to Sharlee. "And he's definitely dead. He and my father were together when the capitol building was overrun by Gralik's forces. They didn't leave any of the leaders alive."

Sharlee offered a noncommittal shrug but didn't seem convinced.

"Without Raveel, the real fighters have gone under water."—My chip re-translated—"... underground. We've been waiting and watching for an opportunity to fight again." Hustan considered us. "Your arrival and your willingness to fight the occupiers is what we have been waiting for," he said. "The Deep Down is at your disposal."

"Deep Down?" I asked.

"The real freedom fighters," Sharlee replied proudly. "The ones willing to do what High Tide can't or won't."

We squeezed through the crevice single-file and descended the winding steps. When we reached the main cavern, Hustan and Sharlee gaped at the *Starfire*. It gave me a chance to admire our ship again, from the perspective of someone who'd never seen it before.

I hadn't really thought about how Tera and Gabe might react to us bringing strangers onboard, but I didn't have anything to worry about. The cargo ramp lowered at our approach, and Tera and Gabe stood at the top, awaiting our arrival. Gabe appeared as stoic as ever, but Tera looked like she might blow a holographic emitter with the excitement of having guests.

We settled the group in the open living area to continue our discussion. Tera was the perfect hostess, visiting and recommending food, while Gabe did all the physical preparation and delivery of anything Tera offered. It wasn't that different from what the real Gabe and Tera might have been like, assuming they had both survived and were hosting a casual alien get-together on a starship.

"We were just talking about striking the quasarium supply," Vrynn explained once we were all settled.

"As crazy as it might have been to drive a hijacked supply truck into the center of Burnee, it definitely surprised the occupiers," Hustan said. "Not to mention the morale boost to our people. I think hitting something else—especially the quasarium—while they're still washing their wounds is a great idea."

Vrynn leaned forward. "The quasarium is what they really want. Maybe if we snatch that away from them,"—she made a rapid grabbing motion—"we can drive them out."

Hustan and Sharlee looked like two kids on Christmas. "How should we do it? Blow up the refinery?" Sharlee asked.

Hustan shook his head. "No. Too many Mareesh laborers work there."

"But that's the perfect opportunity," Sharlee pressed. "We could convince them to sabotage the critical equipment and then get out."

Hustan turned to face Sharlee. "Too many fish make a pod. The occupiers would easily discover the plan."

Sharlee started to object, but Vrynn intervened. "Our strength—especially with the *Starfire*—is air combat. We aren't as strong on the ground."

Hustan and Sharlee both fell silent.

"How do they get the quasarium back to Barchee?" I asked. "Do they use the same transports that bring in the supplies?"

"No," Hustan replied. "A transport from Zerlon arrives every few days to take it."

I shouldn't have been surprised by that bit of information. Zerlon was the location of Gralik's secret Nexus base. The one we'd infiltrated several weeks ago to steal back the Quake Drive.

"Can we track when the next Zerlon transport will arrive?" Vrynn asked.

"I have a friend who works in the spaceport," Hustan said. "I could have him find out."

Vrynn nodded. "Perfect. Just don't get yourself caught again."

Hustan grinned. "I can't make any promises. Last time I was in prison, Sharlee came to rescue me." He squeezed Sharlee's hand. "I wouldn't mind her doing it again."

Sharlee's brow ticked higher. "You think that wave washes the shore more than once?"

The others laughed at what I assumed was a clever Mareesh phrase.

Once we had worked out the details of our plan to attack the Zerlon transport, we sent Mosai, Hustan and Sharlee off on their mission to infiltrate the Barchee base on Mardrys.

After they were gone, I turned to Gabe. "We'd better get the scout ship flying again. It might come in handy for the hijacking."

Chapter Fourteen

H ustan and Mosai contacted us late the next morning from inside the Barchee spaceport, saying that the Zerlon transport had just arrived. It would load the quasarium shipment in less than an hour and then leave immediately.

"That means it's go-time," I said. "Are you ready for some fancy flying?" I asked Gabe.

He tilted his head. "Are you planning to take me with you in the scout ship so that you can ask me at the last minute to take over flying while you jump onto the Zerlon transport despite knowing that my underlying programming does not allow me to pilot a spacecraft?"

I gaped at him. That was exactly what I had planned to do. "That's a very specific scenario. What makes you think I would do something like that?" I casually asked, hoping he didn't notice the change in my skin temperature.

"Tera said that you have asked her to fly the *Starfire* on multiple occasions without giving her appropriate training or time to prepare," Gabe observed.

"Well, I guess I've tried to help you two exceed your programming by pushing you out of the nest every once in a while. Is that bad?"

"It would be if I am not capable of flying."

My stomach sank. We would need to come up with an alternate plan.

Then a mischievous smile spread across Gabe's face. "However, Tera anticipated your behavior. So, she helped me create a piloting skill subroutine that will allow me to execute our mission successfully."

I could feel the tension in my neck and shoulders relax a little. Apparently, Gabe was beginning to develop a sense of humor, mostly at my expense. I shouldn't have been surprised, given how much the real Gabe enjoyed ribbing me.

Once we had taken the *Starfire* out through the underwater tunnel and positioned ourselves near the rocky coast, Gabe and I said goodbye to Tera and Vrynn, and loaded into the small scout ship. The bay door opened, and we flew out over the ocean. Guiding the ship low over the water, I steered us in a somewhat circuitous route toward the spaceport on Mardrys. It was important for us to stay low, avoiding detection, until the right moment. We didn't know exactly what type of fighter escort the transport from Zerlon would have, but given how much accompanied the incoming supply ships, we figured the export ship would be heavily guarded.

"Three Varusian Interceptors just launched," Vrynn's voice said over the comm.

"Yep, I see them," I replied. It wasn't actually true. Just like our first time flying the scout ship, Gabe and I were crammed into the cockpit so tightly that I couldn't see any of the sensor readouts on his side of the display. But Gabe could, and he had already pointed that direction.

"A single transport has just launched," Tera said. "Its transponder signal matches the information Hustan sent."

My grip tightened on the controls. "This is it."

"Don't move in until you see the signal," Vrynn said.

"I know, I know," I replied. "You think I want to get into a dogfight with three heavy interceptors in a small, nearly unarmed scout ship?"

"That sounds like something you would do," Vrynn said playfully. It actually sounded like something she would do, not me.

The transport flew overhead, and Gabe and I followed, hanging back in an effort to appear less threatening. As if a small scout would pose any real danger to a ship that size.

A few minutes into their flight, the transport and its escorts got the first hint that their day would not be going according to plan. Just as they passed through a low-lying cloud bank, a stream of plasma rounds streaked across the sky toward them. I could just make out the *Starfire* high above us, cannons blazing.

Two of the escorts peeled off to intercept the *Starfire*, leaving one escort behind. I wondered whether I'd be able to sneak into position without having to use our only weapon—the defensive auto-cannon.

I took a deep breath. "Cross your fingers that this works."

"The original Gabe's memories indicate that crossing fingers will lead to a successful outcome," Gabe said. "Has this phenomenon been studied in a controlled environment to determine if—"

"Gabe." I cut him off. "Let's worry about the science experiments later. I need to focus on this part."

"Acknowledged."

The single remaining fighter escort took up position above the transport as protection against the *Starfire*. It must not have thought a tiny spacecraft like ours would be any threat.

I pushed the throttle hard, bringing the scout ship directly below the transport in an attempt to keep us hidden from the last escort. As we maneuvered into place, I found the spot on the Zerlon freighter's belly that Tera had said would give me the best chance of going undetected. Of course, it was half the length of the ship away from the ventral access hatch I needed to reach.

I took a deep breath. "This is the part where it gets tricky."

"I will take the controls so that you can climb out," Gabe said.

I released the canopy lock and pushed it slightly open. The sudden inrush of air slammed me backward into my seat. But fortunately, the canopy didn't fly off. Gabe seemed unaffected by the gale-force wind. Of course, he had abs literally made of steel.

He glanced back at me, almost bemused by my predicament, and said, "Bear in mind that the transport has certainly detected our approach and will inform the remaining escort. You have no more than thirty seconds to get onto the hull before it arrives."

"Thanks," I muttered as I struggled through the slipstream. I inched my way back to the gap in the canopy, not making much progress until Gabe pushed me forward with his superhuman strength. "Thanks," I said, unsarcastically this time.

Fighting through the wind, I was finally able to get my head and one arm out. On my third try, my magnetic grip latched onto the hull, and I pulled myself farther out of the cockpit.

"Stay close," I yelled at Gabe as I shimmied the rest of the way out of the scout ship.

The force of the air pressed me hard against the side of the hull, and I hung on tightly to the magnetic grips. A moment later, the sound of plasma rounds exploded around me.

Gabe dove away from the transport as the interceptor fired on him. The scout's little auto-cannon roared to life but did nothing to deter the giant enemy ship.

Fortunately for me, Gabe drew the interceptor farther away, distracting him from the tiny man clinging to the outside of the transport. I refocused my attention on the hatch halfway up the underside of the ship. Keeping each magnetic grip close to the hull and only partially deactivating them, I slowly and painstakingly slid them forward, one at a time, as I inched my way along the smooth surface.

At one point, I made the mistake of looking down—which from the bottom of the transport was actually up—at the blue-gray ocean far below us. It made my head spin. I also caught a glimpse of the *Starfire* streaking in and out of sparse clouds—four interceptors and a Vezor-class runabout in hot pursuit. It shouldn't have surprised me that Gralik had joined the fray. He wouldn't want to see his precious cargo stolen. Not to mention the opportunity to capture the *Starfire*. I hoped Vrynn and Tera could handle him.

Knowing that we might not have much time, I refocused my efforts on the hatch ahead of me. I crawled forward as fast as I could manage, my muscles burning and my eyes stinging as the wind whipped around me.

With my strength nearly gone, I finally reached the hatch and searched for a latch or button or something. Under a smooth recess, I found the actuator and pulled hard. The hatch scraped back and stopped with a loud clunk. I placed one of the magnetic grips against the lever mechanism to keep it from closing on me and reached inside for a handhold to grab.

As I was about to pull myself through, the transport suddenly banked to one side then to the other, jostling me from my inverted perch. Then the transport dove downward, pressing me hard against the hull, making me feel like I weighed five hundred pounds.

Somewhere in the back of my mind, my last rational brain cell alerted me to what was about to happen. Unless the crew of the transport actually had a death wish, the ship was going to pull up—without me inside.

As usual, despite knowing what was coming, there was nothing I could do to change it. The transport pulled up—hard. I clenched my fists over the handgrips, but it was a futile effort. My body was suddenly yanked away from the hull, my hands slipping pitifully from their holds. Thanks for nothing, Sir Isaac Newton.

Gabe and I had been skydiving once before, when we thought the Earth was the only place to do such a crazy thing. Now I found myself falling through the air of an alien world, wondering if the surface of the ocean below me was as hard as water on Earth.

I spread my arms and legs wide, hoping to slow my descent by any means possible. Not that it would make a difference to my body when I hit the ocean—I simply wanted to live a little longer.

Out of the corner of my eye, I saw a glint of light reflect off something. It was the reddish metal of the scout ship. I wasn't sure how Gabe had gotten away from the last interceptor, but at the moment, I didn't care.

The little craft zipped toward me, angling down to match my speed. He maneuvered the ship closer and slightly behind me. I flipped over onto my back to see what he was doing.

It only took Gabe a few seconds to line up on me and start closing the distance. Though I was tempted to glance over my shoulder to see how much time I had, I focused on the gap between the cockpit edge and the canopy. I had come out through that same opening just a few minutes ago, but now it seemed absolutely miniscule.

As the ship slowly inched closer, I spread my arms and legs apart even further, willing myself to fall slower. Then suddenly, Gabe jammed the throttle to full, and the ship shot forward, gobbling me up. I banged a knee against the canopy edge and smashed into the back of the cockpit seat, narrowly missing Gabe's head.

It became obvious that I had landed upside down because, a split second after impacting safely inside the cockpit, Gabe forced the ship into a high-G pull up. The blood rushed to my head, and I felt like my eyes wanted to pop.

"Do I want to know how close that was?" I asked.

"I have no way to determine your desires, but if you would like to know our minimum altitude, I can tell you," Gabe said. "It would have been very close to zero if I hadn't increased velocity at the end."

With some wiggling and shifting, I righted myself in the cockpit seat. "That's all I needed to know," I replied. "Thanks for saving me."

Gabe smiled. "You are welcome."

"Shall we give it another go?" I asked.

Gabe nodded. "This will likely be our best opportunity to reach a successful outcome."

I pointed up at the transport. "Round two."

Despite his earlier joking about not being allowed to fly, Tera had made him a top-notch technical pilot. The only things I brought to the table were randomness and unconventional techniques. Hopefully, my crew would still need those qualities and not replace me with the android replica of my buddy.

Gabe moved us into position below the transport again, a feat that was much more difficult now that they knew we were coming. The cargo ship weaved and bobbed in the air, trusting the overwhelming odds that it would easily survive a mid-air collision with us. Fortunately, with his instantaneous reflexes, Gabe was able to detect and precisely mimic every move the transport made.

Once we were close enough, I slid forward in the cockpit and reached for the hatch. After catching hold of the magnetic handgrip, I didn't waste any time pulling myself into the transport.

I clambered over the lip and leaned against the wall of a narrow passageway. Reaching for my blaster, I discovered that it must have fallen out at some point during my freefall of death. I peered out the open hatch to see if Gabe was close enough to hand me a weapon of some kind.

Plasma rounds exploded around us, and Gabe pulled away. The transport banked hard again, giving me a perfect view of a newly arrived Barchee fighter escort pursuing my friend in the small scout ship. He had fully closed the canopy again, and was attempting to bring the auto-cannon to bear on his new enemy.

The escort had lined up the perfect shot.

"Get out of there, buddy," I muttered, hoping Gabe would make it away safely.

A streak of flame slashed across my view. But it wasn't from the escort ship. A second later, a bright yellow burst flashed in front of me, forcing me to shield my eyes. The escort ship exploded in a ball of flame.

The *Starfire* hurtled by, banking away from Gabe, followed closely by half a dozen interceptors.

I was so grateful that Gabe would be safe that I nearly sank down on the deck right there next to the open hatch.

"Don't move!" a voice behind me boomed.

I held my hands up, hoping that was the universal signal for "don't shoot me, I'm unarmed."

"Turn around slowly," the voice said.

I turned to face the man giving the orders and tried to appear contrite. I certainly felt it when I realized this was a Vanguard Dragoon, one of Gralik's most highly trained soldiers.

"Walk," the dragoon said, waving his plasma rifle down the hall.

I eagerly complied while my mind raced to come up with a way to get off the ship before it left the atmosphere. The armed soldier followed behind me as we moved aft down a long hallway.

"Stop there," the soldier said when we reached a set of doors.

I wasn't sure what was on the other side of those doors, but I knew once I went through, there was almost no chance I'd come back out.

He held his wrist out to the security scanner, and I heard a beep and click right before the ship lurched sideways. Weapons fire impacted the hull, and the entire airframe shuddered.

That was the chance I was looking for. As we both stumbled toward the bulkhead, I used my momentum to swing a fist at the dragoon's face. I missed his face, but fortunately caught enough of his head with my wild punch to slam him hard against the wall. As he staggered, clearly dazed, I pulled him across the passageway and smashed him against the other bulkhead. Expecting it this time, he braced his shoulder against the brunt of the impact. He lashed out with an elbow to my gut, and I doubled over.

Before I could even catch my breath, the soldier kneed me in the side of the head, sending me sprawling on my back. As he raised a foot to stomp on my face, I juked sideways and swept his legs with the most forceful kick that I could manage. I'd like to think my hand-to-hand fighting skills were enough, but the rocking of the ship might have helped, too.

The dragoon teetered and fell against the bulkhead while I scrambled back down the corridor to the plasma rifle he'd dropped. I turned around just in time to see him charging me, a raised knife in his hand. I fired once, catching him in the gut, and he crumpled to the ground.

The transport rocked again, and I rushed on shaky feet toward the front of the ship. When I neared the end of the corridor, a plasma round exploded against the bulkhead next to me. A second dragoon stood at the corner leading to the flight deck entrance.

Taking clumsy aim, I fired at the dragoon, hitting him in the shoulder. Somewhere in the back of my mind, I knew that if the transport was under attack, it had to be Vrynn firing on us. And the only reason she would do that with me still inside was to prevent the ship from leaving the atmosphere and making an intra-space jump.

My time was running out.

I came around the corner to the flight deck and found the pilot frantically weaving the ship back and forth, presumably to avoid being shot down by the *Starfire*.

I pointed the blaster at him. "Don't move!" I yelled.

He held his hands steady, and the transport flew straight again. "If you don't allow me to move, eventually that crazy ship will shoot us down."

"Not anymore. Level the ship and step away from the controls." I brandished the weapon at him so that he'd know I meant business.

He immediately followed my instructions, stepping away from the flight console with his hands raised. "Just so you know," he said as he backed up. "I'll do anything you say. This is just a job for me, and I don't get paid enough to be brave."

"Get to an escape pod, and I'll let you go." I swung the blaster to indicate he should start moving.

The pilot scampered away, and I took over at the controls.

I pulled out my comm device to contact the *Starfire*. "Is Gabe okay?" I asked.

"Gabe's fine," Vrynn replied. "He'll pick you up. I would do it myself, but I've still got Gralik after me."

I nodded and cut the comm. It took a minute to figure out the transport's flight controls, but I soon had the ship pointed back down toward the ocean. I had no idea where on Mareesh we were at this point, but Gabe would hopefully be able to find me.

Bringing the ship low over the ocean, I dropped the speed and activated the thrusters. My landing wasn't as gentle as I'd have hoped, but I didn't really care whether the transport survived. I abandoned the flight deck and hustled around the corner to the main corridor. I didn't see either of the wounded dragoons or the pilot, so I assumed they had made it to the escape pods. Several inches of water sloshed along the corridor from the still-open belly hatch. If that was the only open hatch, the air would probably stay inside the large ship, keeping it afloat.

But that's not what I had in mind.

Halfway down the corridor, I climbed an inset ladder that led to a topside hatch and scrambled out on top of the ship. I closed the hatch behind me because I didn't want to lose my only means of flotation before my ride got there.

A few minutes later, the red scout ship came skimming low across the water toward me. Gabe settled the little spaceship on top of the semi-submerged transport.

As the canopy opened, Gabe grinned at me. "What is the line the original Gabe would have used? Something like 'going my way, stranger?'"

I chuckled. "Sounds like something he might have used on Tera, but I'm not going to complain."

I reopened the transport's top hatch right before scampering over to the scout ship and climbing in. Just as we lifted back into the air, the large cargo vessel laden with half a week's worth of refined quasarium slipped under the waves on its way to the bottom of the sea.

By the time we rejoined the *Starfire* on the far side of Syr, the reality of what we had pulled off was starting to settle in. I wasn't sure our new strategy would be the nail in the coffin for the Barchee occupation, but it was much more likely to be the death blow than cutting off the food supply.

The mood in the cargo bay when Vrynn and Tera welcomed us back aboard was jubilant.

Vrynn bounded across the cargo bay and threw her arms around me. "I can't believe you jumped onto a transport mid-flight," Vrynn said. "Twice."

I was grinning from ear to ear. "And you were amazing in the *Starfire*. You got there just in time to save Gabe."

"Yes. I appreciate your efforts on my behalf," Gabe said to Vrynn as he moved across the cargo bay toward Tera.

"And Gabe, you're an amazing pilot," I said. "Catching me out of midair!" I slapped my friend on the back as he passed.

Gabe didn't seem to be listening to me at that point though, because he had just wrapped Tera in a tight, if somewhat awkward, hug.

As soon as we were back in the cavern, I suggested that we should go to Neevra to make sure Mosai had made it back safely. So, Vrynn and I once again trekked from the cavern back to her hometown.

When we were a few hundred feet from the outer buildings, I noticed some strange activities near the guard station. Vrynn grabbed my arm and pulled me toward a fork in the road.

"I wonder what's going on," I said, casting furtive glances over my shoulder.

Vrynn's brow furrowed. "They're probably looking for us," she said as we veered onto the road that skirted Neevra.

I was simultaneously struck with pride at our accomplishment and apprehension that we'd just made our mission ten times harder. "Can we sneak to Mosai and Bryneen's house without being seen?"

She nodded. "I know a back way."

Vrynn's back way might have been appropriate for a pre-teen sneaking to her cousin's house, but not ideal for two full-grown adults. We were forced to jump three walls, shimmy down a drain pipe, and squeeze through a narrow gap in an alleyway that left scrape marks on the front of my borrowed clothes.

At Mosai and Bryneen's street, Vrynn peeked around the corner. "It looks clear," she whispered before slinking silently along the wall.

A few dozen feet down the road, we reached her cousins' home and knocked quietly. With the sun nearly set, the narrow streets of Neevra were cast into deep shadows, and it seemed like Barchee soldiers would jump out of the murky darkness at any moment.

I felt very exposed standing on their doorstep. Too bad Vrynn's sneak-in plan didn't involve using a back entrance.

When Bryneen finally opened the door, she pulled us immediately inside. Her cheeks were puffy and slightly bluer than normal.

"What's wrong?" Vrynn asked.

"They have Mosai," she said, a small sob threatening to swallow her words.

Vrynn pulled Bryneen over to a couch and sat next to her. "Tell us what happened."

"They were at the spaceport, watching the transport getting loaded, but Barchee security found them right after they sent their message to you. They almost made it to the train, but the soldiers grabbed Mosai and Sharlee just as they were about to board. Hustan was already on, so he was able to sneak back to tell me what happened."

Bryneen broke down in tears and buried her head in Vrynn's shoulder.

"We'll get them out," Vrynn said firmly. "We'll figure out a way."

I wasn't sure how freely we could make a promise like that, but I chose not to say anything. "Where is Hustan now?"

Bryneen shook her head. "I don't know. When the governor's daily broadcast came out, he said it wasn't safe for him to stay here."

"Why? Did Gralik say something about him?" Vrynn asked.

Bryneen looked from me to Vrynn and back, her eyes like saucers. "You haven't seen it yet?"

I shook my head.

She jumped up from the couch and activated her view screen, queuing up a video of the BDF leader that I despised so much.

"I have been very disturbed by recent rogue attacks on our peace," Gralik began. "I had hoped the people of Mareesh could make them stop, but they only seem to be escalating. So I decided to enlist the help of an old friend of mine."

The video cut from Gralik, replaced by a middle-aged Mareesh man in a very casual outfit. It wasn't exactly a Hawaiian shirt, but it seemed to convey that feeling.

"Raveel?" Vrynn sounded like she had seen a ghost.

I frowned. "I thought you said he was dead."

Vrynn nodded absently and shushed me with her hand.

"Good citizens of Mareesh, this is Raveel. It has been some time since I spoke publicly, but recent events on our peaceful planet have forced me to end my silence."

I groaned inwardly. Vrynn huffed. I think we could both tell that this wasn't going to be good.

"I have been enduring my retirement on Nildyr for the last few years," Raveel continued. "And it pains me that I have been compelled to say this. The ship that had been valiantly attacking supply convoys—later engaged by our Varusian enforcers—returned today, aided now by some of our own fighters."

I frowned at the way my implant chip was translating some of the phrases, but it didn't seem like the right time to mention it.

Several videos of Vrynn and me walking the streets of Neevra flashed on the screen. Some of the clips even showed Bryneen and Mosai with us. A moment later, the feed cut to a grainy video taken in the streets of Mardrys showed Mosai, Hustan, and Sharlee moving toward the spaceport. Bryneen stifled a sob when she saw it. My stomach sank.

"When I see these things happening, I am sad," Raveel said. "Please put a stop to this."

In the video, the retired Mareesh leader leaned back in his chair, striking a very casual pose, though it still seemed a little forced. "You know, sometimes we must be patient so that we can become strong." He brought a hand to his forehead as if he were suddenly too tired to handle everything that he needed to say. "That is all for now. Please, do exactly as I say."

Raveel stared intently at us through the screen, then the video feed cut back to Gralik, who had a smug smirk on his odious face.

"I think that's all that needs to be said for today's broadcast. Thank you for your continued support of our peaceful planet." He smiled again, and the screen went dark.

Vrynn sank back on the couch, looking defeated.

"I don't understand what all this means," I said.

Bryneen barely had her emotions under control, which made sense given that her brother was in enemy hands, so I turned my attention to Vrynn, instead. "Why is this such a big deal? Wasn't he just an army leader?"

Vrynn blew out a breath. "Raveel commanded the last of the defense forces near the center of Mardrys when they fell to the Barchee invaders. He was the greatest symbol of defiance against the Barchee. Fighters rallied to him. He was the ultimate leader."

"So how is he now making a video for Gralik?" I asked.

She lifted a shoulder. "Mosai always said he was killed in that final battle. But in the chaos,"—she held a hand toward the dark video screen—"he must have survived."

"And retired to Nildyr before betraying his people?" I asked in confusion.

Vrynn shook her head again. "It just doesn't make any sense. He was the strongest, most stubborn fighter of all. If he had survived, why would he have disappeared?" She stared across the room at nothing in particular. "How could he do this to us?"

After sending Bryneen to a nearby town to hide with some distant relative, Vrynn and I slipped out of Neevra and returned to the *Starfire* to plan our next attack. At least, I thought we would plan our next attack. Instead, Vrynn went to her quarters without eating and didn't come out again. Once I realized that was it for the day, I went to bed, too.

I was awoken from my sleep by a loud crash from the kitchen. I stumbled out of bed, pulled some clothes on, and staggered out into the hallway. For some reason, the lights in the kitchen and living area were on full, daytime-bright. I squinted and glanced around for what was going on. Maybe Gabe's internal chronometer had gotten out of whack. Or maybe I'd never told him to stay quiet at night.

But it wasn't Gabe. It was Vrynn.

She was sitting at the table, a giant mixing bowl in front of her, spooning something into her mouth. How she could stomach eating at this hour was beyond me. But then again, she hadn't eaten earlier, so maybe it was survival instincts kicking in.

I shuffled over to the table.

"Are you okay?" I asked. At least, that's what I tried to say. It came out more like, "Mm kay?" Hopefully, her translator chip knew what I meant.

She stared at me with tear-stained cheeks. "We've lost."

I noticed that her large bowl was actually filled with ice cream, or the ice cream substitute that I'd programmed the food processor to make. Here was the woman I already cared so deeply for, drowning her sorrows in a trough of ice cream. We were a match made in heaven.

Either that, or we were both going to gain a lot of weight in this relationship.

I sat down next to her. "We haven't lost yet. We'll just keep fighting through."

"No. I mean we, the Mareesh people, we've lost the spark to fight. We've lost the memory of what it was like to be free." She paused to take a huge bite. "Who would even want to fight for a people like that?"

She fixed me with an intense gaze, as if the question was meant for me specifically. I put my arm around her and pulled her head to my shoulder. "I would."

Vrynn pushed the bowl aside and wrapped her arms around me. I held her close as she sniffled the last of what must have been hours of crying. I hated to see her like this, but I had to admit that I didn't mind the way it felt to hold her.

After a few minutes, Vrynn let go of me and sat back. I wanted to say something that would make it better, but I didn't really have a lot of optimistic sayings in my repertoire. Of course, I wasn't above borrowing from others. "You know, maybe Raveel was right," I said, trying to sound upbeat. "Maybe we just have to wait for the strength."

Vrynn's gaze shot to me. "What did you say?"

Her sudden reaction caught me off guard. "Sorry. Maybe I shouldn't have mentioned Raveel."

"No. What did you just say?" Vrynn leaned toward me, taking my hands in hers. There was an urgency in her voice.

"Uh . . . wait for the strength?"

"That's not what he said," she insisted. Her gaze was intent on me, but then it drifted as if she was also thinking back to his statement. She stood and began pacing between the kitchen and living areas.

I shrugged. "I mean, that might not be exactly how he said it."

"Because he would never have been allowed to say it," Vrynn added absently. Suddenly, she stopped pacing and ran for the flight deck.

Halfway there, she glanced over her shoulder and waved for me to follow. "C'mon. This is important."

We found Tera and Gabe sitting next to each other on the jump seat behind the co-pilot's chair, Gabe's arm draped around Tera as she snuggled close against his chest. It looked so natural to see Tera and Gabe cuddling close—a scene I'd witnessed many times in my teens and twenties—that I barely thought twice about it.

"Do we need to set a curfew for you two?" I joked.

"Where would you send us at curfew time?" Tera shot back. "It's not like I have a room."

I chuckled. She had a good point there.

"I could place myself in standby mode at a certain time every evening, if that would be helpful," Gabe offered.

Tera frowned at him, then scowled at me.

"Can we talk about all this later?" Vrynn asked. "I really need Tera's help."

Tera straightened a little, proud to be of use.

"Do you have a recording of Gralik's broadcast yesterday?" Vrynn asked her. "The one with Raveel?"

"I don't keep that stuff in my matrix," Tera replied, "but the computer has a record of all local transmissions."

"Great." Vrynn moved to her co-pilot seat. "Could you play it on the display?"

The video of Raveel appeared above the console. I settled into the pilot's chair as he talked about the mystery ship that had been attacking and how the Mareesh people needed to stop the fighting.

When he said the line about having patience and then being strong, I felt justified in the fact that I had mostly remembered it right.

Vrynn pointed at the screen. "Stop there."

The video paused with Raveel's hand having just wiped across his brow. I had initially thought he simply looked tired, but watching it a second time made me realize that his motion wasn't entirely fluid. He seemed to hold his hand against his temple just a split second longer than would be natural.

"Mitch, you saw the clue that I missed!" she said excitedly.

I leaned forward and squinted at the screen. "I did?"

She started bouncing in her seat, all that pent up excitement getting the best of her. "Yes! You remembered what he said about being patient and becoming strong, but you said it differently."

"Nobody's perfect."

Turning to more fully face me, Vrynn grabbed my hands. "That's just it. You did say it perfectly, or nearly perfectly. The actual phrase is 'Wait for strength.'" She lifted one of her hands to the side of her head as she said it. "It's from a famous film in our culture."

Fortunately, the confusion on my face must have prompted more explanation. She held her hand to her temple again. "'Wait for strength' is what the main character says when he is preparing to mutiny against the ship's despotic captain. It's such a classic reference that I can't believe

I didn't catch it. Look. He's even making the motion." Vrynn gestured to the paused holographic display.

"Why would he make a movie reference in the middle of . . ." I trailed off as it hit me. "He's trying to send a message, isn't he?"

Vrynn nodded enthusiastically.

I frowned. "But why not just say it outright? And why wouldn't he have sent the military forces a message long before this?"

Vrynn's expression clouded. "I'm not sure." After a moment, she turned back to Tera. "Can you start it again from the beginning?"

I turned my attention back to the screen, and we listened to the same message a third time.

Vrynn spoke over the middle. "See, he's using phrases like 'compelled to say,' and 'valiantly attacking supply convoys.' If you really listen, it's almost like he's trying to imply the opposite of what he's actually saying."

I had thought something was off about his message. Too bad I hadn't said something earlier.

We watched as Raveel finished his message, eyes boring into us.

"There." Vrynn pointed again. "See that flock of feelja?"

I had only been vaguely aware of the flying animals visible through the window of Raveel's home. They seemed to move over the beach like something between a school of fish and a flock of seagulls.

I leaned in. "What am I looking at?"

"Play the video from the beginning," Vrynn asked.

This time, we all focused on the view of the beach out the window behind Raveel, mostly ignoring his repeated request to the people of Mareesh.

"Right there. See how the flock moved in a swirling pattern." The video continued, Vrynn perched on the edge of her seat. Several seconds later, she jumped, pointing at the flock. "And there it is again. That's the same pattern."

I furrowed my brow as I considered the image. "Maybe the feelers—"

"Feelja," Vrynn corrected.

"—the feelja fly in repeating patterns."

Vrynn's brow furrowed. "Have you ever seen a flock move in repeating patterns?"

"No. But I've seen a lot of things in this star cluster that I couldn't have imagined a few months ago."

Vrynn very intentionally ignored my existential commentary and returned her attention to the video.

I sat back in my seat. "Tera, can you run a pattern recognition algorithm or something like that? Search for repeated clips in the video."

A few moments later, Tera replied. "The speed has been slightly altered, but there is a ninety-six percent chance that the video of the flock has been looped."

"Why would there be a repeating video of flying animals out his window?" I asked.

"Because the window isn't real," Vrynn said.

"It looks pretty real to me." I pointed at the projection. "Are you saying you don't think he's actually on Nildyr? That he's faking his own retirement?"

"Why would a person fake retirement?" Gabe asked. "It would require an extreme amount of effort and subterfuge, which seems to negate the benefits of not working. It would be more logical to not be retired than to pretend to be retired."

I chuckled. "That's some deep pondering right there, buddy."

"He's a prisoner," Vrynn said suddenly, as if the idea had just popped into her head.

My head whipped back to Vrynn, eyes wide. "What?"

Vrynn stood and paced the small aisle next to her co-pilot chair. "It all makes sense. That's why he wouldn't have contacted us earlier. That's why he can't just come out and give us the message. He's a prisoner, and they're telling him exactly what to say."

"Which is also why he didn't say the quote exactly right," I said, catching up. "They might have recognized the reference."

"Exactly," Vrynn said. "He had to be subtle about it."

I whistled. "That was a huge risk. You nearly missed the reference entirely."

"Yeah. But it was a risk for him to try sending a message at all," Vrynn said.

I glanced back at the projection. "Do you think he's in the prison on Mardrys? The one where they're holding Mosai?"

"Possibly," Vrynn said, sitting back in her chair with a contemplative expression.

I leaned forward to scrutinize the video again. A framed photo of an ocean scene on the wall behind Raveel caught my attention. "There's one way to find out." I pointed at the picture. "Tera, can you zoom in on this part of the video?" The projection shifted, bringing the photo into the center and enlarging it. The frame was obviously sealed over with a reflective, glass-like material. I pointed at the phantom reflections in the smooth surface. "Tera, does the computer have an algorithm that can remove the ocean picture so we can see what's reflected from the rest of the room?" I asked.

"No. But I can do it anyway." Her eyes scanned back and forth as she accessed the internal databanks of the ship. A few seconds later, she said, "It will take a minute to process."

I smiled. "Do you mean a literal minute? Or did you mean it figuratively, like it will only take—"

"Finished," Tera announced.

The holographic display shifted, rotating around to show the other half of Raveel's room. This was even better than squinting at the reflection. The computer had extrapolated a three-dimensional mockup. Much of the room was missing, and the forms were weird and misshapen, but there was definitely a person standing across from Raveel, holding up a small device. "Is that the video operator?" I asked.

Vrynn nodded absently as she inspected the scene.

That part was easy. The rest of the room was a puzzle. There were four other nearly humanoid figures in the room, standing just behind the cameraman, two on each side.

"If this person is recording the video,"—she pointed to the one in the middle—"why are these other people here?"

I pointed to each in turn. "Grip, assistant director, director, producer." I smiled at Vrynn, but she didn't seem to get my joke. I shrugged. "If we're right about him being a prisoner, then these are probably guards. Look at their stances."

"I bet you're right. And look at this." She pointed at the midsection of one of the figures. "Does this look like a plasma rifle against his chest?"

I leaned forward and stared at the amorphous distortions. "It definitely could be. And if he really is a prisoner, we have to figure out where he's being held."

Vrynn and I both stared at the projection for several more seconds.

"Can you enlarge this section?" Vrynn pointed behind one of the guards.

"We're reaching the limit of how much enhancing the computer can do," Tera warned.

"That's fine." Vrynn waved off her concern. "Take us all the way to the limit."

The projection in front of us zoomed in and resolved into clearer shapes. It was a door with a sign above it. Vrynn's sudden intake of breath was my first indication that it was a big deal.

"He's definitely on Barchee," she said finally.

"How can you possibly know that?" I asked.

"Look at the writing," Vrynn said, pointing at the squiggle marks on the sign. "It says 'Restroom'."

I barked out a laugh that Vrynn didn't appreciate. "You can tell he's on Barchee because the sign says where the restroom is?"

Vrynn scowled. "No, because the sign is written in Barchee."

"What? I thought you and the Barchee had the same language."

"You did?" Vrynn seemed genuinely surprised. "Haven't you ever heard someone speak Barchee?"

I racked my brain. I was fairly certain I'd kicked a Barchee soldier in the head, but that didn't mean we'd carried on a conversation. "Maybe? But either way, my chip translates over everything. I hardly ever hear the actual words."

"They sound very different," Vrynn said. "Obviously, they're based on the same original language, so they have some similarities, but they've both evolved over the last several hundred years. And the way we write has diverged, too, though not quite as much. You see that swoop there?" She pointed to a curved shape attached to another round shape surrounded by a curvy, round thing.

I gave a noncommittal shrug.

"We don't have that in Mareesh. That's a Barchee character," she insisted.

"I'm gonna have to take your word for it unless Tera or Gabe can back you up," I said.

"There's a ninety-three percent chance that the sign is written in Barchee," Tera said.

"That still leaves a chance that it's not," I said.

Vrynn smiled. "We've gone on less."

"That's true." I let out a resigned sigh. "Okay. What do we do next?"

Chapter Fifteen

"I like this plan even less now that you've finished explaining it," I said to Vrynn.

We were sitting in a dank, back room of Mosai and Bryneen's great great-aunt or something. Hustan was with us, trying to persuade me that the scheme they had come up with wasn't completely insane.

"Trust me, this plan will work. The soldier I know is sympathetic to the Mareesh situation," Hustan said.

I folded my arms across my chest. "One sympathetic soldier isn't going to convince me. What's to prevent him from changing his mind and selling us out at the last minute?"

"Oh, he wouldn't do that," Hustan said. "Not if he wants to avoid the pond."

"The pond?" I asked just as my translator caught up and amended, "the doghouse." That only slightly changed the meaning, and I was still confused.

"This guy married a Mareesh woman. They have a new baby. He's not going to betray us," Hustan said.

I paused to reorganize my arguments. "Fine. So there's a soldier that can help us. I just don't see why we can't use the *Starfire* to go get Raveel. We could be there in two minutes, even with the standard jump drive."

Vrynn placed a hand on my leg. "But we won't be able to get into the prison," she said. "And it wouldn't do us any good to shoot our way in; we would risk killing Raveel and who knows how many others."

"Also, the Barchee military complex in Taleech is vast," Hustan said. "How would you find him? Especially while you had the entire Barchee military after you as soon as you entered the atmosphere."

"Yeah, but this plan doesn't solve that problem," I said. "You still have to find where they're keeping Raveel."

"Yes, but a single person sneaking in"—Vrynn indicated herself—"could have a better chance of finding him before anyone knows what's happening."

I shook my head. "It's going to be obvious what you're trying to do. You're Mareesh. What other reason could you have for wandering around a prison complex asking for directions to Raveel's cell?"

Vrynn cracked a smile at that.

"And why can't we just have this Barchee soldier-guy go for us?" I asked. "He'd have more of a reason to be there in the first place."

"I said 'sympathetic'," Hustan replied. "He's no freedom-fighter."

"Besides, with a little cosmetic help," Vrynn nodded toward Bryneen, "we think I can pass as Barchee."

I leaned back into the couch with a huff. "I still don't like it. What if you can't find him? What if something goes wrong? What if you get caught?"

Vrynn patted my knee. "Don't worry, everything will work out fine."

I scowled at her. "Enemy military prison complexes aren't affected by your optimism," I muttered.

"Then our backup plan will be you swooping in with the *Starfire's* cannons blazing." Her head tilted as she considered me. "You can be my rescuer," she added with a smile.

Her trust in my abilities brought simultaneous feelings of elation and doom.

We took Bryneen with us back to the hidden cavern to help Vrynn get ready for the mission. It made the preparations easier, plus it seemed like the right thing to do. Without Mosai, Bryneen had become listless and sad, which was saying something for a Mareesh. Hustan, on the other hand, was champing at the bit to do something to rescue Sharlee. We said goodbye that morning, telling him to not do anything stupid.

Tera and Vrynn spent most of the morning working through various Barchee dialects that Vrynn might be able to make sound convincing.

"My name is Vureech, special liaison to occupational high command," Vrynn said with a self-assured tone.

"Yeah, I think that one is the best," Tera replied. "It sounds the most authentic. Besides, the lowland accent seems to be the most commonly adopted, and you've just about got it. Don't you agree, Bryneen."

"She definitely sounds like the Barchee I've talked to," Bryneen said. "It's a little bit creepy."

Tera turned to me. "What do you think, Mitch?"

I sighed. "You've repeated that phrase back and forth to each other a dozen times, but every time sounds identical to me."

"That's because you're hearing the translation," Tera said. "If you could hear the way she's pronouncing the words, you'd understand the difference."

I shrugged. "That's probably true, but then it would just sound like gibberish." I nudged Gabe, who was sitting on the couch next to me. "Right, buddy?"

Gabe gave me a polite smile. "Actually, Tera was kind enough to download the Barchee language database into my system, so I have been listening without translation. It sounds acceptable to me."

"I think you're ready," Tera declared. "Now, let's get working on your disguise." She clapped her holographic hands together, looking almost gleeful.

"I brought my kit," Bryneen said, holding up a frilly box.

"That's perfect. And I sent some custom make-up recipes to the fabrication machines," Tera said.

"I think we'd better leave this to the experts." I held out my hands to indicate Tera and Bryneen. "Gabe, let's go down and check the stock of atmospheric missiles."

Gabe stood. "Am I not one of the experts on using cosmetics to approximate Barchee appearance?"

I stopped and faced him. "Oh, sorry buddy. Did you want to stay and help them?"

The corner of Gabe's mouth twitched. "I was attempting to make a humorous comment about how you had singled me out. Based on the transferred memories of the original Gabe, it does seem more appropriate for you and I to go work on weaponry while the ladies do the make-up. Have I ascertained the roles correctly?"

I scratched my head. "Yeah, that's pretty typical, but you can do whichever you want."

Gabe nodded. "I have spent ninety-one point three percent of our time on Mareesh in Tera's company exclusively. Perhaps spending time with you would be beneficial at this moment."

I smiled. "Male bonding, right?"

"Correct."

On our way toward the stairs, Gabe glanced over his shoulder at Tera with a wistful, almost human look in his eye. "Tera does so much to assist me in my duties, often without receiving reciprocal compensation."

"I think that's what you do when you love someone," I said to my friend.

We descended to the lower deck together and made our way to the missile loaders.

"Tera knows that my attachment algorithm has not developed to romantic love yet," Gabe said. "Do you think she would consider it a deception on my part if I did nice things in return, even though I do not feel the emotion?"

I put a hand on his shoulder and smiled. "I think you might be selling yourself short on your algorithmic progress there, buddy. But, no, I don't think Tera would have any problem with you doing nice things for her."

Gabe and I spent the next hour or so in the armory area making sure we had enough atmospheric missiles for the mission. If everything went right, we wouldn't even need to engage the enemy, but it never hurt to be prepared.

As we worked, Gabe's deep thinking about Tera and my own guilt at not having told Vrynn how I felt about her started to gnaw at me. Why hadn't I told her yet? I didn't really have a good reason. Plus, with her about to embark on such a dangerous mission, there might not be a better opportunity.

When Gabe and I returned to the upper deck, I was shocked at what we saw. With a little cosmetics and a stolen uniform, they had transformed Vrynn into a member of the Barchee military.

"Wow," I breathed out. "You look different."

Vrynn's brow went up. "Good or bad?"

"Well, I prefer your regular color to this Barchee skin tone. It makes you look like you're not feeling well. But it certainly looks convincing."

I stepped toward her, wondering how to bring up my feelings for her without it being awkward. I reached for her cheek, but she held a hand up.

"Don't touch. You'll ruin my makeup," she said.

I smiled at her level of dedication. "Are you sure you still want to do this?" I asked in a quiet voice.

It was disconcerting to look at the woman I cared for and see a stranger. She stared back at me with those gorgeous eyes, and then I could see the Vrynn I knew. "My people need an uprising, and the uprising needs Raveel."

"We could always figure out another plan," I replied.

"When the wind blows, the waves rise," she said quietly.

When my chip didn't clarify anything, I tilted my head in confusion.

Vrynn smiled lightly. "It means we all have to perform our duty when the time comes."

I took her hand, making sure not to rub off any of her turquoise coloring. "Be careful," I said.

"I always am."

I was about to object, but she gave me a cute, slow-motion wink. The best one she'd done so far. This woman was very quickly finding a permanent place in my heart. I was tempted to throw caution to the wind and sweep her up in my arms—and possibly more—right then and there.

I shook my head slowly. "You know, I've been trying not to tease you so much lately, but you're making that very difficult at the moment."

She lifted a brow. "How so?"

"Oh, I could say that if it weren't for your make-up, I might have kissed you a second ago."

"That kind of teasing wouldn't work," she replied matter-of-factly.

"Oh?" I said, leaning ever closer to her face, very intentionally glancing at her lips. "Not even a little?"

"No," she said flatly.

For a split-second, I worried that I'd misread all the cues, that maybe she didn't actually have feelings for me after all.

But then she grabbed me by the collar and pulled me toward her, nearly bumping our noses together. "I can always put more make-up on," she said, her tone sultry and intoxicating.

I gulped when I realized that she might actually be serious. My heart pounded as my gaze flitted to her lips. I was certainly willing to kiss her, but was this really the time, in front of Gabe and Tera and Bryneen? She held me there for what seemed like forever but still wasn't quite long enough. Eventually, when she released my collar and put a little space between us, my heart rate slowly started returning to normal. With an endearing little smirk still on her face, she very gently intertwined her fingers in mine. As she considered our clasped hands, her mood turned somber, like the weight of an entire world rested on her shoulders.

It really didn't feel like the right time to tell her how much I cared about her, but then again, maybe she already knew. I let out a long breath. "Seriously though. I need you to be safe and come back to me, okay?"

Our eyes locked, and I saw a moment of trepidation in her gaze. "You, too," she replied. A second later, she pushed up onto her tiptoes and gave me a quick kiss on the cheek before dashing away.

I brought a hand absently up to my face; my cheek was hot where her lips had touched and probably marked with aqua-green makeup, but I didn't care.

From high orbit, I stared down at the tiny island of Mardrys, floating in a vast ocean beneath the *Starfire*.

"Hustan said that the Barchee soldier made contact with Vrynn, right?" I asked Tera. "He didn't change his mind and leave her lying in an alley somewhere?"

Tera nodded. "Yes, he made contact with her. No, he didn't leave her lying in an alley. Hustan's message said they were moving toward the transport and that its systems were brought online a few minutes ago."

Logically, I knew she was right, but Vrynn was deep in the Barchee-controlled base. That made it hard to stay calm. "If the video link isn't—"

Our comm crackled to life as the system finally established a connection with Vrynn's communicator and the tiny video camera embedded in her hair clip.

Tera pointed to the feed. "See, she's fine. It looks like she's in the Mardrys spaceport right now."

Vrynn moved through the sparse crowd of other passengers as she approached the hatch to the transport. A Barchee man in an attendant uniform greeted her. "Welcome Officer Vureech. Please make yourself comfortable in one of our VIP seats."

"Thank you," Vrynn said in a voice of forced seriousness.

"She's boarding the transport." I'm not sure why I whispered it, probably because it felt like the boarding attendant was standing right in front of us.

Vrynn settled herself into a seat near the front—actually, we couldn't see Vrynn at all, but it was obvious what she was doing. A few minutes later, we heard the rumble of the launch, and the transport popped up on my tactical display as it lifted off from the spaceport. We tracked the transport as it rose through the atmosphere and lined up for its intra-space jump to Barchee.

"We'll be waiting for you on the other end, Vrynn," I said through the comm.

She cleared her throat in a way that sounded like an acknowledgement. Then the transport disappeared into intra-space.

I glanced down at my sensor console. "Okay, we've got the coordinates. Match their jump."

We faded into intra-space for the longest fifty-seven seconds of my life. As we returned to normal space, the sensors picked up the Barchee transport in the upper atmosphere. It descended toward the surface and landed at the military complex, just as anticipated.

We watched the video feed as Vrynn exited the spacecraft and plunged into the middle of a bustling transportation hub. Hundreds of commuters marched along to their destinations in what could only be described as organized chaos. It was like the crowd leaving a sports arena had been funneled into a shopping mall.

"Vrynn, according to the description from the Barchee soldier, you should see a hallway branching off from the main corridor to the right," Tera said.

The video feed panned right and held steady on a side hall.

"I bet that's the one." I pointed at the screen then realized how silly it was, considering Vrynn couldn't see me.

"Mm hm," Vrynn hummed back.

The crowd thinned considerably the farther Vrynn went, and the ambient noise slowly died away.

"Okay, I think it's safe to talk," Vrynn whispered. "The hallway is pretty much empty."

"Good. Find a computer terminal," I said. "And be careful."

"It's okay, Mitch. I know how to handle a—" Vrynn abruptly stopped speaking.

The video feed showed someone approaching. I held my breath as a pair of armed guards passed her.

"Try the hallway on your left," Tera suggested. "It looks like there might be some offices down that way."

Vrynn casually turned down the small hallway. She passed several very austere-looking offices, all with workers in them. Finally, toward the end, she found one that was empty. With a quick glance around, she slipped inside and moved to the terminal.

She glanced down at the input interface, a device that looked completely foreign to me. It was like someone had cut a cantaloupe-sized rubber ball in half and laid the pieces down next to each other.

"What if the input interface uses biometrics?" Vrynn asked.

I was glad she asked that question, and not the one that had occurred to me which was "how does this thing even work?"

I glanced at Tera, who was scanning for information. "According to available Barchee military information, biometric interfaces are only installed on about one in five computers." She turned to me. "Are we willing to take a twenty percent chance?"

I shook my head. "No. Especially not with Vrynn in the middle of a Barchee military base."

"What's the worst that could happen?" Vrynn asked, still staring down at the computer interface.

"They could catch you and throw you into prison with Raveel," I replied.

"At least we would know where he was." She said wryly.

I shook my head. "The Barchee military would almost definitely turn you over to Gralik."

The playfulness immediately evaporated from her tone. "I know."

"Maybe we can find the prisoner manifest some other way," I offered.

There was silence on her end of the comm. I would have thought we had lost the connection, except I could see her view moving ever so slightly as she breathed.

"I'm going to try it anyway," she said as she sat at the terminal and placed her hands on the interface.

"Vrynn, don't—"

The video display flashed to life, and the rest of the warning died in my throat. This woman was going to send me into cardiac arrest some day. And yet, I didn't seem to be able to live without her.

"The network connection is still active," Vrynn said, relief obvious in her voice. "Now I just need to find the prisoner list."

Images and squiggly streams flew across the screen.

"There," Tera said. "That last block had a choice for inmates."

The squiggles suddenly flew in reverse, and one of them grew in size. I still had no idea what anything said. I really needed to find an implant that could translate what I saw, too.

"Here it is," Vrynn said. More lines flew across the display. "This is a long list."

"I can read it faster, just pan through the whole thing," Tera said.

The curves suddenly became a parade of swirling lines. How could any information even be conveyed at that speed?

"There's no prisoner named Raveel on that list," Tera said once the vortex of squiggles had ended. "Could he be under a different name?"

"Could he be in a different prison?" I added.

"Either of those could be possible," Vrynn replied as more squiggly curves moved across the screen.

"Actually, Mitch might be onto something," Tera said. "There was an option for High Security on one of the earlier menus."

Vrynn manipulated the interface for a few seconds. "Here it is." New patterns flashed onto the screen and began flying by again. "They don't have many in the High Security section. Maybe they—"

"Stop," Tera cried.

The artistic shapes stopped moving.

"There's Raveel," she said. "In the cluster on the right."

The displayed shapes shifted left and grew to fill the screen.

"Are we sure that's the Raveel you're looking for?" I asked.

Vrynn must have selected something because a mugshot of Raveel popped up on the screen.

"It's really him," Vrynn said. There was a giddy note in her voice. "Where's the high security cell block located?"

"Is there a map in any of that gobbledygook?" I asked.

"Go back a few pages," Tera said.

"Oh, I see it," Vrynn said.

Vrynn selected an option, or at least, that's what I thought she did. A new set of squiggly lines grew on the screen. It took me a few seconds to realize that it wasn't Barchee writing, but a map of the facility. The layout matched the rough outline of the buildings we could see from orbit.

"Pan around the entire thing," Tera instructed.

The map moved side to side and up and down.

"That's good enough; I have it recorded," Tera said.

"Okay, Vrynn. Time to get out of there before—"

"Explain what you are doing here," a stern voice said.

Vrynn's view whipped toward the door, where a man stood framed in the entrance. His expression seemed more curious than suspicious. That was fortunate for Vrynn.

I tried to think of some way for Vrynn to get out. "Tell him you're—"

"I've been assigned to check interface sensitivities on all the terminals in this sector," Vrynn said. I couldn't tell if she'd already thought of that excuse or if she was improvising on the spot. Either way, it was impressive.

His brow furrowed as he considered her. "I haven't heard anything about that."

"It's just a quick check; I'm already finished and moving to the next office," Vrynn said.

The guy's expression relaxed a little. Vrynn stood from the terminal, deftly clearing the information on the screen, and moved toward the door. The guy glanced down at her hand. "You didn't bring any equipment?"

Vrynn's video feed panned the room. I could tell she was searching for some way to explain her situation. "Oh, I didn't need equipment. It was just a standard interface check, verifying connection speeds, that sort of thing." She moved to slide by the guy.

"Wait. I will need to verify your authorization."

Vrynn had nearly passed when the guy grabbed her by the arm. I felt helpless to de-escalate the situation. All I could do was hope Vrynn could get herself out of there.

Of course, Vrynn must not have thought de-escalation was the best option. She flipped his arm around and grabbed it with both hands. But she didn't stop there. In one fluid motion, she pulled his arm behind his back and slammed him against the door.

Apparently, Barchee office workers weren't trained to expect sudden hand-to-hand combat because he crumpled to the ground a second after hitting the wall. Vrynn quickly deactivated the lights and pulled the door closed behind her as she left the office.

"What was that?" I asked in disbelief.

"I'm improvising," Vrynn whispered as she hustled down the hall. "Tera, do you have the location for Raveel yet?"

"The high security cells are in a different part of the facility," Tera said. "According to the map, you'll need to take a transport to the other complex."

"Tell me where to go." Vrynn had nearly reached the main corridor again.

"Turn right," Tera said. "Follow the main concourse to the transport stop."

Vrynn moved quickly through the light crowds back toward the spaceport.

"What if that guy wakes up?" I thought out loud. "You need to hurry."

"I am," Vrynn said softly. "But I don't want to draw attention to myself."

She followed the flow of workers down the concourse. Up ahead, a long train slowed to a stop near a raised platform. It was similar to the high-speed transport that traversed the islands on Mareesh, except much wider and longer.

As the crowd grew more dense, Vrynn fell in step with others around her. The passengers inched forward when the doors to the transport opened.

Then something caught my eye.

Rather than annoy or distract Vrynn, I leaned over to Tera. "Can you play back the feed on my console? I think I saw something in the crowd."

Tera's expression turned worried, but she nodded, and the recorded video appeared at my station. I backed it up about ten seconds and watched as Vrynn's view panned the crowd. I paused and zoomed in.

A security guard stood next to a support column scrutinizing the sea of travelers. But unlike the other guards that Vrynn had passed, this one seemed to focus on her.

I tried not to jump to conclusions. Maybe this particular guard was drawn to Vrynn's striking appearance. I certainly was. I returned my attention to the live feed again, watching for the next time Vrynn glanced that direction.

I saw him again.

He had definitely singled Vrynn out of the crowd, and based on his expression, it wasn't for any good reason.

"Vrynn, I think one of the guards noticed you," I said quietly.

She casually panned the crowd.

"That one," I said, as her gaze swept across the people behind her. "You need to get to the train before he reaches you."

Vrynn fought through the press of people toward the front of the pack. The next time she glanced over her shoulder, I saw the security guard pushing through the crowd, knocking people aside.

Just as she reached the front of the group, rather than board through the open door, Vrynn ducked low and darted back along the side of the transport. She worked across the crowd, cutting in front of people who were trying to board.

The next time she looked back, I was happy to see that the guard seemed to have lost sight of her. At the very last car, Vrynn jumped on the train.

Four long noises that sounded like a child's broken horn carried through the open comm. Vrynn filed along with the others and sat on a bench facing the front.

"I think you're safe," I said. "That guard didn't follow you."

Vrynn lifted a finger and moved it back and forth above her lap, as if she was painting an imaginary landscape.

"She said 'thanks'," Tera interpreted.

My brow went up. I hadn't even considered that Tera could read air-writing. That was helpful.

"Between the guy in his office and the guard on the platform, I think we need to do this as fast as we possibly can," I said.

More writing in the air.

"She wants to know if you think she's going too slow," Tera said before turning to me. "Actually, I don't think she really wants to know that. She probably thinks you're being overly naggy. I certainly do."

Vrynn stifled a small giggle.

"Yeah, well, this is definitely deviating from the plan," I said. "And that makes me nervous."

Vrynn's finger went to work again.

"She says not to worry. Everything will be fine," Tera said.

That was classic Vrynn. I was about to say something witty when she started writing again.

"She's asking for what to do next," Tera said.

"Do you have the location of Raveel's cell?" I asked Tera.

She nodded. "It's in the center of the third cell block."

"Okay, tell Vrynn how to find him," I said.

As the train rocketed along, Tera gave Vrynn detailed instructions. When the transport came to a stop, Vrynn shot out the doors and hustled across the concourse. As she approached the cell block, I brought up the map of this new facility on my console. What I saw did not improve my mood.

"This prison is much more heavily guarded by defensive systems," I said to Tera and Vrynn. "And it doesn't have a prison yard where we can pick you up."

"Maybe there's enough room in this area." Tera pointed at my map. "No, actually, that's much too small for the *Starfire*."

"Can we route Vrynn to this area?" I asked, pointing at a small gap between some buildings.

"Probably. But it's so far out of—"

Tera stopped when Vrynn cleared her throat a second time. We both looked up at the video feed. Vrynn stood facing a security console.

"Use the spectrolight," Tera instructed.

Pulling a small, handheld flashlight from her pocket, Vrynn shined it on the input pad. At first, the pad simply glowed with faint colored swirls, like some kid had drawn a picture of tangled ropes with every color in the rainbow.

"Each color is a different bio-marker," Tera explained. "There are probably more than three dozen code traces left on the panel, but only two of them are distinguishable."

Vrynn nodded. "Okay, give me whichever one you think is more likely to work."

Tera said a strange word that my chip translated as "tell five mountain sneeze." If I had been in Vrynn's shoes, I might have laughed out loud at such a silly security code, but Vrynn simply touched her finger to the screen and traced a pattern that was remarkably similar to the light green line.

The security screen flashed twice, and a moment later, the door slid open. Vrynn slipped through into a much more dimly lit hallway.

"Fifth door on the left," Tera said.

Vrynn walked carefully down the empty corridor. She stopped and faced the fifth door. Rising on her tiptoes, she peeked through the small, inset window. It was a nondescript cell with nothing but an older Mareesh man lying on a cot.

Raveel.

Vrynn considered the security panel embedded in the door. "Will the same code work here?" she asked quietly.

"It should," Tera replied.

Before I could ask Tera the odds, Vrynn had already zigzagged her finger along the surface.

I held my breath until, finally, the screen flashed and the lock clicked. Vrynn quickly pushed the door open. "Raveel," she said as she approached the man lying on the bed.

He slowly opened one eye. "What do you want? Can't you just leave an old man to rot in peace?"

Vrynn stopped and crouched to his level. "Raveel, it's me, Vrynn. I'm here to rescue you."

He lazily opened the other eye. "There is no way that . . ." He trailed off, lifting his head for a better look. "Vrynn, is that really you?"

She nodded. "Let's get you out of here."

"I thought you were dead," he said as he sat up on his bed.

"We thought the same about you," she replied. "Until we saw the transmission."

Raveel rose on moderately steady legs—considering how old he looked. "You must have understood my secret message. But I had hoped you would gather other fighters and go against the occupiers."

Vrynn nodded. "Our forces are scattered. Keelsa has organized a resistance group, but their efforts are weak and diluted. The true fighters won't gather without their leader. That's why we need you." She pulled him toward the half-open door.

"Hurry, Vrynn," I said over the comm. "More moving, less talking."

She stopped and turned slightly away from Raveel. "Despite my flawless execution, this isn't as easy as it looks."

"Sorry. I'm just super nervous," I replied.

When she returned her attention to Raveel, he had a wary expression on his face. "I'm going to assume you're talking to someone on a comm link and that I haven't just been rescued by a crazy person."

"No guarantees on that part," Vrynn replied with a smile in her voice. "But my friend on the starship is right; we need to get out of here."

She checked down the narrow corridor before walking out. Raveel followed closely behind.

"Grab my arm like you're a guard escorting me out of the cell. Otherwise, it looks like we're on an afternoon stroll."

Taking him by the arm, Vrynn pulled Raveel forward to the outer security door. "Same code?" she asked.

"Yeah, keep using it," Tera said.

Vrynn scribbled the passcode on the security input and nothing happened. She tried again, but the screen flashed a message.

"What did that say?" I asked Tera.

"It says the facility is on temporary lock-down," Tera replied.

"You have to get out a different way," I said as I frantically checked the rudimentary map of the facility. "Check the other end of the corridor."

Vrynn and Raveel reversed course, hustling past the long line of cells to the far end, where there was another security door. She tried the code she'd used earlier, but it didn't work.

"The codes are all disabled when the facility is locked-down," Tera said.

"How are we going to get out, then?" Vrynn asked.

"Try the emergency call," Raveel said.

"What's that?" Vrynn asked.

The old soldier pointed back down the hall. "There's a button at each cell door for emergencies."

Vrynn hurried over and mashed the call button. She turned to Raveel and pointed at the ground next to her. "Maybe you should act like you're hurt."

He got down on the floor, though he didn't seem excited about the idea.

"I'll wait until the guards get close enough before attacking them," Vrynn whispered. "But if more than one comes in, you'll have to help."

"What if more than two come through?" Raveel asked.

"Then I might be joining you in that cell," she replied dryly.

With Raveel lying flat on the ground, Vrynn watched the door. A second later, the release clicked, and it swung open. Two guards came through, approaching Vrynn with weapons drawn.

"I don't know what happened," she said to the first guard, pointing to Raveel lying on the ground.

They moved closer, with one guard stepping up to Raveel and nudging him with a boot. "Get up, old man," he growled.

As the first guard leaned over the fallen prisoner, Vrynn punched the second guard in the gut, sending him staggering backward. The first guard whirled on her, but before he could aim straight, Raveel kicked his arm. The blaster fired as it swung upward, narrowly missing Vrynn.

She punched the first guard in the face, then grabbed him by the neck and drove him headlong into the nearby wall. Before he had even hit the ground, she pulled his weapon and took aim at the second guard, who had now regained his footing. Her shots hit him twice in the chest just as he fired. He flew backward and slid several feet down the hall as his rounds bounced harmlessly off the walls.

Vrynn glanced around the corridor. "Where's Raveel?!" she exclaimed.

"Vrynn," the elderly commander called from the security door. He'd had the presence of mind to catch it before it slammed closed again.

Shouts echoed from the opposite end of the corridor. A pair of guards had entered from that end and started firing at them. Vrynn scampered after Raveel, narrowly avoiding the blaster fire, and ducked through the security door with him. After pulling it closed with a clank, Vrynn grabbed Raveel by the arm and walked down a small hallway toward the front of the facility.

"Don't go out the way you came in," I said, consulting the rough outline of the buildings. "Find a service corridor leading to the loading docks."

"My friend wants us to go out through the dock area," Vrynn said to Raveel.

"Good idea," he replied. "This hallway will take us that way," he said, pointing the other direction.

The narrow corridor was decidedly utilitarian with pipes and conduits hugging the walls and ceiling. After half a minute, the hall dumped them into a larger, warehouse-looking area. Several transports sat in their bays, waiting to be unloaded.

"We could always steal a truck," Vrynn whispered.

"No, that would definitely draw too much attention," I said. "Just slip out onto the city streets, and we'll find a place to meet you." I turned to Tera. "Make sure the Quake drive is online. As soon as they find a place big enough for the ship, we'll target their location."

Vrynn and Raveel crouched behind a cargo truck and crept along the side of the loading yard.

"I haven't been in fresh air in several years," Raveel said.

"No time to enjoy it yet," Vrynn said.

They scampered around a nearby corner and made their way down a narrow alley.

"How far to the nearest open space?" Vrynn said.

I consulted my tactical display. "The best spot is several miles from your location, on the outskirts of the city."

"That's not going to work, Mitch." The video panned back to Raveel. "Raveel will be easily recognized as a prisoner. Besides, he can't run very far in his current condition."

"I can run a short distance," Raveel objected.

"Okay, uh, hang on." I panned around the map of the city. There were a few small open areas but none large enough for the *Starfire* to fly through a portal into. They were barely large enough for the *Starfire* to set down. "Could we open the portal above the city and then land in one of these spots?" I asked Tera, pointing at one of the plazas.

"They'd see us right away," she replied in a defeated tone. "Do you want to have to fight through the entire Barchee fleet?"

"What else can we do?" I threw my hands up in frustration.

"What if you open a portal in one of these streets?" Vrynn suggested.

I scrutinized the video feed. "We would fly right into a building."

"No. Just open the portal, and we'll walk through it to you," she said.

"Is that possible?" I asked Tera.

She shrugged her holographic shoulders. "Technically, the *Starfire* doesn't have to go through the aperture."

I turned back to the video feed. "That's perfect, Vrynn. You can just jump through the portal to us. Hang on, we'll target your location."

"Are you still in orbit?" she asked.

"Yeah," I said. "We were waiting until . . . oh, we can't open the portal from here. You'll get sucked into space."

"Yeah, that wouldn't be good," Vrynn replied drily.

I grabbed the controls. "Okay, we'll find a place to land. Just a minute."

As I approached the edge of the Barchee atmosphere, the screen flashed with an incoming communication.

"That's Barchee control," Tera said. "They probably want to ask what you're doing."

"Ignore them," I said, focusing intently on getting the ship down to some patch of ground.

"If we ignore Barchee space control, they will send ships to intercept us," Tera said.

"As soon as they identify our ship, they'll send ships anyway," I said. "Hopefully, we'll be long gone before then."

"Mitch?"

I returned my attention to Vrynn's video feed. I had been vaguely aware that they were winding back and forth in the city's alleys, trying to put some distance between them and the prison complex. But now, all I could see on the video feed was a dead-end.

"What happened?" I asked.

"The guards were on our tail, and I must have made a wrong turn," Vrynn said.

"I'm trying to get us down as fast as I can." I turned to Tera. "How long before we can land somewhere?"

"Two minutes," she said.

"We don't have two minutes," Vrynn complained.

I scrubbed a hand across my face. "Uh, what if we just open the portal here in the air? Are we low enough in the atmosphere?"

Tera's eyes scanned quickly, probably checking the exterior sensors. "Yes. The air is breathable, but barely."

"Okay, target the aperture to Vrynn's location in the alley," I said, decelerating the *Starfire* to a rapid halt and switching on the hover emitters.

"Acknowledged," Tera said a moment later. "Also, three Barchee fighters are on their way."

My head jerked back to her. "How long until they get here?"

"Three minutes," she replied.

"Hurry Mitch, I think the prison guards are just around the corner," Vrynn said in an urgent whisper.

"Activate the portal!" I could feel my heart about to beat out of my chest.

The aperture gradually widened in front of the ship. But instead of the usual star field or planet, all I could see was a dirty alley wall with Vrynn and Raveel standing on the edge of the aperture.

For several seconds, Vrynn and I stared at each other across the wide gap of thin air between the *Starfire* and the portal it had opened.

"Now what?" she asked.

"Hang on." With a quick move on the controls, I spun the *Starfire* around to face backward. "Open the cargo door," I said to Tera. "And Gabe, get down to the cargo bay and help Vrynn."

"Yes, sir." I didn't have a chance to see if he'd saluted, but it wouldn't have surprised me.

I shifted my attention back to Vrynn's video feed, where I could see the *Starfire* hanging in the air in front of her. I was struck by how strange this entire situation was. I bet the Barchee had never seen a prison break quite like this before.

With the *Starfire* lined up in front of them, I gently pulled back on the stick to slide us closer to their perch.

Vrynn beckoned with her arms. "A little more, Mitch. It's still too far to jump."

"Barchee fighters will be in weapons range in sixty seconds," Tera said.

The ship suddenly shuddered, like we'd been hit by something.

"Look out, Mitch!" Vrynn cried.

I checked her feed and saw Vrynn and Raveel huddled against each other for protection, bricks and dust falling around them. I must have backed the tail end of the Starfire through the open portal and crunched against the alley wall.

"Is it close enough yet?" I asked.

"Fifty seconds," Tera announced.

"Still too risky for Raveel," Vrynn yelled.

Until this moment, I hadn't really considered the inconvenient placement of the cargo bay, slung low under the tail of the Starfire. It meant I couldn't get the bay door any closer to them because the tail stuck too far through the portal.

"Can you slide the portal away from the wall?" I asked Tera.

She shook her head. "Not without closing the portal and opening a new one."

"We don't have time for that," Vrynn said.

"True," Tera replied. "Now we only have forty seconds."

The comm connection to the cargo bay crackled on. "Can you tilt the ship forward?" Gabe asked. "And downward a little bit?"

I could see where he was going with this.

After double-checking that the hover emitters were still at full power, I pushed our nose toward the ground.

"Thirty seconds," Tera said.

It was like the zero-G maneuvers I was always practicing, except for the gravity. I was about to slide out of my seat and faceplant against the front glass of the flight deck.

"You can jump now," Gabe called out.

I glanced at Vrynn's video feed. Gabe was braced against a row of shelving, arms open wide. Raveel leaped from the edge of the alleyway above us—with a small push from Vrynn—and landed on Gabe.

"Twenty seconds," Tera announced. "Actually, missiles fired."

"I thought you said twenty seconds!" I yelled back.

"It's an estimate," Tera replied. "How am I supposed to know when they're actually going to fire?!"

"Vrynn, get in the ship," I called over the comm.

An explosion lit the video feed. Vrynn glanced back down the alley where the prison guards were closing in, plasma rifles firing. She screamed, and then the video was tumbling, and I couldn't tell what was going on.

"Gabe, what's happening?" I yelled. "Do you have Vrynn?"

"She is not all the way in the ship, but she is no longer on the other side of the aperture," Gabe explained. "I recommend we close it."

"Tera, close the portal," I said, nudging the *Starfire* forward.

The aperture closed just as the guards arrived. I checked Vrynn's video and saw that she was clinging to the edge of the cargo door, while Gabe was inching toward her, his hand outstretched.

"Missile impact in five seconds," Tera said. "Approximately."

I focused on Vrynn, hoping that my zero-G abilities had improved enough to make this work. I eased off on the hover emitters, allowing the *Starfire* to slip into a freefall. Vrynn and Gabe both floated upward as we fell. Then I gently eased the hover emitters back on to slow our fall.

The maneuver went perfectly, except for Vrynn's impact with Gabe and Raveel. But bruises aside, I was just glad they were all safely inside the cargo bay.

"Close the cargo door," I said. "And make sure the defensive lasers are targeted on those incoming missiles."

I pulled up and banked hard away from the incoming fighters. The lasers were able to take out a few of the atmospheric missiles, but I really needed Vrynn next to me. As if I had conjured her by the thought, Vrynn appeared at my side and slid into her seat. The sight of her with artificially aqua-tinted skin made me do a double take, but she had her cannons activated just in time to take out a nearby Barchee fighter.

We opened a portal to Mareesh, and a few seconds later, flew into the calm skies of Vrynn's homeworld.

As we floated gently down beyond the south end of the island chain, I glanced over at Vrynn. "I can't believe that worked," I said breathlessly.

"I told you, all it takes is a little confidence sometimes," she said with a grin.

I shook my head but decided not to disagree with her. "What's next?" I asked after a moment.

"We organize a rebellion," Raveel said, suddenly appearing at the flight deck door.

Chapter Sixteen

As word of Raveel's escape from prison spread, messages from Deep Down liaisons in each town began to come in. Not only that, but each of these contacts reported an eagerness on the part of their networks of fighters to actually do something against the Barchee occupiers. It was quite the turnaround from just a few days ago when we struggled to find more than half a dozen people willing to fight.

Of course, breaking Raveel out of prison also had its downsides. The number of Barchee soldiers patrolling the streets of Neevra tripled instantly. Video displays in various locations throughout town flashed his picture along with the reward for his recapture. And worse, Mosai and Bryneen's home was under constant surveillance by occupying forces. They must have connected our involvement in the prison break back to Vrynn's cousins.

With half the occupying soldiers on the hunt for Raveel, he could only move through the streets at night, and only very cautiously. He couldn't stay in any of the regular homes in Neevra for fear of being discovered, so we found an alternative. But after one night spent in a cramped cellar on the edge of town, the newly freed leader decided he'd rather camp in the grain fields outside of town rather than live one more hour in what felt too much like a prison cell.

Besides keeping Raveel's location secret from the Barchee and Gralik in particular, we had an uprising to plan. Not long after returning to Mareesh with the rebel leader, we received a message from High Tide—specifically from Natheem.

Apparently, Keelsa wanted to see Raveel.

That was why, early one morning a few days after bringing Raveel back to his home world, we found ourselves traipsing up a windswept hillside along the eastern edge of the island.

"Are you sure this meeting . . . is really worth it?" I asked Raveel between breaths. We were at a particularly steep part of the hill.

"What do you mean?" he replied calmly. How he could still be in such great shape after eight years in prison was beyond me.

"I mean, Vrynn and I haven't been fighting the occupation as long as the rest of you." I paused to wave my hand vaguely toward the valley below us. "But Keelsa's group hasn't been very effective in the fight against the Barchee. Are you sure they even have anything to offer?"

"Regardless of the water's source, it is still wet," he said.

Vrynn and Bryneen and the other fighters all nodded at this. There must not have been an equivalent saying in English because my translator didn't give me anything else. I had to assume it was some wise Mareesh adage.

We reached the top of the hill a few minutes later, and I gazed in awe at the view around me. I had been on Syr long enough that the view of the valley's green landscape strewn with densely clustered towns had become familiar to me. But from the hilltop at the eastern edge of the island, I could also see the wide expanse of the Mareesh ocean. It was breathtaking.

"Raveel, I have a question," Bryneen said deferentially. "Will part of our plan be to free Mareesh prisoners?"

Raveel gave her a sympathetic look. "You're worried about Mosai."

Bryneen nodded energetically.

"We obviously need more fighters," Raveel answered, "but I can't promise that it will be our first objective."

His reply appeased Bryneen, and she seemed to relax a little. "Thank you," she said.

Below us, a band of Mareesh trekked up the hill from the direction of Leenai, Keelsa leading the way. Natheem walked next to her—his large frame easy to spot.

Raveel had asked Vrynn and me to welcome the High Tide group and begin the formal part of the discussion. I had no idea what that meant, so I decided I'd let Vrynn do most of the talking.

Natheem and another fighter that I vaguely recognized from our truck hijacking mission stepped to the front of their group.

"Hello, Vrynn," Natheem said once he was close enough. "Good to see you again."

"Natheem," Vrynn replied. Her tone was cold. I wasn't sure if that was part of the protocol for a meeting like this, or if she was simply upset with him.

"I wasn't sure you would actually come," Natheem said.

"It wasn't my choice," Vrynn replied. "Raveel insisted."

Natheem straightened to his full stature. "The High Tide would like to offer its help."

"Why do you think we need help?" Vrynn asked.

"You're obviously going to make an attack on the occupying forces," Natheem pointed out. "You could always use more soldiers."

Vrynn glanced away momentarily, considering her response. "Even if you're right. What makes you think we would want help from the High Tide?" Vrynn was laying the disdain on fairly thick.

Natheem shrugged, attempting to ignore the snub and act nonchalant. "You might not, but Keelsa insisted that we offer. We can add to your numbers."

I hadn't really been participating much in the ceremony so far—I wasn't even sure if I was meant to—but this seemed like a good time to say something. "It's important to have wet water," I offered. I couldn't remember the exact phrase Raveel had used, but hopefully their translators would fix the saying if I'd misquoted it.

Natheem gave me a puzzled look, as did his companion and the other High Tide fighters behind him. Vrynn stifled a giggle.

I must not have said it quite right.

"I see you brought the old codger with you," Keelsa called over Natheem's shoulder. "He hasn't seen combat in eight years. I'll be surprised if he lasts two minutes in our first battle."

Without missing a beat, Raveel replied, "They needed me to talk some sense into a loony woman who can barely meet societal expectations of basic hygiene, much less dress herself in anything remotely acceptable to be seen in public."

Keelsa pushed between Natheem and his companion, disdain evident in her expression. Raveel stepped up into the gap between Vrynn and me, obviously unhappy. I glanced back at Natheem and the other fighters in his group. They seemed equally worried that this meeting had suddenly taken a turn for the worse. In fact, I was concerned for Raveel's safety until I caught a slight twitch at the side of Keelsa's mouth.

Raveel's face broke into a wide grin. He moved quickly, closing the gap to his former lieutenant. "It's good to see you, old friend."

Keelsa matched his step, a deranged smile on her face, and they embraced each other, much to the relief of everyone else on the hilltop. I hadn't really considered what we would do if the meeting had gone south.

Raveel pulled back, holding Keelsa at arm's length. "You haven't changed a bit, you crazy old woman."

"You just look old," Keelsa shot back.

Raveel laughed. The rest of the group joined in, and the tension on the hilltop seemed to dissipate. Raveel pulled Keelsa aside, and they began an animated conversation. Fighters from both sides intermingled, renewing long-dormant friendships and making new acquaintances.

Keelsa and Raveel's discussion seemed to be going well, except that she didn't appear to believe what he was telling her. A moment later, Raveel motioned us to join him.

"Explain again—for the benefit of my senile friend"—he gave Keelsa a patronizing pat on the arm, and she scowled at him—"how you were able to open the portal to the streets of Taleech when you rescued me."

I gave her a brief explanation about how the Quake Drive worked and some of the things we'd been able to do with it.

"How many people could you send through this opening?" Keelsa asked. Her wild mannerisms were slightly less pronounced up close when she was puzzling through a problem. But all in all, she still sort of looked like a crazy woman.

"Hundreds, maybe thousands," Vrynn replied. "It all depends on how large we make the aperture and how long we leave it open."

Raveel nodded in satisfaction, and Keelsa seemed ready to burst with glee.

I held up a hand. "But we don't have limitless power to leave the portal open. And large distances also quickly deplete our power reserves."

"The distance we have in mind would not be very great," Keelsa said. "Only from one island to another." She held out a hand toward the silhouette of Mardrys on the northern horizon.

I began to understand what they had in mind.

Raveel fixed us with his wise gaze. "Once we decide the location of the other end of the portal, can you work out the best starting point?"

Vrynn beamed, and I knew her answer immediately.

"Yes," I replied. "Just tell us when."

Late the next afternoon, dressed as day laborers, Vrynn and I rode the train to Mardrys.

The first part of our plan required someone to be in person to target the terminus of the portal. And that meant making our way through the narrow streets of Mardrys.

We had also moved the *Starfire* as close as we could get it to Mardrys—the rocky shore of a small, protected cove on the north end of Syr. Not only did this cut down the distance of the portal jump—and therefore the power required—but it meant we didn't have to share the secret location of the *Starfire* with the entire Mareesh rebel movement.

I glanced down at my hand as the train glided smoothly along its track. Bryneen had given my hands and face a quick makeover in hopes that I wouldn't draw unnecessary attention to myself during the mission. At least I knew what I might look like as a Mareesh.

The sunlight disappeared as we entered the tunnel through the side of the Mardrys caldera. Vrynn grabbed my hand, and I squeezed back. The critical part of our mission was just ahead.

As we passed into the interior of the caldera, I could see the capitol building looming in the distance. It had looked so beautiful on my first trip into the city—its pearlescent white walls gleaming in the sun—now it seemed foreboding and impenetrable.

We exited the train and walked through Mardrys on our way toward the capitol. The streets were scattered with people on their way to jobs or errands, none of them aware that we were, hopefully, about to start an insurrection. The Barchee soldiers that we passed seemed equally oblivious to our efforts, which was a good thing.

By the time we started up the street toward the capitol, I started worrying about the mission. The *Starfire* was in position—I'd flown the ship myself. Gabe and Tera had understood the very detailed instructions we'd left them, so that shouldn't be a problem. But I had no idea if all the combined Deep Down and High Tide forces would reach the *Starfire* in time. And would they know how to organize themselves to move efficiently through the portal when we were ready for them? How long did it take to gather all the willing fighters from the southern island into one location? And could they do it all without alerting the Barchee forces?

Vrynn must have sensed my anxiousness because she reached out and took my hand as we climbed up the steepening street. I offered her a weak smile.

"It'll be fine," she whispered.

My English would ruin the Mareesh disguise, so I didn't reply. I didn't have anything helpful to say, anyway.

We reached our assigned position, just across the street from one of the security stations built into the high wall of the capitol building. It wasn't the main public entrance to the capitol; that one had too many visitors and too much security. This was a small, auxiliary entrance that didn't see as much traffic. And hopefully, they wouldn't have a very bright soldier manning it.

Vrynn turned and embraced me, presumably to hide the fact that she was speaking into a communicator. I wasn't going to argue.

"We're in position, Tera. Is everything ready on your end?"

"We have about a hundred people milling around outside the ship," Tera said. "Gabe is trying to keep them entertained, but they don't seem to appreciate it."

Gabe jumped in on the conversation. "Considering the parameters of my assignment, and the dangers that these individuals are facing in their forthcoming mission, it is understandable that they are not responding well to my hospitality . . . or my jokes."

My eyes bugged out at the thought of Gabe telling the Mareesh freedom fighters any of the stupid jokes the real Gabe had so frequently employed in awkward social situations back on Earth.

Vrynn stifled a laugh. "That's great, Gabe. We'll be ready for them in a few minutes."

"Position lock?" I whispered, furtively checking that no one was around to overhear me.

Vrynn nodded her understanding. "Tera, you've still got the lock on our position, right? How close will you be able to target the aperture?"

"I have your position within two meters. Targeting the aperture inside a large room should be fine," Tera replied.

"Acknowledged. Standby." Vrynn took a breath, her energy obvious in every movement. "I think we're ready."

We walked across the street to the auxiliary entrance, playing the part of a cute couple out for an afternoon stroll. When we reached the glassed-in security station, Vrynn slowed. There was only one soldier on duty inside the small room. He would be easy enough to neutralize with a blaster shot, but the protective glass made that impossible. At least, not before he alerted the rest of the capitol's security forces.

Vrynn stepped up to the security window. "Can you hear me through this?" she asked slowly, tapping on the glass.

The guard seemed mildly annoyed. "Yes, what do you need?"

"I've received a summons to come here . . ." she pulled out a thin, gray slate with squiggles on it—apparently the Mareesh version of paper. ". . . from a Deputy Cheethra? Am I saying that right, Cheethra?" She tilted the slate toward the soldier, but not steadily enough for him to read it.

He squinted at the slate. "I've never heard of any Deputy Cheethra assigned here."

"But that's what the summons says," Vrynn complained, lifting the slate and waving it at him. Her performance was convincing enough that I almost believed there really was a Deputy Cheethra who had summoned Vrynn to the capitol.

The soldier stood and leaned forward. "Let me see that."

Vrynn waved it in his direction again, acting nervous enough to be mildly helpful while not actually letting him see the words on the slate.

The soldier frowned. "Come over here." He motioned her to a side window, which obviously had to be opened from the inside.

While the guard was still in the motion of unlocking the window and pushing it open, Vrynn lifted her foot up near my knee and urgently whispered, "Boost."

I knew better than to question. I bent forward and grabbed her boot, forming a stirrup with my hands. She immediately launched herself through the now-open panel in the security station.

I wasn't sure she had fully planned out the move, though it was certainly graceful to watch. She arced expertly through the air and crashed into the soldier's midsection, knocking the guy off his chair and landing in a heap on top of him. As the guard attempted to extricate himself from under Vrynn, I pulled the blaster from my jacket and leaned in through the window, training my weapon directly at his chest.

"Don't try anything," I said to the guard as he reached for the emergency button. At least, I assume that's what it was. Apparently, hiding the emergency button under the counter was a universal constant.

His mouth fell open in obvious surprise at hearing an alien language spoken by someone who appeared Mareesh.

"Vrynn, can you find the door release?" I asked. The console looked like a preschool art project.

Back on her feet, Vrynn scanned the console and pushed the button. "There."

There was a click inside the door on my right, and I pulled it quickly open.

In the brief moment that Vrynn let me through the auxiliary door, the guard's hand shot toward the emergency button. Instinctively, I fired to stop him. My round only grazed his shoulder. Vrynn reacted quickly, too, delivering a withering knee to the guard's nose and knocking him back to the floor.

But it was too late. He'd successfully activated the alarm.

"We have to get the portal open," Vrynn exclaimed.

We left the unconscious guard behind and raced into the capital's outer courtyard. It was a maze of miniature rivers and fountains flowing in all directions. There were a handful of Barchee officials walking along pathways to wherever they were going. We ignored them as we sprinted for the inner structure. They couldn't do us any more harm than the guard that had sounded the alarm.

Halfway across the outer courtyard, Vrynn veered away from the main doors that seemed like the obvious choice to me. A moment later, I understood why as a dozen Barchee soldiers marched around the opposite side of the central structure. I stuck close to Vrynn as she wound through more rivers and ponds. She pushed open a single door between two waterfalls and we snuck into the main building.

I'm not sure why I had been expecting something similar to a capitol rotunda; the Mareesh had different historical experiences and building materials. They wouldn't have anything like Greek architecture. The main building was cavernous, with an incredibly high ceiling that glowed like a yellow sunset. In the center, there was a raised cone like a mini volcano with a pulpit in the middle.

Vrynn must have seen my amazement. "It's the assembly room—the seat of our government."

She pulled me toward one of three raised gallery areas. The gallery platform nearest to us wasn't flat and uniform like a stage or stand in Earth architecture. It looked more like a wide boulder about five feet tall and thirty feet across had been plopped right there in the assembly room. Two similar rock-like platforms sat on the other side of the expansive space.

Once in place behind the boulder platform, Vrynn pulled out her communicator. "We're in position, Tera. Target our location."

"Acknowledged," Tera replied.

A moment later, the familiar aperture appeared about a dozen feet in front of us. The view through the portal was of dozens of Mareesh fighters standing on a rocky shoreline, Raveel and Keelsa in the center.

I approached the portal and could feel the ocean breeze swirl through the opening. I waved them in. "Two at a time," I said. "And hurry, they've already sounded the alarm."

Freedom fighters surged forward, more or less in pairs, and stepped through the aperture. Vrynn had chosen this location wisely. We were able to use the boulder platform to conceal the size of our ever-growing force, just in case someone happened to enter the assembly room while we were still coming through.

Though obviously not enough concealment.

"Security breach in the assembly room!" a voice yelled from across the enormous hall.

We only had about twenty fighters through the portal with at least double that still waiting. Plasma rounds streaked across the room, impacting the edges of our platform-turned-rampart.

Raveel surveyed the fighters hunkering around him. "This room is the foothold. We must take this room, then we take the capitol, then all of Mareesh." He pounded his fist against the boulder for emphasis. "Vrynn, lead team one to the governor's pinnacle." He pointed in the direction of the central pulpit. "From there, you can direct us to the Barchee forces. Keelsa, take the rest and flank the enemy forces. Remember, this room is our foothold."

Vrynn and Keelsa nodded and gathered their groups.

My first impulse was to go with her, but Raveel grabbed my arm. "Mitch, I need you to stay here with the portal until all the fighters are through."

I glanced back at the aperture. More than half of our force was still waiting to join the fight. Their speed through the portal was slower, more cautious, now that the fight had begun. I took up position at the nearest edge of the boulder platform and started taking shots with my blaster.

Keelsa's main group was a third of the way around the assembly room, hiding behind one of the other boulder platforms. They were in a heavy firefight with Barchee soldiers coming in through the main doors.

I risked a peek at the central podium and saw that Vrynn and several members of her team had reached the tiny space at the top. They fired on the Barchee soldiers entering through the far door.

Tactically, our enemy was at a significant disadvantage, being fired on from two directions, and Vrynn's small group was a big part of that. Even though they were few and not as well fortified, they fought with much more impact than the enemy anticipated. Most of the soldiers foolish enough to enter the hall were cut down at the doorway.

Once Keelsa's team could move forward and flank the doors, the Barchee would certainly have to give up the assembly room as a lost cause. The first step toward victory for the Mareesh felt easily within our grasp.

Just when I thought the Barchee soldiers might pull back, a second door, part way around the circular room, was thrown open, and more soldiers pushed in. The Mareesh freedom fighters no longer had the advantage of two groups firing on one. Vrynn's team immediately came under fire from the new, closer door, which was out of range of Keelsa's group.

"Bring more force against the second door," Vrynn said through the comm.

Raveel surveyed the situation and gathered a group of fighters around him. "We will flank the occupiers' new position." He pointed toward the last boulder platform, closest to the newly opened doors. "Go."

As his group flowed across the assembly room toward the third platform, Raveel said to me, "Send the rest of the fighters wherever Vrynn says. And stay safe." With that, he disappeared around the side of the boulder. Plasma rounds flashed by, hitting dangerously close to the Mareesh leader, but he pushed ahead.

"Mitch, Mitch, can you hear me?" It was Vrynn on the comm.

"Yes. Are you okay?"

"A new group of soldiers just snuck through the second door," she said.

"That's fine. Just tell me where to send our fighters," I replied.

"No, you don't understand. It's a squad of dragoons."

My stomach sank. Even a small force of Vanguard Dragoons could turn the tide of this battle quickly. "What can I do? Where are they?" I asked Vrynn.

"They're moving high along the outside wall," she replied. "I think they're trying to flank your position."

With a quick glance around the side of our makeshift bulwark, I located the squad of dragoons. I didn't get a chance to count their numbers before plasma fire forced me back, but they were definitely moving around the wall toward our position. I wasn't sure why they would choose this strategy; they would be as exposed during the flanking maneuver as we would be.

I glanced through the portal. We had nearly emptied the beach; only twenty or thirty fighters still needed to come through. I caught the attention of the next two Mareesh exiting the aperture. "Take position here and stop those soldiers." I pointed at the dragoons, who were now in open view from our rallying point.

The two fighters knelt next to me and unleashed a firestorm of plasma rounds on the dragoons. The enemy squad broke ranks, some returning fire, others advancing along the wall out of view. We continued firing on the dragoons we could see, but I had the suspicion some had slipped by in the chaos. How many, though, I wasn't sure. Eight? Maybe ten?

"Vrynn, I lost track of some of the dragoons," I ducked when another plasma round hit the platform above my head. "Can you still see them?"

There was a moment's pause. "Three made it all the way to the outer door we entered through. They're right behind you."

I whirled around toward the aperture but couldn't see anything besides the half a dozen Mareesh fighters waiting on the distant beach. They were the last to come through the portal and join the fight for the capitol. "Where are they?"

"They just disappeared." Vrynn's voice was frantic now. "You didn't see them?"

I looked again, but I still couldn't see them. Could the dragoons have snuck up on us using the portal as a screen?

Hunched low, I scampered back toward the circular Quake Drive opening, doing my best to not come near the edge of the aperture. We still didn't know what would happen if half of a person tried to go through the portal, but the other half didn't. And I didn't want to be the guinea pig.

I peeked behind the portal.

Nothing.

I moved back around to the front just as Natheem, who had stayed to bring up the rear, stepped through the aperture behind the last pair of fighters.

Except for the *Starfire*, the beach was now empty.

Or it should have been.

Over Natheem's shoulder, something caught my eye.

Three Vanguard Dragoons crept away from the beach toward the ship.

"The dragoons are on the beach," I yelled in the comm. "Tera, Gabe, dragoons are coming your way. Fire on them."

Tera said, "We're not allowed to—"

"They'll steal the ship," I cried. "This is an emergency!"

The plasma cannons fired, kicking up plumes of gravel and sand into the air. The dragoons scattered. Hopefully, that would keep them at bay for a minute or two, at least until we could solidify our control of the assembly room.

Almost simultaneously, half a dozen doors around the perimeter of the assembly room slammed open and Barchee soldiers poured into the room, firing on us from all directions. Despite being completely surrounded and outnumbered at least four to one, our band of freedom fighters continued firing back.

A loud voice boomed through the room's audio system, rattling my last nerve. "Cease fire!" Gralik said.

He stood framed in one of the open doorways yelling into a type of microphone device. The onslaught of rounds from the surrounding soldiers dwindled then stopped.

A second later, one of Vrynn's comrades, perched up on the central podium, took a pot shot at the Nexus leader. The round struck at Gralik's feet, and he dove behind the doorway. Dozens of nearby Barchee returned fire, peppering the podium's parapet wall with plasma rounds. The other freedom fighters on its top hunkered down for cover, but the impulsive would-be sniper wasn't quite fast enough. He was struck in the melee and thrown from the tower.

"Vrynn, are you okay?" I yelled into the comm.

I watched the battered podium for signs of movement. There had been three or four fighters—including Vrynn—crowded into the small space at the top, but I couldn't see them.

"I'm okay," she replied quietly over the comm.

I nearly sank to the ground in relief at the sound of her voice.

"Don't test my patience." Gralik's magnified voice returned. "If that happens again, I will just kill all of you and be done with it."

I turned my attention back through the portal to the shore of Syr. To my dismay, there were several more dragoons moving across the beach toward the *Starfire*. I fired on them with my blaster, but my aim was no good at such a long range.

"Vrynn, more dragoons just went through the portal somehow," I said. "They're going for the ship. I have to get you out of here so we can stop them."

There was a short pause. "There's no time, Mitch. I'm pinned down here. You have to go back without me. Close the portal and stop them from taking the ship."

". . . no one has to die today . . ." Gralik droned on, saying something about surrender.

"I can't leave you here to be captured," I pleaded with Vrynn.

"We don't have a choice," Vrynn said softly. "If you stay here. They'll capture you, too. And then the ship."

"I'm sure I can get to you. What if I—"

"No," she replied firmly. "You have to keep the *Starfire* safe." Her voice softened. "Then you can come back and rescue me."

A heavy fear clutched at my chest. We both knew that wasn't likely to happen.

Even if I was successful at fighting off the dragoons, I'd have to wait until it was safe enough in the assembly room to open the portal again. And from the way the battle was going, unless it took a sudden turn in favor of the freedom fighters, the capitol building would remain under Barchee control.

What was left of the dragoon squad moved quickly across the room toward our position. They would reach the aperture in less than ten seconds. I took a fortifying breath and picked a plasma rifle from a downed fighter. Grabbing Natheem and another fighter, both hunkered down near the portal, I dragged them back through the opening onto the rocky beach.

"Close the portal, Tera," I yelled into the comm.

"But how will Vrynn—"

"Close it now!"

The portal behind me quickly shrank and vanished. In the spot where it had disappeared, stood two dragoons facing the other direction. They wheeled around and all five of us fired on each other from point blank range. One of the rounds caught the fighter next to me in the chest at about the same time as his shot downed one of the dragoons. The other dragoon fired twice before Natheem and I took him out. But one of his shots sliced across my arm. It felt like someone had lit a fire near my shoulder.

I looked at our downed comrade and knew immediately there wasn't anything we could do for him. I glanced at Natheem and saw that he'd reached a similar conclusion. I checked the hole in my jacket. My arm was still intact, but a patch of angry red welts had already formed on the skin. I would just have to live with the pain and consider myself lucky that I still had my arm at all.

But we weren't out of the woods yet.

I pointed at the dragoons circling the *Starfire*. "We can't let them get the ship."

As we ran toward the *Starfire*, I tried to formulate a plan. The outer airlock hatch and the cargo bay door would both stay closed until I asked Tera to open them. Would the dragoons be able to force their way in?

The dragoons noticed our approach and fired at us. Natheem and I dove behind a nearby outcropping, rocks and pebbles exploding around us.

I called on the comm. "Tera, you've got about ten soldiers surrounding the ship. Natheem and I are trying to get there to help. Keep firing on them. But try not to shoot us," I added as an afterthought.

"I don't want to shoot anyone!" Tera cried.

The plasma cannons were still firing, but not very accurately. I wasn't sure if that was a limitation within Tera's algorithmic programming or if she was legitimately not interested in hitting her targets.

I took aim and fired on the closest dragoon, taking him down with a few shots. The remaining soldiers moved farther away from our position, toward the back of the ship. That left an open path to the *Starfire*. But with that much open beach between our rocky cover and the ship and at least half a dozen dragoons waiting for us, we would never make it to the *Starfire* without being shot.

A moment later, a barrage of plasma rounds hit the ship near the closed cargo ramp.

"What's happening?" I asked Tera.

"They're firing on the door!" she yelled.

"Will it hold?" I asked.

"I don't know. I've never had to test it out," she said.

I considered the situation. I couldn't get to the ship without being shot, and I couldn't stop the soldiers from attempting to cut their way inside.

"Take off," I said through the comm. "Get out of here."

"What?" Tera asked.

"If we fly away, you will be stranded," Gabe added.

"The most important thing is to keep the *Starfire* safe. You have to get away from the dragoons."

"But I'm not supposed to fly," Tera complained.

"Neither is Gabe, and he's a great pilot," I shot back. "Get the ship out of here now. Take it under water, then go to our hiding place. I'll meet you there when I can." Another set of concussive shots hit the back of the ship. "Go. Now."

The *Starfire* rose gracefully—assuming getting pounded with plasma rounds while trying to float could be considered graceful—and sped away from the beach.

"Is there another way off the beach?" I asked Natheem. "That way is blocked by dragoons." I tilted my head in the direction of the main path to and from the beach and the pack of dragoons moving toward us from that direction.

"There's a smaller path this way," Natheem replied. "Follow me."

We crouched low and scampered across the beach, away from the dragoons. Plasma rounds ricocheted off the pebbles at our feet. I held my plasma rifle across my body and fired wildly at the enemy soldiers. That didn't stop them from shooting at us, but their aim got much worse.

We reached a rocky cliff about two hundred feet from where the *Starfire* had been. A narrow path clung to its side, leading up to the ridge above our heads.

Natheem ducked behind a stone jutting from the cliffside. "You go up first; I'll cover you," he said as he began laying down suppressive fire along the beach.

I scampered up the path, trying not to slip off the edge at the narrowest part, and found a large rock about halfway up. My position commanded most of the beach below, and to prove it, I took aim at the nearest group of dragoons and fired several rounds. They dove for cover; some returning fire.

"Natheem!" I yelled, waving him up the path as I continued to keep our enemies pinned down.

He ascended quickly to my position. As he approached, I tilted my head toward the rest of the path. "Cover me from the top."

With our roles reversed, I fired at any dragoon foolish enough to show his face in the rocks below me. A minute later, plasma rounds streaked past from somewhere above me, and Natheem yelled from me to follow.

I ran as fast as I could up the rest of the trail, glad that the burning in my legs meant I was still alive, and joined my fellow fighter at the top.

"That's the town of Teelno," Natheem said, pointing at a cluster of houses about half a mile down the green hillside. "If we run, we might reach it before the soldiers can follow us."

We ran as fast as we could down the small path that connected the town to the seaside cliff. My breath came in ragged gasps by the time we reached the nearest homes. Before turning the first corner, I glanced over my shoulder back up the path toward the cliffside. A small cluster of dragoons stood silhouetted against the sky. They hadn't started down the path after us. In fact, they seemed unsure where to go.

Natheem pulled me around the side of the house, and we settled into a brisk walk as we navigated the roads of the quaint little town. As my heart rate began to subside, my brain finally started catching up to my body, trying to make sense of everything that had just happened.

"How did the Barchee know we were planning a—"

He held up a hand to silence my question. "Not here." He glanced around, looking nervous that we would be overheard.

We wandered randomly through town before turning into a narrow alley and knocking on the door of a dilapidated row home.

An old man, with completely blue hair, answered the door. He took one look at Natheem and me, grunted in obvious annoyance, and turned away from the door, leaving it ajar.

"My uncle," Natheem said quickly as he motioned me inside. We walked through the living area of an obviously neglected dwelling to a small back room about the same size and character as a college dorm room.

We both collapsed—Natheem on a ratty bed, me onto a rickety chair. After a few moments, I blew out a long breath. "How could everything have gone so wrong? How could they have known?"

Natheem heaved a deep sigh, and I could tell something was off because he wouldn't meet my eye.

I stood and paced the floor of the small, dirty room. "How could that many soldiers have been waiting for us in the capitol building? I didn't even think the Barchee had that many soldiers on all three islands!" I gave vent to some of my frustration. Turning back to Natheem, I let my arms fall to my sides. "They must have known we were coming."

He shook his head. "We've had efforts go bad before. That's the nature of fighting against an entrenched enemy."

"But how could they have known?" I moved closer to him. "Does the High Tide have a leak?" A moment after I said it, I realized how silly that phrase would have sounded if translated literally.

But apparently, Natheem's chip did the job right. His back stiffened at whatever translation his implant had given him. "Just because things go poorly doesn't mean we have a traitor to the cause."

I ran a hand through my hair. "You know what? I can't stay here. I have to get back to my ship and make sure it's safe." I moved to the door but stopped when I heard an alert sound on the house system. We both glanced over at the symbols flashing on the video display.

"What's that mean?" I asked Natheem.

He scowled. "It's a planet-wide broadcast."

"Maybe it's—" Before I had even finished my thought, the display flashed again, and a video appeared.

Gralik sat staring out of the display.

I had a visceral reaction to seeing his face. My first instinct was to slam my fist through the screen. My next impulse was to sprint, full-speed, back to the *Starfire* and track him down. But neither of those ideas would help Vrynn, so I pushed them to the back of my mind.

"Greetings, citizens of Mareesh," Gralik's annoying voice began. "It's unfortunate that I have to speak to you again so soon. Despite the great pride I take in fulfilling my responsibility as your governor, at times my enjoyment is marred by situations like the one we have right now."

He stood and walked around his desk, the camera moving with him. "A grave threat to our peace has reared its ugly head, which is unfortunate because of how many years I've been here serving you, trying to bring prosperity." Gralik held a hand out, and the camera panned across a large room to a group of prisoners lined up against the wall—hands bound in front of them, heads bowed in defeat.

It only took a second to realize these were the freedom fighters. I saw Keelsa, Raveel, and several others I recognized. Some of them had bruises, others had more serious wounds that had been hastily patched.

Natheem shook his head. "This wasn't supposed to happen," he muttered.

I threw my hands up in exasperation. "Yeah, obviously, Natheem. The battle was supposed to be our foothold in defeating the occupiers. Instead, all of our fighters have been captured," I declared, holding a hand out toward the video. "It must have been a trap."

Gralik continued blustering to the camera. "Some of these citizens—who haven't made a habit of resisting my efforts to bring order to your planet—will spend a few weeks in prison and then be released."

Natheem seemed to relax a little at this news.

"Others—who have chosen chaos and anarchy over peace and civilization," Gralik continued, "will not be allowed to return to our society for much, much longer." He stopped and cast a glance toward Raveel. "If ever."

I knew which category Gralik would put Vrynn in, and it wasn't the one getting out for good behavior. Natheem continued staring at the display, shaking his head.

Finally, the camera panned across Vrynn, and my breath caught. Unlike the others, she still appeared defiant, glaring at Gralik as he passed. Then she stared straight into the camera, almost as if she was looking right at me.

"Still others have been at the root of all of our recent problems." Though he spoke to the citizens of Mareesh, he sneered at Vrynn. "And we can't have that. As much as it pains me to do it, certain insurrectionists must be executed for their crimes."

"No! You can't!" Natheem yelled at the screen.

I stood there in stunned silence.

Gralik was going to execute Vrynn.

Natheem sank into a nearby chair, his face in his hands. "I don't understand. It wasn't supposed to happen like this." After a moment, he looked up at me, pain evident in his eyes.

On the video feed, Gralik spoke again. "However, there is one way to save her." He walked toward the camera and stared straight into it. His expression turned gravely serious. "Give me the starship," he said.

Natheem shot back to his feet. "That was never part of the deal!"

I turned my attention to Natheem. "Hang on. What did you just say?"

He turned to me. "We have to find the ship," he said, his eyes half-wild. "We have to give it to him. To save Vrynn."

I grabbed Natheem by the shoulders and shook him, hoping to bring his focus back to reality. "What are you talking about, Natheem? What did you do?"

Gralik spoke again. "You know who you are, alien-man. And you know I'll make good on my promise." He backed away from the camera and turned toward Vrynn, but he was still speaking to me. "Give me the ship, or she dies." The last part came out in a sneer, as if he was savoring the threat.

I could see the flash of fear in Vrynn's expression, but it was quickly replaced by determination. Her eyes shot daggers at Gralik. Then she shifted her attention to the camera. "Don't do it, Mitch. Don't listen to him. Take the ship and—"

Her defiance was cut short when Gralik smacked her across the face.

Gralik stared at the camera—at me—as he spoke. "You have until tomorrow at midday."

The broadcast terminated.

Natheem stared at the blank screen as if he had gone into shock. "They promised they wouldn't hurt her," he said softly, almost to himself.

I took a step toward him. "What did you do?" I asked in a cold whisper.

Suddenly, his expression changed from dismay to superiority. He turned his narrowed gaze on me. "I did what had to be done, what I've always done. I prevented more lives from being lost. I prevented another war. But I wouldn't expect you to understand."

I shook my head slowly, realization sinking in. "You betrayed your own people?"

Natheem shook his head. "No. I'm supporting my government—the rightful government—in an attempt to save my people from themselves." His voice was thick with condescension. "I'm not the traitor here; the rebels are. Gralik is the governor. Everyone needs to come to terms with that."

I was too dumbfounded to speak. I stood there gaping at Natheem, barely able to process what he had just said.

Then a pit opened in my stomach as the terrible reality of Vrynn's situation came crashing down on me. How was I ever going to get her out of a Barchee prison? Particularly if Gralik had her and planned to execute her.

Anger over what had happened during the raid on the capitol boiled up inside me. Anger and rage for the one who had done it.

I looked back up at Natheem, and something inside my brain snapped.

Without thinking, I lunged forward and punched him dead in the nose.

His head snapped backward with a satisfying pop as he crashed into the wall and slumped to the floor.

"That was for Vrynn," I yelled down at him, pretending my knuckles weren't throbbing in pain.

Natheem groaned as he shifted up to a sitting position. He looked dazed, as if he'd never been punched before—which, given his size, maybe he hadn't. He wiped a trickle of blue blood from under his nose and struggled back to his feet. "Vrynn wasn't supposed to be captured," he declared loudly.

"So, was this a general betrayal of your people?" I asked. "Or did you make a deal about Vrynn specifically?"

He ignored my jab. "They were going to hold everyone for a few days, just until things cooled down—and certain individuals with powerful starships were convinced to leave." He looked pointed at me. "Then they were going to let everyone go."

I shook my head. "Vrynn never would have agreed to that. She would have stayed and fought for Mareesh regardless of any underhanded deals you made."

"Not if you'd left with your starship," Natheem shot back.

"Don't count on that," I muttered.

He ran a hand through his blue-highlighted hair, refusing to meet my eye. But he didn't deny it. "None of this matters now anyway. You have to give Governor Gralik the ship to save her life." He moved to grab my shoulder, but I pushed his hand away.

"Do you think we can trust Gralik?" I asked. "He just betrayed you. Do you think he's going to let Vrynn go if I give him the ship?" I took a half step toward Natheem and lowered my voice. "Besides, she would rather die than for Gralik to have the power to enslave more worlds like Mareesh."

He blew out a breath and glanced around the small room as if hoping to see something that might save the situation. Finally, he sank back onto the couch. "You have no idea how hard it's been seeing her with you," he said with a defeated sigh. "I wish you'd never brought her back here. You got her hopes up that she could somehow defeat the occupiers and free Mareesh."

"Is that what you think happened?" I asked with a laugh. "You think I brought her to Mareesh? You think I talked her into doing any of this?" I held my arms wide, indicating our entire situation. "If you think that, then you must not know Vrynn very well."

He slumped further into the couch, a hand over his face.

When another surge of anger threatened to erupt inside me, I moved to stand over him. Looking down at his pitiful form through narrowed eyes, I said. "Someday you'll answer for what happened today, Natheem. But just know this, if you ever do anything to hurt Vrynn again, I can promise I'll do far more than punch you in the face."

My communicator buzzed, reminding me that I still didn't know what had become of the *Starfire*. I grabbed the comm and connected the link. "Tera? Gabe? Are you okay?"

The sound of Tera's voice was a huge relief. "We're fine. Just hanging out in this dank cave until you tell us what to do next."

"I'm just glad you got away safely." I glanced out a nearby window, attempting to gauge the time of day. "I'm not sure how fast I can travel in the dark, but I'll get there as soon as I can."

"I guess that's fine," Tera replied. "Also, we just got a message for you from someone named Shariamy. Do you want to hear it?"

"Finally." I exhaled in relief. "Yes, play it for me."

"The message isn't just audio, there's video, too," Tera said.

I glanced over at Natheem's display screen. I had a hard enough time on Earth trying to get my phone to play something on my smart TV; how was I supposed to figure out alien technology? "Go ahead and send it, but I may only be listening to the audio."

There was a pause on Tera's end. "Okay."

Natheem reached over and tapped the control console of his video screen, and my communicator magically connected. It was nice to know that advanced civilizations had somehow solved that puzzle.

A video of Shariamy popped up on the screen. Her cheeks were as round and rosy-pink as I remembered them. And the pearlescent hair piled high on her head seemed even more shimmery in the light of her video studio.

"Hi Mitch. I'm so glad you contacted me. It sounds like you're out there with your crew having incredible adventures. Makes a girl a little jealous." Her expression was part teasing, part suggestive. I chose to ignore it. "Anyway, I've been busy with some negotiations out in one of the halo systems, and I'm just getting back to all of my communications. I thought your first message with my assistant was adorable. She does look so much like me that people get us confused." Shariamy smiled as if this was entirely on purpose. "Initially, I was planning to just drop a word at BDF command that Gralik should get a very demanding assignment somewhere far away from the Barchee system, but your second message has me concerned."

The Shariamy in the video paused long enough that I nearly responded. It almost felt like we were having a conversation.

She shook her head. "I know Gralik personally, and he isn't the governor of Mareesh." She made it sound like that was the silliest thing she'd ever heard.

My eyes went wide, but not as wide as Natheem's.

"At best, he's an unremarkable, mid-level military commander who thinks he has a long shadow." My chip kicked in. "... who's too big for his britches." I couldn't help but smile at that particular translation.

"If I recall correctly," Shariamy continued, "he was sent there to halt an invasion by the neighboring planet. After a few days, he reported back that the invading army had been stopped and had returned to their own world."

"What?!" Natheem said, leaning forward as if he were talking to the display. "That's not what happened!"

Shariamy talked over his outburst—because obviously she couldn't hear him. "I did some digging and found in his submitted report that a Commander Raveel was elevated to governor in the aftermath of the fighting." Shariamy leaned forward, fiddling with some controls, and an image of a decade-younger Raveel, in full dress uniform, flashed on the screen. "So that's who the Bonara central government currently has listed as the governor of Mareesh."

I was dumbfounded. If Shariamy was to be believed—and I couldn't think of any reason she would lie about all this—Gralik was an imposter. Posing as governor to keep the Mareesh people under his control. Not only that, but he'd imprisoned the real governor, probably to keep up the ruse.

The Shariamy in the video—completely oblivious of the bombshell she'd just dropped on us—continued with her message. "I'll check with the BDF to make sure they haven't given him some additional assignment as liaison to the governor, but I can tell you with absolute certainty that he is not governor. According to the records in the Bonara government system, the appointment of Governor Raveel became official when it was approved by the senate seven years ago." A very official-looking image flashed on the screen, accompanied by a sharp gasp from Natheem.

"I'll begin an inquiry into Gralik's conduct on Mareesh," Shariamy said. "You can help by gathering any evidence of his unauthorized actions and transmitting it to me, but not through the normal BDF channels. Send it to my office in Vasielle." She lifted a shoulder. "Well, that's all I have for now. Good luck on your adventures." Shariamy waved, and the message ended.

"Did you see the Bonara seal?" Natheem asked in awe.

That seemed like a strange thing to notice about that exchange. Shariamy's hairstyle, for one, was worth remembering. I lifted a shoulder, unwilling to betray my lack of knowledge to him.

"It means that was an official government transmission," he said.

I didn't have time to figure out the intricacies of how he knew that, or what would keep a bad actor from simply transmitting the Bonara seal in his communications; I was just glad Natheem believed what Shariamy had said.

His eyes lost their focus, locked on the ground at his feet. "I can't believe Gralik isn't the real governor. That he's a fraud." He glanced down at the smudge of blood on his hand. "How could I have been so wrong?" he whispered.

With a fair bit of suspicion, I scrutinized this beaten down traitor as his worldview shifted around him.

"I didn't know," he said, shaking his head. "If only I had . . ." he trailed off to silence. Then his expression hardened, and he stood and faced me. "It's my fault that the real governor is locked away again. I want to help you free Raveel and the others."

"What makes you think I want help from you?" I hissed. "I don't want to be anywhere near you."

Natheem drew back at the obvious sting in my words, then his gaze dropped. "I don't blame you, considering what's happened." A moment later, he squared his shoulders and looked back at me. "I know you might not believe me, but everything I've done was meant to bring order and stability to my people. To follow the law and prevent more suffering and death." He pointed at the now-blank screen. "It's true that I was tricked by Gralik's lies. But it's not too late to fight him. We can still change all of this. We can come up with a plan to break them out of prison."

I shook my head. "I don't know how to trust you again."

Natheem nodded sadly. "I understand." Then he fixed me with a penetrating gaze. "But you need to rescue Vrynn, and I'm all you've got."

We stared at each other for several long moments as his declaration hung in the air between us.

I hated that he was right.

Chapter Seventeen

That night, I tossed and turned, unable to really fall asleep. It might have been the hard mat that Natheem's uncle had given me to sleep on, but I think it had more to do with knowing that Vrynn was lying somewhere in a prison awaiting her execution the next day.

And the fact that I would be forced to trust Natheem again if I ever hoped to get her out.

My mind swirled with thoughts of failure.

Before light had even hinted at the arrival of day, I was up and on my way toward Neevra and the *Starfire's* secret cavern. But not before I gave Natheem very specific instructions on when and where he and the last free remnant of his High Tide force needed to be that morning.

All the way back to the ship, I was tormented by thoughts of what might go wrong that day, and what would happen to Vrynn if all my worst-case scenarios came true.

What if I never got the chance to tell her how I felt? Obviously, I was fairly sure she knew my general feelings for her, but I'd never really told her how much more she meant to me now. What if I couldn't rescue her? How would I go on without her?

Those thoughts—and several other unhappy endings—kept me company on my run back to the cavern. Fortunately, thoughts of catastrophes were driven from my mind as I focused on preparing the ship to go to battle. My brain zeroed in on one important fact—I had a girlfriend to save.

By mid-morning, the *Starfire* was skimming low over the ocean waves on its way toward Mardrys. Tera stood next to me on the flight deck, scrutinizing the video feed coming from the commandeered satellite.

"Are you sure we can trust this guy?" Tera asked, pointing at the small dot that represented Natheem's comm device.

It might have been just a simple question of curiosity, but it hit me hard.

Truth be told, I didn't trust Natheem.

I contemplated telling Tera and Gabe everything that had gone wrong with the capitol raid and who had been responsible for it, but I decided that information would only make Tera trust Natheem less, and that was the last thing we needed.

Natheem was crucial to our plan.

So I decided to distract her with misleading facts. "He's nearly to the warehouse in Mardrys." I held out a hand to indicate his progress through the city toward the High Tide's dilapidated building. "I doubt he would have gone this far if he simply wanted to betray us."

"Maybe he placed the device on a small animal and sent it along the street," Gabe suggested. "Or perhaps he paid a child to carry the comm to the warehouse."

Tera looked appalled. "Are you suggesting he would intentionally put an innocent child or small animal in danger?" She turned back to the projection. "He's even worse than I thought."

If she only knew.

I held up both hands in an attempt to calm them. "Hang on. I don't think he's doing either of those things." I pressed a button on my console to activate the comm link. "Natheem, how are things going?"

A moment later, a quiet reply came. "We're nearly to the warehouse. The Barchee patrols are heavier than normal this morning, but the soldiers don't seem to care about a shabby group of Mareesh workers from the southern island."

"Good," I replied. "We'll wait for your signal." I cut the link.

I turned to Tera and raised a brow, challenging her to contradict what she just heard.

Rolling her eyes, she finally said, "Fine. I guess he's helping us." She folded her holographic arms. "But I still don't see why you didn't send a larger group. What good are a handful of rebels going to be against an occupying army?"

"Given how many freedom fighters were captured in the capitol attack last night, we're lucky to have any," I said. "Natheem has been spreading the word about Gralik's illegitimate government, but we can't expect people to change their minds overnight. This is what we've got at the moment." I leaned forward and watched his progress on the projection again. "Besides, all we need Natheem and his compatriots to do is retrieve some of their stockpiled weapons."

Tera huffed. "Oh, is that all."

I did my best to ignore her as the *Starfire* flew over the northern coastline of Syr and along the underside of the bridge leading to Mardrys. The Quake Drive had already opened a portal through the Mardrys caldera—it had even jumped us to the opposite side of Mareesh, but I figured I'd get us as close as possible to avoid the targeting inaccuracies and additional power requirements that came with greater distance.

A few minutes later, the comm clicked on. "We're in position," Natheem said.

"Send the exact coordinates where you want the portal opened," I replied. "And stand back."

The transmission with the coordinates came in.

"Are we sure you can program two sets of portal jumps into the Quake Drive at the same time?" I asked Tera.

"Technically, we aren't," she replied. "I'm holding the second portal location in the computer's memory and waiting until after the first portal closes to activate it."

"I guess I'll trust you on that one." I opened the link to Natheem again. "Standby." Then I nodded to Tera to open the first portal as I pushed the throttle forward.

The aperture expanded in front of us, and we sailed through the portal and right into the Mardrys caldera, directly over the airfield of the Barchee base. At the end of the long, narrow base, the capitol loomed high on its hill.

"Target laser systems on the comm towers," I said. "I'll handle ground fire with the cannons."

Given that the top of the caldera was covered with a defensive plasma grid, I wondered if the capital city even had any defensive systems. They would hardly need them. What starship—besides the *Starfire*—would be able to get through?

My assumption was incorrect.

The aperture had barely closed behind us when the threat warning blared on my console. Several small auto-cannons within the spaceport perimeter began firing at us. Those weapons didn't pose any immediate threat to the ship, but I raked across the emplacements with the plasma cannons just to get rid of the annoyance.

The fighter ships, waiting on alert, were a different story.

"Keep zigzagging us, Gabe," I said as I quickly switched from cannons to missiles, firing one at each fighter on the airfield. As the missiles streaked toward their targets, I switched back to the plasma cannon, amazed at how Vrynn was always able to manage the complexity of the *Starfire's* weapons so effortlessly. I fought back the pit in my gut of wishing she was sitting in the seat next to me. If we were successful, she'd be there with me soon enough.

As we swept over the spaceport, I let loose a barrage of plasma rounds on the row of troop transports next to the airfield and on as many hangared ships as I could.

"Barracks next," I directed Gabe.

He brought the *Starfire* low over the barracks building—maybe a little too low considering that we started taking fire from several medium-sized defensive cannons—and I raked the area with the plasma rounds.

"Right side shields at ninety percent," Tera announced after a particularly brutal hit from an anti-starship gun.

"We don't have time to deal with every last auto-cannon. Just fly low toward the prison; I'll take out what I can on the way." I panned the sights to the rear, tracking the guns as we overflew each one. Obviously, my accuracy on the cannons wasn't as good as Vrynn's, but I felt like I'd done well enough.

I looked out the front windows at the buildings below us. "There," I said, pointing at the wide prison yard next to the long cell-block building. "Activate the portal to Natheem's coordinates and target that spot."

A moment later, the aperture expanded, and I could see into the interior of the warehouse several miles away.

I activated the comm link. "Go Natheem."

Several trucks and Veechus drove through the portal onto the prison grounds. The Barchee guards may have initially been shocked to see so many trucks appear out of thin air, but it didn't take them long to figure out that this wasn't a friendly mission. Soldiers with plasma rifles spilled from the prison entrance, and Natheem and his small group started taking fire.

Gabe brought the *Starfire* into a hover above Natheem's group, and I fired at the enemy soldiers, taking down half a dozen and scattering the survivors.

My warning system blared, and I checked the tactical readout. Even though we were inside the prison grounds, the guard towers must have been equipped with their own plasma cannons. I swiveled the crosshairs towards them and reduced both towers to rubble.

With the area momentarily secured, I switched back to flight controls and set the *Starfire* down behind Natheem's line of vehicles.

I jumped out of the pilot's seat. "Hopefully, I'll just run in there, grab Vrynn and the others, and be back out here before you need to do anything else."

"What if you die?" Gabe asked.

"Then make sure to save Vrynn," I said as I grabbed a plasma rifle.

"What if she does not make it either?" he replied.

"I don't know," I said on my way out of the flight deck. "Fly off to a remote star system and live out your wildest dreams together."

As I ran to the ladder and slid down to the lower level, I heard Gabe call out, "What if I do not have any dreams?"

I rushed to the line of freedom fighters hunched behind vehicles and quickly found Natheem.

When he saw me, he pointed. "That was amazing."

I didn't know if he was talking about the fancy flying, or the expert cannon work, or maybe the trip through the jump portal, but I hardly had time to stop and talk about it. "Let's get in there."

Natheem nodded and motioned for his team to follow. We hurried across the narrow gap to the prison entrance. About halfway there, we took fire from the doorway, but there wasn't any cover, so we ran straight at the entrance, guns very literally blazing.

We took down several soldiers in the doorway, but one of Natheem's fighters was hit on the way in. Plasma rounds streaked toward us from the long hallway behind the security checkpoint, and I dove behind a nearby desk for cover.

I waited another few seconds, then jumped up and fired twice, taking out the guard standing in the hallway. More shots hit the wall next to me, and I dropped to my stomach. Shots from the doorway took out the second guard. Good thing Natheem and his friends were there to back me up.

We regrouped near the entry to the main hallway. From the layout I'd studied, I knew that the majority of the prison cells would be deeper into the building, down the long corridor. Of course, that long corridor would be the perfect place for an ambush.

I raised my rifle as we moved forward. "Stay alert, everyone."

Halfway down the corridor, bright blue lights began flashing overhead and a loud screeching sound—that I assumed was an alarm—blared in our ears. We flattened ourselves against the side walls, the only cover available, and continued inching forward.

Plasma rounds erupted from the far end of the hallway. We returned fire, hoping to keep them back from the doorway long enough for us to press ahead. A moment later, I heard shouts from behind us. Another group of soldiers was moving toward us from the rear.

"We can't stay here!" I yelled at Natheem. "They'll have us trapped."

He nodded, and our squad surged forward, hugging the walls and staying low. When we were within forty or fifty feet, one of Natheem's fighters pulled out a small metal device about the size of an orange, squeezed it, and tossed it through the doorway.

The hallway was immediately filled with shouts of dismay, and I could see guards scrambling farther down the hall to avoid whatever that device was. I glanced over at Natheem to see what he thought we should do next. He and the others were all prone on the ground with their heads down.

I quickly mimicked their position, figuring that they knew a lot more about weapons on this planet than I did. I barely had the thought cross my mind whether the hand grenade was a universal constant when there was a bang and a bright flash that swept along my vision like a photocopy machine. It left my skin hot and tingling. Then everything went dark.

A moment later, I felt a tap on my shoulder. I opened my eyes, and it was like night had arrived early. The corridor wasn't completely dark; more like the brightness setting on my vision had been turned down to minimum. In the dim gray, I saw Natheem standing over me, gesturing for me to get up.

"What was that?" I asked, but my voice sounded muffled.

He motioned our group forward. As I glanced back down the corridor, I saw a blindingly bright wall of plasma sweeping slowly away from us. I turned and followed Natheem and the other fighters as they pushed deeper into the facility.

We reached a branch in the hallway. Doors lined the walls in all directions. How were we supposed to figure out where our prisoners were? I pointed to two of the fighters and the hallway on the left, then another pair and the corridor straight ahead. They all nodded and moved down their assigned halls.

Natheem and I took the right branch, and I hoped we'd find our captured fighters before the entire base arrived to stop us.

When a guard entered at the far end of the corridor, I raised my rifle and fired twice. The plasma rounds that left the end of the barrel seemed weaker than usual. My shots missed the guard, and he fired back, hitting the door next to me. His rounds caused a small shock wave that knocked me sideways.

I was lucky not to be dead.

Natheem's aim was better than mine; his shots threw the guard backward, smashing him against the wall and knocking him unconscious. At least, I assumed he was unconscious; he didn't have any physical damage from the plasma rounds.

As Natheem helped me back to my feet, he must have seen the bewildered expression on my face. "The damping wave!" he yelled, though it sounded like he was speaking to me through a pile of blankets. "It's temporary."

From his pack, Natheem pulled out a device that looked like a hand-held wood router and gave it to me. Then he pulled out another one for himself. The idea of drilling through these cell doors using only a sharp drill seemed absurd, but I watched Natheem and followed his lead. He activated his tool, spooling up the cutting bit to incredible speeds, and jammed it into the door by the lock. With a few careful movements, he cut the latching mechanism free and pulled the door open. He nodded toward the door on the other side of the hall.

I quickly copied his trick.

The first several cells we opened were empty, but by the fifth door, we found one of the Deep Down fighters. He was ready to join the fight, so Natheem handed him a weapon from his pack.

As we worked on the cell doors, I noticed the lights seemed to grow brighter. Or it would probably be more correct to say they were returning to normal. Sounds were a little louder, too.

By the time we reached the end of the hall, we had amassed a respectable group of fighters. We even had weapons for most of them, thanks to what we'd picked up from the downed Barchee soldiers.

"Guards!" one of the fighters yelled, though it still came out like a speaking voice.

We took up positions hunkered behind open cell doors and fired back. The fighter just in front of me took a plasma round to the chest and fell backward. Another prisoner grabbed his weapon and returned fire, taking down the guard.

The firefight only lasted a minute or two, but three of our number were injured, one critically. I realized that they were only still alive because of the effects of the damping wave. That wouldn't last much longer. Of course, the enemy soldiers were still alive, too. We dragged their limp bodies down the corridor and locked them in nearby cells.

"Move forward!" I yelled at Natheem. "We need to find the other groups."

A fighter next to me tapped me on the shoulder and pointed at my hip. I glanced down at my comm unit and saw the connection light flashing. I held the comm up next to my ear.

". . . in only about one minute," Gabe said. The sound of his voice was tinny and muted.

"Gabe, what's going on? I can barely hear you!" I yelled.

"Eight Varusian interceptors entered the atmosphere about five minutes ago," he said. "They are not broadcasting transponder signals, so we assume they are operating as Nexus. They will reach us in less than a minute. You must come back to the ship."

At that moment, there was an explosion at the end of the hallway, and guards and prisoners exchanged fire again.

"I can't get to you right now," I said. "Besides, I still haven't found Vrynn."

"What are we going to do, Mitch?" Tera exclaimed over the comm. "Gabe and I can't fight eight interceptors."

Vrynn and I might have been able to hold our own against that many ships, but only with a lot of luck. I certainly couldn't ask Gabe and Tera to accept a suicide mission like that. Or worse, send them into a Nexus net.

"Fly away," I said.

"Should I stay close enough to support the battle?" Gabe asked.

"No, not with that many enemy fighters," I replied. "We can't let them capture the *Starfire*."

"Where would you like me to fly?" Gabe asked.

An idea suddenly occurred to me. "Go get help," I said. "Find Shariamy on Varus Prime. Hopefully, maybe she can bring someone with the authority to remove Gralik."

"Acknowledged," Gabe said, and the comm link ended.

I hoped they could get away in time, but I couldn't worry about that at the moment. We had to get the rest of the Mareesh fighters out.

With our wing of the prison under control, we pushed back down the hallway to where we had split our small group. We were greeted by fighters from the other two cell blocks. They crowded together at the intersection of the corridors.

I elbowed my way through our gathering force, frantically searching for the one person I'd done all this for. It was a sea of blue-highlighted hair, which made it difficult to distinguish the one Mareesh I cared the most about.

I found Raveel deep in conversation with Natheem.

"Where's Vrynn?" I asked, trying to control my panic.

Raveel's face was somber. "The guards took her away early this morning."

"Where?" I asked.

"She was going to the governor's enclave for her execution," he replied.

I felt like I'd just taken a plasma round to the gut. I knew I wasn't the most optimistic person in the world—or galaxy—but I guess I always figured I'd be able to save her.

Raveel put a hand on my arm. "There is still time to rescue her. But first, what is this that Natheem tells me about Gralik's governorship?"

I explained about Shariamy's message and the revelation concerning Gralik and his apparent lack of authorization from the Bonaran government.

Raveel nodded and moved to the center of our rebel group. He held his hands high and called for order. "Mitch has information that will aid our fight." Raveel then turned to me. "Tell them."

I cleared my throat. "Gralik's position is illegitimate," I said loudly. Confused faces stared back at me. Some appeared genuinely bewildered. While for others, my words seemed too fantastical to be believed. "We don't know how it happened, but he was never officially appointed governor of Mareesh."

The fighters buzzed with excitement. This news obviously strengthened their cause, and they knew it.

Raveel raised his hands again. "You are some of the few who know that the occupiers rule without true authority," Raveel said, his voice loud and commanding. "But if we are successful in our mission today, the news will ring through the islands. And we will gather our people, strong and united, and drive the occupiers away forever."

A cheer erupted from the small group.

The leader turned to Hustan and Sharlee, who stood together nearby. "You two take the front. Lead the main group out into the prison yard and secure our position. No doubt the Barchee will send fresh soldiers into the fight."

The pair nodded their understanding.

Raveel considered his small band of freedom fighters. "Stand together. Hold your brothers and sisters close in ranks, and we will not fall." He hefted his rifle and swung it toward the front of the prison. "Forward to the fight!"

The fighters surged down the hall, picking up more weapons from fallen guards. At the exit from the prison, volleys of plasma fire erupted as they met Barchee soldiers entering the compound. Our force rushed out to the vehicles Natheem and his fighters had brought from the warehouse, using them as makeshift barricades.

As the front ranks that Hustan and Sharlee had organized began laying down suppressive fire against the enemy, more fighters poured out of the prison and fell in behind them. Fortunately, High Tide had brought a veritable armory in one of the trucks, and more weapons were quickly distributed.

The Barchee soldiers had taken up position across the prison yard behind a line of barricades and fired intently at the line of Mareesh. The freedom fighters answered right back.

Raveel moved to a window and glanced outside. After a moment, he turned back to those of us still inside awaiting orders. "Natheem, take a team and find another way out." He pointed toward the side of the prison complex. "We need to flank the Barchee line."

Natheem snapped to attention. "Yes, sir." He saluted and ran off with several others down an auxiliary hallway.

I was next to receive Raveel's instructions. He also called Mosai and Bryneen over. "You three will need to sneak past the fighting to reach the governor's enclave in time to save Vrynn." He pointed in the direction of the capitol building. "After she's safe, bring back whatever help you can find. We need to defeat the Barchee forces before we can take the rest of the city."

It was a good thing Raveel gave me this assignment because I would have done it anyway, with or without his permission.

After several minutes of sustained fighting between the Mareesh fighters and the Barchee soldiers across the yard, the pitch of the battle changed. Natheem's small group had reached a flanking position, and were pouring heavy fire into the Barchee lines. The enemy soldiers shifted the focus, retaliating against Natheem and his small group for their attack. Natheem and several others were hit.

"This is our chance," Raveel said to the fighters still with him in the prison entry. "Push the Barchee line back."

The rest of the freed prisoners spilled out of the doorway and into the yard, eager to join their comrades in the fight. Mosai, Bryneen, and I followed close behind them, landing in the middle of chaos. Plasma rounds and blaster bolts streaked across the yard in both directions. Most of the Mareesh fighters had found cover behind various vehicles and other objects on our side of the battlefield.

I hated to leave our comrades in this jeopardy, but we had the chance to slip away and we needed to take it. I led my small group through the firestorm along the perimeter toward a protective berm near the prison fence. Hunkering down for protection, we concentrated our fire on the prison fence, blasting a hole large enough to crawl through.

I had studied the general layout of the Barchee base and knew that the small access road outside the prison fence would lead us along the perimeter back toward the capitol building. Once we were all through the fence, we hustled down the narrow lane. I had no idea how busy the base was under normal operations, but I hoped the massive prison break would keep everyone busy while Mosai, Bryneen, and I worked to find Vrynn.

Halfway to the governor's enclave, a truck loaded with soldiers suddenly turned onto the lane, heading right for us. We all dove behind the short stone wall bordering the road. Obviously, a head-on attack against a troop transport would have been futile, but as the truck trundled past, Mosai and I shared an unspoken look. We weren't about to let this opportunity pass us by.

When the truck had gone about fifty more feet, I nodded to him, and we both jumped up and brought our rifles over the edge of the wall, firing at the retreating vehicle. Bryneen quickly joined us, and with our combined fire, we caused enough damage to send the truck careening off the road into a nearby building.

Without stopping to inspect our handiwork, we jumped back onto the road and hurried toward the governor's compound. When we reached the building, we ducked behind some nearby foliage just within sight of the front. It was a broad, three-story building constructed of the same pearlescent-white stone as the capitol. A high wall encircled the property, making it difficult to see how many soldiers might be inside. Two were guarding the gate.

"How are we going to get in?" I asked.

"We could blast our way through," Mosai suggested, patting his plasma rifle. "It's three against two, and we have the element of surprise."

"What if we sneak around the side? We might be able to scale the wall," Bryneen suggested.

Not that I was opposed to brute force from time to time, but I liked the sound of Bryneen's plan better. We backtracked down the road until we reached a side street. Crouching low, we worked our way along a narrow alley until we reached the building adjacent to the governor's compound. Hopefully, the owner of this particular structure was a loyal Mareesh citizen and wouldn't mind us sneaking through their property as part of the effort to overthrow the illegal governor. If so, Gralik should have picked his neighbors better.

We entered the neighboring courtyard, and I pulled myself on top of the wall bordering the compound to get a peek over. There was one soldier facing away from me, obviously patrolling the rear of the building. I couldn't see any other guards on patrol.

After a whispered explanation to Mosai and Bryneen, we waited until the lone soldier was turned away again, then the three of us helped each other quickly up over the wall. Flattening ourselves against the side of the building, we inched along, searching for some way in. Unfortunately, with the Mareesh architectural style of having windows made of the same material as the wall—only transparent—we couldn't break in that way.

Halfway along the side wall, we came upon a side door.

"It's locked," Bryneen whispered.

We still had our plasma rifles, so brute force was always an option. Then I remember the small drilling device Natheem had given me to cut through the cell doors. I checked my pack and found that, fortunately, I must have stowed it there at some point during the excitement of the prison break.

The side door on the governor's compound was easy to cut through, though the noise seemed much louder now that I wasn't under the effects of the damping field. We pushed through and found ourselves in a long hall, richly decorated in vibrantly colored wall ornaments and paneling. The floor was a muted gray with swirls of shimmering pinks and greens. To me, it was a psychedelic nightmare, but maybe this was the height of opulence on Mareesh.

Wide openings on both sides led away from the long hall, but I had no idea which way would take us to Vrynn. We crept carefully along the corridor, weapons at the ready. A moment later, a short man with bright blue hair—definitely Mareesh—came around the corner carrying a tray of food.

He breathed in sharply, and for a moment, I thought he might raise the alarm. Instead, he tilted his head, beckoning us towards him. "If you're looking for the prisoner scheduled for execution, she's on the second floor just above us," he said in a low voice.

"Thank you," Bryneen whispered back.

"There are two guards in that hallway. I was on my way to bring them their meal. Maybe you can use that as a distraction."

I nodded my understanding.

"Oh, and the vehicle access tokens are kept in a locked box just inside the garage door." He nodded toward the back of the building.

I didn't quite understand what that meant, but Bryneen and Mosai seemed to, so that was good enough for me.

The Mareesh server walked down the side hall and up a narrow staircase with the three of us following several steps behind. At the entrance to the second level hallway, he paused and indicated we should wait. He walked briskly into the hall and approached the two soldiers standing against the wall.

"Here is your morning meal," the server said.

Both guards reacted with sounds of eagerness in anticipation of their food. A moment later, the three of us slipped from our hiding place and approached the guards. They were so intent on their food that they didn't even look up to see us coming until it was too late.

The first guard caught the butt of my plasma rifle against the side of his head and crumpled to the ground. Bryneen and Mosai incapacitated the second guard in a similar fashion.

I pulled out the router tool and made quick work of the lock then pushed the door open.

Immediately, I heard a voice cry out, "Mitch!"

Vrynn sprinted across the small room and jumped into my arms.

"I'm so sorry I couldn't keep you from being captured," I said. It wasn't the most romantic phrase that had ever been uttered, but it was all I could think about for the last day. And given that I finally had this woman in my arms again, I decided to tell her more. "Vrynn, I'm not just a little bit falling for you." Her brow furrowed in confusion. "I'm completely, one hundred percent, wholeheartedly in love with you." Her mouth spread with a wide smile. "I wish I'd told you a while ago; I just never found the right time. But I figured it was important that you should know how I feel, before—"

Apparently, she had lost interest in my rambling confession.

Without another word, she pressed her lips to mine.

The effects of the damping wave had definitely cleared because the feeling of her kiss caused an explosion of sensory overload in my brain. I pulled her closer, kissing her back as hard as I could.

"Save it for later, you two," Mosai hissed from the doorway.

I pulled back from the kiss and smiled, somewhat embarrassed that we'd gotten caught up in the moment.

"Where's the ship?" Vrynn asked, glancing absently at my lips. Her eyes danced with excitement.

I shook my head. "I sent Gabe and Tera away when Nexus fighters came out of orbit. I didn't want them to catch the *Starfire*."

"You're wonderful," she said with a wide grin.

"Wait until you hear the next part," I said, grabbing her hand and pulling her toward the open door. "Gralik was never appointed governor of Mareesh."

Vrynn frowned. "Then who was?"

"Officially, it was Raveel, though I'm not sure anyone ever told him." She was clearly confused, so I continued. "Really, it's possible that the Bonaran government doesn't even know what's happening here."

Vrynn's brow furrowed. "But the messages for help? Our appeals to the chancellor?"

"Lost in the bureaucracy. Intercepted by Gralik's lackeys." I shrugged. "We don't know what went wrong, but at least now your people will be justified in fighting back."

Vrynn's gaze darkened. She turned and stared down the hallway at some unseen foe. "Let's end his rule as governor right now."

I understood why she felt that way, but I shook my head. "We're here to rescue you. We can't take on Gralik right now. Let's get back and help the others."

With additional prodding from her cousins, we finally convinced Vrynn not to set out on a suicidal rampage of vengeance. We hurried back down the stairs and toward the rear of the building. In the garage, we found a secure box, and, after short work with the handheld cutter, we discovered a collection of small plug-like objects inside.

"Grab the one for the armored Veechu," Vrynn said to Mosai.

Clearly, these must be the Mareesh equivalent of a car key. I turned to see what she was talking about, and there in front of us was a utility vehicle—like the Veechu we'd driven in the truck hijacking—with a giant, double-barreled plasma cannon mounted above the rear bed.

Suddenly, a soldier came through the garage door and pulled up short. He lifted his weapon, but fortunately, Mosai's shot caught him before he could aim. His plasma rifle went off as he fell backward into the hall. The noise must have alerted other soldiers because I could hear shouting from down the hallway and outside on the grounds.

We didn't have much time.

Not surprisingly, Vrynn jumped into the raised rear seat and powered up the plasma cannons. A moment later, the turret began swiveling back and forth. "I'll wait until we get outside to test them," she said with barely contained enthusiasm.

"Thanks for that," I said, as I jumped into the cab of the truck.

It looked similar enough to the Veechu I'd already driven. I flipped the switch for the main power, and everything lit up. The familiar hum of energized motors reached my ears. I gripped the sticks and nudged one forward. The vehicle lurched ahead eagerly.

Sounds of approaching soldiers grew louder by the second.

"Let's go already!" Vrynn yelled.

Mosai scampered around the Veechu to the passenger side while Bryneen activated the garage opening and then dove for the jump seat right behind me.

I slammed the throttle. "Here we go."

The truck sprang forward, crashing against the edge of the garage door and ripping it free. A second later, the truck shuddered with the sound of plasma rounds. For a moment, I thought we'd been hit by enemy fire but quickly realized it was our own weapon. I glanced behind me and saw Vrynn grinning from ear to ear.

"This might be almost as good as air support," she said.

I pushed the throttle forward and steered toward the rear gate. As we sailed past stunned soldiers who scurried out of our way, Vrynn turned the cannons on the governor's building. She poured round after round into the upper floor, presumably Gralik's realm, until we were far enough down the road to be out of range.

The main entrance to the Barchee base loomed ahead of us. Unlike our quiet exit from the prison battle, I intended to reenter the fray by driving right down the base's main thoroughfare. No sense in treading carefully with a beast like this.

"Take out the gate!" I yelled to Vrynn.

She pivoted the cannon forward and fired several rounds at the obstacle in front of us, shredding most of it as we smashed through what was left.

"Yeehaw!" I yelled, swerving a second later to avoid a warehouse building next to the road.

We cruised along the central street straight back toward the prison. Hopefully, the Mareesh fighters had successfully overcome the occupiers. But if not, the cavalry was here.

As we approached, I could see the battle still raging. Coming at the fight from the back of the enemy line, we caught the primary Barchee force completely by surprise. Infantry units scattered in seconds as Vrynn's onslaught continued. I was tempted to punch straight through their lines to reach our freedom fighters, but at the last second, I swerved away.

"Keep firing," I said to my passengers. "Maybe we can draw enough attention that our forces can overwhelm their line."

Bryneen and Mosai joined in the effort with their plasma rifles. Mosai even took a few shots across me, aiming at targets through my open window. We must have looked like a spinning firework as I drove in wide circles with Vrynn and her cousins firing rounds in every direction.

The squads of occupying soldiers that had been pressing closer to the Mareesh fighters just a moment earlier were now forced to deal with us. They peppered the exterior of the Veechu with plasma rounds, but the armor held. And Vrynn scattered each group as they fired on us.

Vrynn had just blown a hole in one of the Barchee barricades when Bryneen said, "Uh oh."

My head whipped toward her. "What?" But I didn't need to hear her answer. From the airfield about a mile deeper inside the base, a pair of Barchee escort fighters jetted toward us. I hadn't thought I'd left any ships intact, but I must have missed these two.

"Vrynn, we've got incoming aircraft." I said, pointing in their general direction.

Vrynn turned the cannon on the enemy jets and sent out a stream of plasma rounds. The best plan I could think of for protecting ourselves was to find cover of some sort, so I drove the truck into a nearby alley, hoping to minimize the vehicle as a target while still allowing Vrynn to shoot back.

"Hey!" Vrynn cried as her line of fire was abruptly blocked. Her rounds struck the wall of the alley and showered us with debris. "Too far. Back up a little."

I tapped the throttle, and the Veechu inched backward.

Despite the range to the escort fighters still being too far, Vrynn sent a plasma barrage screaming at them anyway. Surprisingly—or perhaps not surprisingly—she hit one of the ships in the winglet as it attempted to dodge her streams of plasma rounds.

The second ship bore down on its strafing run. Vrynn quickly shifted her aim and fired another prolonged burst. The rounds connected with their target, and the fighter exploded in a ball of flames.

"Nice shot, Vrynn!" I said.

"Missile! He got off a missile!" Vrynn yelled back. "Drive, Mitch!"

I grabbed the throttle and jammed it forward. When the Veechu's drive system didn't respond immediately, I instinctively let off, thinking I'd flooded it. Glancing down at my instrument panel, I searched for something wrong. Obviously, that was an Earth-technology thought, but things happen in the heat of the moment.

"Mitch! Why aren't we moving?!" Vrynn screamed.

"Sorry," I called back as I threw the drive into full-forward again. The motor kicked in and the Veechu lurched forward, but it wasn't soon enough.

With a deafening explosion, the missile slammed into the building we'd taken cover behind. The alley wall collapsed, showering chunks of gray material down on us as Bryneen screamed.

Once the avalanche of stone had stopped, I turned around in my seat. "Is everyone okay?" Bryneen and Mosai looked fine, though shaken up. "Vrynn, are you hurt?"

"No, but I am stuck," she replied dryly. Her end of the Veechu had taken the brunt of the building's collapse.

While Mosai worked to break through the front windshield, I crawled into the back seat next to Bryneen. Vrynn had gotten into the turret from the top, but there did seem to be a way to access the turret's bubble from inside the vehicle, too.

We banged and clawed at the enclosure's internal hatch, but with little success. By this point, Mosai had crawled through the broken windshield out onto the front hood. I looked at Vrynn through the transparent material, unsure what else to do.

"Back up. I want to try something," she said, her voice muffled by the enclosure.

Bryneen crawled out the windshield to join her brother, and I retreated to the front seat to see what Vrynn would do. There was a long pause, then the turret's hatch exploded off its hinges.

Vrynn slid down into the back seat, a wisp of smoke coming from the barrel of her plasma rifle and a broad grin on her face. "That worked," she said.

We climbed through the broken glass and stood on the hood of the buried Veechu, surveying the damage.

"It was fun while it lasted," Bryneen said.

That was exactly how I felt.

By the time Vrynn, Bryneen, and I started scaling the pile of debris, Mosai was already at the top, hunched behind a wall fragment, firing at the Barchee soldiers below. "Hurry. Our forces have started to break through the Barchee line," he called over his shoulder.

We climbed up and added our firepower to Mosai's. Our crazy maneuver with the armored Veechu must have caused such chaos in the Barchee ranks that they were now scrambling in confusion, trying desperately to hold position. From half a story above the street, and behind what was left of the Barchee line, we picked off the occupiers as they attempted an organized retreat.

Once there were no more Barchee soldiers in range, my small group clambered down to join in the chase. What could have been a long and drawn out battle for the Barchee base was turning into a rout. We chased the soldiers down the main thoroughfare toward the spaceport airfield. The few times the enemy tried to stop and regroup, we pushed harder and overran their positions.

At the gate to the spaceport landing strip, the Barchee soldiers were joined by reinforcements from the nearby barracks. They held their position at the gate, and the Mareesh fighters formed up across the plaza behind several destroyed vehicles and other obstacles.

Raveel moved down the line, giving encouragement. "We need to break through, fighters! If the occupiers can hold the spaceport, they can bring in reinforcements. We'll never be rid of them."

I glanced around, searching for a vehicle or something we could use to push our line forward. Part of me wished I hadn't sent Gabe off to find help. I should have told him to just hide under water until the Nexus fighters left him alone.

In the distance, I could hear the familiar whine of a starship engine core. I glanced at Vrynn and could tell she was hoping the same thing.

Maybe it was the *Starfire*.

As we scanned the sky for any sign of a ship, the engine noise increased. It got to the point where I could tell that it was the sound of more than one starship coming. So unless Gabe and Tera had somehow commandeered another ship, it probably wasn't the *Starfire*.

All eyes turned to the narrow gap in the caldera wall. The defensive plasma grid near the spaceport momentarily flashed off, and a pair of transports flew through. Instead of landing at the airstrip, the ships continued low over the base, circling our position and touching down just behind the airfield gate. A moment later, we could see troops unloading from the transports. Dozens and dozens of them.

"They must be pulling reinforcements from the other islands," Vrynn said.

I watched in dismay as the new soldiers pushed to the front. "Not just regular reinforcements," I said, pointing across the wide street that had become our narrow battlefield.

Mosai groaned. "Not dragoons again. Why can't they just leave us alone?"

The fighters around us hunched lower behind our makeshift barricades. I cast a grim glance at Vrynn and tightened my grip on my plasma rifle.

The dragoons, holding large full-length metal shields, formed into a tight formation in the center of the line. They looked like an anti-riot squad or a Roman legionnaire wall. Each shield had the muzzle end of a plasma rifle protruding from the middle, and as the dragoons started forward, they unleashed a torrent of plasma rounds.

"Return fire," one of the Deep Down commanders yelled.

We opened up with everything we had, but it didn't really have much effect. Some dragoons shuddered under the impact of multiple plasma rounds, but the formation continued to push forward.

"Aim for the gaps and the ground!" Raveel called out. "It might be—"

A blaster bolt struck him in the shoulder, knocking him backward onto the ground. A nearby fighter ran to help. The rest of the Mareesh continued firing, desperately hoping to stop the dragoons.

The first group was halfway across the open square and still marching, when a second group of dragoons formed a shield wall on the far flank and began moving toward us.

"Pull back the flank!" Hustan yelled. "Pull back the center!"

Fighters around me shifted formation, moving to take up new positions, and I did my best to move with them. We found new cover behind an overturned Veechu.

"Their wall can't be perfect," Mosai said. "Aim for the gaps next to the center dragoon."

Vrynn and Bryneen joined us, concentrating our fire all on the same spot. After a few dozen rounds, the lead dragoon faltered and stumbled. But just when we thought we might break their formation, the entire line of dragoons turned their embedded weapons on our small group.

I pulled Vrynn down just as the corner of our barricade exploded. The rest of our line was in similar chaos. Dozens of fighters had fallen, some injured, some likely dead.

Suddenly, another volley of plasma rounds struck near us, but from behind this time. I turned around and saw another pair of transports sitting on the main road between us and the prison, disgorging even more enemy troops. Already, a full platoon of Vanguard Dragoons had formed up and were marching down the main road toward us.

We were trapped in the middle of the Barchee base with mercenaries closing in on us from every direction.

"In here!" someone yelled. A Deep Down fighter had opened the door of a nearby warehouse. The rest of the Mareesh freedom fighters ran or dragged each other to the relative safety of the building; the stronger ones pushed equipment into the doorway to form a makeshift barricade; the injured were pulled farther inside.

Raveel sat against the far wall, his face pale, even for a Mareesh. Sharlee moved among the fighters, offering words of encouragement and defiance.

Vrynn grabbed my arm. "We have to do something," she said.

I glanced around the dirty warehouse, taking stock of the situation. I slowly shook my head. "Vrynn, I don't think there's any way out of this."

"Those soldiers aren't part of any legitimate occupation," Vrynn yelled, pointing toward the street and the waiting dragoons. "They're thugs!"

I nodded. "Yeah, but right now, they're thugs with better weapons who outnumber us two to one."

Vrynn didn't seem to be fazed by this reality. "If we can only—"

"Attention Mareesh insurgents!" a booming voice said, echoing around the street outside.

All the fighters turned their attention to the sound of the voice.

I didn't have to look to know it was Gralik.

"You have all fought valiantly, but it's time to stop this nonsense." Gralik stood across the wide street behind a row of dragoons, speaking into a megaphone-looking device. His voice was friendly and patronizing at the same time. "After all, why are you fighting? You wouldn't even be here if it weren't for your ancestors from Barchee. Their technological advancements made it possible for you to thrive here on this world. You should be uniting with them. There shouldn't be Barchee and Mareesh, you should be one united star system. Stop resisting the inevitable."

"Oh, that's a load of treckla dung," Bryneen said. "They've been spewing this propaganda in my school for the last eight years, and I'm sick of it." She fired a few shots toward the sound of the voice.

In response, dozens of rounds immediately pelted our pitiful rampart, throwing sparks and shards of metal into the air around us. After a few seconds, the barrage died down.

"If you test my patience again," Gralik yelled, "I will kill every last one of you!"

Bryneen glanced at us. "Sorry," she whispered, though she didn't look very sorry.

Gralik continued his speech, sounding more flustered than before. "But I'm a benevolent governor. I'm willing to forgive all of these transgressions under one condition."

Vrynn's expression hardened, mirroring my own. We knew what was coming.

"Hand over the insurrectionists and their starship, and I will let all of you return peacefully—without your weapons, of course—to your homes."

"Don't listen to him, Vrynn," Mosai said.

Others nearby echoed the sentiment, offering Vrynn and me words of encouragement.

I scanned the warehouse. Members of the Deep Down and High Tide crouched shoulder to shoulder behind the barricade. Streaks of blue blood marred the unswept floors leading to the dozens of wounded and dying slumped against the back wall. They were fighting for their freedom, but they were also fighting to protect us and the ship.

Could I really let them die when I had the power to save them?

I turned to Vrynn. "Maybe we should do it," I said.

Her eyes were murderous. "What? Are you crazy?"

I held up a hand to stop her before she got too mad at me. "I'm not talking about giving him the *Starfire*. We would never do that," I said point blank. "But look around, Vrynn." I held out a hand to the rest of the warehouse, filled with wounded and beaten fighters. "I don't see how we can fight our way out of this. They will all die unless we surrender ourselves."

Vrynn considered the other Mareesh around her, and her expression turned to sad resignation.

"Don't do it, Vrynn," Natheem yelled from across the room. "You can't trust Gralik. He's not going to let us go free just because he has you."

"He is right, you know," Vrynn said. "What are the chances Gralik lets them live?"

I felt my throat go dry. "Not good. But what are the chances they survive if they continue fighting? At least if we agree to Gralik's terms, there's a chance they'll live."

"But we aren't really agreeing to the terms," Vrynn pointed out. "We aren't giving him the *Starfire*."

"Yeah, but he doesn't know that yet. Maybe we could string him along for a while. Tell him the ship's hidden off the coast of Nildyr." I offered her a wry grin.

"He'll never let us go until we give it to him."

"I know," I replied somberly.

Vrynn took a breath and nodded. "If there's any chance to save the rest of the fighters to return another day, then I'm willing."

I took Vrynn's small hand in mine, and we slowly stood from behind the barricade.

Vrynn considered the small band of freedom fighters huddled behind us and nodded with satisfaction. For once, I knew what she was thinking. Our lives for theirs would be worth it.

From the back wall of the warehouse, Raveel held up a hand in farewell, gratitude evident on his face. I returned the gesture.

Bryneen stood and threw her arms around Vrynn, tears streaming down her cheeks.

"Keep up the fight," Vrynn said to her young cousin. "And stay strong." Her voice choked on the last word, and she hugged Bryneen tighter.

Vrynn released Bryneen and gave Mosai a hug, too. "Keep each other safe."

He nodded, doing his best to fight back tears.

I handed my plasma rifle and my blaster to Mosai. "If I survive this, I'll want these back." It was an uncharacteristically optimistic thing to say, but in the face of certain death, I couldn't help myself.

Vrynn looked up at me with a sad, watery smile.

It was time.

Together, we walked cautiously toward the enemy lines. I found my pace slowing, probably because I wanted to savor every last second of life and the feeling of Vrynn's hand in mine. To my surprise, as we stared down the enemy line across from us, step by tortuous step, time felt like it slowed down.

Halfway across the battle-ridden street, my comm beeped. I glanced at Vrynn as my step faltered.

She looked down at the comm device then up at me. "Gabe and Tera?" she asked in a whisper.

I gave a subtle nod.

"What's going on there?" Gralik yelled. "Why are you whispering? I can tell you're talking to each other. Don't try to make some stupid plan to escape."

Suddenly, I had an idea.

With my free hand still raised in surrender, I called out, "It's the AI on our ship. They're trying to communicate with us."

I couldn't see the nuances of Gralik's expression, but even from forty feet away, there was no mistaking the eagerness in his face.

"Order it to land here," he commanded.

"Okay, hang on." I very slowly reached for the comm device on my belt, trying not to make any sudden moves in the face of dozens of weapons trained on me. I activated the link. "Gabe? Is that you?"

"Affirmative," he replied.

"I sure hope you're nearby with an armada of reinforcements," I said wryly.

"No and yes," my android buddy replied.

I might have laughed if I wasn't in such a dire situation. "Tell me what's going on, and bear in mind I'm standing in the middle of the Barchee base surrounded by enemy soldiers."

"We are approximately eight and a half light-years away, currently in orbit of Varus Prime. We opened a pinhole portal in the sky above Mardrys so that we could send a comm signal through," Gabe explained. "We do have help with us. Should we target a larger portal at your location and bring all of the ships through right now?"

"Yes!" Vrynn nearly shouted.

"Why are you excited?" Gralik called from across the street. He turned to the dragoons next to him. "I'm tired of this. Go get them."

I held my hands up higher. "Wait. Wait. The ship is on its way right now."

Before I had even finished speaking, the familiar Quake Drive aperture appeared in the sky above our heads. A split second later, the *Starfire* zoomed out. It was such a relief to see that I nearly jumped for joy.

A second later, fighter ships began streaming through the portal, first five, then ten. Soon there were at least thirty starships flying overhead. All Varusian Interceptors. My gut reaction was to worry they were chasing the *Starfire*, but Gabe said they were with him, so these must not be Nexus-affiliated starships.

The last ship to come through was one I'd only seen once before, at the spaceport on Ludros Beta Five. But it was the one that told me Gabe had successfully accomplished his mission. Shariamy's gleaming silver transport sailed over our heads, pulling all eyes to it. I couldn't help but notice, though, that she'd been hiding some tricks up her sleeve—or her hull—because the ship was now bristling with cannons and missiles. It wasn't a simple, unarmed transport after all. It was closer to an attack ship.

The Nexus forces on the ground opened fire at the newly arrived ships, and the street erupted in utter chaos. Gralik yelled something at his dragoons, but I couldn't hear it over the melee. Vrynn and I crouched low and hurried back to the warehouse door, where Mosai and Bryneen tossed us our weapons.

The interceptors and Shariamy's ship rained down plasma rounds on the lines of dragoons and Barchee soldiers, who quickly scattered for cover.

The line of freedom fighters stood from their positions behind the barricade, ready to pursue the retreating occupiers.

"Look," Keelsa pointed back down the wide road toward the center of the Mardrys caldera and the hill of the capitol building.

Even from several blocks away, we could see mobs of Mareesh pushing up the streets toward the capitol walls. Word of Gralik's illegitimate rule must have spread.

Raveel trudged over to us, one arm over a fellow fighter for support. "Keelsa, lead the High Tide forces to retake the capitol. Organize the citizens there. I will join you soon." He searched the rest of the large group. "Hustan, take our Deep Down force and hunt down the occupiers." Raveel glanced at the skies overhead, filled with Varusian fighters attacking the Barchee soldiers. "You might want to stay at a safe distance until these ships finish their work, though."

Vrynn stepped toward Raveel. "I want Gralik," she said through gritted teeth.

The last we'd seen of him, the Nexus commander was slinking away down the street toward the airfield.

"I'm sure we'll get him," I said, pointing at the ships above us. "Look at the odds. No one is getting out of this."

"I don't care. I want to personally make sure he doesn't get away." Vrynn turned her attention back to Raveel. "Please."

The old rebel leader smiled. "Go. And take whatever help you need."

Vrynn gave a curt nod and took off through the chaos, hot on Gralik's tail. I did my best to keep up with her, knowing that despite the momentum shift in our favor, Vrynn would be in grave danger if she found herself in the middle of a group of dragoons or Barchee soldiers. Fortunately, there were dozens of freedom fighters pressing ahead, pursuing the enemy into the spaceport.

Blaster fire and plasma rounds exploded all around us as we ran after Gralik. Once we passed through the airfield gate, I finally caught up to Vrynn. She pointed at a group far ahead of us. Gralik raced across the landing strip with several of his dragoons.

I paused and raised my plasma rifle.

"No!" Vrynn said, grabbing my arm. "I want him alive to face his punishment." Her expression was full of wild fury.

"You're willing to risk that he'll get away?" I asked.

"No, I'm going to catch him before he does," Vrynn replied as she blasted past me.

A pair of allied interceptors circled the airfield—one at each end. Maybe that would keep Gralik and his goons from escaping. A troop transport that I hadn't noticed before landed in the middle of the field and began unloading its soldiers. They definitely appeared Varusian, or at least I could tell they weren't Barchee or Mareesh. And their uniforms matched the BDF personnel I'd seen on my visit to Varus Prime.

"Hurry. He's heading for the last hangar," Vrynn called over her shoulder.

I wasn't sure what could be waiting for Gralik once he reached it, but I knew it wouldn't be good for us, so I picked up the pace, pulling even with Vrynn. I took a few potshots at the walls near the fleeing dragoon squad, hoping to slow their retreat without killing Gralik.

"Good idea," Vrynn said and pulled out her own blaster.

Even with pieces of building exploding in front of them, Gralik and his dragoons pressed on. They ducked inside the last hangar—which I had unfortunately missed in my initial attack on the base. Two dragoons took up a defensive position next to the door. Vrynn and I dove to the ground, narrowly avoiding the rounds from their plasma rifles.

I activated my comm. "Gabe, we could use some help here."

"I am currently covering Mareesh fighters surrounding a group of enemy soldiers."

"Gralik is about to get away if we don't stop him," I said.

"I will come to your position immediately," Gabe replied.

Fortunately, Gralik's escape attempt caught the attention of the interceptors covering the airstrip. One swooped low, activating thrusters, and pointed directly at the hangar Gralik had entered. Several plasma rounds from the interceptor neutralized the remaining dragoons. With the approach to the hangar clear, Vrynn and I rushed forward to stop Gralik.

But before we even reached the hangar, the main door exploded in plasma rounds, not from the waiting interceptor, but from inside. A moment later, two atmospheric missiles streaked out. The allied interceptor was hit and fell in a burning fireball back to the airfield.

As the smoke cleared, Gralik's runabout rammed through the hole in the hangar door and out onto the pocked airstrip. Its main engine powered up, preparing to launch.

I couldn't believe we were this close to stopping Gralik, and he was still going to escape.

Suddenly, the *Starfire* swept over the airstrip and fired a few plasma rounds at the runabout.

"Gabe, target the runabout with the harpoon," I yelled.

"Acknowledged," he replied.

The runabout's thrusters fired, lifting it off the ground. He would be at full speed within seconds. Just as Gralik transitioned to forward power, the harpoon from the *Starfire* struck the hull of the runabout and held tight.

"Perfect shot!" I yelled.

The runabout's engines went to full power, but a second later, it hit the end of the harpoon tether, jerking against the *Starfire's* mass.

"Now what?" Gabe asked as Gralik's ship pulled and strained against the line.

"Bring him down. Don't let him get away," I said.

"Even with my superior reflexes on the controls, I am having difficulty keeping our ship stable," Gabe replied.

"Open the cargo door," I said, running toward the spot where the *Starfire* hovered over the field, Vrynn close on my heels.

I wished I was the kind of guy who could tell the woman he loved to stay behind where it was safe, but there was nowhere I would rather have her than by my side. Besides, she deserved to be the one to bring Gralik down.

We made it to the ship, but even with the ramp lowered, it was still about ten feet too high for us to reach.

HelperBot rolled up to the edge of the cargo bay. "How may this unit be of service?" it called out to us.

"Get a rope," Vrynn yelled back, and the small automated cart disappeared into the cargo bay.

"Can't you bring it a little lower?" I asked Gabe over the comm.

"The runabout's thrust is fluctuating randomly; I am being forced to manually adjust our altitude to hold this position."

HelperBot came to the edge of the cargo ramp, a coil of rope between its loading arms.

"Uh oh. The tether," Gabe said.

I looked at Gralik's ship—pointed nearly straight up at this point—and saw that the tether was now directly below his engine nozzles. The cable glowed white hot in the super-heated exhaust.

A second later, the tether broke with an ear-splitting bang. I grabbed Vrynn and pulled her back just as the *Starfire* slammed hard into the ground.

HelperBot floated for a split second in the cargo bay opening, then crashed against the deck, amazingly able to keep his wheels under him. Vrynn and I scrambled up the ramp just as he threw the rope at us. "This unit has delivered rope, as requested," it said in its chipper announcer voice.

"Close the ramp and get us back in the air," I yelled as we dashed through the cargo bay toward the ladder.

We were airborne once again and racing after Gralik by the time Vrynn and I reached the flight deck. Vrynn jumped into her seat, sliding right through Tera's holographic projection.

"Sorry," Vrynn said absently as she grabbed the control sticks.

I was about ready to jump into my own seat when I realized I wouldn't slip as smoothly through Gabe—who was now occupying the pilot's chair.

"Mind if I drive?" I asked.

Gabe slid over, giving me space to take over the controls.

"Where is he?" I asked Tera.

"He just flew through the spaceport gap," she replied. "He's already heading for orbit."

I pushed the ship to full throttle. "Then let's go after him."

"Unfortunately, the plasma grid over the gap has reactivated," Tera said. "And by the time we contact whoever is controlling it, the runabout will be nearly out of the atmosphere."

I gave her a sidelong glance. "Well, do we have a Quake Drive or don't we?" I asked.

Vrynn smiled, and Tera nodded, understanding my implied request.

An aperture opened right in front of us, taking the ship through the caldera wall and popping us out above the runabout.

"Can you damage him enough that he has to land?" I asked Vrynn.

"Definitely," she replied with a grim expression.

Vrynn opened up with the plasma cannons, but she wasn't aiming to kill this time. Her shots went wide as Gralik banked and dove to dodge the incoming fire. After a few maneuvers, he tried to regain altitude, but Vrynn hemmed him in with cannon fire again. We definitely had the upper hand, but it was a tricky business to shoot down a starship without killing its occupant.

Just as the runabout angled upward for another attempt, its left engine nozzle began pouring out smoke.

I turned to Vrynn. "What happened?"

"I didn't do anything," she said with a shrug.

We both turned to Tera. She glanced innocently around the flight deck before saying. "Well, apparently my lockout algorithm doesn't prevent me from using the defensive lasers to target the engine regulator flaps of an enemy ship." She allowed a small smile.

"Nice job, Tera," I said as we dove to follow Gralik's spiraling runabout.

At the rate he was losing altitude, it was obvious that Gralik had very little control over where he was going to crash.

"Better ready another harpoon," I said to Vrynn. "That is, if you still want to bring him to justice." I eyed her to see if she had changed her mind. I wouldn't lose any sleep over letting Gralik be another casualty of one of our air battles.

"I'll get it ready," she said, jumping up from her seat. "He's absolutely going to stand trial."

Vrynn had the second harpoon loaded in plenty of time, but I had the immense satisfaction of waiting until the last second to spear the runabout and prevent it from slamming into the ocean. I only wish I could have been there to enjoy Gralik's terror.

We hauled Gralik back to the Barchee base—now fully under Mareesh control, thanks to the BDF forces. As soon as the runabout touched the tarmac, it was immediately surrounded by dozens of soldiers. By the time we set the *Starfire* down a few hundred feet away and joined the gathering, Gralik had already been dragged from his ship and put in restraints. He yelled and insulted and threatened, but no one listened.

Shariamy walked over to us, a pair of BDF soldiers flanking her. "Thank you for bringing all of this to our attention," she said. "Apparently, the diplomatic corps relies too heavily on the military to get news about outlying worlds. We might need to change that in the future."

"We're just grateful you've finally freed us from the Barchee occupiers," Vrynn said.

Shariamy—or rather, Consul General Razome—glanced around the base as Mareesh fighters escorted streams of Barchee soldiers into the compound for deportation. "Actually, I'd say you freed yourself. I'm just here to make it official." She gave Vrynn a genuine smile. "Despite the help we might have given you in rectifying the situation here on Mareesh, the diplomatic corps is deeply in your debt for what you've done. So it would seem, I now owe you two favors. Let me know if I can ever help."

"Thank you," I said as I put an arm around Vrynn, "for everything."

She looked from me to Vrynn and back. "My original offer still stands," she said with an exaggerated raise of her brow.

"I think I'll hold on to what I've got," I replied, pulling Vrynn closer.

Shariamy smiled broadly. "Good choice." She turned and waved at us over her shoulder as she walked back to her shiny ship.

Chapter Eighteen

T he Mareesh forces didn't fully retake the islands until near the end of the day. Most of the Barchee soldiers, upon hearing that the occupation had ended, were more than happy to hop on the next transports bound for their home world. But there were some holdouts.

Vrynn and I shuttled several dozen Mareesh freedom fighters—crammed into the cargo bay of the *Starfire*—to the small town of Burnee, where a particularly ferocious mid-level Barchee commander refused to acknowledge the illegitimacy of the occupation.

Hustan brought the platoon into position surrounding the small barracks, and Sharlee led the charge inside. The skirmish was over by the time Vrynn and I escorted Raveel to the center of town. We arrived just as the last of the Barchee soldiers were taken into custody.

Hustan approached us, holding out an arm toward the line of soldiers. "That's all of them." He turned to Raveel, a broad smile on his face. "We finally did it, sir."

Raveel nodded, his smile a bit more reserved. "Yes. We did."

"Now all that's left to do is round up the collaborators so they can face justice," Hustan added.

Raveel's brow furrowed. "Collaborators?"

"You know, the Mareesh who helped the occupiers," Hustan said. "Or the ones who pretended to resist the occupation but actively opposed our efforts, like Keelsa and Natheem."

"I don't think Natheem will be facing anything," Vrynn said, her expression sad. "I saw him fall during the battle."

After a moment's pause, Hustan somberly said, "I suppose that's justice enough."

Raveel considered his fighters in turn. "Natheem was wounded badly, but the injury was not fatal," he said finally.

Vrynn was as surprised as I was to hear that news. From what I'd seen, I hadn't thought Natheem had survived, either.

"Then he *will* be held accountable for his crime," Hustan declared.

Raveel rubbed his chin, a pensive expression on his face. "Let us wait to condemn until we fully understand."

Hustan's brow furrowed. "But, sir. He betrayed us. Are you saying he won't be punished?"

Raveel shrugged. "No, I cannot say. That will be determined at a future day. What I can say today is that Natheem fought valiantly to win back our freedom, and he will bear the scars of the battle for the rest of his life."

Hustan didn't look convinced, but he nodded in deference to Raveel's judgement.

The silent moment was broken by an alert on my comm device. I stepped a little away from the group. "Yes?" I asked.

"Mitch, we just received a transmission from Consul General Razome," Tera said.

"Okay, go ahead with it," I said.

When Tera spoke again, her tone was unusually somber. "You're going to want to come back to the *Starfire* to see it."

Sensing something was wrong, Vrynn moved to my side, and together, we hustled back to the ship.

Once on the flight deck together, Tera played the transmission for us.

The video of Shariamy—bright face, pearlescent hair, and all—appeared in the air in front of us. "Mitch, Vrynn, I've got some bad news," she said. "Somewhere between the point that we delivered him to BDF security on Varus Prime and when his ship was meant to arrive at the processing facility . . ." She paused as if unsure how to tell us. ". . . Gralik disappeared."

My eyes went wide. "No," I whispered.

I glanced across the narrow gap at Vrynn. She shook her head, part in disbelief, part in resignation.

Shariamy continued, "He has officially been relieved of duty. All privileges and clearances revoked. A warrant has been issued for him to appear before the high tribunal. And we have a team of trackers searching for him, but that's no guarantee." She paused and blew out a breath. "I think I underestimated how deep the Nexus corruption within the BDF actually goes. I'm sorry. We'll do our best to catch him, but I thought you two deserved to know." She shook her head sadly, and the recording ended.

I stared off at nothing in particular, feeling like I'd just crossed the finish line of a marathon and someone had handed me a bicycle and said, "you can do another hundred miles, right?"

I realized I'd never felt so tired before in my life.

I also realized that people who do triathlons are crazy.

"It's not so bad," Vrynn said with that aggravating optimism.

My eyes probably bugged out of my skull. "How can you say that?"

"He doesn't have any more power on Mareesh," she said. "And he's a fugitive on any planet where the Bonara Defense Force has a presence. He's not nearly as dangerous as he used to be."

I shook my head. "Nexus hasn't exactly worried about that before," I insisted. "They're still dangerous."

She shrugged. "Sure. But nothing we can't handle."

I wanted to argue, but she reached across and grabbed my hand. That was enough to silence whatever I was going to say. I might not have had her level of confidence, but I was happy to have her by my side as we continued the fight.

The celebrations on the Mareesh islands lasted for at least a week, though I may have lost count of the days after four or five.

With Gralik driven from power, Vrynn and I felt free to take our time on Mareesh. He would certainly come hunting for the *Starfire* again, but at the moment, he was a fugitive on the run. We felt safe to enjoy a few days of relaxation in Vrynn's hometown. And when he did come after us again, we wouldn't be alone. We had allies now.

"Mitch is a very strange name, did you know that?" Mosai said as we stood visiting at the hundredth celebration party we'd attended together. "There's nothing like it in Mareesh culture."

I shrugged. "It's pretty common for a human."

"Well, there are going to be many, many Mareesh boys, and maybe even some little girls, who will grow up with a very strange, non-Mareesh name."

My mouth dropped open as his words slowly sank in. "Really?"

A wide grin spread across Mosai's face. "Oh, definitely. I know of one already. His mother is a friend of Bryneen's. He was born yesterday."

"Hopefully, he grows up to be brave and strong, just like his name-sake," Vrynn said as she joined us, threading her arm around my waist.

I pulled her close against me. "That optimism of yours keeps coming up against impossible barriers," I said with a smile.

She laughed and rose up onto her tiptoes. "What would I ever do without you, dirt boy?" She gave me a light kiss on my cheek then turned to Mosai. "Make sure some of the other guests have a chance to speak to our hero, cousin." Before she turned away, she gave me a perfect wink. Not too obvious to be awkward, not too fleeting to be missed. Just the perfect, subtle wink.

That wink was such a small thing, nothing that would alter the future of the galaxy. But to me, the fact that she'd even tried to learn that minor Earth gesture spoke volumes about who she was. If I hadn't already been head over heels in love with this woman, that certainly would have sealed the deal.

Without thinking, I grabbed Vrynn and pulled her back to me. Leaning down, I gave her a long, lingering kiss. I'd already let too many days go by without letting her know how I really felt.

Today wouldn't be one of those days.

Vrynn wrapped her arms around my neck and returned the kiss with a passion. We stood there in the middle of the party for several seconds—or maybe minutes—completely oblivious to what was happening around us, until Mosai loudly cleared his throat in my ear.

Reluctantly, I pulled back and released Vrynn. She looked as breathless as I felt. With an expression that conveyed an utter lack of remorse, she gave my hand a squeeze and walked to a nearby group.

Shaking his head at us, her cousin moved to join her, but I stopped him before he walked away.

"Mosai, can you help me with something?" I felt my heartbeat suddenly increase with what I wanted to ask him. I took a deep breath. "I'm not completely familiar with Mareesh customs yet, so I wanted to know if I need to ask Vrynn's . . ." I stopped myself when I realized that Vrynn's parents had both been killed in the First Battle of Mardrys. "Who can I talk to about my intention to date Vrynn?"

"Date her?" Mosai asked, his brow furrowed.

Obviously, his translation chip didn't know how to fix that phrase. Maybe I would need to learn how to speak Mareesh at some point. I attempted a better description. "You know, when someone wants to pursue someone romantically with the intent to create a permanent relationship. That's what I want with Vrynn."

Recognition lit Mosai's expression. "Oh, right. You've already become entangled with her, so there's no need to do anything else until you're ready to wrap yourselves together."

"Entangled?" It was my turn to be confused.

"When you pursue someone and all that stuff you just said," Mosai replied.

I couldn't help but smile.

Vrynn and I were pretty entangled, and I didn't mind that at all. Even though jumping to the Bonara Cluster had been a complete accident, now I couldn't imagine what my life would have been like without Vrynn by my side.

And I couldn't wait to see what adventures the future held.

I knew if I did my best to help people who needed it and fight the bad guys wherever we found them, I might be able to stay tangled up with Vrynn for a long, long time to come.

1.5 Novella and Reviews

T hanks so much for reading my book. I hope you enjoyed it.

If I could ask one quick favor. Please leave a book review or even just a quick rating on Amazon.

After that, you can sign up for my newsletter to get all the behind-the-scenes information and news about my writing (www.myles christensen.com/starship2). Also, you may have noticed a few references to part of the storyline that isn't in book 1 or book 2. The story of Mitch and Vrynn trying to set up their home base on Thetis Max (between books 1 and 2) is told in a free novella that you'll receive when you join the reader newsletter. This isn't a new novella, it's the same one I offered at the end of book 1. I'm just adding it here for readers that might have missed it the first time.

Acknowledgements

Thanks to my readers. You were really begging for the next book, and that was a huge motivator for me.

I appreciate the early feedback that I got from my beta readers: Ryan_Reads, Ross Jaburg, Maddy216, and BingeingonBooks. You helped me find those spots that still weren't quite right.

Thanks to my family for supporting me in my writing efforts. Your encouragement means the world (or the universe)

As always, my biggest thanks go to my sweet wife. Your help with brainstorming, and your suggestions during edits made all the difference.

M yles Christensen loves to write exciting adventures because he loves to read exciting adventures. The hopeless romantic in him will usually sprinkle a teensy bit of romance into his stories. While writing, he listens to music that matches—and sometimes inspires—the storyline.

His mild-mannered alter ego is a product development engineer, university professor, and game inventor. He lives in Utah with his wife and children.

Printed in Dunstable, United Kingdom

65822762R00188